I0744783

Printed in the United States of America

Burton Blake

Robert Tucker

For My Parents and Grandparents

I THE LEGACY

Chapter 1

Taxi Dancer

1940

Kristina Holtzman was not a great social dancer, but she was beautiful, so the men patiently waited their turn to thrust their ten-cent ticket at her to claim the next dance.

What she was good at was typing. Her mother, a journalist, had taught her how to type and Kristina had found a low-paying job in the secretarial pool of the Chicago municipal government. Her assignments exposed her to many departments that supported the city and gave her an understanding of how the award of contracts were determined, how money changed hands, and how corruption flourished. Her low wages forced her to look for another way to supplement her meager income, so she danced.

She contributed most of the weekly twenty dollars handed to her in a sealed envelope at the cashier's window to help pay her mother and father for food and other household expenses. At eighteen, she was the youngest of five children. Her two older brothers had moved to California to find jobs several years ago. Her two sisters were married to husbands who worked in local Chicago factories.

With the crash of 1929, her father Conrad Holtzman, had lost his position as a foreman in a textile factory. Each day, he joined the lines of unemployed men hoping to be chosen to work loading and unloading freighters at the waterfront docks or any factory where an announcement had been made that temporary labor jobs were available.

Writing under her maiden name, Julie Josephson, her mother continued to work after three decades at a greatly reduced wage for the Chicago Tribune.

Early each morning, Kristina and her mother left their small house on the west side and rode the trolley to the downtown loop where they went their separate ways among the desperate hungry crowds.

For the first few weeks when Kristina had begun working, she had not covered her head with a cap or a scarf. The sight of her long blonde tresses drew whistles and catcalls from homeless street vagrants, drifters, and men queued at unemployment lines and soup kitchens. When she concealed her hair with a cloche hat, the rude expressions stopped, but the looks of appreciation did not.

The monolithic clatter of typewriter keys and syncopated ringing of carriage returns had diminished over the past year to where only a dozen women produced their output quota of letters and official government documents while the remaining Underwoods gathered dust on deserted desks in silence. As the employment of eighty-eight other typists was terminated four and five at a time, the fear of losing their jobs left those who had survived the lay-offs tense and submissive.

That morning, Kristina noticed that the stern-faced typing pool supervisor, Mrs. Griffin, was missing and her co-workers conjectured as to whether she had been "let go" as well.

Kristina rolled a familiar form onto her typewriter and began the repetitive task of reducing the pile stacked in her 'in' basket which was expected to be empty by the end of the day. Her long elegant fingers struck the black, brass imprinted metal keys with rapid reflexive strokes that required little concentration and resulted in consistently error-free documents. Her skill allowed her the luxury of letting her thoughts wander to counteract the incessant boredom of her task in the bleak gray office. High soot encrusted windows admitted only a suggestion of sunlight blocked by the daily overcast of smoke from factories. Hanging globe lights cast a weak yellow glow, inadequate illumination that caused severe eye strain among the women.

Born into a working-class family surrounded by discussions of labor issues with union officials who often came to the house to meet with her father, she perceived life as a struggle against poverty in a society ruled by men who manipulated and controlled the economy in support of their wealth.

Her indoctrination originated and grew from the vivid stories her parents told her and her brothers and sisters about their activist days in the Chicago ghettos.

At five o'clock, she left the municipal building and walked four long city blocks to meet her mother for the return ride home on the trolley.

"How was work?" her mother asked.

"The usual, but the supervisor was let go."

"Mrs. Griffin?"

Kristina nodded. "I just learned today that she's been a widow for the past eight years. Her husband died working in a packing plant. One of the other typists knew her, but never said anything to the rest of us. Mrs. Griffin would have fired her for gossiping."

"How unimportant. Everybody has bad experiences, but it sounds like she had her pride."

"She didn't want anyone to know she was a widow."

"What's the purpose in that? I don't know." Her mother stared out the window at the familiar streets along which the trolley swayed and clanged, throwing a shower of electric sparks from the overhead cables at intersections. Despite accepting the deplorable conditions of The Great Depression, she had lost the inner fire that fueled her young spirit in fighting social and economic injustice. Her own depression settled in. *Perhaps a fact of getting older,* she thought. *Nothing much has changed. No jobs. No food. Another war.* Huddled along the sidewalk, men and women wearing layers of patched tawdry clothing ignited memories of forty years ago.

Handing out seditious pamphlets in the tenements and hawking them on street corners in the business section of the city had been Julie's daily task. Teeming with life, the city exerted a force of its own, a vast filthy dark presence shrouded in its own smoke and factory dust. Laid over with the stench and pall from the stockyards, it ingested hordes of hungry, ragged immigrants who disappeared into the labyrinthine bowels of sprawling tenements and sordid existence.

And now, forty years later, Julie's own daughter had proposed that she become a taxi dancer to earn extra money. The reputation of taxi dancers was unsavory, since many of the young women operated as prostitutes on the side and used the taxi dance venues as places to meet men who would afterwards take them to hotels or sleazy apartments.

Julie did not believe her daughter would ever succumb to the proposals made on the dance floor or on the street as the girls departed from the "dancing schools" and "ball rooms." Kristina had persisted that she could make money strictly on the dancing and would never degrade herself by selling her body.

There had been much discussion and negotiation with her parents, who finally agreed to allow two nights during the working week and Saturday nights she could taxi dance. But there were conditions. She could dance only at an upscale ball room that attracted a better class of male customers. She would stay with a friend, Sally Glover, from work and they would go to the establishment together. Kristina's father, Conrad, would meet them at the door promptly at eleven and drive them both home in his Model A Ford. There would be no post dance dating, which led to drinking at night clubs and the inevitable hotel room.

Kristina and Sally checked their overcoats at the cloak room, received their claim tags, then proceeded directly to the ladies dressing room. Their interview with, Cornel Grant, the ballroom manager, a dapper dressed middle-aged man with protruding front teeth, recessed chin, and oily slicked back hair, had been a degrading experience, but one they had to accept as the price of admission.

"There are rules," he said. "Here's how it goes. The dance floor is everyman's land. Any chap asks you to dance, you take his ticket and dance with him. The dance tickets are ten cents each. Customers buy what they want at the door, but there's no free dances. No ticket, no dance. Got that?"

The girls nodded.

"We got other rules. What you do outside the ball room is your business, but you come in here to pick up marks and I hear about it, you'll be out on your ass. The Aragon is a class establishment. It's not a whore house and I don't let whores in here. So, any thoughts you have along those lines, you lookin' for fish and to play the sex game, put it out of your mind. You got that?"

Again, the girls nodded.

"You're dime-a-dance girls. When a customer comes up to you and gives you his ticket, you dance with him for only one song. That's all, one. If he wants another dance, that'll cost him another ticket. You get a commission on every dance ticket you get from your dance partners. Half the price of that ticket pays for the orchestra, the ball room, and my operating expenses. You get the other half. The more dances you have, the more money you make. You give any free dances, you lose money and I lose money. If I lose money, you'll hear from me. I run a business, not a charity. You got that?"

The girls nodded.

"This is a high class place. The customers expect to see high class women. So even if you ain't, you show up here lookin' like one. If you don't have a gown or two, you better get one or don't show up. It's okay to wear makeup. Just don't overdo it. Not too heavy on the eye shadow and lipstick. Don't want you lookin' like whores. Blondie, you're such a natural beauty, you don't need to wear no makeup, but your friend can use some help, a lot of help. Hope you have the personality to overcome your face. Customers like to have a good time, laugh a little while they're dancing. So talk to 'em. Ask 'em about theirselves. But if someone don't want to talk, don't push it with 'em. A lot of men come here because they don't have the gumption to talk to a woman anywhere else. Here, it only costs 'em a dime. But there's shy ones and some don't even speak English. You won't see any niggers, no black and tans. They have their own dance halls and clubs. If you're seen talkin' to any outside the ball room, even out in public, don't bother to come back. That gives us a bad reputation that Aragon girls will sleep with niggers and spics. Like I said, what you do outside after the dance is your business, just don't let other customers see you and don't let me hear about it.   You do and you're out. Be here an hour before we open the doors. We change bands from time to time, but we got only the best. Big names want to play here. The rest of the country gets to hear 'em on the radio. That's all I've got to say. Keep your nose clean. Follow the rules and you'll do okay. Any questions?"

The girls shook their heads.

"Good. Some of the girls are Aragon veterans. Some are nice and they'll talk to you. But you're competition, especially you, Blondie. What did you say your name was?"

"Kristina."

Cornel bobbed his head. "Yeah, Kristina, you're competition. Okay, we're done. Get outta my office."

Kristina rose from her hard-back chair. "Thank you, sir, for the opportunity." Trying to conceal her sudden tears, Sally moved quickly to the door. Her tears did not escape Cornel's notice.

"Sure, sure, you gotta have a thick skin, girlie, for this business."

Once they were on the street, Sally paused to wipe her eyes. "What an awful, horrible man. I hope we never have to talk to him again."

"He'll be the one who gives us our money."

"As long as I don't have to listen to him. So awful. So awful. You are so lucky. It's a sin to not be beautiful."

"But you've got personality. You're peppy. Peppy Sally." Kristina laughed.

"I'm not peppy. I don't have clever things to say."

"I think the idea is to get your dance partners talking."

"I suppose I can do that. I would certainly never insult them, not like Corny."

"His name's Cornel."

"Corny fits him better."

Kristina laughed. "That's a girl. Peppy."

"Oh, go on. Here comes your trolley."

"See you at the door."

On their first night, the established Taxi dancers greeted them with derision.

"Hey, princess, where'd you come from? You lose your way and wander off a movie set somewheres?"

"She ain't no princess. She's an ice queen. Look at them eyes."

"She ain't no ice queen. That's for sure. Those baby blues could melt ice. What's your name, princess?"

"Kristina."

"Princess Kristina, perfect. You got a last name?"

"Holtzman."

"Holtzman – you a kraut?"

"Swedish and German."

"You got the right kinda mix all right. You sure you ain't a swell from the north side come down here to slum with us got nothings?"

"I'm not a swell and I'm not slumming. I came here because I can't make enough in my regular job."

"What's that?"

"Secretary."

"Secretary. Most of us here worked in the packing house or lost our sewing jobs in the sweats and textile factories."

"You better be able to move your feet here, doll. Better wear comfy stompers. Customers don't pay a dime a ticket to make googly eyes at you. You know how to dance?"

"I'm not a professional dancer, if that's what you mean. I had an older brother and sister who taught me when I was growing up. They learned from my Aunt Beth."

"Where'd she learn? She a taxi dancer too?"

"No, on the stage. She performed in operas and musicals twenty to thirty years ago. She was a good dancer – ballet and tap."

"What's her name? She still around?"

"Beth Peet."

"Never heard of her, before my time."

"She got married and moved back to Minnesota."

"You from there?"

"I was born and raised here in Chicago. My mother's from Minnesota. My father's from Germany."

"Ain't it somethin' that we all come from somewhere else?"

"You dance like they do on the stage, ballet and tap?"

"No, I never had lessons like that. But I do know the modern ones, foxtrot, two step, jitterbug, waltz, Charleston, the Lindy stomp."

"Well, some customers, all they want to do is hang on to you and shove you around the floor. Get as close as they can to you. Some are creeps, but we dance with 'em anyway. A few guys come in here who really know how to move, especially the Flips. They ain't just here to grope the merchandise, but you dance with 'em too often, the white customers 'll think you're a share cropper havin' sex with 'em on the side. Flips really like blondes, so they'll be hot to dance with you."

"What's a Flip?"

"You must be one of those innocent church girls. You raised by nuns or somethin'? The Flips are Filipinos. There's scads of 'em in Chicago. Come over from the islands just to date American girls. Easy to fish. You play 'em right and they'll spend money on you, take you out for Chinese and buy you nice things. In case you're wonderin', since you didn't ask, name's Margaret Janezewski. Known as Maggie. Best ducky shin-cracker dancer at the Aragon."

The ordinary features and less than spectacular gown of Sally Glover relegated her to being unnoticed and, therefore, not a competitor. She looked up to Kristina and admired her. Sally had hoped to further strengthen their association at work by suggesting they become taxi dancers, a venture she was not confident enough to attempt alone. She felt graced by Kristina's kindness and unconditional acceptance of her. It made her feel capable of being peppy.

All too soon, the roll of drums set a steady rhythm that instantly seeped into the primordial core of every man and woman like an auditory drug coursing through their brains and bodies that set them moving reflexively in time to the beat. A fanfare from trumpets, trombones, and two French horns called them out onto the spacious bent wooden floor, spongy under foot on a structural cushion of cork layered with felt and springs that accentuated the sensation of floating weightlessness.

The wail of a saxophone expanded the sound and the cascading warble of clarinets and treble trill of flutes joined the musical dialogue in the rising momentum and volume that eclipsed all else and set the dancers and their partners swirling in a kaleidoscope of tribal energy under radiant crystal chandeliers, mosaic tiles, bright red and gold and green colored plaster, a terra-cotta ceiling and the fantasy of a Spanish palace courtyard surrounded by a regiment of graceful Romanesque arches.

The deep resonant thumping of a bass and tinkling riffs on a piano infiltrated the overt driving dominant brass and romantic melodic jazz style of swing.

Kristina's head-turning Nordic elegance drew a surge of men thrusting their tickets at her, beseeching her favor as their dance partner. "Hey, doll, let's dance." "Me first, beautiful." "Where did you come from?" "I ain't seen you here before." "You sure move nice, smooth." "Give me a chance." "What's your name, Greta Garbo?" "Take my ticket. The next dance is up." "The song's started." "I'm waitin' right here for you, babe. I'm next in line."

Chapter 2

Neptune's Court

The recent events of Joseph's life moved too quickly, beginning with his bold approach to speak to the driver of a model A Ford waiting for Kristina and Sally at the curb. When he asked her if she would like to go for some coffee and pie after the ballroom closed, she told him politely that she did not date any of the patrons and that her father would be waiting outside to take her home, an arrangement unheard of among taxi dancers seeking after-the-ball-is-over opportunities to make more money or manipulate their dates for gifts, such as a dress or a new coat.

Humbled and chagrined by her response, he did not pressure her or push his invitation, but he was curious that this beautiful young woman would be met by her father and assumed he was just being overly protective. At the sight of the man's thinning gray hair and still youngish Germanic features, Joseph determined not to be intimidated despite what Kristina had told him of her father's prowess as a bare-knuckle fighter. He moved quickly to the open driver's side window and bent slightly to better see him.

"Sir, my name is Joseph Blake. I would like to marry your daughter."

"What did you say your name was?" Conrad's roguish blue eyes assessed him up and down.

"Blake, sir, Joseph Blake."

"How long have you known her?"

"About a week, sir. I come here to the ballroom just to dance with her, nobody else. I've fallen in love with her, sir."

"How do you know she loves you or even wants to marry you?"

"I don't, sir."

"Then why are you asking me? Why don't you ask her?"

"I would like your permission to court her, sir."

"Court her. Don't you think asking me is a little old fashioned?"

"No, sir, I don't. I honor and respect her and you as her father."

"Well, I'm impressed, young man. What did she tell you about me?"

"Well, sir, she said that when you were a young man, and you were a bare-knuckle champion. I'm not a violent person and I respect you for that."

"So, you're afraid I'll punch you out if you hang around my daughter?"

"Something like that, sir. But even if you weren't a bare-knuckle fighter, I would still want to court her, with all due respect, sir."

Conrad noticed that Kristina and her friend, Sally, were trying desperately to keep from laughing. He looked back at Joseph.

"So, you want to call on her?"

"Yes, sir. She said she lives at home with you and your wife. I would just need to know the address and when it would be appropriate to come and see her."

"You see her here at the Aragon."

"It's not the same, sir. When I give her my ticket, we have only a few minutes, one song's worth.   Then there's a whole army of men waiting to dance with her. She's very popular."

Conrad looked at Katrina. "What do you say, daughter? Is it okay if Joseph Blake comes to the house to call on you?"

Kristina smiled and leaned toward the window. "I'll let you know the next time we dance."

"I'll be first in line."

"That's all for now," said Conrad. "It's late. We're headed home."

His face wreathed in a silly grin, Joseph watched the car pull away among waiting taxis and other automobiles loading up with dancers and their dates. He plunged his hands deep into his pockets and, whistling a dance tune, joined the thinning crowd making the long walk back to their boarding houses.

He was among the thousands of single, impoverished young men who lived in the city, renting cheap rooms, and working in available jobs as clerks, plumbers, electricians, stock yard herders, meat packers, factory assemblers, on railroad crews, traveling salesmen, stevedores and sailors in port while freighters were unloaded. They were drawn to the ballrooms and dance halls to escape their daily existence of survival to savor a few hours of heart pounding music and romantic fantasy.

Joseph had started as a shipping clerk, making deliveries to packing houses and other suffering businesses. In 1940 with the introduction of war production and the re-opening of factories, he was promoted to the position of shipping manager in a machine shop that converted into a weapons factory. He had big dreams.

Kristina's parents immediately liked the young man who came calling on their daughter. The impending war and institution of the military draft accelerated Joseph's and Katrina's wedding plans. Within a few months of their modest civil ceremony, Joseph was drafted into the army. Because of his two years at the University of Illinois, he was put through officer training and graduated as a lieutenant assigned to a supply squadron based in Australia to support the Pacific campaign against the Japanese.

Kristina continued to live with her parents and listened to the daily news on their Zenith Stratosphere radio about the progress of the war, listening for any news that might affect her new husband.

Two Navy seamen from the wartime troop transport blindfolded Joseph Blake with a black cloth that did not admit even a clot of light. They escorted him barefoot up the steep metal steps from the ship's hold and, each gripping his exposed arms, guided him across the deck as it gently rose and fell from the rolling swells. The hot humid air pressed down on him, exacerbating his sensation of anxiety and claustrophobia. He raised his head slightly, seeking a wisp of westerly sea breeze so he could breathe more easily through the suffocating fabric.

His handlers stripped off his summer tan uniform down to his shorts, then maneuvered him onto a wooden crate. He heard the whirring of electric clippers, a sound that rekindled his memory of basic training. The metal roughly raked his scalp and he felt his wavy blonde locks fall away. The intense sun raised a heavy sweat on his brow that seeped down under the cloth into his eyes which instantly bubbled with tears from the stinging salt.

Suddenly a deep commanding voice announced over a bullhorn, "Hear ye, hear ye, you are now to be judged in the court of King Neptune, god of the seven seas. Since until this day you have not crossed the equator at the 180th meridian, you are guilty as charged and will be punished by being thrown overboard into the open sea to be devoured by fish and turtles ruled by King Neptune. If you survive your ordeal and can return to the ship, you will no longer be a Polliwog, but will be promoted to the rank of Shellback with all privileges allowed. Are you prepared to meet your fate?"

Joseph vigorously nodded his head and mumbled through the cloth, "I am, sir."

"Good! Fellow Shellbacks, march the Polliwog to the side and push him overboard."

"On your feet, wog," one of the handlers ordered and helped Joseph to a standing position. He heard laughter and applause from the bystanders crowding the deck but lost his sense of direction as he was repeatedly spun about. Disoriented, he staggered and reached out for support as the cries from the watching men escalated, "Throw him overboard! Throw the wog overboard. There's sharks waiting for 'im down there! Hope you know how to swim! It's a long way back to the states!"

He felt himself being pushed backward into empty space and braced his body for a long fall. His metal dog tags rattled against his chest as he was brought up short with a splash in the half-empty swimming pool at mid-deck. He went under. His feet touched bottom and he immediately bobbed to the surface. Two sets of strong hands guided him to the poolside ladder.

"Up you go," a voice chuckled against his ear.

As he climbed out onto the deck, other hands immobilized him while the blindfold was removed.

The voice on the bullhorn boomed. "Welcome back, Lieutenant Blake. You are now promoted to a Shellback!"

A roar of approval accompanied the enthusiastic applause.

Joseph grinned and wiped the water from his eyes.

Chapter 3

Yanks

Joseph joined the soldiers pressed against the rail as the troop ship eased into Brisbane harbor shared by a carrier, Navy destroyers, commercial freighters, flying boats and small maritime vessels. A cheer went up at the ship's sidelong contact with the dock. Minutes later, a continuous line of uniformed men shouldering heavy duffel bags streamed down the gang plank and were directed by a greeting sergeant clutching a clipboard into an adjacent open warehouse where they clustered like a tight herd of cattle until the shouted directions by another sergeant moved them in the direction of a line of tables manned by lower ranking corporals and privates who processed their paperwork and moved them along to a convoy of waiting military trucks on the street.

Miles of army tents blanketed what had been the Ascot race track now converted to a bivouac and staging area for thousands of soldiers undergoing training for the campaign to take back New Guinea, held and fortified by the Japanese.

Just before he clambered down from the back of the green canopied supply truck, Joseph momentarily scanned the tent city and long lines of brown and tan-uniformed men coming and going quickly along the narrow aisles like a colony of oversized ants.

"Lieutenant!"

Joseph grasped a young cherubic-faced corporal's outstretched hand reaching up to him and eased himself with a light hop to the dirt race track now gouged by wide tire marks from the lumbering transport convoys that arrived and departed daily delivering troops and supplies. His eyes watered from the acrid odor of burned oil and diesel fumes undulating from the chugging engines invading the nearest field tents. He followed a rapidly growing line moving in the direction pointed out by the corporal. "HQ's the fifth one down, sir. You process in there."

"Thank you, Corporal." Joseph returned the brief salute.

Shouldering his duffel bag, he trudged through the dust that coated his shoes he would soon trade for jungle combat boots. A clerk reviewed the written orders Joseph handed to him and showed him his tent location on a wall diagram that also identified the kitchen and dining mess, shower and sink tents, and strategically placed rows of latrines at the outer edges of the track downwind from the main sleeping areas.

The sun-cooked humidity raised a sweat on his brow. He stepped along slightly raised wooden slatted walkways providing dry passage over stretches of mud from frequent rain storms that darkened a blistering blue sky before passing on.

The door to his cabin tent stood open. A tall balding man wearing a white tee shirt, tan slacks, and brown shoes rose from where he was seated writing a letter at the edge of his cot. Giving a brief salute he came forward to greet his tent mate.

"Welcome, Lieutenant. I'm Elmo Reed, first sergeant. I've been assigned to your unit. We'll be working together over on the island."

Joseph dropped his duffel on the opposite bunk and extended his hand. "Joseph Blake."

"Long boat trip."

"It was that."

"Your hair's growing back. That's a good sign. Neptune sailors didn't have to shave mine off." He laughed and ran his palm over his exposed shiny scalp. We have chronic baldness in my family on my father's side. Saves money on haircuts."

They both laughed. Elmo's warm brown-eyed expression established an immediate kinship with the lieutenant who was a few years younger than himself.

"Where you from, Joe?"

Joseph accepted Elmo's immediate familiarity after months of addressing other soldiers by their rank and insignia. "Chicago. Yourself?"

"Minneapolis."

"Cold winters."

"Oh, yeah, Chicago runs a close second."

"It's the wind off the lake."

"We get wind too, but it comes down from Canada."

"We must miss it. Here we are in the tropics talking about winters back home. How long have you been here?"

"Two months."

"You must know your way around."

"Oh, yeah, I'm a Yank down under. Aussies have a hard time getting' used to us. They'll raise a glass to us in town. They're glad we're here all the same, except for the Negro soldiers. They're quarantined as soon as they get off their segregated troop ships. They don't come over from the states with white soldiers. They're confined to a base outside the city. They don't see combat with us either. Army won't give 'em guns. They're used to build roads in the jungle or anyplace else."

"The brass let American soldiers mingle with the Australians?"

"Oh, yeah, we're in a holding position until MacArthur figures out what he's going to do. Aussies have been fighting the war since before we arrived. We're fighting right along with 'em now, especially the air war. MacArthur doesn't want us to get stir crazy, so we can get town passes just about every night."

"Do we have mail delivery?"

"About once a month. Usually comes with a troop ship arrival. You expecting mail?"

"I married just before OCS. My wife traveled with me until I shipped out. You married?"

"Three years. Two kids, a boy and a girl."

"That's wonderful. My wife's due," said Joseph.

"Sorry you can't be there. It's a great experience."

"Hate to miss it. I'll make up for it when I return."

"Yeah, we have to hold on to that." Elmo glanced at Joseph's duffel. "You want to unpack first or would you like the grand tour?"

"Grand tour."

"The mess tent and the latrines are the two most important places."

"We about at lunch time?"

Elmo checked his watch. "We'll stop by there first. Everyone eats in shifts."

Joseph opened a canvas briefcase side bag and sifted through a thin stack of documents. Looks like we have a meeting at headquarters tomorrow morning at 08:00 hours."

"That will be in town, the AMP building. General MacArthur works from there. We won't be likely to meet him. We have a major down the chain who's our contact. I've had two meetings with him. He's been waiting for your arrival. We've got a big job ahead of us, a logistics nightmare."

"Well, I don't mind a challenge."

"Me neither, but there are serious issues getting what we need for the troops. We're a long boat ride from the states. Takes forever from the factory. We've been stocking up inventory at Amberley Airfield to take over to Port Moresby on C-47s. We won't fly alone though. They give us P38 escorts to chase off Jap Zeroes."

"Have you been over there yet?"

Elmo shook his head. "We'll be going together. First time for both of us."

"It will be good to work with you, Elmo."

"Likewise. Ready for the tour?"

"Lead the way."

Large and small military trucks and jeeps interspersed with a few Australian civilian cars, trams and buses jammed the main road into Brisbane. As their jeep crawled along Queens Street in bumper to bumper traffic, the five to seven story brown brick buildings, small shops and the display window of a department store reminded Joseph of a typical American small town invaded by an army.

Since his arrival four months ago, Joseph and his friend, Quartermaster First Sergeant, Elmo Reed, had made the daily trip by jeep downtown to the AMP Building where General MacArthur had established his headquarters to direct the Pacific Campaign.

The meeting had gotten off on the wrong footing.

After one week, Major Donaldson, to whom Joseph reported, promoted him to the rank of captain. "I'm glad you're here, Captain. You have no idea how glad I am you're here. I was gonna have to take my ass over to that God-forsaken island until you showed up. I have a good thing going for me here on the mainland. Shacked up with an Aussie broad who says she'll marry me if I promise to take her back to the states when the war's over. So, I promise her, but this war ain't gonna be over for a long time. Japs have dug in for the long haul. We're at the bottom of their shit pile. I'm givin' you two bars in place of the one you came over with. Your first sergeant is an asset to you. He knows the ropes, right Top?"

"Yes, sir," Elmo gave a curt nod.

"The way it goes here, you take care of me, and I'll take care of you."

"We'll do our job, Major," said Joseph.

"You now own the responsibility to establish and manage a supply chain in support of Fifth Air Force and ground troop operations based at Port Moresby."

"First Sergeant Reed will get you orientated."

"He has already been most helpful, sir."

"The General is making a big push. He does not tolerate failure, absolutely none."

"We'll address the problems as we encounter them, sir."

"Until you leave for Moresby, I want a weekly report of your progress on my desk."

"Of course, sir."

"Otherwise, I don't want to see your faces in this office. It's assholes and elbows. Is that clear?"

"Very clear, sir."

"If you should need anything, First Sergeant Reed knows where and how to get it. Just don't come to me."

"Understood, sir."

"Good, it's important that we understand each other."

Joseph wondered how the major had won his cluster in the first place and secondly, how he could live with himself. He clearly didn't want to take any risks where other men could go out and do his work for him and maybe die in his place for their efforts. Joseph didn't trust the shifty-eyed man. His head periodically twitched at the conclusion of a directive statement, at which moment his right hand quickly shielded his trimmed brown mustache as an involuntary gesture that he was concealing something.

Later, when he and Elmo were returning to Camp Ascot, Elmo offered, "He's a bit of an asshole."

Joseph nodded. Although profanity was a common expression among soldiers, he never used any himself.

"There are two reasons he doesn't want to go over to Moresby. He's afraid he'll get his ass shot off and he's bucking for a spot on

MacArthur's staff. On top of that, he's married and has a kid back in the states. He's just leadin' on the Aussie babe he's shacked up with."

"Well, I guess it takes all kinds," said Joseph.

"Yeah, it takes all kinds."

Seated in a forward passenger section of the fuselage, Joseph and Elmo watched through the rain streaked canopy as the two prop engines of their C-47 aircraft coughed to life. The spinning velocity of the blades crescendoed from a whine to a roar, as the heavily loaded cargo plane lumbered along the tarmac and lifted slowly into the gray overcast sky.

From ten thousand feet, they looked down on a miniature flotilla of naval warships, battle ships, destroyers, cruisers, gunboats, torpedo boats, patrol boats, oil and gasoline tankers, a hospital ship, spread for many miles barely moving northward away from Queensland's Cape York Peninsula across the Coral Sea.

 The thrum of engines combined with the metallic vibration and heat within the plane lulled Joseph into a restive doze until Elmo gently shook his arm to wake him.

"We're coming up on the island."

Joseph twisted in his seat for a clear view through his window. Far below, the coastal topography of cane and spear grass savannahs blended into malarial swamps of mangrove, sago, and nipa palms that collided with jungle rain forest covering the jagged volcanic peaks and deep valleys of the Owen Stanley mountain range.

"Japanese forces hold the north side of the island at Buna-Gona," said Elmo.

In one of their briefings back at Brisbane, Major Donaldson had told them, "Port Moresby can't be used for anything more than an operations staging area. It's a small advanced headquarters to support combat operations. MacArthur considers Moresby at great risk of being strafed and bombed from the air and then overrun by Japanese infantry. The Japs have fortified and hold all the high ground, including Milne Bay to the east and Papua to the west."

Wanting to elude automatic ground fire from Japanese soldiers hiding in jungle foxholes and bunkers, the pilot put the C-47 into a steep descent and made a short landing at the Port Moresby airstrip.

The engines faded to silence. Coming off the plane, Joseph and Elmo watched a long line of wounded soldiers. Some were missing limbs, others had their bodies partially covered with blood-soaked bandages, pressed tight to hold exposed viscera. One moaned through the bloodied remains of a face. Many were carried on stretchers to another waiting C-47 for evacuation to Brisbane. Joseph and Elmo walked quickly past fly-encrusted corpses waiting to be flown to Australia for burial.

Oppressive heat assaulted the two men as they thrust forward against an invisible wall of humidity that sucked the strength from their bodies. A confusion of sound spun them around to watch P-38 fighter aircraft taking off and rising into the airspace over the bay to come together in squadron formation on a bombing run to the east.

As they lugged their duffels to lines of tents infiltrating the dense encroaching jungle that threatened to creep out over the airstrip, they saw unshaven emaciated bearded men wearing tattered uniforms stained with mud, diarrhea and jungle rot, oozing festering open sores on arms and legs, their fingernails gone, consumed by mold and damp.

"They're going through shit out here," said Elmo.

A ragged solider with no visible rank insignia slowly stood, as if in great pain, from a log as they approached. "That a supply plane?"

"Yes," said Joseph.

"Bout time. What's the hold up? We're dyin' over here."

"Long ways from the states," said Elmo. "Takes two months by ship."

"I'm Captain Busmer."

Elmo started to raise his right hand to his forehead.

"We don't salute here, never. Not even if General MacArthur walks by. He'd be a fool to do it and a sitting duck if he tried wearin' his stars and ribbons. Though from what we know about 'im, we're never gonna see him. He's tryin' to fight the war from behind a desk by sendin' us out to do his dirty work. Best advice hide your bars, Captain. Sniper'll take you out in a heartbeat."

"Thank you for the warning." Joseph quickly removed his Captain's bars and stuffed them deep into his pocket. "Blake," he extended his hand, "Joseph Blake."

"Bill – Bill Busmer."

"Elmo Reed." Elmo shared a handshake.

"Good to meet you. Biggest problem we have here is not enough of anything and what does get through is rotten with mold. Have to throw most of it away. You wouldn't happen to have a load of sirloin steaks on that goony bird?" Busmer asked, referring to the C-47. "Damn sick of eatin' bully beef over here. You open a can, it'll turn your stomach. Not even beef. The mutton those Aussies cram in the cans we just throw it away. It's god damn putrid, makes you sicker 'n a dog. Hear the Navy eats good. Too bad MacArthur don't feed us grunts better, since we're doin' his god damn dirty work. Anyway, you didn't come over here to hear me gripe. Native carriers 'll unload the plane for ya. They carry our shit in the jungle. They're used to livin' out here like animals. We aren't. They don't look like much, all skin and bones, but they're stronger and can outlift and out march any one of us. You need to get acquainted with 'em. Make your hardass life easier. There's an empty tent down along the trail. Must have your name on it. Don't leave a flashlight or lantern on inside at night. Makes you a target. You won't be alive come morning."

"The Japs that close to us?" Elmo asked.

"Our patrols can go out only so far. Japs hold all the high ground. We're stuck in the swamps. Have to fight off snakes and crocodiles as much as Japs. Never bargained for this. Japs are jungle fighters. Snipers get in close. Can't see 'em 'til it's too late. Camouflage. Mostly we never see 'em at all. They live in the ground, come up out of holes, some in trees, pick us off and disappear. You see all the wounded being evacuated when you came in?"

Joseph and Elmo nodded.

"Trip wires with grenades and land mines in the bush everywhere. That's why you saw legs missing."

"How's the receiving end on supplies?" asked Joseph.

"Not enough and not steady enough. Ask anyone. Can't use half of what we get. Jungle rot. Nothin' dries out here. Between that and the leeches droppin' down out of trees crawlin' up your legs, suckin' on your balls and crawlin' up your ass and the mosquitoes, we're fightin' what we can't see and losin'. Jungle's as much of an enemy as the Japs. Every soldier here's got malaria. Makes us so sick we can't fight."

"What about quinine?"

"Not worth a damn. Pop a dozen of the damn pills and parasites still eat your guts from the inside."

"What about atabrine?"

"No one wants to take it. Turns your skin yellow. Makes us look like Japs. Rumor is it ruins your manhood. More than a rumor. Can't even get your dick up."

"We brought over a lot of DEET," said Elmo.

"Bug bombs help a little, but they don't last. Even when you spray inside your bed net, the bastards find a way to get to you. Rub it on your skin and it sweats off."

"None of the tents are marked and no flags. Which one is HQ?" asked Joseph.

"Fifth one down the path," said Busmer. "But if you're lookin' for Colonel Sebastian, you're more likely to find him at maintenance or the fuel depot, about a half mile down the airstrip. He's hands on workin' with the men here. Don't spend time sittin' behind a desk like MacArthur."

After leaving their duffels on mosquito netting covered cots in their tent, Joseph and Elmo hiked along the edge of the tarmac in the direction of several canvas covered wood sheds pointed out to them by Captain Busmer

With no rank insignia displayed, they did not recognize the lanky soldier in a sweat-soaked camouflage uniform among six privates and non-coms rolling large barrels of petroleum from storage to a staging area in preparation for refueling a B-17 bomber while other crew members loaded arsenal onto racks in the bomb bay.

Not knowing whom to address, Joseph intercepted a sergeant headed in their direction, "We're looking for Lieutenant Colonel Sebastien."

"Yes, sir, that's him over there pushin' with the others. He's in the middle."

"Thank you, sergeant."

As the colonel walked back to assist with another barrel, he noticed the two men waiting for him. "You two just arrive? You look lost. I can put you to work."

"I'm Captain Joseph Blake, sir, and this is First Sergeant Elmo Reed. We just came over from Brisbane."

"Must have been on the goony bird that landed."

"Yes, sir."

"See you got rid of your bars. Good thing. Welcome to Port Moresby, gentlemen, and welcome to whatever supplies you brought with you." His full mouth parted in an energetic smile as he shook hands with each of them. "Let's head back to the main camp and I'll brief you on what we're doing here."

As they returned to the camouflaged tents and outbuildings bordering the tarmac, he waved his arm and pointed out features of the camouflaged storage areas and anti-aircraft guns.

"Moresby is General MacArthur's beach head, his stepping stone from Australia to take back the islands and move north to the Philippines. We support all Air Corps supplies for petroleum and salvage of parts. We do routine maintenance for fighters, light bombers, transports, and any transient aircraft that can't make it back to its base. If we can't repair it, we ship it to Australia." His crisp blue eyes blinked rapidly at the buffeting trade winds whipping them from offshore.

"We house and feed combat crews at the Arcadia Transient Camp, just west of where you're bivouacked, and we operate three air depots, Jackson, Moresby, and Milne Bay. We have five other airdromes on other islands to salvage damaged aircraft. We do welding and sheet metal, some machining and engine repair. Getting what we need when we need it is the biggest problem. We can't do the mission without resources. Procurement and logistics with supply sources back home aren't up to speed. But we have to figure out ways to move on. And when materiel does arrive, we must deal with inadequate storage and transportation issues, tactics, our resupply points, and the weather. With the rain and humidity, perishable food spoils overnight. Tents leak like a sieve. We've had to dump thousands of cans of food. And the insects – the god damn insects get into everything."

As the next few weeks progressed, Joseph grappled with what Elmo had described as a "logistics nightmare."

They supervised crews from transport ships transferring food and medical supplies for portable hospitals, arsenal, ordnance, cannons, 60mm mortars, Thompson .45 caliber submachine guns, .30 caliber machine guns, howitzers, Browning automatic rifles and cases of pineapple grenades. Quarter ton trucks carried combat equipment and supplies to aid stations in forward areas. Elmo instructed his men on dispensing camouflage uniforms, helmets hung with green mosquito netting, and other supplies, including mail.

Joseph opened the envelope. When he removed the black and white photograph of his three month old son, several other photographs, a news clipping, and a folded letter from Kristina, he had to leave his shared tent and find a secluded spot where he could sit and read and, through his tears, absorb the image of his wife holding their baby boy, Elias, starring wide-eyed at the camera.

When the photograph was taken, a slight breeze had blown a lock of Kristina's wavy, shoulder-length blonde hair across one eye, rendering a coy expression. Her long shapely legs descended from a light floral print summer dress to small feet propped up in canvas wedgies. To Joseph, she looked like a movie star.

He unfolded and read the news article written by his mother-in-law, Julie Holtzman, clipped from the Chicago Tribune. It was titled, *A Goldbrick Papa Enjoys His Role.*

Elias Blake was deeply loved by the circle of adults who sheltered him. His father was on the other side of the world in New Guinea fighting against the Japanese. The year was 1944. Kristina showed him photographs of Joseph, young and handsome, looking back at him with a wide confidant smile and a depth of gentleness in his warm brown eyes. His father had a great shock of wavy blonde hair that made him appear dashing and cavalier in his captain's uniform

Elias and his mother lived with her parents in a white two-story frame house on a narrow, shaded street on the west side of town. He was never left alone. Either his mother or grandmother or a visiting aunt watched over him, even while he napped. When he became ill, coughing and gagging on mucous with tiny infant coughs, his mother never slept.

He knew who his mother was and could differentiate her from the other adults. Her voice was the gentlest and her slender face smiling and solicitous whenever she looked down at him or lifted him close to her. He knew her blue eyes and the sweet fresh smell of her flawless rosy skin. His stubby little fingers pulled and entangled her long sleek blonde hair and he burbled and chortled at its texture.

He knew milk and when he saw its shape approaching his face, he clutched the bottle and held it tightly while his puffy lips sucked and squeaked the rubber nipple. The warm liquid coursed down his throat and curled in his stomach, expanding with well-being and contentment. She handled him gently when she changed his diapers and he talked to her with his incoherent cooing and belching sounds.

When she took him outdoors, the sense of motion, the multitude of smells in the air, the colors of the sky and lawn and flowers and the high-pitched melodic bird calls mingled with the slow chug of passing cars assaulted his senses as she pushed him in his baby carriage and sang to him.

These impressions of the world outside the house left him in awe, desiring more. On the inside, the pungent garlic, onion, meat and fresh dough and paprika food smells of his grandmother's European cooking and the occasional bang of pots and the crackling of grease and blistering pop of stews and gravies filled his senses. So, life beckoned him. And so did death.

As the pediatrician left the house, he told Elias's mother and her parents that nothing more could be done for her baby. Thousands of infants and children across the country were succumbing to the polio virus. All they could do was pray for him.

They prayed fervently and wept and went without sleep. They took turns holding him all through the night and never laid him down for fear he would stop breathing. They sponged his small quivering body with a cool wash cloth in an attempt to reduce the discomfort of his raging fever.

His eyes did not open.

Elias began to die.

His mother was beside herself with grief. She refused to let anyone else hold him, as though she alone could protect him from death. Her husband would never see his child, only photographic prints just as the infant had seen him only in a photograph. Her emotion choked her so that she could no longer pray. She heard the rapid words of prayer uttered by her mother and father. As her child faded, so did her faith.

The doctor had told them that if her baby lived for twenty-four hours, there was a remote chance that he might survive, but with the crippling effects of polio. By late morning, the infant began breathing more easily. His mother detected a soft sibilant snore and his skin was no longer hot to the touch.

He continued to live.

Elias enjoyed the feel of the grass between his tiny toes as, under his mother's watchful eye, he careened about the back and side yard. His chubby legs protruded from bulky swathed diapers and pumped him along with a rubbery flexibility until he toppled forward or sometimes just sat down with a soft bump.

The discovery that he was the creator of his own feces was a marvel to him. They became his treasures that he did not want his mother to find and take away from him. He cunningly would crawl behind the couch to do his business and play with the squishy greenish-brown substance, his early experience with the equivalent of molding clay. He did not know how his mother could discover his clandestine activity which he had so cleverly hidden himself. But he had not yet reached the age to understand the nature of evidence, in this case the movement of drapes, the sour-sweet odor wafting from behind the couch, and the telltale smearing on his face and body.

Elias was growing, but still hadn't met his daddy. He had seen one particular photograph of his father so many times that the image was imprinted in his mind, along with a helpful prompt from his mother, "He's your Daddy."

*   *   *

Togugawa Ichirou waited patiently for the American patrol to pass from sight on the jungle path. An advance scout of the Tsukamoto Battalion, he left his bunker under the concealment of darkness and penetrated the perimeter of the camp spread along the edge of the Port Moresby airstrip and extending for several miles along a cleared dirt track to allow the passage of supply trucks and men.

His mission was to establish a presence as an unseen sniper, constantly changing locations and taking out individual enemy soldiers over a period of five days to create fear and havoc among their ranks.

He used a type 97 *Arisaka* bolt action rifle. The 6.5 X 50mm cartridge traveling through the long barrel burned the propellant, emitted little smoke or flash and rendered him undetectable with a bullet velocity and accuracy up to one hundred yards.

Seeking to maximize his view of the main camp, he camouflaged his helmet and body with fronds and leafy branches, burrowed into a shallow foxhole, and waited, dozing during the day. In the inky blackness of nightfall, he quietly climbed into a tree. He removed a coil of hemp rope from his pack and tied his left leg to a branch to keep from falling. He listened to a sudden light rain rattling against the leaves and thought of how he, as a *Shinto* warrior, honored his Emperor by risking his life which he would gladly sacrifice in combat according to the *bushido* oath he had taken to never surrender.

Joseph and Elmo woke to the metallic roar of a P38 squadron taking off for a bombing run.

"Morning," mumbled Joseph. He disliked the fetid smell of his unwashed fatigues. He hoped to get in a quick outdoor shower and a shave at the latrine tent before starting work. He and Elmo were beginning to take on the sallow haggard appearance of the other troops.

"Early start," said Elmo, pulling on his boots. "Need a cup a coffee to crank me up. At least we didn't have an all nighter."

"Hard to sleep in this heat," said Joseph.

Elmo grunted, stood up from his bunk and tightened his web belt. "I think the mosquitoes eat their way through the netting."

"Might get some mail today," said Joseph.

"I'm due a letter," said Elmo. "Haven't gotten one in a month."

Joseph finished lacing his boots. "Colonel Sebastien wants to meet with us after the C-47's come in this morning."

"Think they'll be on time? They're a week overdue."

"He wants to talk about a plan to improve management of the supply chain from Brisbane. Once the goods come off the ships, they sit in a warehouse for two weeks before they get sent to us. He wants us to coordinate so they go directly from the transports to the aircraft and can be delivered the next day."

"That means talking with Major Donaldson in Brisbane," said Elmo. "He'll actually have to do some work to organize it. Can you reach him from the com center here?"

"I'll try an interim ship to shore transmission. We're too far away. Otherwise, it will have to be a written request signed by Sebastien. He outranks Donaldson. If I sign it, Donaldson will just ignore it."

"Did you hear if he made it to MacArthur's staff?"

"I would doubt it," said Joseph. "MacArthur wants go-getters under him, not slackers."

The cacophony of early morning shrieks and whistles of tropical birds echoed and re-echoed through the surrounding jungle forest.

As Joseph and Elmo stepped out of their tent, through the clustered trunks of palms, they heard a sonic wall of droning engines and watched three C-47 supply planes, land and taxi over to maintenance and ground crews gathered, waiting at the end of the tarmac to service and unload the aircraft.

Joseph and Elmo walked along the dirt trail toward the latrines, located well past the kitchen and mess tent where the aroma of hot coffee competed with the penetrating odor of rot and decay from the encroaching swamp. Elmo said he was stopping off for a cup. Joseph continued on alone.

He heard a sharp crack from the nearby jungle canopy. He slapped at his neck thinking a large flying insect had attached itself to him. He fell sideways into the mud freshly created from the night's rain. He remembered the photo of his wife and their son, Elias, and remembered and remembered and remembered until his memory faded to eternal darkness and was gone.

Hearing the shot, Elmo ducked, spilling hot coffee. From the mess entrance, he saw Joseph lying flat on the ground and figured he had dropped at the sound of the rifle shot. He waited to see if there would be any more gunfire.

An infantryman spotted the Japanese sniper and killed him with a single shot. Togugawa's rifle bounced through a network of branches to the ground. The infantryman pumped three more rounds into the dead soldier's body, as he fell from his perch and swung at the end of the rope tied to his leg.

When Joseph didn't move, Elmo ran out to him, shouting, "Joe! Joe! Are you hit?" Elmo saw the blood pool seeping from Joseph's neck at the base of his head. He knelt beside his friend. "Oh, God. Oh my God. Medic!" he shouted, knowing it was too late. "Medic! Over here!"

Later that morning, Elmo gathered Joseph's personal letters and the photos of his wife and child. If he survived the war and made it back to the States alive, he would return them to her and share in her grief.

11 ICONS

Chapter 4

Awakening

The pressure directly over Kristina's heart increased and a sensation of numbness and a loss of feeling seeped outward to her arms and legs. She could not move or call out. Her shallow breathing puffed in short bursts. She dreamed she was floating through a dark void of endless night. This place was death. This was where she would find Joseph.

A warm summer night breeze lifted the white lace curtains like a silent benign ghost billowing over her bedside night table where the spring of a clock unwound second by relentless second with a loud affirmative 'chock' echoing from the wooden floor and walls of her childhood.

Other than assisting her to the bathroom, her mother could not coax her from her bed. She would sit up and eat a small bowl of chicken and vegetable soup when Julie brought it to her and sipped water from a glass next to the telegram on the table.

She had not bathed in a week. Her once beautiful hair hung in greasy strands parting to expose pathways of pink scalp. Sweat stained her nightgown in yellowish brown blotches and the odor of decay had begun to rise from her sheets and blankets.

She was only vaguely aware of the rosy-cheeked cherubic face of her one-year-old son, Elias, peering over the top of her mattress and chortling at her in a language she didn't understand. When she opened her eyes and smiled at him, he laughed and laughed and she wondered why he was so happy. But then he did not know about the telegram, what it said, and what it meant and what had happened to their lives. He was just happy to see her open her eyes and look at him.

She noticed how similar her son's excited brown eyes and expressive mouth were to his father's. A realization that Joseph continued to live through their son began to incubate. She reached out and gently touched his blonde curls.

She was aware of her friend, Sally Glover, coming to sit with her and commiserate, although few words passed between them. Sally would pick up Elias and seat him on her lap as the center of attention. Kristina did not want to hear any more news about the war. When she finally ventured downstairs in a somnambulant state to the kitchen and living room, her mother removed the newspapers with their blaring headlines about the European and Pacific campaigns. Her father ceased playing the radio announcements and went next door to listen.

Two months later, she began taking Elias for short walks in his stroller around the neighborhood. When people who knew her approached her to express their condolences, she smiled politely, thanked them, and quickly moved on.

One morning, before Julie could dispose of the daily newspaper, she caught Kristina reading a feature story she had written, one of a series about women on the home front.

"How long have you been writing these?" her daughter asked.

"I started a few weeks ago. When we heard about Joseph, I became interested in women who are waiting the outcome of the war, because of you."

"Are you writing about me?"

"No, my darling, of course not. Our personal family life is not for public consumption."

"What about these other women?"

"I include them only if they are willing. The purpose is not to be voyeuristic, but to show their strength and fortitude. Women are doing marvelous things on the home front to take up the slack while the men are gone. What they are accomplishing will change the status of women in this country forever."

"How do you mean?"

"Women will no longer allow themselves to be treated as second class citizens suitable only as sexual objects, giving birth, raising children, cooking and cleaning and essentially being domestic slaves for men."

"What does that have to do with me? I'm no longer a wife. I'm a widow and I'm only twenty-one."

"That's the point. You have a whole life ahead of you in which you can do something remarkable. You have a beautiful child, a son you can love and nurture. You yourself are a beautiful young woman. You're also intelligent and have skills that can gain you meaningful employment, maybe even lead to a career."

"What kind of career? I don't think I can be a journalist like you."

"You have to discover what you want to do. It takes a little research, but one thing for sure, you have to pull yourself together and get out of the house. You don't have to become a riveter on an aircraft assembly line or enlist in the military as a WAC or a WAF or even become a nurse. Because you have a child to take care of, there are certain limitations on what you might do, but not many. Some might require more education and that's always possible. Did Sally Glover tell you she has a job at a bank now?"

"No."

"Before the war, only men worked in banks. If you're interested, you might talk to Sally about it. From the time you were a little girl, you've always been good with numbers. You speak and present yourself well. If you started working in a bank, who knows where that might lead."

Kristina bathed, washed her hair, and put on the summer dress that she had worn in the photograph taken with her holding her baby, the picture that she had sent to Joseph in New Guinea. She slipped on a pair of flats and walked outside into the back yard where her mother and father maintained a victory garden.

As part of the war effort, the government rationed sugar, butter, milk, cheese, eggs, coffee, meat and canned goods. Labor and transportation shortages restricted the harvest and movement of fruits and vegetables to market.

Julie, her mother, had been raised on a wheat farm homesteaded by her parents on the Minnesota prairie during the late 1890s. Growing and preserving garden crops had provided them their primary source of food along with the chickens and livestock they raised and slaughtered.

From the time she was a small child in Chicago, Kristina had helped her mother plant and harvest produce in their backyard garden plot. Their industry   predated the call to make gardening a family and community enterprise to support the needs of the war by saving commercial canned foods for the troops.

The regulations and constraints reminded Kristina that her husband had been a supply officer and depended on the availability of raw material resources for all the soldiers who were out there fighting in Europe and in the South Pacific.

Citizens across the country cultivated twenty million urban gardens that produced ten million tons of fruits and vegetables in private yards, parks, public spaces, empty lots, and on building rooftops. Magazine publications provided instructions on how to preserve this copious output by canning, a process in which Kristina had years of experience working alongside her mother.

She knew how to operate a pressure cooker with a tight lock down lid to prevent the escape of steam and maintain the high temperature necessary to kill bacteria in the food. She would transfer the processed food into glass canning jars sealed with lids and bands.

The growing and harvesting and preservation of food prompted her to become more aware of the war-time economy, the community effort of children in schools and Scout troops pushing wagons and wheel barrows collecting scrap metal in sponsored drives to contribute to the millions of pounds of aluminum to build fighter planes, steel to build battle ships, and kitchen grease for the extraction of glycerin to make explosives for bombs and ammunition.

War production procured textiles, wool needed for military uniforms and silk and nylon to make parachutes.

The War Production Board issued regulations and guidelines to clothing manufacturers to save the amount and length of fabrics. Violation of the restrictions resulted in the prosecution, fines, and imprisonment of garment makers, which became rare in civilian life.

The Office of Price Administration oversaw the rationing of foods, metal, gasoline, and shoes. The military needs for leather and rubber restricted buyer consumption to three pairs of shoes per year.

Kristina realized there was more she should and could do. It was time for her to rejoin the living.

Kristina noticed that the line inside the bank was growing longer toward the end of the day, mostly women and only an occasional late middle-age or elderly man. She easily distinguished those customers from mills and factories wearing work boots, coveralls, shirts with rolled-up sleeves, and short cut hair tied back with red or blue bandanas, from the shop girls and office workers modeling gray polyester business suits or skirts and blouses and emulating the luxurious wavy long hair, mascara, and red lipstick of the leading glamorous female movie stars, Hedy Lamar, Veronica Lake, and Lauren Bacall.

Friday was payday and every one of the ten bank tellers transacted a steady stream of deposits and cash withdrawals. While their men fought overseas, the women made money at home. The Chicago Trust and Savings Bank enjoyed a thriving continuous flow of business. The manager had extended the Friday service hours to six o'clock to accommodate the army of female employees stopping in from work on their way home.

Kristina manned a teller position next to her friend, Sally Glover, who had recommended her to the overweight fifty-year-old manager, Dwight Sampson, and arranged an interview. Impressed by her beauty and respectful comportment, he had immediately hired her and assigned Sally to train her at the teller window.

Kristina surprised herself at the ease with which she fit in working with the other female employees. She discovered she had an aptitude for the efficiency required in implementing financial rules and regulations.

Promptly at six o'clock, the armed bank guard locked the front doors and let the finishing customers leave a few at a time.

"After the next one, I'm closing out here," Kristina told Sally. She completed the transaction, put up her closed sign, and counted out her cash drawer hand balance. She signaled to the supervisor in charge of cash that she was ready to enter the safe according to their double locking procedure. She entered the verified amounts of her notes and coins in the reserve cash register which she and her supervisor signed. When the last customer had departed and the bank closed for the day, Sally, who was the head cashier, each teller, and the head supervisor checked and confirmed all items of the cash balance. Upon completing his review and agreeing with the figures, the manager signed the cash balance book.

"I've observed how well you handle customers at the window," said Dwight, tugging at his wrinkled brown polyester suit coat. We're going to be needing another loan officer in the next few months and

I'd like you to start training with Myra Blankenship. You've met her before."

"Yes, thank you, sir."

"I've discussed it with her. She foresees that at some point she's going to need an assistant and she's in agreement. You'll report to her Monday morning."

"Thank you, sir. I appreciate the opportunity."

"Have a nice weekend, Kristina. We're fortunate that Sally brought you to us." Dwight pulled at his long nose as a punctuating gesture.

As they walked along the crowded street to take the elevated light rail, Sally grinned and said, "Never fails, Kristina. Stick with me, kid, and you'll go far."

"You keep opening the door for me, chum."

"It's not me. You sell yourself. People are attracted to you, just like when we were at the Aragon."

The light in Kristina's blue eyes faded.

"Oh, I'm sorry I mentioned it."

"It's okay. That's okay. I'm dealing with Joseph's death a little at a time. I just have to accept the fact and move on."

"I'm still sorry."

"I have Elias. I have our son."

"You're lucky. You're very lucky."

"When the war's over and the men come home, you'll find your man, Sally. Whoever he turns out to be, he'll deserve you."

"I haven't given up hope."

Kristina put her arm around her friend's shoulders and gave her a brief hug just before they climbed the platform steps to the elevated transit, known as the 'L'.

"My husband is one of those men who doesn't want his wife to work," Myra Blankenship said as she opened a legal document and riffled through several forms on her desk. "We had a hasty courtship before he was drafted. Thank God I didn't get pregnant or I wouldn't be sitting here." She adjusted her glasses.

The slanted tortoise shell frames reminded Kristina of cat eyes. She leaned forward from her chair to peruse a page that Myra turned to in the loan operations manual.

The discussion when Kristina entered Myra's spacious office that morning had begun with an exchange of appropriate greetings. Containing her awe at Kristina's tailored beauty presented in a gray business suit and secretly admiring the younger woman's coiffed blonde French twist, Myra had motioned her to sit in one of the three chairs lined up in front of her desk. Kristina noticed a second empty desk separated from Myra's by several feet near a side wall and assumed that would become her work area.

Myra's reference to her husband had come about as a way of bridging her perceived social gap with Kristina, who looked more suitable to appear on a movie screen than in the formal confines of a Mid-west bank. Myra's recessed undistinguished features and attempt at a glamorous hair style, hampered by an explosion of frizzy reddish-brown curls, did not succeed in creating the impression of attractiveness she desired. So she opted for compensating with a manner of tough efficiency and too much red lipstick. Placing a copy of the Chicago Tribune front page conspicuously on the corner of her desk provided a reference and entrée to the ensuing conversation. The headlines announced a victory in the Navy's island campaign in the South Pacific.

"Mr. Sampson spoke highly of your work as a cashier."

"My co-worker, Sally Glover, trained me well."

"She's diligent and steady. Never makes a mistake."

"I was reading the morning paper just before you came in. Do you follow the war news?"

"I used to, but I haven't lately. My mother is a journalist on the Tribune, so I get updates."

"My husband was wounded," said Myra.

"I'm sorry. My sympathy to you."

"There might be nothing to be sympathetic about."

"Was he badly wounded?"

"Enough to give him his ticket home."

"Well, at least he's coming home. My husband won't be."

"I know. Mr. Sampson told me you're a widow. I apologize. I won't dwell on the topic."

"It's okay. I've learned to cope. It's one of the reasons I came to work here in the bank. You have something to celebrate. What's your husband's name?"

"William – Bill. He was a gunner on a battleship. A Navy man. He told me in one of his letters he liked being in the Navy. He liked working together with his crew. It suited him. I don't know what he'll do when he comes home. He'll be handicapped. Lost his right arm in an explosion. He's not left handed."

"My husband's name is Joseph. He was a supply officer, a captain in New Guinea. The war office told me in a letter he was killed by a sniper."

"You have a son."

"Yes, I have a son, Elias. He's three years old. His grandfather takes care of him during the day and sometimes a neighbor woman watches him."

Myra's gaze cast down to the news headline. "Seems like we all met our men, then there was this mass exodus like we're a society of insects. I won't give up my job when Bill comes home. If he tries to force me, I'll leave him. I'll just leave him. How did you and Joseph meet?"

Kristina did not immediately respond.

"There I go again," Myra brushed her hand across the desk. "I said I wouldn't dwell on it and I'm still talking about it."

"That's okay. I don't mind. We met at the Aragon Ball Room. I was a taxi dancer."

"A taxi dancer. How romantic. How thrilling. I can picture you as a taxi dancer."

"It was fun. Sally was a dancer too."

"Sally Glover, a taxi dancer?"

"We were working as secretaries then. Dancing made us a little more money when times were hard."

"It's like you led another life, a secret life."

"I guess it was kind of another life, not so secret though."

"I mean you took your life into your own hands. That's what I did getting into banking and I don't want to give it up. You inspire me, Kristina. You inspire me."

Kristina grinned and shook her head slightly.

"Bill mentioned New Guinea in one of his letters. When his ship left Australia, they were going to the Coral Sea. That was my last letter from him." Myra caught Kristina's glance at the operations manual on her desktop. "Well, on to more mundane matters." That Kristina might think less of her for her lack of enthusiasm about her husband coming home, she said, "It isn't that I don't miss my husband. I do miss him. I miss holding him at night and making his breakfast in the morning."

"I understand. I miss my husband too."

"Listen. There's a lot here to learn about loans. I'll be walking you through the procedures, but you might find it helpful to read each section first, then we'll talk about it and look at documentation."

"I'll get started." Kristina received the manual from her, opened it on her lap, and began to read, quickly familiarizing herself with such terms as loan-to-value and loan-to-cost.

She carefully read the section entitled Loan Officer Duties and Responsibilities.

In soliciting mortgage loans, she would be taking information from prospective borrowers and completing the loan application form, analyzing the borrower's income and debt and pre-qualifying the borrower by collecting financial information to determine the maximum affordable mortgage amount.

She would inform the borrower regarding the home buying and financing process, advise about the different types of loan products available, and explain how closing costs and monthly payments could vary from one loan to another.

She would be the primary contact between the borrower and the bank, collect financial information and related documents that were part of the application process, order appraisals and maintain correspondence with the borrower, realtors, and the lender, between the application and point of closing.

She would also have to comply with Federal regulations and enforcement. There was a lot to learn, but she felt confident she would be able to perform the duties required of her.

By reading the daily news and listening to radio broadcasts, Kristina became more aware of the sacrifice Joseph had made along with thousands of other American and Australian soldiers.

She read what later came to be known as Operation Cartwheel, the combined strategy of General MacArthur moving northward from the South Pacific, Admiral Nimitz from the Central Pacific, and Admiral Halsey moving Marine and Army forces island by island northwest from Guadalcanal along the Solomons chain to New Georgia.

Through 1944 and 1945, the names and locations of South Pacific islands in the news had become as familiar to her as the names and locations of neighboring states. At times, she wished she'd never heard of them.

Chapter 5

Houses

The faded black Ford pickup struck another pothole, jolting Carl Hofstadter upward so that his head struck the roof of the cab. He glanced over at his father's weathered noncommittal face emerging from under the sweat-stained broad brimmed hat he had worn for years, plowing and harvesting the fields.

The truck needed new springs and shock absorbers to replace those worn years ago. The truck itself needed to be replaced with a new one. Other than it could still lurch along the narrow two-lane country road, it was junk and belonged in the scrap yard among other retired farm machinery and equipment.

The potholes needed fixing. The entire road needed to be resurfaced to withstand even the meager traffic over its long country miles. Times had changed. Times were different now. The hard-economic times were behind them. The war was behind them, leaving torn and ravaged lives in its wake.

Potholes.

They reminded him of bomb craters on hastily constructed landing strips and roads he and his Seabees unit had laid down along island coastlines and in the midst of sweltering disease-infested jungles. The bomb craters had enraged him. Their appearance meant no progress had been made against the enemy, since their planes continued to return and destroy what he and his men had built.

He hated bombs. He hated the necessity of war. But bombs had ended the war and set him on this road home. Bombs had decimated two entire Japanese cities, their life and culture, vaporized innocent civilians into lumps of char and left their shadowed imprints on walls.

He braced himself against the dash as the truck approached the next pothole. If no one else was going to repair this road, he would. The impulse to do something positive and constructive had consumed him from the moment he walked down the gangplank of the troop ship and set foot on the dock in San Diego, California.

The embedded thought stayed with him on the long train ride across the Southwest upward through the plains states northeast into the Middle-West to the end of his rail travel in Chicago. He dozed through most of the Greyhound bus ride the last leg of his journey to Rockford. He called his parents to let them know he had arrived, then waited at the bus station for two hours until his father's ancient truck crawled into the gravel parking lot.

Carl tossed his duffel bag into the rear among a few bales of hay and a rake and shovel. As he climbed up into the passenger side of the cab, he met his father's extended hand.

"Good to see you, son. You made it."

Carl grasped his hand with a single firm shake and settled onto the worn leather seat.

"How was your trip?"

"Long."

"Ma'll have food on the table when you git there."

Carl nodded. "Looking forward to it. Forgot what real food tastes like."

"You look fit."

"It happens in that line of work."

"Soldierin'."

"Soldierin'." A drop of salty sweat wormed its way from his hairline down the back of his neck into the stained collar of his tan uniform soiled from the weeks of travel since he had shipped out from Brisbane, Australia. The Mid-west summer heat and humidity were not nearly what he had endured in the South Pacific. Pacific but He felt displaced and unfamiliar with the hundreds of acres of corn fields. Dense armies of green stalks taller than a man were occasionally interrupted by sweeping vistas of hay and grain fields and pastures dotted with grazing herds of black and white spotted dairy cattle.

A hot wind rushed through the open window enveloping him with the sweet greenish scent of freshly turned loamy soil and new mown hay. A ring-necked pheasant rose up out of the cornfield ahead of them in an explosion of variegated rust and gold plumage tipped with black extending into its long trailing tail feathers. The bird lifted in a graceful arc high over the moving truck and descended into the wall of corn stalks on the other side of the road.

"Purty sight," said his father. "Be on the dinner table come fall."

Hunting.

Carl didn't want to pick up and handle a gun again, not even to hunt deer and game birds. He had been trained on weapons, rifles, grenades, and a side arm and had been expected to fight if he came under attack, which happened all too often. He had been fired on while laying landing pontoon bridges to establish beachheads and strafed and fired upon while rolling tarmac for airfields. He had seen his men hit and falling around him. He had narrowly escaped slicing shrapnel spinning through the air lodging in bodies and amputating limbs. Life was perilous. Life was vulnerable and momentary. Death was forever. He did not again want to hear the sound of gunfire.

His father slowed the truck for a right-hand turn onto a half mile gravel driveway bisecting a pasture and a hayfield. Rivulets from a recent thunderstorm puddled in the ruts that established a track to a two-story white frame house and barnyard outbuildings sheltered by elm and oak trees from the relentless wind coursing across the flat land.

Carl could see his mother push open the screen door and step out onto the porch. She waved a dish towel.

As he braked the truck to a stop in the yard, his father turned to him and said, "Glad you're home. Gittin' a bit old and stiff to work the farm myself. Glad we can do it together. Time to greet your ma."

Forgetting that she could no longer move quickly, she stumbled coming down the steps and caught the handrail to maintain her balance.

"Ma!" Carl shouted at her. "Take it easy! You don't have to hurry!" He reached her with three long strides and took her in his arms.

"Oh, Carl, Carl, you don't know how I've prayed for your safe return. I put my faith in the Lord he'd look after you." She swiped at her sudden gush of tears.

"Someone looked after me. Might as well be him."

"It was. It was. I'm sure of it."

"I smell apple pie." The aroma of apples cooked in cinnamon and sugar and creamery butter wafted through the open kitchen window.

"I just took it out of the oven. Oh, let me look at you." She stepped back at arms length, not letting go. "You're just as I remember you, only thinner. You've lost weight."

"Navy cooks don't know how to feed us like you do."

"I am going to make anything and everything you like."

"What's for dinner?"

"A prime rib roast with biscuits, gravy, corn and mashed potatoes."

"Farm cooking – my favorite." He gently rubbed a smudge of white flour from her cheek, rosy from the oven heat. Her dumpling features appeared to have risen from the mounds of dough she kneaded and rolled to metamorphose into the daily ritual of baking breads, rolls, cakes, and pies. He knew she donated most of them to church socials and needy families in town. Her pies and jams were consistent winners of awards at the county fair.

He noticed her thinning hair had turned gray since he had last seen her crying and waving her white handkerchief goodbye to him as he looked down from a passenger window of the departing Greyhound bus. His father with unchanging coveralls and denim shirt hanging on his stringy body had aged, as well, and now moved more slowly than Carl remembered and with a slight limp.

Later when Carl commented on it, his father said, "Pulled somethin' in my back," he pointed, "down here. Never thought a hay bale would do that to me."

As he hoisted his duffel bag and crossed the small living room furnished with an antique floral cushion couch, wooden end table and old handmade cane wooden rocking chairs, Carl paused to look at a framed eight by ten black and white photograph of his sister smiling back at him with an exuberance that unlocked a flood of buried memories.

Growing up with few friends who traveled on horseback from distant farms to congregate in a small one room school house, until they reached high school age, Carl and Greta had relied on their own compatibility and resourcefulness to fill their young years with the riches and loneliness of an isolated rural childhood.

What Carl missed and remembered most about his sister was her indefatigable enthusiasm and cheerfulness. He had never known her to be sad, or at least not to express any depression she might have felt but kept well-hidden.

The photo had been taken at the onset of spring. She wore a long green woolen scarf patterned with snow flakes. Even with a single wrap around her neck against the morning chill, the tails of the scarf hung down to her knees. Two long blonde braids tumbled from under her snug red ski cap giving her the aspect of a comely young maiden from a Swiss mountain village.

The chug and sputtering cough of the John Deere tractor Carl was driving that morning muffled Greta's yelp. A sudden uneven pull of the machine prompted him to glance back over his shoulder. The tail of her scarf had become tangled in the churning blades of the disc harrow and jerked her off her metal seat where she had been operating the handles and levers to raise and lower the discs.

With a sharp cry, Carl hauled back on the emergency brake to stop the machinery. He leaped over the tall rear tire to the ground and dashed to his sister, twisted among the blades. Her unmoving eyes bulged from strangulation.

Carl unwrapped the scarf and gingerly lifted her limp body into his arms. Blood leaked through her clothing. By the time he stumbled across the furrows of the plowed field one hundred yards to the house, he knew she was dead.

In the back of the truck, he cradled her lifeless head and shoulders on his lap during the ride to town that pushed the truck to its limits.

He blamed himself for not saying something about her scarf. He blamed himself for knowing better, but not noticing, not paying attention. "I should have said something to her. I should have told her." His body shook with sobs. He refused to be consoled by his mother and father. Other than barely functional exchanges, he stopped talking to them. He stopped seeing his friends and spent his time alone, roaming the woods and fields and sitting in solitude by the stream that meandered through the land.

Although he worked with his father in the fields, haying, planting and harvesting, he grew to hate the farm and, with an irrational impulse of distorted vengeance, vowed that one day he would destroy it.

The uneven wooden stairs to his room creaked under his weight. He dropped his duffel on the narrow bed and stared through the window. As a young boy, on hot summer nights, he had sometimes crawled out onto the slanted green shingled roof of the front porch which extended the length of the house. He was too tall now to fit through the window and had no desire to make a futile attempt to step into his past.

He looked briefly at his maroon and gold high school pennant pinned to the wall and the framed black and white football photograph nestled among three trophies he had been awarded as an outstanding quarterback and captain of his team. Although he had aged from the stresses of war, he was still recognizable as the ruggedly handsome young man standing in a cavalier pose. His former shock of blonde hair now showed signs of receding at his temples, an inheritance from his father. The gray-green luster of his eyes had dimmed and no longer projected the bemused challenging expression linked to the fresh broad smile of the youth gazing back at him.

In the bathroom he and his sister had shared with their parents, he listened to the water rushing through the plumbing leaving a small whistle of trapped air. He washed his hands and face. The aroma of his mother's cooking drew him down the stairs.

His father waited at the kitchen back door. "Up to giving me a hand with the milking?"

"Nothing I'd like better. Makes me feel right at home. Taking up where I left off."

He followed him out the screen door, letting it fall shut with a remembered bang. A Labrador Retriever and a nondescript herd dog trailed after them as they walked a well-worn path from the house to the barn. He gave each of them a pat on the head as they came over to sniff at him in greeting. A flock of feeding crows shattered the air with raucous caws as they rose on lazy wings from a nearby field.

Carl heard the cows lowing and mooing. From years of habit and repetition they lined up at their stalls where they thrust mucous dripping bewhiskered black nostrils into their feed. Upon entering the barn, he paused at the rising acrid odor of urine and dung nested in the yellow straw scattered about their hoofs. The flutter of pigeons cooing in the rafters and loft mingled with the sounds of the cows in a repetitive choral composition.

Carl reached under a cow to connect a milking machine to her udders. His head pressed against her grassy bovine-scented hide. He moved to the next cow and maneuvered the hose and suction cups into position. He listened to the steady grinding crunch of molars on hay grabbed with a swish from the feed rack by probing lips.

After the machine finished pulling the milk from the sac of each cow, Carl and his father tugged and stroked the udders to eject any remaining vestige of milk into a pail for its butter fat content and to prevent the growth of bacteria causing a mastitis infection in the animal.

After sealing the tops of a dozen milk cans in the refrigeration room, they returned to the house for dinner.

The aroma of prime rib infused with garlic and fresh garden herbs smote them as they entered the kitchen through the back door.

"Mouth watering, Mom," said Carl and kissed her on the cheek enroute to the sink to wash his hands. "Mouth watering."

"It's right at that point of medium, the way you like it."

Carl's father waited for his turn at the sink, then opened the pantry cupboard and brought out a bottle of Tennessee bourbon which he poured liberally into two juice glasses. Holding the neck poised over a third glass, he asked, "One for you, Mother?"

"You know better, Lucius. I don't take spirits."

"This is a celebration, for Carl's homecoming."

"Did you think to ask Carl if he might prefer a lemonade. He might not care for spirits after fighting in the war. I'm sure he didn't drink any in the Navy. There's a cold pitcher of lemonade in the icebox."

Carl laughed. "Spirits are fine, Ma. They make things feel better."

"I know you didn't care much for Pastor Schmidt before you left, but prayer makes you feel better too and it doesn't make you inebriated."

"I'm sure I said a prayer or two out there, but I'll take a drink anytime, especially to raise a glass with Pa."

"See, Abby, he's a man of the world." Lucius clinked his glass against Carl's outstretched to him.

Carl smacked his lips. "Good stuff, aged."

"Only bring it out for a special occasion. Nothin' more special than you comin' home alive."

"I'll drink to that." The men laughed.

"Time to sit down." Abigail shook her apron at them as though shooing chickens.

Once seated, she led them in a quiet statement of grace, prominently including their gratitude for the safe return of their son.

Few words passed between them as they devoted themselves to the diligent ingestion of food, chewing, swallowing, dwelling on the warmth and expansion in their bellies.

After dinner, Carl and his father sat out on the porch in the fading twilight and listened to the rising chorus of crickets harmonizing with the clink of dishes and pots and pans being washed in the kitchen behind them. The slow steady momentum of his rocker accompanied Lucius' narrative about the weather, crops, their rural neighbors, and local events.

"Mother went to see the doctor 'bout a month or so ago."

"What was it?"

"Had some pain in her chest."

"Her heart?"

"Doc didn't really say, but he gave her some medicine to take every day."

"What kind of medicine?"

"Little pills of some kind. To help keep her blood pressure down," he said.

"She feelin' better?"

"I think so. Don't talk about it much. She never was a complainer. Keeps things to herself. She says prayer 'll keep her goin' more than them little pills."

"If it helps, it helps." Carl began to think about what this information meant. His mother and father were aging and wouldn't be able to maintain the farm for many more years and he had no desire to become like his father and work the land for a living.

His mother came out carrying a cup of chamomile tea and joined them in her rocker for a brief interlude. "Couldn't ask for a nicer evening."

"So how you doin', Ma? Pa said you saw the doctor."

"It's nothin' to concern yourself about, son. Just a woman's ailment," her voice fell with a note of weariness.

"You and Pa are always a concern to me."

"We get along all right."

"That's good."

"It helps that you're home now. Pa won't have to take everything on his shoulders."

"Yes."

"Don't know what your sleep habits are," said Lucius. "We have to be up at dawn to feed the stock and milk the cows. Ma takes care of the chickens. Brings in the eggs."

"I'll hear you movin' around. I'll be up."

"Smell of bacon and eggs and coffee and hotcakes should get you out of bed."

"Better than an alarm clock."

"Well," Lucius stood from his rocking chair. "Good night, then. Sleep well."

"Good night, Pa." Carl watched his father open the screen door and go inside.

"Hear that? Whippoorwill," said Abigail at the sound of the familiar bird call.

"All this comes back," said Carl.

"Good to have you home, son. Good to have you home."

Carl nodded.

After his mother had gone inside and upstairs to bed, Carl noticed a headline in the local paper about a "New Highway Planned." He picked up the paper and positioned it to catch the light through the window from a living room lamp.

Carl had been too far removed from events on the home front to have any emotional attachment to the announcement made by the carrier commander that their President, Franklin Delano Roosevelt, had died. What more significantly registered in Carl's thoughts was that the President who replaced FDR had conclusively ended the war. Japan had surrendered and he was alive, mustered out of the Navy as a Chief Petty Officer, and going home.

Because of his background, among the first questions he had been asked by the recruiter when he enlisted was whether he could operate heavy equipment. His affirmative answer landed him in a Seabees construction battalion bound for the South Pacific. He gained experience constructing fuel tank farms, airfields, supply depots, storage dumps, Quonset village housing, hospitals, staging and training areas and other facilities to support military action in the Coral Sea and island campaigns.

After three years of construction, including the distinction of working under fire, he decided he was no longer interested in driving John Deere tractors and combines and harvesters. But what he had learned with the Seabees provided him an unexpected seed to become an entrepreneur.

He read in the Rockford Morning Star that the city council was considering plans for new highways to be constructed around the city to provide access to the downtown area as the residential boundaries began to push outward. He looked at the map diagramming the proposed route and saw that it touched the boundary of their farm.

During the remaining summer days just before the fall harvest, Carl made a trip into town to buy surveying tools and acquire a copy of the deed and plat map of the farm. When he returned, he spread the seven map layers on the kitchen table, drawing the curiosity of his parents.

"Why'd you go into town for that?" Lucius leaned over to peruse the terrain and elevation markings.

"I have an idea about the farm."

"An idea? What do you mean? What are we looking at here?"

"One thousand acres."

"I know how big it is."

"You read that article in the paper?"

"'Bout the highway?"

Carl nodded. "When I was at the city hall, I stopped in at the planning office. They gave me more details. We have an opportunity to do something more with the land."

"You didn't tell me you were going to the planning office."

"I know. I want to do a little surveying."

"What for? You want to plant some new crops. I already rotate."

"It's not about crops, Pa. It's about houses."

"Houses?"

"I want to build houses."

Lucius stared at him. "You shell shocked, son? Houses have nothin' to do with the farm. Is it you don't want to be a farmer?"

"Something like that. The war changed me, Pa. It changed a lot of us. The country's not the same as when we shipped out overseas. It's changed for all of us who came back. The vets need jobs and they need homes to live in and raise families, get back to leading normal lives."

"You talk like you want to put houses on our land."

"Not all of it. Just some of it."

"The farm's been in the family for three generations. It's your inheritance. You should be grateful, not try to throw it away."

"I'm not throwing it away. A thousand acres is more than we can manage. I've taken the truck out and walked the woods and fields. You've been farming only a few hundred acres, about one third of the land."

"It's enough. It's all I can handle. It pays for what we need. Now that you're home, we can use more of it. When I saw the map, that's what I thought you were talkin' about."

"We don't have to touch the land you're farming. I'm talking about one or two hundred acres that are near the highway that goes to the toll road the state is planning to build. Businesses are moving east to get close to the road. We have a chance to be part of that, providing homes."

Glancing up from under the raised hood of the Ford pickup, Carl noticed the lone man climb down from the back of a hay wagon being towed by a tractor. Looking neither to the left or right, he walked with a purposeful stride up the long driveway. Carl wondered if the suitcase bumping against his left leg at each step contained tools or household products the man wanted to sell. Wiping a streak of black grease from his hands with a rag, he came forward into the front yard and waited to greet the stranger, who did not alter his rapid pace even as he approached Carl, as though to do so would undermine his resolve. He stopped abruptly and politely removed his brown ivy cap.

"My name is Dimitri Woijcek. I am here to build houses. I am staying with friends in town. My English not good, but I can read. I see your message in paper you want a builder of houses. I am that one. I build houses in my country after the war until Russians come. When Germans gone, we build everything, houses, roads, bridges, railroads, buildings that Nazis bombed. When Russians come with tanks and guns, I leave country. I have enough of war. I come to America with my wife and child. We stay with other Czech people in Racine, Wisconsin. There is no work for me in Racine. So I come to Rockford to find work and I see your message. So I am here."

Carl studied the stocky man's Slavic features. Keen milky blue eyes confronted him over high flat cheekbones spread from a narrow delicate nose. Carl extended his hand. Dimitri quickly transferred the cap to his other hand holding the suitcase handle and grasped Carl's with a confident strong grip.

"I'm Carl Hofstadter."

"You will give me a job"?

"I will give you a job."

"I am sorry to ask, but I will need a place to sleep."

"I'm not ready to start building yet. I'm only in the planning stage."

"I do not have a way to travel from town."

"There's a side room with a cot in the barn. You can take your meals with us, me and my mother and father."

"You are a kind man."

"I have to survey the land, then get the money to build. You can help me."

A sudden grin matched the enthusiasm from his eyes.

"Follow me," said Carl. "I'll show you the room. When did you leave Czechoslovakia?"

"Six months ago. It was hard. I still have family there, brothers and sisters. They could not get out in time."

"I can pay you only a small wage to get started. More later, much more. But you'll have room and board here."

"Until now, I had nothing. I am thankful. You have much farm here."

"In the beginning, I want to start small, then grow the development, depending on the demand for houses. There is more than enough land."

"As far as my eyes can see."

"Once we get underway, I'll provide temporary housing for the construction workers, for those who want it. Racine isn't too far away to visit your wife and child. Do you have a boy or girl?"

"Boy, Milos. He is three years."

"You're a lucky man."

"I am thankful."

Chapter 6

The Vision

A sharp autumn wind kicked loose chaff across the harvested corn field flicking in and out of the microscope's vision field as Carl rotated the knurled ring and slightly angled his viewing eye to confirm there was no motion of the target toward or away from the cross hairs. He double checked that the bubble of the Alidade was centered. He noted the position and indication of the stadia arc and the interval on the perpendicular rod being held by his assistant, Dimitri, standing one hundred yards away, providing him the horizontal distance and elevation. He then jotted the computation in the notebook he carried and waved to the young man, who carried the rod to the next position.

He listened to the sliding cadenza trill of a meadowlark.

Less than a month ago, Carl had been driving an Allis Chalmers corn picker down the long rows, clipping ears off the stalks and skinning away the husks. The ears dropped into a wagon towed behind the picker. When the wagon was full, Lucius hooked it to his second tractor and hauled it to a corn crib near the barn.

Carl had not anticipated that fifty acres of corn grew on the land he needed to begin his development project. He had convinced his father that other acres could be planted for the next year's harvest.

Carl and Dimitri left the farm at dawn to make the one-hundred-mile drive to Chicago. The survey was completed. Their appointment was at 10:30 to present their proposed housing development to a bank loan officer. Carl's early inquiries discovered no banks in Rockford had sufficient loan capital to underwrite his project. The initial investment would require ten million dollars with a budget allocation over the next two years. As soon as ground was broken, advance print advertising in Illinois, Wisconsin, Indiana, Iowa, and Missouri city newspapers would attract buyers to purchase a phase one Hofstadter Home under construction and move in after six months.

Gas was becoming available and cheap. Carl was pleased to see cars passing his truck chugging along the highway to Chicago. The appearance of more automobiles meant that returning veterans were getting jobs. The post war economy was becoming a reality. People needed homes. He didn't want to let the opportunity pass him by like the cars passing his father's old truck.

Accompanied by a Czech folk tune, Dimitri alternatively whistled and sang to fill the rural monotony of the long drive until they reached the outskirts of Chicago. His effusive optimism filled the cab with an inability to sit quietly. He squirmed and wiggled and cast glances at the speedometer needle wavering at 50 miles per hour, the truck's top speed.

Carl worried that the periodic shuttering and rattling of the frame was a precursor to a breakdown that would leave them stranded at the side of the road. Not showing up for the interview would undermine his plans. He wanted to make a good first impression to the extent he had taken Dimitri into Rockford and had outfitted them both with gray flannel business suits, including Fedora hats.

A woman's voice at the other end of the line had caught him off guard in response to his phone call. He had expected to be talking to a male loan officer. He questioned what a woman would know about a large business transaction. He assumed she would have a boss, a supervisor or bank manager, a man who would handle the contractual arrangements and management of his loan.

"My wife, Jaramila, say she is happy for us and will pray for us today. I call her on phone last night. You hear me call her in house."

"Yes, I heard you." Carl grinned. "Didn't understand a word of what you said. Does your wife speak English?"

"My Jaramila, she is learning, but not so fast as me. She stays most of time with Czech people in Racine. I go out travel around to find work. I am man of world."

Carl smiled and nodded. "You are that, Dimitri. I want the loan officer to meet you and know you have the skills for construction. We'll have to hire a crew to work with you, builders, plumbers, electricians. You can't undertake a project of this scope alone."

"I know how to boss others. I did back in my country, twenty, thirty other workers. We make large buildings and houses. People know me. I do good work."

"Hopefully, it won't take much to convince the lady we're going to meet."

"Jaramila's praying will reach her and she will like us."

"Just like my mother. She says the same thing. Women think praying is the answer to everything. Has nothing to do with business. Guess it makes 'em feel like they're helping us."

"It is good to have God with us in this thing."

"Sounds like he keeps you happy."

"I have never been so happy since leaving my country. As soon as we start building houses and making money, I move Jaramila and our son, Milos, here from Racine. I tell her it will not be long."

"Let's hope so."

"When you meet, you will like them and they will like you."

"I'm sure of it."

"Jarmila like to cook like your *mateřský*. Your *mateřský* is good cook. Jarmila is good cook. She tell your *mateřský* how to make *Svíčková* and *Ovocné Knedlíky*. You will like. When you build houses and make money, you need wife to take care of you. Who do you know to make your wife?"

"I can't be concerned with marriage for a while. I don't know anybody. Most of the girls I knew back in high school are all married or they lost a husband in the war. My first priority is this housing development. I'll worry about a wife later."

"Jaramila know a good woman for you in Racine. She is Jaramila's cousin, Duska. Very beautiful. Czech women have beauty. My Jaramila has beauty. Many want to marry her, but she would only look at me. Our son, Milos, is handsome boy, like me and his *matka*. When he become man, girls will like him one day." Dimitri tipped his Fedora back and forth on his lap. "Hat is nice. I can wear to work."

"You wear it with a suit, not work clothes. It'll just get dirty."

"I like hat. If it get dirty, Jaramila can wash it for me."

"It's up to you."

Dimitri positioned the hat at a rakish angle on his head and grinned. "Make me look like boss."

"You're the boss all right."

"I see tall buildings." Dimitri pointed at the distant Chicago skyline beginning to come into view.

"We're getting close. This is a long drive. Hope we don't have to make it too often."

"We stay at hotel in the city tonight? Duska say many Czech people live there."

"No, depending on how our meeting goes, I want to get back. I've been in touch with an architect. He wants to meet with us after our bank loan meeting. He'll be important to design options and to estimate costs and pricing. We'll also be talking with the owner of a heavy equipment company in Rockford tomorrow. I'd like to cut a deal with him, maybe bring him in as a partner. There are five more phases after phase one. Lots of land to excavate, seven hundred acres. He needs to know if we're getting the money. He'll want some up front. Need to talk with city planning about power and water and sewage. Need to have pipelines run out there. We don't have any time to spare. My mother and father have had a well and septic tank from the beginning. Might have to use septic tanks. We'll see."

Carl didn't want to park his battered old truck in front of the bank in case the bank officer should see them drive away in it at the conclusion of their meeting. He parked out of sight a block away. He and Dimitri walked quickly along the windy streets overshadowed by massive multi-story gray stone and steel buildings and entered the financial fortress through heavy imposing oak doors they hoped were the gateway to their fortune.

Disoriented by the size of the main floor entrance and long row of teller cages, they cast about seeking a source of information. Carl spotted an engraved sign on the closed door of one of several side offices, Loans.

"That's it." He nudged Dimitri's arm, a gesture that moved them together in that direction. Unsure of what to do next, they stood in front of the door, until a uniformed bank guard approached them.

"May I help you?"

"We have an appointment with the loan officer," said Carl. "Can we just go in."

The guard knocked gently. A female voice responded, "Yes, please come in."

The guard opened the door and beckoned them forward.

Both Carl and Dimitri could not hide their expressions of shock and amazement at the sight of the beautiful Germanic blonde woman wearing a shapely business suit who rose from behind her desk and came forward to greet them with a warm welcoming smile. They quickly removed their hats.

"Good morning, gentlemen. You must be Carl Hofstader and Dimitri Woijcek." She shook each of their slowly extended hands. "I'm Kristina Blake. Please be seated." She walked past them and closed the door. Returning to her desk, she graced them with her elegant voice. "I understand you had a long drive all the way from Rockford. May I offer you tea or coffee?"

Both men nodded vigorously. "Coffee," said Carl. "Coffee," Dimitri repeated. They watched her pour them each a coffee in china cups from a sterling silver pot on a side table serving tray. Without spilling a drop walking in her high heeled shoes, she carried the coffees to them in each hand. "There are also cookies, if you'd like."

The men nodded. Flustered, Carl tried to collect his thoughts. She handed them a small plate displaying a variety of cookies. They each selected two and she returned the plate to the serving table. Moving back to her executive chair, she leaned forward slightly against the desk top and engaged them with her full attention.

"Now, how can I help you?"

Carl nervously cleared his throat, placed his coffee cup and saucer on the front corner of her desk and handed her the portfolio. "We're here to talk about a development loan. Here's our proposal." He opened and turned the presentation portfolio, so she could see and read the documents it contained.

Dimitri attempted to hang his hat on the left arm of his chair, but it immediately tumbled to the floor. He reached down to scoop it up and placed it on the nearest corner of Kristina's desk until he saw her eyeing it with a slight frown, then removed it to perch on his knee.

Kristina took a yellow legal pad and a sharpened pencil from her desk drawer and wrote a comment. "I see you've met with your local planning council." She referred to the top document. "And your proposed use of the land is to develop and sell four hundred single family residential homes in five phases over the next four years and that phase one will be for fifty homes."

"That's right," said Carl.

"And you own the land for development."

"It's in my father's name, Lucius Hofstadter. One thousand acres of prime farm land. He's getting too old to maintain it and has agreed to parcel it out for development, except for one hundred acres around the farm house and barns. There's a legal document in there. He's been a dairy farmer all his life. I'll be the sole inheritor when he and my mother pass. He doesn't want to retire and move in to town. Given the demand for housing and the growth of business in Rockford and surrounding areas and the new toll road being built between Rockford and Chicago, our development is an opportunity that speaks for itself."

"We'll discuss the financial details in a moment, but what is the amount you're requesting?"

"Ten million dollars." Carl paused. "It's all budgeted out in the proposal."

"Do you have an accountant?"

Carl shook his head. "Dimitri and I worked everything out. We both know construction. Me, from the Navy. I was in the Seabees for the duration of the war. Dimitri has built hundreds of homes and commercial buildings during the reconstruction in Czechoslovakia until the Russian occupation. He's new to this country, but he fits right in."

Kristina smiled. "We're all immigrants or children of immigrants. My parents came from Germany and Sweden in the late 1890s. My maiden name is Holtzman. My husband, Joseph, died in the war. Welcome, Dimitri."

"*Danke Schone*. I learned German when the Nazis occupied my country during the war. I am sorry about your husband."

"I've learned to cope."

"Do you have children?"

"A son."

"What is his name?

"Elias – Elias Blake. He carries his father's name, although he will never meet him."

"It is sad. I know what it means to not have a father," said Dimitri. "Mine was tortured and killed by the Nazis for being a member of the communist party."

"Shall we continue?"

"Ja, Danke."

"I'm going to take you through the loan process and I'll need you to explain your planning," said Kristina.

"We're ready," said Carl nervously. Kristina's resemblance to his deceased sister was uncanny. He had to repress the impulse to reach across the desk and hold her hands. "Please go ahead."

"First – let's review your loan to cost assessment."

"The budget begins on the next page."

Kristina studied the figures. Then looked up. "You excluded the land from your hard costs."

"I didn't put that in there, because my father and I own the land."

"It's still part of the overall value. Can you provide an estimate of what it's worth undeveloped and what it would be worth with residential development?"

"I can only guess. I don't really know what the current market is, and it's likely to change now after the war. More men working, more jobs. They'll be buying homes using the G.I. bill."

"We'll still need an appraisal of the land as a requirement of the loan."

"Is that something you do?"

Kristina smiled at his guilelessness. "Of course, we provide that service. But we need to add it to the soft costs in your budget. I see you have estimates for legal fees, professional fees, marketing, and general overhead costs. Your hard costs do include excavation of the land and putting in pipe lines for water and sewer. Did you arrive at these figures based on quotes?"

"Just conversations with companies and the city would subcontract the pipeline work. They provided those estimates."

"We'll have to verify their accuracy."

"Whatever you'd like."

"I don't doubt the figures. It's just standard procedure in processing the loan."

"If I were to guess, the land has got to be worth several million dollars just as farmland."

"I'm sure it is," said Kristina, "but we need to arrive at an officially determined value. It will take into consideration other factors like location demographics, proximity to services and material resources, transportation, and other current and planned commercial developments."

"Rockford had major weapons manufacturing during the war," said Carl. "It's rapidly converting to a peacetime economy, and there's the toll highway being built from there to Chicago. And there's the railroad."

"We'll take all those factors into consideration. You've put in what appears to be all your material costs for construction of the homes. Did you calculate those on a cost per home basis?"

"We plan to build homes that are pretty much all alike," said Carl. "Buyers can choose from three or four different models and interiors. We have an architect working with us on the designs."

"Are the designs available?"

"There are sketches and formal drawings in the package. No construction drawings. We'll have those after the loan is approved."

Kristina sifted further into the stack of documents and unfolded and spread the blueprints across her desk. She studied them for several minutes. "These look interesting. They appear to be utilitarian and affordable, given the features and dimensions. Is the three-bedroom model your largest?"

"We can add bedrooms and bathrooms. But the largest in the first phase will be three bedrooms and one bath."

"How many more phases are you considering?"

"Four more to make it five, but we have a vision."

"What's your vision?"

"A nine-hole golf course to be expanded to eighteen holes and a country club a few miles from the tract."

"That is visionary."

"In the next phases, the houses will be larger and more like custom luxury homes, especially near and around the country club and golf course."

"You haven't costed those out."

"Well," Carl grinned sheepishly, "like I said. It's a vision. We hope to make it a reality based on the success of phase one."

"It's a good thing to be visionary."

"I'm certain we can get there, but we have to start at the beginning."

"I'll also want to examine your estimate for your interest reserve. It's a cost of the project and needs to be included in the budget as a part of the total cost, although the loan will cover only the construction period. Amortization won't begin until the units are sold. What is your revenue source to pay the monthly interest of the construction loan?"

"I'm negotiating with Lewis Murtagh. He owns and operates an excavation company for streets and roads and commercial development. He's close by in Rockford. He has the heavy equipment, earthmovers and the like. We've had a couple of conversations. I've asked him to become a financial partner, not a full partner. Dimitri is also my partner. The capital for interest payments would come from Murtagh."

"Has he agreed to a partnership?"

"Not yet. He wanted to hear the result of our meeting with you."

"Unless you have some other source of capital, his involvement would be essential to the bank granting the loan."

"He stands to make a great deal of money as my partner. I don't think he'll walk away from my offer. But if it came to that, would the bank consider ownership of a land parcel?"

"That's a possible alternative. Would Mr. Murtagh also cover contingency reserve costs for changes during construction?"

"As the partner, yes. That would be included in our agreement."

"I'm going to have to take a look at the land before I can proceed with the loan application."

"Anytime you want."

"And I'll need a notarized copy of the partnership agreement with Mr. Murtagh, unless you pursue the alternative option of giving ownership of a land parcel to the bank."

"We're meeting with Lewis tomorrow morning. I hope to wrap things up. When do you want to come out and see the land?"

Kristina perused a calendar on the side of her desk. "What about next Wednesday?"

"That's good for us."

"I'll need directions."

"Can I have a piece of paper? I'll draw you a map."

Kristina tore a page from her yellow tablet and handed it to him along with a pencil.

"Now I think you will not meet Duska," said Dimitri, as they climbed up into the truck cab. "You have found your woman. Am I right?"

"Let's just say I saw her. I can't say I've found her. She might not have any interest in me."

"You must woo her, my friend."

"Woo her? Is that what you do in Czechoslovakia, woo a woman? That's something was done about two hundred years ago. Woo."

"Well, then, my English is not too good. You can court her. Do you court here in America?"

"That's old fashion too. I could ask her out on a date, but I doubt she would go with me. She's a war widow, remember? She has a kid."

"She also needs a husband and you need a wife."

"Did you see her? Did you hear her?" Carl started the truck and put it in gear. They moved into traffic. "She's smart. She's not a housewife. She's a business woman. And she really knows her stuff."

"And she is beautiful."

"Roger that."

"Who is Roger?"

"It's just an expression. Something we said in the Navy."

"What does it mean?"

"It means we agree."

"Mmh – Roger that. Roger that."

Although he would never admit Kristina's resemblance to his deceased sister, Carl had recognized it instantly. He knew he could love this woman, this war widow and her child. Convincing her would be a challenge. She was a woman of quality. He had grown up on a farm and had little more than a high school education. She was a sophisticated lady. He didn't know what he would even say to her in a social situation.

Elias had not cried or fussed when Kristina explained to him that she was going on a business trip and would not be home as usual after work that night. He had grown accustomed to her leaving in the morning while he ate his cereal and toast and drank his juice. His grandmother and grandfather were always there to take care of him until she returned in the evening. Then he enjoyed her undivided attention all the way up to being tucked in bed, read a story, sung a lullaby, and drifting off to sleep. And she was at his bedside when he awoke, went potty, and, holding her hand, padded down the stairs in his bunny pajamas.

He had reached a point where he didn't want her to carry him. She understood he was discovering and beginning to assert his independence. He didn't seem to notice that his left foot was slightly twisted inward out of position at the ankle from his polio illness. She never called the slight abnormality to his attention. If it didn't bother him, and she wouldn't let it bother her. Every other physical thing about him was perfect. He was her beautiful child.

The map Carl had drawn and the terse written directions were easy to follow. The red and gold autumn colors of the woods and countryside through which she passed reminded her that the days were growing shorter. Although she handled her father's car without difficulty, she preferred not to drive at night. She found the headlights of approaching vehicles disconcerting coming toward her in the darkness on narrow streets and two-lane highways. The aggressiveness of drivers coming up behind her in the sleek new cars being manufactured in Detroit frightened her. But she refused to pull off the road to let them pass, even when they impatiently honked. She made them wait until the next lane over was clear to safely go around. She feared for the one's who disregarded the solid center lines, especially on blind hills. What could a few moments gain them if they died in a head-on crash.

colder, She assumed she would be walking around on the farm property and wore flannel slacks, a light tan sweater and a green windbreaker, and flats. Heels and a suit would not have been suitable. She didn't want to arrive looking like a citified businesswoman. Carl lived with his parents. They were farmers, although his mother might frown on her wearing slacks instead of a simple dress.

Kristina wondered why she was concerned about making an impression. She was just doing business with a customer, but she had detected a recognizable expression in Carl's eyes and his occasional faltering in discussing the development project until she redirected the conversation. She had seen those amorous looks and glances many times when she had been a taxi dancer back before the war. No matter how men looked at her after her marriage to Joseph and even now, as a widow, she didn't take notice and avoided any approach and casual conversation. Her demeanor was all business with any men she encountered in the bank. Outside, she openly snubbed them and was socially off-putting, and heard more one refer to her behind her back as an "ice queen."

Her memories of Joseph were too recent. Even though he would never come back, she felt loyal to him, to their marriage, and to their son. Regardless of the vow 'til death do us part', she would never shrug him off like a dime-a-dance partner.

Three hours later, she turned off the main highway onto the numbered rural route identified on Carl's map. An endless sea of harvested corn fields and fallow hay fields stretched to the horizon delineated by low rolling hills. With the exception of an occasional farmhouse marked by a barn and a silo jutting high above the peaked roof, there were no landmarks until she came to a junction with a general store and filling station pump standing forlornly with weeds sprouting at its base in the front gravel parking lot. She stopped, then made a right turn at the crossroads as indicated on the map and continued her journey into the rural hinterland.

The map showed the Hofstadter farm located three miles from the junction. She watched carefully for a metal mailbox with a painted number two on its weathered side. Coming upon it seemed to her to take a long time. She began to wonder why anyone would want to live in a house in a suburban residential development way out there in the country. But she knew from demographic studies that inner-city housing was not adequate to meet the demand for returning veterans and their long waiting families. So many of them, like herself, had moved in and lived with parents and relatives for the duration of the war. She considered Carl and Dimitri applying at her bank for a loan to be a fortuitous sign.

Finally, the sought for mailbox rising next to a ditch choked with dying wheat grass came into view on the right shoulder of the road. She slowed and turned in at the narrow gravel driveway that led up a slight elevation for a quarter of a mile to the barnyard and house where she could see Carl and Dimitri waiting on the front porch to greet her.

She turned off the motor, stepped out of her car and took a deep breath of the crisp autumn air, as the two men walked over to welcome her.

"How was your trip?" asked Carl. "We're glad to see you found us."

A smiling Dimitri raised his hand and touched his hat in a casual salute.

"I had my doubts, but your map was clear," she said. "It's a long drive out here. I didn't realize how far from the city it actually is."

"The new highway will pass close by that junction where you made the turn. It will be an easy commute for people living out here. And, of course, the corn and hay fields will eventually be gone and there will be roads signs, so residents have directions and can see where they're going."

"There's no question you have plenty of land." Her hand pushed aside an errant strand of blonde hair snatched by the breeze and deposited over her left eye.

"We'll take you around in the truck to see some of the property, especially where the phases are planned. But first, would you like to come in the house and meet my parents. And after such a long drive, you might need – well, you can use the bathroom, if you want."

"Thank you. I will need that."

"Roger that," said Dimitri.

As they walked to the house, she wondered at Dimitri's remark and that he was wearing his fedora, which appeared somewhat comical and out-of-place with his farm clothes. But she surmised he must really like the hat.

Off in the distance, she saw Carl's father driving a faded green John Deere tractor towing a plow along the lane of a fenced pasture containing a scattered herd of brown and white Guernsey dairy cattle.

Abigail Hofstadter could not hide her astonishment that the banker whom her son brought into the house was a woman, and that she was wearing pants. She hesitantly shook Kristina's extended hand, as Carl introduced them to one another.

"It's a pleasure to meet you, Mrs. Hofstadter. You have a wonderful farm and those are wonderful smells coming from your kitchen. I imagine you're a fantastic cook."

"I do spend most of my time in the kitchen. It's my place. You work at the bank?"

"Yes, I'm a loan officer. Carl and Dimitri met with me last week. We're taking the next step in considering the loan application. It's important to see what the land looks like."

"It's always been farmland. I can't picture it with houses on it."

"Well, from the plans I've reviewed, you aren't likely to see the houses. Your son just wants to reduce the size and scale of the farm. Your home and the barns and the near surrounding land won't be touched."

"That's a blessing. Lucius and me don't want to go nowhere. We want to live out our lives here. Carl is doing what he wants. The war changed him I think."

A slight momentary grimace passed across Carl's face. "We're taking a ride out to look at some of the land."

"Be sure you're back in time for lunch. We're having pork chops, sweet corn, and potato salad. I hope you have a good appetite, Miss. I make sure we eat well here."

"I do, Mrs. Hofstadter. I look forward to sampling your cooking."

"There's apple pie too. My apple pie has won blue ribbons at the county fair."

"I'll bet it has." Kristina grinned and turned to Carl. "Shall we then? Lead the way."

They went out through the kitchen back door and crossed the barnyard to Lucius' old pickup truck.

"Not much to look at and it's a terrible ride. Still runs okay with a little mechanical help."

"It's a tight fit for all three of us in the cab," said Dimitri. "I'll ride in the back."

Kristina gripped the side of her seat with one hand and braced herself against the dash as the truck lurched along the rutted lanes that formed the boundaries of the harvested fields. They finally stopped on a low rise and stepped out truck, so Carl could point to and locate the terrain represented on the maps he spread across the vehicle's hood.

When they returned for lunch, Lucius eyed Kristina with a kind of wariness and awkwardness in the presence of her beauty. He said nothing while they ate at the dining room table. Mostly they ate in silence with the exception of Carl's mother hovering and encouraging everyone to eat more.

Although she sincerely liked the Hofstadters, she felt oddly out of place among them. She attempted to relate by telling them a little about her parents and siblings and how different her life was growing up in Chicago than she imagined life on a farm. Carl filled in where he could with an anecdote or two about his high school days. Lunch ended on a positive note with Kristina's accolades for Abigail's apple pie washed down with a cup of coffee.

She, Carl, and Dimitri moved into the living room to discuss further details of the loan application documents she had brought with her and Carl produced his partnership contract with Lewis Murtagh, which met the interest reserve and contingency cost requirements for the bank.

Carl and Kristina went out the front door. Dimitri joined Lucius walking to the barn to milk the cows. He had discovered he enjoyed the task, including the aroma of warm milk streaming from the animals' teats, the oats and hay, even the bovine grassy odor of urine and cow dung deposited in the straw at the morning and late afternoon milkings.

Outside standing in the driveway, Carl fumbled in his mind for something appropriate to say. "Are you driving all the way back to Chicago tonight?"

"No, tomorrow morning."

"Where are you staying?"

"The Faust Hotel, in downtown Rockford."

"I know of it. Would you like company for dinner?"

"I appreciate the offer, but no, thank you, Carl. I don't date customers of the bank."

"I wasn't thinking of it as a date. Just company."

"Again, it's nice of you to offer, but to do so would be against bank policy for its employees. It's to prevent any conflict of interest, perceived or not." She had made up and used this excuse before.

"Oh, I'm sorry. I didn't know. It's good that you explained."

"I'm very happy to have met your parents."

"I'm sure they were surprised and impressed. I didn't tell them that the banker who was coming to see the land was a woman."

"I think the situation was a little awkward for your mother, and especially for your father. I don't think he knew what to make of me."

"Oh, well, Ma's old fashioned. Grew up on a farm and been a farmer's wife all her adult life. Pa is more comfortable around cows and tractors than people."

"Are there other children in the family?"

"My sister. She died when she was a teenager. It was an accident. I don't talk about it."

"I'm so sorry. You must miss her."

"It was a long time ago, but yes, I'll never forget her."

"Well, I must be going. I don't like to drive after dark."

"You've got a good three hours before the sun goes down. Not much traffic between here and Rockford."

"So I noticed coming out."

"Won't stay that way once we break ground."

"The loan approval will take another week or two."

"I understand. If there are any problems or you need more information, you'll let me know?"

"Of course. The bank encourages economic growth. Your development will measurably contribute to that in this area of the state."

"That's the whole idea."

"Thank you again, Carl." She extended her right hand. He grasped it with a firm gentle shake accompanied by a warm smile.

"I look forward to doing business with you," he said.

She smiled and climbed into her father's car. Carl wondered why she was driving such an older vehicle when she could probably afford one of the new models being made in Detroit. She was a banker. Although he was temporarily stymied in getting to know her, how she might be living her life intrigued him. There was more to her than an eye-catching hair style and a business suit.

When she arrived home the following morning, after getting down on her hands and knees to hug and kiss her ebullient beaming little boy, she half-listened to what her mother was telling her.

"A man came to see you yesterday."

"A man? From where? Who was it?"

"He said his name is Elmo Reed. He said he and Joseph were good friends during the war. They were stationed and worked together in Australia and New Guinea. He's a tall soft-spoken man, going a little bald. I could see him and Joseph getting along."

Kristina slowly rose to a standing position. Her hand lingered caressing her son's golden curls.

"Why did he come here?"

"He left these for you." She pointed to a medium sized box on a side table. They're letters and news clippings you sent to Joseph. And this."

Kristina carefully opened the sealed envelope. "Money. Quite a lot of money. There's several thousand dollars here."

"Mr. Reed said Joseph was an inveterate gambler. Those are his winnings. Apparently, he meant to use it for a down payment on a house, according to Mr. Reed."

"Did this Mr. Reed give you an address or some way to reach him?"

"He wrote his address and a phone number. He had to catch a train. I told him you were expected home. He lives in Minneapolis. He has a wife and two children."

"Joseph mentioned him in one of his letters."

"What are you going to do with the money?"

"Nothing, at least for the present. I'll put it in a savings account for Elias. By the time he's eighteen, it will accrue a great deal of interest. I think Joseph would want that." Kristina wiped at a sudden tear.

"I think he would too."

Chapter 7

The Tract

The excavation and construction scene reminded Carl of a war zone, oversized earthmoving equipment carving out and shaping the landscape for the placement of cement foundation pads at equal lot-sized intervals along winding dirt truck trails that would later become the paved streets throughout the housing development.

He and Dimitri and their partner, Lewis Murtagh, moved in to three large construction trailers, with one serving as an office. Carl reveled at the sight of hydraulic lowering and raising of bull dozer scoops loading two-and-a-half-ton dump trucks, back hoes clawing into the earth to create long trenches for pipelines, and observing Dimitri inspect the arrival of building materials moved into large storage sheds to preserve them from the elements, particularly a snow forecast that warned them of an early winter.

Within days after concrete was poured, Dimitri instructed his carpenters to begin building the wooden infrastructure, the studs, beams, braces, roof rafters, and floor trusses of the first phase homes. He organized his crew to work in teams on each segment of the construction and move from one house to the next like an assembly line. Once a frame was in place, the electricians and plumbers descended upon the half-completed structures. The scurry of activity underscored by the staccato rhythm of pounding hammers and the rasp of saw blades cutting lumber, coupled with the comings and goings of material laden flatbed trucks and unloaders created the impression of a human ant colony. Everywhere he looked, Carl could see men and machines in motion. Even if it snowed, he would continue building, as long as a major storm didn't shut them down.

The advanced promotional advertising had paid off. Every unit had been sold and buyers were clamoring to get in on the subsequent four phases. In another three months, the phase one segment of the project would break even and begin to show a profit. Kristina had informed him that the bank was satisfied with the progress he was making.

Other than a ground-breaking ceremony, infrequent phone conversations and written progress reports, he had little personal contact with her. She promised to come and see the first houses as the walls went up and roofing was laid.

A reporter from The Rockford Morning Star had visited the construction site three times to take progress photos which appeared in the paper and sparked further buyer interest along with the update that the new highway passing through the area would be completed by the following spring, allowing commuters quick efficient access to and from the city. Pictures and descriptions of the single-story, pitched-roof rooms with built-in garage, wood or brick exterior walls, sliding and picture windows, and sliding doors leading to patios had instant appeal and provoked a steady stream of phone calls to the sales office.

Even though all fifty houses in the first phase were not completed, Carl decided to have the grand opening of the tract before the first snowfall, which might curtail interest, at least until spring. He realized that over the next two to three years, he had the potential to expand the business and establish a residential and commercial real estate empire that would yield him a vast fortune. He set himself the goal of becoming a multimillionaire.

True to her promise, Kristina attended the grand opening. She had followed the news features and read the sales figures and managed the flow of interest revenue into the Hofstadter Homes loan account.

What she had thought would be a marginal success had escalated into a huge marketing potential. Carl's vision was becoming a reality. She told him the bank was fully behind him and would support the expansion of his development projects. Then Carl surprised her with the offer of a job as vice president of marketing for Hofstadter Homes and his newly formed Hofstadter Corporation at three times the salary the bank paid her, plus a benefit package including stock options.

She explained, "I can't immediately respond, Carl. Your offer is certainly generous, but I have to carefully consider my other fiscal responsibilities, as I'm sure you understand."

"I do understand. Even if you turn it down at this time, the offer remains open. When I first came to the bank, you said something about my being a visionary. I project that I'll be worth three million in three years and my corporation will grow way beyond that. I'm not confining myself to residential real estate. There are other industries to pursue and I want to be the first."

"What other industries do you have in mind?"

"Petroleum, power and energy. Detroit can't bring cars off the assembly line fast enough. Cars need fuel, an endless supply of fuel and all the new homes being built need gas and electricity."

"That's very ambitious and shows insight."

"I want you to be with the company, to be a part of it, to be with me. I know we're just sitting here in a construction trailer, but by next summer, I'll have a ten-story office building in downtown Rockford. You'll have a suite on the top floor. Take your time. Think about it. That office will be there waiting for you."

*   *   *

Kristina studied the menu and avoided Sally's accusing look as they waited for their lunches to be served.

"Why are you still reading the menu? We already ordered. Did you change your mind?

"No, just thinking."

"About what? You've been acting distant since you returned from the groundbreaking."

"I'm sorry. I don't mean to be distant, especially with you. I'm just preoccupied."

"Is it Carl Hofstadter? I saw how he was the last time he came into the bank. He's like a different person, confident and loud. He turned heads."

"Success can do that to some people."

"Something happened out there, didn't it? I can tell. You don't have to keep it from me. We're friends. Remember?"

"Of course, why would you say such a thing?"

"I get the feeling there's something you don't want me to know."

"I'm Mr. Hofstadter's loan officer."

"Mr. Hofstadter? You know him well enough to call him by his first name. You do when he comes to the bank."

"I'm concerned. There could be a conflict of interest."

"You're kidding. What possibly?"

"I just want to avoid any liabilities."

"Something legal?"

Kristina nodded.

"You? What is it? What's your concern?"

"What I'm telling you can't go any further. It has to stay between us. No office gossip. You can't say anything to anybody."

"What's so mysterious? I promise I won't tell anybody. If we have a secret, it's our secret. It's safe with me."

"I have to be very careful that Carl doesn't jeopardize his own loan."

"Are you having an affair?"

"Gracious, no, Sally. How could you?"

"It was beginning to sound like it. Did he bribe you? Are you getting a kickback? Is he paying you off?"

"You've been reading too many pulp fiction novels. No. And I mean a big No."

"I'm teasing. You're being overly serious. That worries me."

"I'm always serious, especially when it comes to finances."

"I know. That's why I said overly."

Kristina stirred her ice water with a straw. The half-melted cubes clinked against the glass. She waited until they came to rest. "I'm thinking of resigning."

Sally stared at her in disbelief. "Something did happen. You better come clean with me."

"Carl offered me a job with his company."

"I knew it. I just knew it, but I wanted to hear you say it. What kind of job?"

"Vice President. He recently incorporated."

"You're going to be an executive with all the perks, just like the big boys."

"I haven't accepted."

"But you're going to."

"I don't now. I'm really torn about this, Sally."

"What's to be torn about?"

"The way it will look to the bank officers, like I'm in cahoots with Carl or something. I don't want to risk them taking back the loan."

"The bank is already realizing revenue and the officers have seen the projections. If something happened to you, let's say you met an untimely death, would they rescind the loan? No, of course not. There's nothing for them to be suspicious about. You're honest and above board. You're an ethical person, a highly regarded employee."

"I'm still concerned about what they would think of me."

"You're following a career opportunity. Men do it all the time. Being a woman shouldn't hold you back. Let them think what they want. It's your life."

"I suppose it is."

"It just is. You're very fortunate that this is happening."

"I'm not used to this sort of thing."

"Of course, it's never happened to you before."

"I'm not sure how to handle it."

"You know what I think, Kristina dear. I think he's offering you more than a job as vice president of his company."

"What do you mean?"

"Oh, come on. You must know perfectly well. The man's in love with you."

"I'm not ready for that. I don't love him, Sally. He's a nice man, kind, likeable, very ambitious. Maybe a little too ambitious."

"And damn good looking."

"That's not important."

"What is – important to you."

"My son."

"It sounds like Carl Hofstadter can provide him with a great life, all the advantages - a better future. He can attend an upscale suburban school which will give him educational advantages over a Chicago inner city school. He'll learn middle class values through his friends and their families. You'll be living the kind of life you deserve."

"I could never love him like I loved Joseph."

"You're not expected to. I don't think he would ask that of you. You barely know Carl. But if you're working with him everyday, you'll get to know him and he'll get to know you."

"I wish he wouldn't have offered me a job."

"It's an opportunity. You can change your life for the better. You don't want to work here in a bank forever. And you need more outside your work than going to see a movie with me once in a while. And by the way, I may have a dating arrangement."

"You met someone?"

"He came into the bank yesterday and opened a savings account. And he made googly eyes at me and called me Miss Glover, very respectable, don't you think?"

"Did he ask you out on a date?"

"Not yet, but he will. I know it."

"Is he a vet?"

"A marine. He made sure to tell me that. Kind of rough face, but nice-looking guy, nice eyes. You can tell from how tight his shirt is he's really built from the neck down. Bet no one tangles with him."

"I'm happy for you, Sally. I hope things work out."

"Next time he comes in, I'll ask a leading question."

"Like what?"

"If he's married."

"It's pretty obvious he isn't."

"Have you ever known me to be subtle?"

"Not much."

"He doesn't strike me as the kind of guy who likes a girl to, you know, act shy and coy, things like that."

"You know how to read 'em, Sally."

"We had a lot of practice at the Aragon."

"We did at that."

Carl stared out the window of the model home, serving as the sales center of the tract, overlooking the annual ceaseless bird migrations at the end of autumn. Across the road beyond the green backed gold-lettered Hofstadter Homes billboard sign, spreading wings of flocks of birds lifted like a massive dark blanket from brown dead fields where they had stopped to feed on the last remaining kernels of fallen grain and scurrying insects that suffered the misfortune of not being underground.

He was alone in the office. The young saleswoman he had hired to provide guided tours of the five model homes would not arrive until ten. There had been two calls so far that morning, a man asking about financing and another wanting to know when the golf course and country club would be completed and if membership would be restricted. The third call came as an unexpected surprise.

"Hello, Carl? This is Kristina."

He lurched to a ramrod upright sitting position in his chair. "Kristina, Kristina, I'm glad you called. I was just thinking about you. It's Saturday. You said you didn't do business on the weekend."

"I had to come in to work. The bank has a huge backlog of loan applications of all kinds, houses, new businesses, construction, more corporate loans, and they all have to be processed by the end of next week. There are three of us working them now. My friend, Sally Glover, was promoted. She's here with me."

"Do you need more information regarding the corporation?"

"Not for the bank, for myself."

"About the position."

"That's right, about the position."

"Did you call to tell me you accept?"

"I need more information. I'm considering your offer. Before I make a decision one way or the other, I would like you to provide me with a legal proposal, a contract detailing the offer."

"This is wonderful news, Kristina, music to my ears. I'll have my attorney draw up the document first thing Monday morning and I'll drive it over to you."

"You don't have to come all the way to Chicago. There's no rush. Just drop it in the mail. Even if I accept, I can't immediately leave the bank."

"You can write your own ticket, Kristina. The terms will be very generous."

"I can appreciate what you're doing."

"The excavation has started on the corporate building. We're hoping to be ahead of the winter freeze. You can move into your office by spring."

"My son and I will need a house. If we move ahead with this, I'll make a down payment on one in the tract."

Carl laughed. "You can even approve your own loan. And by the way, you don't have to buy. I'll give you a house as one of your perks."

"I could not accept that. The bank would view it suspiciously."

"The bank has nothing to do with it. You'll be working for me. It's my decision."

"Actually, it's mine."

"Whatever you say. Whatever makes you happy."

"It's not about being happy. It's about being ethical."

"This really isn't about ethics. I do want you to be happy."

"And I do have to get back to work. I didn't want to keep you waiting."

Carl laughed out loud. "Listen, I'll wait 'til the cows come home."

"How are your parents?"

"Each time I stop by, they talk about their aches and pains, but nothing serious. Pa still milks the cows twice a day, though I think I've convinced him to bring on a hired hand. Lifting is getting too hard for him."

"How's Dimitri?"

"He's moving his wife and son down here from Racine next week. He's building a house for them out near where the golf course will be. My architect is working on the design for mine. More than a tract home. Posh, really upscale, a split-level showplace, five bedrooms, three baths, three car garage, even a landscaped swimming pool. I selected a one-acre lot, also right next to what will be the fairway to the eighth green. Did I tell you I'm talking to Trent-Jones about designing the course? Just got a letter from him last week. He wants to come by and see the land. He's building one in Florida right now."

"I don't know much, if anything, about golf courses."

"Oh, listen, you'll learn. And you'll love the game. I'm taking a look at a golf pro to hire for the club. You can have private lessons from one of the best."

"You paint a nice picture, Carl. Sally's waving at me. I have to get back to work."

"Thank you for calling. Thank you so much for calling. Your contract is as good as in the mail."

"Have a nice weekend."

"You too, Kristina, you too." Carl hung up the phone with a loud "WHOOP!" jumped out of his chair and ran outside onto the sidewalk. Raising his arms into the air, his wide yellow and green necktie flapping in the wind, he looked up at the gray pre-winter sky and shouted, "Yeah! Yeah! Yeah!" Then he rushed back inside to the phone and called his attorney at home.

Chapter 8

Trauma

lias was upset, but he didn't know why. The source of his feeling came from watching his mother nervously packing belongings in boxes and, with the help of his Grampa, carrying them outside to a new car, a dark green Hudson, parked in the driveway. He had looked out the door at the car from the safety of the elevated front porch. The hunched hulking lines of the vehicle intimidated him, and he went back inside to play with his plastic toys on the living room floor. He wanted his mother to stop doing what she was doing and sit down and play with him like Grampa did on the mornings she went to work. He knew she wasn't going to work, because she wasn't wearing those business clothes. She was wearing pants and a sweater and shoes that didn't make her grow taller and teeter when she walked.

To his shock and surprise, on her return trip into the house, she began gathering up and packing his scattered toys into one of the remaining empty boxes. He jumped to his full three-year-old height and grabbed at them with a loud wail, "No! No! My toys! Mine!"

"I'm not taking them away, dear. You'll have them again. We're taking them with us on a little trip."

Elias didn't know the word 'trip' and was wary of his mother and becoming frightened that some impending doom was about to happen to him related to the car. He reached into the box for his deposited toys.

"Elias," his Grampa, Conrad, raised him into the air and held him in his arms against his chest. "Let's go out in the back yard and pick some flowers for Gramma."

Elias pointed down at the box his mother was rapidly sealing shut. "Toys! My Toys!"

"Your toys are okay. They'll be with you all the time." Conrad carried him away through the dining room and kitchen and out the back door. He felt secure in his Grampa's strong arms and didn't fuss and kick and cry.

They went down the back wooden steps to the vegetable garden bordered by colorful autumn blooming flowers whose flaring petals were beginning to droop at the touch of cold descending temperatures at night. Conrad knelt down corralling his grandson between his arms and knees face to face with a cluster of golden mums. Elias reached out and touched one.

"Go ahead. Pick it for Gramma." He helped the boy snap it off several inches down the stem, long enough to insert into a vase. "How about one for your Mama. He plucked another. When we go in, you give it to her." He raised Elias into his arms again and they returned to the house, entering through the back door.

Continuing on through the living room, they went out the front door and down the steps to where his mother and Gramma were standing next to the car. Gramma Julie took him into her arms from his Grampa and hugged and planted a rapid succession of kisses on the top of his head and all over his face.

"You and Mama are going to live at a different house," she said. "We will come to visit you often."

Not understanding what she said, Elias stilled sensed that he was being tricked and manipulated, that his three adults were doing something to him against his will, something he didn't like. Large globular tears rolled down his chubby red cheeks.

"He knows, but he doesn't know," said Julie. "It's best you get under way and call us when you arrive. He'll feel better when he hears our voices on the phone."

"It'll be hard for him for awhile. This has been his home. We'll miss him."

"He knows you love him and he won't forget," said Kristina, blinking away a tear. Seeing her cry would only make the separation from his grandparents worse for Elias.

"How soon will he meet that little boy you mentioned, Milos."

"Tomorrow. I'll have his mother bring him over."

"Having a friend to play with will make all the difference in the world."

"It'll be his first," said Kristina. "Up to now, we've been it."

"He doesn't have to grow up too fast, you know," said Julie.

"I know. He'll take it in stride just like we all did."

"Be safe, but don't over protect him," said her father. "As soon as he's old enough, I'll teach him how to fight." Conrad referred to his youthful days as a bare-knuckle street fighter in the Chicago ghetto.

"Oh, no you won't," said Julie. "One fighter in the family has been enough. He should learn to play the piano or violin instead."

"He needs to know how to defend himself," said Conrad. "He's likely to meet some boys in school who'll make fun of him." He referred to the daily reminder of his grandson's hobbling walk caused by the child's bout with polio as an infant. "That shouldn't stop him from putting down a bully."

"They're going to be living in a nice neighborhood," said Julie. "He's not likely to encounter that kind of boy."

"Maybe not. You have a safe drive, *meine liebe*," said Conrad and embraced his daughter. Julie sandwiched Elias between her and Kristina with a firm hug and transferred her sobbing grandson to her daughter's arms. Kristina immediately turned and placed Elias on the front passenger seat and carefully closed the door as he woefully looked up at her through the window. The doom he feared had descended. He was going away.

Kristina got in at the wheel and started the engine. She clutched the gear into reverse and with a fierce wave to her parents, backed out of the driveway and drove quickly down the street.

Chapter 9

Conformity

1955

Elias studied the red pimiento-stuffed olive lopped over at the apex bottom of the empty martini glass. A second empty glass kept it company, touching rims, but without an olive. He had watched his stepfather with his head tipped back consume it in a single gulp and chew it, making juicy noises with his mouth.

Both his mother and stepfather had left him sitting alone in the family room watching *Leave It to Beaver* on the black and white television. His mother had said they were going out to dinner that evening at the country club, but Elias was concentrating on 'The Beave' and the olive and barely heard what she was saying except that Milos Woijcek and his mother were coming over to be with him rather than hiring a sitter for the evening.

With both of his parents momentarily out of the room, Elias determined that if he wanted to get the olive before his mother returned and took away the martini glasses, he had to make his move. He quickly rolled to his feet from where he was lying on the floor, scooped the soggy olive out of the glass and popped it into his mouth. His eyes widened with disgust at the sour taste. He mentally debated whether he should run to the bathroom and spit it out into the toilet and flush it down, which would cause him to miss an important part of the program or or spit it out and hide the half-chewed mess. He decided on the second option and scooted it out of the sight under the couch. He could retrieve it later after his parents left and toss it in the garbage.

The Beaver had gone to the barber shop but and had lost the two dollars and twenty-five cents given to him by his father. Out of concern that his dad would be angry with him, The Beave had gone home and attempted to cut his own hair with catastrophic results. With the help of his older brother, Wally, they tried to figure out a way to keep his head concealed until the hair grew back.

Elias laughed at The Beave's predicament. He identified with The Beave as a boy somewhat like himself and the mother and father similar to his own parents. His stepfather wore a gray flannel suit and a tie when he went to work, just like Hugh Beaumont, who played The Beave's father. He wore a tie when he mowed the lawn. You never saw him wearing tennis shoes. His mother wore dresses and high heels, even around the house, just like The Beave's mother played by Barbara Billingsley. She wore high heels when she did the laundry, ironed clothes, vacuumed the carpet, dusted, cooked their meals and washed the dishes.

The only relationship Elias didn't have which would complete his identification with the Cleavers was a perfect big brother, like Wally, played by Tony Dow. Elias himself would have been a big brother if any other children had been born after his mother married Carl Hofstadter six years ago. But Elias sensed something was not the same with them like his favorite television family.

His closest likeness to having a brother was his friend, Milos Woijcek, who was at home practicing the piano. Milos wouldn't be allowed to watch television until he came over that evening. In addition to completing his school homework, he was required to practice for at least two hours after supper. What bothered Elias was that Milos actually liked to play the piano.

When he and Milos were in first grade at the local elementary school, the music teacher heard Milos picking out tunes on the music room upright and adding chords and left-hand accompaniment without ever having had a lesson. He could hear a song on the phonograph and play it by ear. Miss Wollencroft had advised his parents that their child was musically gifted. Within one year, Milos was driven to Chicago for a weekly lesson with a recommended professional Russian pianist, Aleksei Greschenko. Milos practiced on a new ebony Steinway concert grand installed in a special music room added to the in the sprawling ranch style house built by his father one block from the Hofstadters and backing on the country club golf course.

Carl and Dimitri had watched the excavation and creation of their golf course with great anticipation. Dimitri and his contractors had completed the club house pro shop, restaurant, ball room, Olympic size swimming pool, diving board and high platform and locker rooms months ahead of the ribbon cutting ceremony that opened the course. From the sports world media messages, the influence of Ben Hogan and Arnold Palmer on the need and importance of businessmen to play golf to be successful caused membership enrollments to surge. Not only did business owners from Rockford and nearby communities enjoy the club amenities, but the ten thousand dollar annual fee per family was an affordable figure for many of the local suburban middle class residents.

While Dimitri continued to manage commercial and residential construction projects, Carl spent as much time playing golf as at the office directing the development of his oil exploration and extraction projects in Southern Illinois and expanding into neighboring Kansas.

Seven years ago, Kristina realized that Carl's hiring her to be his vice president of marketing and finance was a ploy to get her to agree to marry him. Although she acknowledged his ulterior motive, she did not reject the arrangement, but controlled the timing and development of their relationship on her own terms. She did not make the proposition for him an easy one. And now that she had stopped working, she had settled into the routine of being a wealthy housewife and local socialite.

That evening, as she looked at her image in the mirror and attached her pearl necklace and diamond earrings, she thought back on her decision and the advantages it had ultimately brought her and her son.

Kristina swiveled around in her high-backed leather executive chair and looked out through her bay window over the incrementally growing sprawl of the city. The skyline along the Rock River on either side of the bridge had changed during the past seven years from the few squat brick main street department stores, shops, and doctors and lawyers and dentist offices of a small Mid-West town to a burgeoning center of interstate commerce linked by highways and railroads to the east through the smokestack iron and steel industrial cities of Indiana, west across prairie farmland to Iowa, Kansas and beyond, and north into the neighboring state of Wisconsin dairy farms, and south into Missouri connecting with long trade barges traversing the Mississippi River from New Orleans to St. Paul, Minnesota.

Sally had told Kristina that if there had been any innuendo when she resigned from the bank to take a job with a major customer, such comments would have been uttered only behind closed bank executive doors or at their private dinners and cocktail parties. But Sally had heard nothing mentioned among her rank and file peers. If she had, she would not have shared the information with her friend. She was convinced that Kristina had made a wise decision, appropriate for her present circumstances and for the future.

Kristina had discovered that the local press became just as interested in her as in the Hofstadter Homes development. Her photogenic beauty immediately became associated with interviews and press articles about her as a leading businesswoman, an executive. She had broken the gender mold.

Upon realizing the effect of her image, Carl placed her smiling photograph in the media advertising, marketing brochures, and on the welcoming sign at the tract development entrance and sales site. Her promotion caused a mixture of disapproval by some husbands that Kristina was violating the traditional role of housewife and mother and sending the wrong message to their daughters. At least half the wives and mothers envied and admired her. She received letters at her office expressing both positions. After a time, she stopped reading them.

The ranch style tract homes sold out for all five phases. Then one day as Carl was reviewing the sales figures and reading over the contracts to see who the buyers were that Kristina had qualified for loans through local banks, he came across one that caught him by surprise, Kristina Blake. A tremor of apprehension seized him, but he quelled the impulse to jump up from his desk with indignation and storm into her office next to his and demand an explanation. She was ruining his plan or at least getting in the way of it. He realized early-on in their working relationship that he could not be forceful with her. She was a strong and independent woman with a mind of her own. If he ever hoped to marry her, he had to proceed carefully, almost delicately.

When she first moved to Rockford with her son, at Dimitri's recommendation, she rented a small two story frame house on a quiet street lined with tall elms whose root structure pushed up at the concrete sidewalk creating a series of trip hazards for the unwary. The long established neighborhood was home to returning war veterans and their young families and several elderly couples and was only a few houses away from where the Woijceks made their temporary lodging until the completion of their sprawling residence near the country club.

Dimitri's wife, Jaramilla, who insisted she be called Millie so her name sounded like an American woman, offered to take care of

Kristina's son while his mother was at work. The instant bond he formed with Milos, who was the same age, eased the anxiety of separation. Elias looked forward to spending each day at the Woijceks with anticipation and excitement and barely acknowledged his mother's departure when she left him at the Woijcek household.

Millie paused in kneading the large lump of dough for baking bread and listened for the boys' voices where she had left them minutes earlier playing with small model plastic cars and trucks on the living room floor. Something had silenced their constant jabbering and spluttering motor noises and diverted their focus in the moment. Upon looking around the corner of the kitchen door, she saw the attraction, a ragged looking gray and white dog with soulful brown eyes peering from his furry mustached face at the two boys who had crawled over to the screen door. The dog's pink tongue tried to lick at them through the mesh. His body wriggled frenetically and his stub of a tail stuttered back and forth with short spasmodic jerks. His sharp bark pierced the silence.

"Well, what have we here?" said Millie crossing the room.

"A dog, Mom," said Milos. "He wants to come in and play with us."

Millie smiled down at the blonde blue-eyed likeness of the boys. *"They could be brothers,"* she thought. Even at three, Milos mimicked her husband's stocky chest and muscular arms and legs and the smooth pronounced Slavic beauty of her well-defined face. When they had been shopping at the corner Piggly Wiggly grocery market, a woman had commented what a "pretty boy" he was. The reference concerned her. Being called a pretty boy was not necessarily a good thing in America where most of the boys and men she had seen had rugged good looks whether they wore suits to work in an office or denim overhauls to work in a factory.

She did notice differences between the boys. Elias tended to be more vocal and directive in their imaginary play than Milos, who trailed after him. Detecting Elias's slight physical handicap with a precocious withdrawn demeanor and respect, Milos would still tease his friend from time to time by pinching and poking him and, giggling, leaping away just out of reach when Elias tried to retaliate.

Weather permitting, they would bundle on their jackets and Millie would walk them to a nearby park only a few blocks from the house.

Occasionally lapsing into Czech commenting to herself , she rotated pushing the boys on the swings, helping them get started and getting off the teeter totter so as not to be catapulted onto the dirt, and spinning them on a dizzy merry-go-round. She closely monitored Elias in his awkward attempts to follow Milos climbing the jungle gym like a small monkey. Watching Milos scamper up the sliding board ladder while he had to laboriously climb one slow step at a time frustrated him. Unable to keep up with Milos charging around the playground, he would stop, sit, and silently watch.

Back at the house, Millie fed them a hearty lunch of fresh baked bread dipped in paprika and garlic flavored thick tomato gravy with floating chunks of bologna sausage. She smiled as they laughed at making milk mustaches while they munched warm chewy chocolate chip cookies for dessert.

She would read a simple children's story to deter them from fussing and resisting nap time. Within minutes following a brief bout of tickling and giggling on Milos's bed, the boys would simultaneously fall asleep, their blonde heads touching each another.

When Kristina arrived at the end of the day to take Elias home, he and Milos would play hide and seek with her, laughing and dodging away and refusing to let her get a hold of him. Sometimes, she acquiesced and let him stay overnight with the Woijceks and the boys would run off shrieking through the house.

The appearance of the stray dog on the front porch was an amazing event. Neither Elias nor Milos had ever had a pet. They had occasionally seen a dog being walked on a leash by its owner and a large black retriever that came and went as it pleased, roaming the neighborhoods and establishing its territory with repetitive strategic stops to pee. But the dog at the door was new.

"So who do you belong to?" Millie asked leaning down over the boys for a closer look. "Do you have a collar? Are you lost? Did someone forget to close the door?"

From the appearance of the animal, Millie suspected its owner had dropped it off somewhere to get rid of it.   The pooch looked a little thin, like it had been scavenging for several days. "Are you hungry? I bet you're hungry."

"He's hungry. Let's feed him, Mom," said Milos. "He's hungry. He's telling us he's hungry."

"Okay, but you have to get up off the floor so I can let him in."

The boys scrambled to their feet. She opened the door. The mutt raced inside and reared up in an ecstasy of wriggling and licked the boys' faces as they threw their small arms around the dog's neck in loving acceptance.

Millie gently placed her hand on the dog's head and he twisted upward to lick her dough and flour scented fingers. "Food is what you want. You must be hungry. Bring him along to the kitchen, boys."

They followed the dog who sensed she was moving to the source of food. He looked up at her chopping cooked meat and potatoes covered with gravy into a bowl. The boys crowded in close continuing to pet the dog.

"Okay, boys," said Millie, carrying the bowl to a corner of the kitchen and placing it on the floor. "Move back and let him eat. Don't bother him while he's eating."

Her extended arm directed the boys in a reluctant shuffle away to the table. Their dancing eyes watched the dog's muzzle thrust into the bowl and giggled at the rapid slurping and chewing noises. Millie place a second bowl filled with water near the first and backed away to watch with the boys.

"He needs a bath," she said.

"We can do it," said Milos.

"You can help. We'll use the hose outside in the back yard."

Pushing the bowl across the floor, the dog finished lapping up the last streak of gravy. A loud belch erupted from the back of his throat sending the boys into a paroxysm of laughter.

As soon as the stream of water gushed from the hose, the dog snapped and gulped at it in play, which again regaled the boys who reached in to help Millie scrub the animal's tangled black and white fur with sudsy warm tap water she carried out in a metal pail. A thorough rinsing followed with the dog's body violently shaking an explosion of spray over Millie and the boys. The dog topped her efforts to dry him with a towel with a vigorous roll on the grass. He suddenly sprang to his feet and madly raced in circles around the yard prompting the shouting boys to chase him. After a few minutes, he plunked down panting at Millie's feet and his puckish face looked up at her.

"Okay," she said. "Back inside." She gathered up the pail and towel, turned off the hose at the spigot, and held the back door open for her trio led by the dog who scampered ahead of them and laid down spread-eagled on the kitchen floor. "We have to give you a name," said Millie, as the boys entwined their fingers in the dog's coat. "Something that tells who you are. How about *Radek*. It is Czech for happy and you are so happy?"

The dog licked the boys' faces as they repeated the name. *"Radek, Radek, Radek."*

When Kristina came to the house to pick up Elias, the dog greeting her at the door surprised her.

"Showed up on the porch today," explained Millie.

"Me and Milos have a pet," said Elias stroking the dog's back.

"His name is *Radek*," said Milos. "It means he is happy."

"What a charming little face you have, *Radek*," Kristina bent over to scratch him behind his ears.

"The boys have had a good time with him," said Millie. "We gave him a bath."

"Are you going to keep him?"

"Oh, yes, we will keep him. Get him shots, a leash and a collar so we can go on walks and he can run around the playground. He is very fast. He likes to run."

"He ran in the yard," said Elias.

"Zoom! Zoom!" Milos sliced the flat of his hand through the air.

"Sorry to have to take you away," Kristina said to Elias, "but it's time to go home."

"*Radek* will be here for you tomorrow," said Millie, manipulating Elias's arms into his jacket.

"Tomorrow," said Elias kneeling down to look into *Radek's* eyes. "I see you tomorrow."

"Thank you, Millie. Looks like you have your hands full."

"I am glad for it. A pet is good for children."

Kristina nodded. "Okay, my boy. Ready to go?"

Elias took her hand. "Bye, Milos. Bye, *Radek*."

Milos waved. "Bye."

"Bye, see you in the morning," said Millie, "bright and early."

"Bright and early," echoed Elias.

Kristina noticed that Elias hummed a kind of tuneless song on the drive home.

After she had given him a bath, read a story, and tucked him into bed that night, she put on her nightgown, robe, and slippers and went to the kitchen to pour a glass of whiskey and soda. Then she selected a record album to play on the phonograph and settled on the couch to sip her cocktail and, with the volume turned down low, listen to Frank Sinatra crooning her favorite songs, *I'll Be Seeing You* and *I'll Never Smile Again*, she remembered from the war years.

* * * *

Carrying a double scotch and water, Carl took a leisurely stroll through his newly completed house, admiring its large rooms, over-size picture window views of the golf course fairway fifty yards away meandering along the border of his landscaped property. He paused to sit on a leather couch and gaze out from the living room past a poolside gazebo nestled among sculptured boulders and climbing pink floral vines. Agitated and restless, he rose from the couch and circumvented several white leather stuffed easy chairs with ottomans and contrasting red, orange, and burgundy cushions on his way to the spacious tiled kitchen appointed with the latest top-of-the-line appliances and an overhead wrought iron rack adorned with polished copper pots and skillets.

He continued through to his well-stocked bar in the adjoining dining room and refreshed his drink before continuing his lonely tour of the eight thousand square foot house, ending up in the palatial master bedroom. He stared at the king size bed and the second of two walk-in closets intended for Kristina, if he could ever convince her to marry him. Her lack of response to his romantic overtures alarmed him.

Ever since joining the company, she had acted distant and socially inaccessible, refusing dinner invitations and going with him and other staff to business lunches only. What troubled him immensely was that she considered their relationship just a part of the business and had suggested as much by her words and actions.

His evenings were increasingly spent diluting his angst with scotch and martinis or attending an occasional dinner party at the home of his financial business partner, Lewis Murtagh whose wife never missed an opportunity to criticize Carl in a snide way for using the attractive image of his company vice president on billboards, posters, advertisements, and figuring her prominently in the local society section of The Morning Star, a small city newspaper.

"Her image has sexual implications," Irene Murtagh accused him. "If she wants to be a movie star, she should go to Hollywood, don't you think?"

"There's nothing sexual about her," Carl immediately regretted his drunken comment, fearing Irene would use it in the exchange of ceaseless gossip among her women friends thriving on innuendo and damaging fabrications to stimulate their mundane ordinary lives.

"I think using Kristina is a great idea," said her husband, trying to defuse any resentment by Carl from Irene's narrow-minded criticism. "A stroke of genius. She's created a recognized identity for the homes that has meant millions in sales, which, let me remind you, is why we're in business." He poured another glass of Bordeaux, forked a bite of rare sirloin into his mouth and mixed it with a gulp of the dark fruit flavored red wine. He brushed a droplet from his black mustache attached above his upper lip like a caterpillar wriggling with Lewis's chewing motions.

He had not known nor met Carl Hofstadter and Dimitri Woijcek until the day the younger men had walked into his office with a proposal for a housing development. Lewis had recently submitted a successful bid on a segment of a major highway development project. Carl had explained that the news announcement of the award to Murtagh had brought him to the compound populated with heavy road construction equipment next to a rambling single story brown brick building at the edge of the city on the west side.

"I have eight-hundred acres of farmland a few miles west of here. The highway you're building will pass close by. I'm planning to build a five phase housing development and I'm looking for a financial partner."

Lewis shifted a half-smoked cigar from one side of his mouth to the other and peered up at Carl and Dimitri through his bifocals. He rose slightly from his desk chair and reached across to shake hands with the two men. "Have a seat, gentlemen."

"Looks like you have drawings."

"We do," said Carl. "We've completed surveys and are preparing a presentation to the planning commission. We'd like to strike a deal with you."

"Let's see what you've got. I gather you've come to me for the excavation."

"That and more," said Carl spreading the drawings across other paperwork cluttering Lewis's desk.

Lewis traced the topmost terrain map with a stubby finger. "Lot of land. Pretty ambitious. I need to see it before I commit to anything. You financed?"

"Not yet. We're talking to a bank in Chicago. Chicago Savings and Loan."

Lewis nodded. "How soon."

"Next week."

"You have time to take a drive out there?"

"We're living on the farm. My parents'."

"But you own it."

"It's in their name. They're getting old."

Lewis nodded in understanding. "You know I have the highway to deal with. Equipment is going to be tied up for a while."

"We'll work with you on that. The highway's important to the development."

"Gotcha."

"We'd like to have you with us on the proposal."

"I'll let you know after I see the land. If it's a go, you can write me in."

Events had moved quickly once the loan was established. Kristina had visited Lewis and his accountant and local banker to go over his company finances to confirm its solvency in covering the interest costs. Lewis ended up buying more equipment to accommodate the housing development excavation along with the scheduled highway construction. A year later, he recognized that something was going on between Carl and Kristina when he visited Carl's ten story office building in downtown Rockford and discovered Kristina sitting in a large expensively appointed executive suite with her name and title of Vice President on the door.

In addition to Kristina's promotional skills, Lewis approved of her involvement in the company because she was a looker, a real sexy dame, the kind he would pay to spend the night with, if he did that sort of thing. But he believed he could have his fantasies about her and recalled his younger days back in the 20's when his buddies called him Murt the flirt. He had been a ladies man then, having a "swell time" at wild raucous parties that lasted all night and sometimes into the next morning with a second round of raunchy sex to assuage his edgy horniness from a hangover.

Then he had a full head of curly dark hair, a pencil thin mustache, and was a fancy dresser and dynamo dancer. Then, he couldn't get enough sex and had his hand exploring up a girl's skirt almost every night, until he met Irene, who was capable of fulfilling his insatiable demand, until she married him and they raised three children. The physical excitement faded over the years as though it had never existed between them and disintegrated into a perfunctory defensiveness of petty criticisms and stinging emotional darts that exacerbated the scabrous wound of their marriage.

Lewis indulged his fantasies in a secret library of Playboy Magazines kept hidden in his safe at the office. He removed the centerfolds only late at night after his handful of administrative staff had long departed. He clipped the blinds to shut off all indications that anyone remained inside the building, then spread his selected favorites across the conference table. Stripping off his clothes, he would stride naked around and around the table, exercising his penis into maximum tumescence until he was about to ejaculate. Then he would lie on his back on the floor and watch his jism spout into the air and land on his belly that had boasted six clearly articulated abs twenty-five years ago.

The news that their son had been killed on the beach at Normandy short-circuited something in Lewis's brain. Given the shortness of a life, a compelling need to pursue hedonist pleasures consumed him. Trying to cope with the loss of her son drove Irene into the religious clutches of well-intentioned catty church women whose main discourse was to make negative comments about Kristina Blake, comments that reached a fever pitch with the appearance in The Morning Star of her announcement to wed Carl Hofstadter.

Chapter 10

Marriage

Sales of the Hofstadter Homes had soared beyond expectations for all phases. Kristina disclaimed Carl's crediting her for the financial success. "The availability of the homes themselves, the returning vets, and the changing times we live in sold those houses," she said. "I had little to do with it."

"On that point I sharply disagree," said Carl. "I'm proud of you. Everyone in the company is proud of you. You put us on the map. The press and media promotion put you on the map."

"However it happened, you have become the image, the spokesperson, of the company, the modern woman."

"I'm not any more modern than any other women."

"Oh, but you are. You're a new breed, a front runner, a career woman."

"You make me sound like a horse."

"You're not like most other women, Kristina. You're a thoroughbred."

"I really don't care being compared to livestock, one of the herd. Do I get fed a special brand of high performing oats?"

"No, no, not at all. Let's just say you're special, really special, especially to me."

Kristina looked around her office. "At least I keep a clean stall. You don't have to pick up after me."

"Okay, let's drop the horse nonsense. I apologize. This is not what I came in here to see you about. Something far more important for both of us."

Kristina inwardly tensed. Whenever Carl alluded to mutual involvement, her guard came up. "What is it?"

"I was going through the housing contracts and came across one with your name on it."

"Yes, I can actually afford to buy one. My husband was a military veteran so I can use his GI bill benefits."

"I'm not the most sensitive person," said Carl.

"So I've noticed."

"I accept that. But you are. That's why you're here. I need you in my life."

"As I explained before, we have a workable business relationship."

"That's not what I'm talking about. I want you in my life, my personal life."

"I already have a personal life."

"Being a young widow with a son. Don't you feel you're missing something?"

"No, not really."

"This isn't just about me. How about his future. How about opportunities for him. Doesn't he miss having a father?"

"He never knew his father. The closest person he has known as a father is his grandfather, who he misses very much. Fortunately, his grandparents come to visit him once or twice a month."

"I'm thinking of a father who would be with him every day."

"You mean you."

"I can't be any more obvious, but I'm almost afraid to ask you to marry me. I'm afraid you'll turn me down. I'm really not such a bad guy."

"I've never called you a bad guy?"

Kristina's compressed grin caught him off guard.

The ball disappeared at the succinct powerful impact and rose in a long high trajectory until it was no longer visible as though absorbed into the vast blue sky. It suddenly appeared as a tiny white dot with a brief single bounce at the lip of the sand trap bordering the approach to the green.

Carl slowly lowered the driver from his frozen follow-through position, retrieved the tee, and stepped back.

"Great shot, Carl," the approving voice of the pro acknowledged. "You're in a good position for a birdie. Chip to get on and one in the cup."

Wendell Jones had coached him through a series of lessons since the opening of the country club five years ago and now occasionally joined him and two of Carl's business associates in a round of eighteen holes. He discreetly never commented or gave advice to Carl's invited guests unless asked. Once they observed his skill and style of play, they always requested his feedback.

Upon recruiting and hiring Wendell, Carl had given him carte blanche to establish the tone and caliber of the club covering everything from the clothing and equipment sold in the pro shop to the hiring and management of employees to maintain the rolling emerald fairways and greens that spanned over two hundred acres. Carl would not hire young Negro men to work at the country club as caddies or in the restaurant as cooks and waiters and kitchen help. All the grounds keepers were Caucasian. He claimed that members did not want to see color in their club or on the links.

He also posted a strict dress code for men and women who played the course. Men were required to wear slacks and a collared shirt or long sleeved shirt and tie and could add a light full or vest sweater. A hat was optional. Women had to appear in a blouse and skirt with an option of a light cashmere sweater. During the hot humid summer months, they could wear a sleeveless blouse and Bermuda shorts.

The course had been designed to take advantage of low lying hills and narrow forest strips of oak and elm trees bordering manicured greens and fairways occasionally intersected by a meandering creek that curved and switched-back across the terrain.

A large black and white photograph of Carl, Wendell Jones, Kristina, Dimitri, and Lewis Murtagh at the opening ceremony had a prominent place on the wall near the pro shop entrance. The photo had been taken a week before Carl's wedding. Apprehensive that Kristina might change her mind, he hired a wedding planner from Chicago to manage the arrangements, since Kristina seemed disinterested in having a gala affair. She told him a small civil ceremony would be adequate and that he didn't need to turn the wedding into a prominent local society event that enhanced the visibility of Hofstadter Homes and the corporation.

Five years ago, Elias was uncertain about Carl. He hadn't really understood his mother's attempt to explain the nature of her relationship with Carl and how Elias fit in. He didn't understand how this stranger could suddenly become his father. He felt more of a kinship with Dimitri, Milos's father, who was easy going and fun loving and treated him like Milos's brother. The man his mother introduced as Carl, soon to become her husband and his stepfather, was not at all like Dimitri. He seemed tense and nervous and reluctant to touch him other than to pat him on the head and shake his hand. Dimitri always grabbed him in a laughing bear hug and planted two loud lip-smacking kisses on his face that brought a rush of blood to his cheeks, a sparkle to his eyes, and a giggle to his throat. Elias loved how the open goodness of those greeting embraces made him feel when he went to spend the day with Milos.

He didn't understand what was happening when Carl drove him and his mother out of the city into the countryside and stopped at a house ten times larger than the one in which Elias and his mother currently lived and was told this would be his new home.

"I don't want to stay here. What about Milos?" he asked.

"Milos and his mother and father will still be neighbors," Kristina explained. "They are also moving to a house near this one. You can see it from here," she pointed across an expanse of landscaped yard to a house of similar size and architecture fifty yards away.

"Milos will live there?"

"Yes, that is where Milos will live and he will still be your friend."

"Okay."

"Shall we go inside," said Carl. "We'll show you your room."

The size of the entry and the expansive living room stunned Elias. He grasped his mother's hand and feared he would become lost if he ventured into the labyrinth alone. They followed Carl through the living room and attached dining room offering a glimpse of the large kitchen in passing and down a long hallway with many side bedrooms until they stopped and entered one of them. The first thing Elias noticed was a stained wood bunk bed along the far wall. He released his mother's hand, walked across the hardwood floor partially covered with a large tan throw rug, and climbed the short ladder to the top bunk. He clambered onto the mattress, turned, and smiled.

"Milos can sleep down there."

Elias had never been in a church before and he had never worn a snug-fitting gray and maroon plaid sport coat and a collared white shirt fastened at his throat with a snap-on yellow bow tie. His mother had told him he looked very handsome and dashing. He felt better about the discomfort of the tie when he saw Milos wearing similar garb when the Woicjeks arrived at the filled Lutheran church parking lot. Jaramilla stayed with the boys and let them run around the churchyard for a few minutes while Dimitri joined Kristina and Carl and went inside through the wide hand-carved door rising to a Gothic peak.

Elias saw a woman wearing a mauve-colored dress and a spring hat with a floppy brim arrive. He remembered meeting her once when she visited his mother at their small house. He knew her name was Sally and he had liked her. He waved, but she didn't notice him as she entered the church escorted by a man Elias didn't know. Once Jaramilla took the boys by their hands and lead them inside, Elias couldn't distinguish the man from the others, since they all wore similar suits.

Millie guided the boys to the front row of pews and sat between them with Elias squeezed in next to his grandmother, Julie, who placed her arm around him and drew him close for a kiss.

"Gramma, I didn't now you would be here. Where's Grampa?"

"You'll see him. Wouldn't miss it. Shh, we have to be quiet."

Impressed by the surrounding silence, cascade of flowers at the altar, a bronze statue of a crucified Jesus Christ against the backdrop of the stained glass window rising to the apex of the cathedral ceiling, the boys glanced at each other only once across Millie's lap and refrained from being silly. They remained intimidated and silent at the sudden exploding sound of a pipe organ expanding and filling the spaces of the church in an emotional mind-numbing religious cantata. Elias felt the music pressing him down into the hardness of the wooden seat against his bottom. His body involuntarily squirmed. The pressure of Millie's hand on his arm steadied him.

At the sudden lilting cadence and melody of the traditional Lohengrin wedding march, which he had never heard before, he lifted his chin and opened his clenched eyes. A white-robed minister cradling a Bible had appeared on the raised red-carpeted steps in front of the altar. Elias noticed his thinning gray hair and pale serious expression. He saw Carl and Dimitri rise from the opposite front row seated next to Carl's parents and move into position on one side and Sally Glover on the other side of the minister. He wondered what they were doing up there until he sensed and heard the shifting of everyone seated in the church twisting to look at his mother escorted by her elderly father, Conrad Holtzman, walking slowly down the aisle toward the altar. Her father's broad generous smile beamed out to the congregation. Kristina's best effort was a compressed grin and a tolerant expression in her eyes. Rather than a bridal gown, she wore a mauve business suit and small hat visually linking her to Sally as her maid of honor.

Elias tried to stand up on his seat and wave at her, drawing a ripple of laughter from the solemn gathering of adults and a benign smile from the minister. His grandmother gently pressured him back onto his seat.

As his mother and grandfather arrived at the steps, the music faded to silence and the minister began to speak. Elias didn't understood his words, but realized the ritual formality was transforming Carl and his mother into a husband and a wife and that Carl was now his stepfather.

Carl considered the country club his personal domain. The single story brown brick structure covering one acre on a rise overlooking the first tee of the golf course bore his family name in a large wrought iron sign of inspired scrollwork at the front gate.

A massive glass chandelier hung from the ballroom ceiling. The floor design and heavily draped plum-colored décor in the restaurant and bar were intended to accommodate large crowds for social gatherings.

Carl had orchestrated the wedding to feature the country club venue and invited members of the press from Rockford, Chicago, and local regional cities and towns in Missouri, Iowa, Kansas, Wisconsin, and Indiana to publish articles and society photos in their newspapers.

Although Millie kept an eye on the boys, Elias and Milos sampled desserts within easy reach from the buffet and wandered freely among the grownups. The reception dinner progressed and the twelve piece big band orchestra music prompted the dancing, drinking and raucous laughter and toasting of the bride and groom.

Drawing smiles of amusement, Elias and Milos hopped about near their table imitating the twisting partners and gyrating out onto the dance floor. Carl's elderly mother, Abigail, appeared lost and sought the security of sitting with the pastor and his wife. No alcoholic beverages for them. Lucius grew drunk and danced a polka with Kristina. Kristina's parents, Julie and Conrad, ate heartily, drank beer, and congratulated Kristina and her husband and exchanged partners during a Viennese waltz.

Elias barely noticed his mother and stepfather leaving the reception since he had dozed off sitting in his chair at the dining table with the Woijceks. He was staying with them while his mother and Carl went away on a week long honeymoon.

Carl and Kristina began the night drive to their resort destination. Both were quiet and subdued, not acknowledging one another. Kristina characterized the distance between them with a ferocious yawn and stared out her window at house and farm lights they passed in the isolated countryside until their infrequent appearance among stands of tall pines further north. Carl decided he was feeling too drunk to drive and pulled over. He asked Kristina to take the wheel. She complained that her night vision was not very good. "I told you I don't like to drive at night. Remember?"

"Has to be better than mine, at least tonight."

"Maybe we should just go back to the house and leave tomorrow morning. That would be sensible."

"We just got married. Who wants to be sensible? It's our wedding night."

"I do, Carl."

He laughed. "We already said that at the altar."

"Don't be funny. We want to get there in one piece. This is not pleasant."

"All right. You're right. I just celebrated a little too much and you're not much of a drinker. You do what you think is best. We have a reservation waiting for us at the resort and we've already driven thirty miles. It's only another twenty. It's farther to go back than to go on. There's almost no traffic on the highway. All you have to do is take it slow, stay on this side of the line."

"I know how to drive."

"I know you know. At this point in time, I trust your driving more than I trust mine, which is a compliment to you, because I'm a damn good driver."

"At least you're smart enough to pull over. All right, we'll keep going."

"That's my girl."

"I'm not a girl, Carl. I'm your wife."

"And a serious one at that. Did you enjoy the reception?"

"I enjoyed watching Elias and Milos jumping around to the music and your mother and father dancing a two-step."

"Your Ma and Pa sure held their own."

"They were young once."

"And you and Sally lit the floor on fire. Sorry I couldn't keep up with you. I never learned to dance like that."

"Sally and I were taxi dancers before the war."

"I remember hearing that somewhere."

"I told you, or maybe Sally did."

"Her boyfriend sure knows the steps. Where'd he learn."

"In the Marines."

"Oh, come on."

Kristina grinned. "Sally taught him. They met about a year ago. They're getting married next month."

"Good for Sally."

"What's that supposed to mean?"

"Just good for Sally. She's your best friend. She deserves to have a good man at her side, just like you."

"Don't think too highly of yourself. Remember who put you on the map."

"Of course, I'm joking. Not only do I love you, I am indebted to you."

"You are," she grinned for the second time. "And don't you forget it."

"Somehow I don't think you'll let me."

Kristina put the car in gear and looked back to check the nearest lane as the double-fin Cadillac edged off the gravel shoulder back onto the two lane highway.

Kristina stared past her husband's empty breakfast plate, juice glass, and coffee cup and saucer. The remnant streak of yellow-orange egg yolk clinging to the plate in the wake of the wiping pattern of his toast nauseated her and she quickly raised her eyes to stare out over the expanse of blue lake shimmering in the morning sunlight. A lone gull coasted down to momentarily rest on the placid surface, then rose with a high-pitched sharp cry and continued its search for food.

She finished her second cup of coffee, then left the table on the dining room balcony and walked down the open steps to a dirt path through a stand of pine that brought her to the beach. She slipped off her loafers and, carrying them with one hand, walked barefoot to the edge of the water gently lapping the shore. She waded in to her ankles and absorbed the cool liquid sensation against her legs. Her bare arms rippled with goose bumps from the summer breeze. Her tan Bermuda shorts and sleeveless white blouse gave her only an outward sensation of freedom of movement and a sense of escape.

Carl rushed through breakfast and gulped down several cups of coffee to erase the edginess of his hangover, then drove off to town in search of an open pharmacy where he could buy condoms.

Arriving at the Lake Geneva Resort late the previous night, Kristina had to check them in and support her stumbling half-asleep husband up the elevator to the third level and along the hall to the bridal suite with a view of the lake. Once inside, Carl collapsed onto the large bed with a steady stream of snores. Kristina pulled off his shoes and rolled him over to occupy one side of the bed and left him sleeping in his clothes until morning. She did not put on the nightgown she planned to wear, but her usual cotton pajamas, used the bathroom, brushed her teeth and washed her face, then slipped into bed under the covers and slept with her back turned toward him.

His hand pawing at her breasts woke her the next morning. He had shed his clothes in the bathroom, relieved his bladder, and wanted to have sex. His foul alcohol-tainted breath and rough beard scrapping her face drove her to throw back the blankets and erupt from the bed.

"What do you think you're doing?"

He looked up at her with a sheepish grin. "What we couldn't do last night."

"What you couldn't do."

"Well, I'm ready now." He glanced down at the erection probing upward through the fly of his underwear.

"I prefer that you shower and shave and get yourself cleaned up. Get yourself sober."

"Oh, except for my head, I'm sober enough."

"We're not going to start off this way, Carl."

"What do you mean. This is our honeymoon."

"Drunk."

"I'm not drunk."

"Last night."

"Last night was the reception. We were celebrating. You were drinking champagne too."

"I could barely get you up to the room last night. The bell hop had to help me. It was rather embarrassing."

"Did you give him a tip?"

"Yes, I gave him a tip."

"I hope it was a big one. He was moving important cargo." Carl emitted a snort of laughter. "Much bigger now."

"You're just being rude and gross. It's not becoming."

"Sorry, I do apologize. I don't usually make comments like that. It's the headache talking. We have some getting acquainted to do."

"I think the timing will be better later today."

"I'm feeling pretty spry at the moment."

"I'm not feeling – spry. You're not being at all romantic or attractive."

"I do have my moments."

"This is not one of them."

Carl grinned. "Remember what the minister said, a wife will obey her husband and submit to his will."

"You certainly can't believe I take that seriously. Those were only words."

"Yeah, they were words." He noticed his erection receding into a mound of soft skin.

"And another thing. Did you bring condoms?"

"I have to use a condom? We're husband and wife. It won't feel as good."

"No condom, no sex."

"What about children?"

"We should have discussed this before. No children. I have my child. I don't want any more children."

"I guess we should have talked about it, but I can live with that. I married you for you, because of who you are. You're someone special to me. Sound romantic? Not just that, I mean what I'm saying."

"I know. I appreciate what you're saying."

"I'll get cleaned up and we'll go have breakfast. I'm starving."

Followed closely by Milos and his four year old little sister, Duska, named after her aunt in Racine, ignoring Kristina's greeting, *Radek* rushed through the open front door and went wriggling and wagging in search of Elias. Discovering him in the family room seated on the floor, the dog gave him a quick lick on the face, then ranged back and forth across the carpet like a canine vacuum cleaner searching for the source of a scent in the thick pile.

Milos dropped to the floor and joined his friend in watching the conclusion of *Leave It To Beaver*. Duska flopped down next to her brother. Behind them, *Radek* rooted out the half-masticated olive from where Elias had shoved it under the couch and swallowed the tangy flavored pit.

"You look very nice," Millie complimented Kristina as she entered and followed her to the kitchen. Kristina maintained her envious slender figure by swimming and playing tennis at the club.

"Thank you so much for coming over," Kristina's heels clicked across the wooden floor. "I made some snacks you can put out for Duska and the boys and there's milk in the fridge. You're welcome to anything you'd like."

"You and Carl have a good time at the dinner party and don't feel you have to hurry to get back."

"Is it okay for Milos to stay over? Elias was hoping he could."

"Of course. I can come by for him in the morning. He deserves a little break from piano practice, but not much. He has a recital next month at the music school in Chicago."

"Such a talented boy. We'll probably be late returning, if that's all right."

"I can sleep on the couch."

"You and Dimitri should join us at the club sometime. We could hire a sitter to watch Duska and the boys."

Millie's mouth drooped in a deprecating grin. "We do not like so much those parties. We like to stay home."

"I always feel better knowing you're with the boys anyway."

"We have fun. We have a good time."

"You're a good neighbor, Millie. What's Dimitri up to tonight?"

"He go bowling with friends. This their bowling night."

"I can't interest Carl in bowling. He just prefers golf. All his business associates are golfers."

"Dimitri try, but he not like golf much. Ball is too small. Bowling ball much bigger."

"You could try golfing with me sometime."

"Same reason, ball is too small. I take care of house, cook, work in garden."

"You're very good at those things. My mother was a great cook, I've never been that interested, although I don't' get complaints from Elias and Carl. I don't think they're very discriminating when it comes to eating anyway."

"Elias have good appetite, better than Milos. Eat more than Milos."

"The boys are growing so fast."

Carl came along the hall from the bedroom to the kitchen. "Hi, Millie, we appreciate you coming over again. It's our turn the next time you and Dimitri want to go out."

"Hi, Carl, we go see Milos play in concert. We can take Elias and Duska and maybe you like to come sometime."

"We'd like that, wouldn't we, Kristina?"

"Very much. You need to give us his schedule."

"We did see him on Ed Sullivan," said Carl. "He was a hit, famous overnight."

"He doesn't think about famous. He is still good boy."

"I don't think the spotlight will change him," said Carl. "Not with the great parents he has. You help him keep a good head on his shoulders."

"Elias is a good boy too. He has a good head."

"Kristina gets most of the credit for that. Are we ready, dear? Shall we go?"

"Let me grab my purse and we should say goodnight to Elias."

"Of course, where are the boys?"

"Family room."

"Meet you there." Carl left the kitchen. Upon entering the family room, he stood watching Elias and Milos with Duska and the dog snuggled between them. Kristina came in a few moments later and went over to the boys who were oblivious to her bending down to give them each a kiss and a pat on their tousled blonde heads. But Radek thrust his nose up at her and she rubbed his ears and Duska jumped up to give her a hug, then promptly sat down.

"Your dad and I are leaving now, Elias."

"Okay, have a good time."

"Milos is staying over."

"I know. He already told me."

"Millie has snacks in the kitchen whenever you get hungry."

"Can she bring them in here?"

"You'll have to put them where *Radek* can't reach them."

"Don't put them too high or I can't reach them," chirped Duska, a cherubic blonde version of her brother, only half his size. The bib and straps of her pink coveralls concealed most of her blouse decorated with tiny farm animals.

"My mom brought him a bone to chew," said Milos. "But he likes cookies better."

"We're thinking of coming to your recital next month," said Kristina.

"I'd like that. You can sit in the front row with my mom and dad."

"Maybe we could come over to your house sometime and get a preview," said Carl. "Time to go, Kristina."

"Okay, boys, Duska, enjoy yourselves."

"We will, goodbye," said Elias.

"Bye, Mrs. Hofstadter," said Milos.

Kristina angled across the room to Carl, who took her arm and escorted her to the front door.

"Bye, Millie," said Kristina. "We're on our way."

"Goodbye, be careful driving."

"Always," said Carl.

The door closed behind them and they were gone.

Millie went to check on the children, saw they were intently watching television, then went to the kitchen to prepare their snacks on small paper plates. To avoid spilling and staining the beige carpet, she decided not to take glasses of milk out to them. They would have to come to the kitchen when they were ready to eat their chocolate chip cookies.

As much as she respected and admired Kristina, she wished Kristina would stop trying to invite her to social affairs at the country club. Kristina recognized Millie's embarrassment and discomfort, but asked out of courtesy, given the friendship and business relationship between Carl and Dimitri. Millie reminded Kristina of her Swedish mother, Julie Holtzman, and her old world kindness and good-hearted values which did not fit in with the WASPish country club wives and their preoccupation with class distinction and fashion. Other than stories in Life Magazine about Dior, Chanel, and Givenchy and seeing advertising on television commercials, Millie knew and cared little about the famous clothes designers.

Her purpose, her focus was raising her children and being a devoted wife to Dimitiri. Despite her trepidation leaving her extended family in Czechoslovakia to come to America, what her husband had accomplished within a few years exceeded her imagination. He had brought them from a low income immigrant community to an upper middle-class home and a living standard that left her feeling out of her element. She didn't voice her insecurity to Dimitri and never complained. He would be angry and think she was ungrateful for all that he had done for his family.

Dimitri knew he didn't fit in with the social class of men and women for whom he had built magnificent luxury homes, but he didn't dwell on what his wife, Millie, thought of as a stigma, their ethnic heritage, their broken English, and avoidance of posh parties.

Since he and Millie had escaped political repression in their home country, he wanted nothing to do with American politics and had cautioned her to not talk with anybody about their origin. He had been following the McCarthy hearings aired on television and written about in The Morning Star. He feared that coming from a communist country, he and Millie would be branded as communists themselves and would be deported, losing everything. He could see that the Senator Joseph McCarthy was just like the dictators and bureaucrats from whom he and Millie had escaped. He would never have guessed that the man who could conceivably destroy their lives came from just over the state line in Wisconsin.

Having a business association through Carl with Lewis Murtagh concerned him. Lewis openly praised the McCarthy hearings, especially when he tossed back a few beers with Dimitri and some of the crew after work. He never alluded a direct accusation to Dimitri, but the innuendo haunted him to the extent he avoided contact with Carl's business partner whenever possible. Lewis noticed the change in Dimitri's behavior and thought he was being secretive, trying to hide something about himself. Lewis watched for an opportunity to validate his suspicion. He would not tolerate having a communist working in his company, even if he was a minor twenty-five percent vested partner.

He privately voiced his concern to Carl, who immediately rejected his accusation. "Why would you think that? You have no reason to think that. Dimitri is a good friend and a loyal member of this company. In case you've forgotten, he built all those houses and shopping centers that have made us millionaires. And, by the way, he's a United States citizen, both him and his wife."

"I don't trust him."

"What reason do you have for not trusting him and in what way?"

"Their boy."

"Milos? Are you out of your mind? He's ten years old. He knows nothing about politics. Where do you get this, Lewis. Where's it coming from?"

"I hired a private detective to do some investigating."

"You what? What's the matter with you, Lewis? What's going on here? I don't like what you're telling me."

"Then you won't like this. Every Saturday, Dimitri drives his son to Chicago to take piano lessons from a Russian who came from Russia. His name is Aleksei Greschenko and he's a communist. I think he's a spy come over here to steal secrets and send 'em back to his pinko comrades."

"You really need to let go of this obsession, Lewis. I don't want to lose my best friend over this because you're paranoid."

"I am not paranoid. I have proof."

"You've got nothing but your own opinion and you believe that propaganda bullshit McCarthy is passing off as truth to make himself important and stir up the country. I didn't fight in the war to let a dirty politician smear the names and reputations of good honest people."

"I know you're not a communist. You just want to protect your friend. But you wait and see. I've got proof."

"Lewis, leave Dimitri alone. He's a good honest man and he loves this country. He came here to escape demagogues like McCarthy."

"We'll see. We shall see. And by the way, McCarthy is not a demagogue. He is a great man, a great leader. I hope he runs for President."

"Let me make this a little stronger, Lewis. You do anything to hurt Dimitri and his family, I'll sue you and dissolve your portion of the partnership."

Lewis grunted, rose from his chair and walked out of Carl's office. "Like hell you'll sue me," he muttered under his breath.

From the beginning of his partnership with Carl and Dimitri, Lewis had never envisioned the financial success they had achieved. He didn't understand the forces of supply and demand and dynamics of the post war culture and economy that provided the foundation for real estate development on such a huge scale. He had taken a risk, going in with Carl. It had paid off and now he wanted a bigger share.

Because he had provided only the excavation of the Hofstader land for development, he had accepted twenty-six percent ownership of the company, only two more than Dimitri Woijcek, a communist. He resented that he was not a senior partner on equal footing with Carl Hofstadter. He had tried to negotiate incorporating his excavation business as a division of the Hofstadter real estate enterprise. Lewis silently raged at Carl's refusal to even consider the offer. Carl saw the move as a ploy to gain more leverage in his company.

His distrust grew that Lewis might try something underhanded, especially now that he admitted he was spying on Dimitri. Carl had also offered to buy out Lewis's twenty-six percent of the company for five million dollars. Lewis had scoffed and walked away. He had much bigger plans. He and Carl had not spoken to each other since, which was fine with Carl, who warned Kristine to keep a close eye on the corporate books. He told her he believed Lewis was not past embezzling the company.

When the television program ended, Millie shepherded the children into the kitchen for their milk and cookies served at the table. She promptly gave Radek his bone so he wouldn't beg. Duska always shared a morsel of her food even though she had been instructed not to. Radek dropped his bone, gazed up at her with alert loving eyes, and waited. As soon as her mother glanced away, Duska obliged with half of one of her cookies that Radek lipped from her small fingers with quick delicacy. Then he picked up his bone and lay down under the table to gnaw on it.

After the snack, the boys returned to the family room and opened a Monopoly game on the carpet. Elias distributed the play money while Milos positioned the cards. They each selected their favorite icon from the box, Elias the small metal shoe because it reminded him of his crippled foot, and Milos taking the train engine because it reminded him of a percussive musical rhythm.

Millie sat aside with her daughter on the couch and watched her add bright colors with precision to the people and bird and animal shapes in her coloring book. Millie also pulled several children's books from her canvas bag for Duska to read when she tired of directing the dull points of her crayons.

Frustration festered in Lewis like a searing hot coal that flared up and fueled his anger every time he thought he was unable to have what he wanted. Throwing violent tantrums as a child had evolved into winning at all costs as an adult with no regard for the consequences to others. Others were always competitors, people who denied him or stood in the way, despite his attempts to manipulate them. His narcissistic self-absorption consumed him with a sociopathic intensity that drove him to stop at nothing.

Having worked with heavy excavation equipment and trucks and turning cars into drag racers, Lewis knew everything there was to know about automotive systems. He watched and waited to lethally strike back at Carl. A nighttime soiree at the country club provided Lewis the opportunity.

Halfway through the party at the country club, the teen-age parking attendant with hair Brill-creamed in a precisely combed duck tail stepped from behind his podium and approached Lewis Murtagh as he lit up a cigar. "Should I bring up your car, sir?"

"Uh, no, thanks. A friend asked me to get something for him from his car." Lewis held up a set of keys he pulled from his pocket.

The attendant moved back to his station. Lewis scanned the full lot dimly illuminated by three overhead street lamps spaced around the perimeter. He saw Carl's gold Cadillac among other cars sequestered to an area labeled and roped off for valet parking only. After a few puffs on his cigar, he crossed to the section with an unhurried walk and sidled in between the cars. Pretending to drop his keys, he placed his still smoking cigar on the car hood, stooped down, then quickly lay on his back and scuttled under the Cadillac.

Removing an ice pick from his inside suit coat pocket, he positioned the sharp point against one of the welded air ducts and pounded upwards with the palm of his other hand to puncture the duct. After repeating the vandalism on a second duct, he crawled out from under the vehicle. He dusted himself off, straightened his suit jacket and noticed a spot of grease on the cuff of the right sleeve. He removed the jacket and draped it over his left arm. He started to walk away, then remembered the cigar resting on the car hood.

The parking attendant watched him return puffing vigorously on the cigar.

Four hours later, the insistent ringing of the front doorbell and Radek's loud ferocious barking roused Millie from a doze. She thought she heard sirens in the distance. She slipped her arm away from her sleeping daughter, lunged up from the couch and, encouraged by Radek racing back and forth between her and the entry way, hurried to the door.

"Shush, Radek, it's okay. Shush, you're making too much noise," to which the dog swallowed his bark into a deep threatening growl as she grabbed him by the collar and opened the door. Expecting to see

Carl and Kristina, the sight of the blue uniformed police officer and the flashing red and yellow lights behind him on the roof of his car startled her. "Yes, officer, is something wrong? Did something happen?"

"Do you know Carl and Kristina Hofstadter?"

"Yes, yes I do."

"Are you a relative?"

"No, I'm a family friend, Millie Woijcek. I'm taking care of their son while they're at the country club party tonight. My children are here with me. They're all asleep."

Radek had quieted, but a low growl gurgled in his throat.

"I'm afraid I have bad news."

"Yes?"

"Mr. and Mrs. Hofstadter died in a crash."

Millie choked and could not speak.

"They were coming down that steep hill from the country club. The road has sharp curves. They appear to have lost control of the car. It went off the road down a high embankment and hit a large tree. They were killed on impact."

"Oh, my God, poor Elias, their son. How am I going to tell him?"

"How old is he?"

"Ten, like my son, Milos. They are like brothers."

"Do you need some help? Is there a pastor or minister?"

"It is better to hear it from me. I've known him since he was little boy. I will call my husband. He loves Elias like a son. He will help me. The boys are sleeping. I tink we wait until morning."

"Probably best."

"When can we see Carl and Kristina?"

"After the coroner completes an autopsy."

"Why autopsy?"

"To determine the cause of the crash. According to the investigating officer, there was a lot of heavy drinking going on at the country club, some kind of celebration. It's possible that Mr. and Mrs. Hofstadter had too much alcohol. The coroner will determine that."

"That is why I tell my Dimitri drinking is not good. It can come to this."

"Is there anything I can do for you, Mrs. Woijeck?"

"No, I will let her family know. She has brother and sister and her friend in Chicago, Sally. Her father is not alive no longer and her mother is in a rest home. Kristina told me her mother doesn't remember her."

"I'm truly sorry, Mrs. Woijeck. The police department will assist you in any way we can. The coroner will provide the death certificates. Will you and your husband be arranging for the funeral?"

"I don't know. Maybe Kristina's friend, Sally, can help us. I will call her in the morning."

"Sorry to have to bring you this, Mrs. Woijeck."

"You are a nice man. You just do your job."

"Goodnight, ma'am." He returned his hat to his head and walked away to his car. At the open door, he called in to his dispatcher.

Millie closed the front door, released Radek's collar and stumbled to the kitchen phone. Wiping a torrent of tears from her eyes, she dialed her home number and waited for five rings before Dimitri's voice came on the line.

"Dimitri," she choked and sobbed into the mouthpiece. "Carl and Kristina died in car crash. You must come now. Come now."

"I am coming." The phone clicked to silence at his end.

Chapter 11

Demagogues

Inhaling the suffocating aroma of mums and white lilies that he would forever associate with funerals, Elias peered over the edge of the caskets the mortuary attendant had opened for viewing. He tentatively reached out and touched his mother's face and was surprised to discover she felt like stone.

"Mommy," he called to her. "Mommy." He turned to look up at Millie. "Why doesn't she wake up?"

Before driving to the funeral, Millie and Dimitri had tried to describe and prepare him for what to expect. He had not reacted with tears. He looked at them, listened attentively, then stared out the living room window at the back yard and golf course fairway where a foursome, two men and their wives, were walking past with their golf bags in tow. Later, during the viewing at the funeral home, even as he registered the lifelessness of his mother and stepfather, the image of the golfers associated with the country club, his parents' Cadillac, and his mother's empty martini glass with the lone olive he had filched remained with him.

Millie and Dimitri accompanied him to the open casket. Sally followed and stood close behind him with her hands gently resting on his shoulders. "She's beautiful, Elias. Your mother is always beautiful. She loved you more than anything or anyone else in the world."

"I know." These were the first words Elias had uttered since Millie and Dimitri had explained to him what had happened on the morning he and Milos and Duska had awakened and wandered into the kitchen for their milk and Cheerios. He didn't question that his parents had died, but he had not grasped that reality until the moment he touched his mother's frozen face.

Millie and Dimitri stood aside with Elias and Milos between them and observed the line of friends and business associates who filed in to the mortuary viewing room to pay their respects. Among the visitors, Dimitri noticed that Lewis Murtagh barely glanced at him and ignored Elias. Dimitri thought Lewis should have offered some words of condolence to the boy, but he purposely avoided him. Dimitri wondered why.

There had been discussions and a meeting with a social worker and a judge at the Rockford courthouse where Sally had provided notarized legal documents that named her as the guardian for Elias and executor of Kristina's will. Carl's will had been established independently with clauses that related to the corporation and his partners, Dimitri Woijcek and Lewis Murtagh, who were present at the reading.

Sally and her husband, Web Dawson, were awarded a stipend of one-hundred thousand dollars a year until Elias reached the age of twenty-one. They would also live in the house bequeathed to Elias and continue to raise him as surrogate parents. Elias stayed with the Woijeck family until Sally and Web arranged to move from Chicago, bringing their three year old daughter, Lizzie, into his life.

Dimitri glanced up at the rearview mirror and caught the edge of a short ladder, a shovel, and a gray metal tool chest in the bed of his Ford pickup. For a moment he looked away, then immediately back again at the dusty white Chevrolet sedan that was following him again. He had caught only a glimpse of the driver, but he recognized the snap-brim hat and the manner in which a limp cigarette dangled from the left corner of his mouth. The narrow blade of his pointed aquiline nose extended from under his lowered hat brim as an outgrowth of glowering brows shading dark eyes. His face reminded Dimitri of an insect. Dimitri was certain he was the same man who had followed him into the diner where he had stopped for lunch.

The man's shirt sleeves were cuffed half way up his arms and he didn't remove his hat. He ordered a hamburger and coffee and read a newspaper while he ate at the far end of the counter and seemingly ignored him. He finished and paid for his lunch at the checkout just before Dimitri, who lingered for an extra minute perusing the pie display as though he might order a piece of coconut cream custard meringue. A queasy anxiety oozed from the pit of his stomach and bile stung the base of his throat at the sight of the man lighting up a cigarette as he sat and waited in his car.

"Why the hell are you watching me? What do you want?" Dimitri silently voiced to himself, tucked his head down, and walked quickly to his truck. To his relief, the man did not follow him home. He paused and looked up and down the street before pulling into the driveway, then hurriedly entered the house.

An energetic Bach sonata rippled from the music room where he could hear Milos practicing the piano. He saw Durska playing with her dolls on the family room floor visible from the kitchen where Millie was preparing the ingredients for an apple streudel. From his expression and agitated movement, she immediately sensed his distraction. Shaking loose flour from her hands, she turned to him.

"What is it? Something has happened. I can tell. This is not how you come home."

Dimitri gripped the back of a kitchen chair. "I'm being followed."

"Followed?"

"A man has been following me."

"Why? Who is this man?"

"I don't know, but I think Murtagh has something to do with him."

"Murtagh?"

"He thinks I'm a communist. He so much as accused me without saying it."

"But you are not a communist. We are not. Does he know we came to America to escape from them?"

"He's an ignorant man. He thinks because we came from Czechoslovakia we are communists. He has been listening to that mad man always in the news, that Senator McCarthy who calls everyone he doesn't like a communist so he can have them arrested and deported. He's a fascist like the Nazis."

"Here, in America?"

"Here in America."

"How can that be?"

"I don't know, but it is and we are not safe from Murtagh and this man. He can ruin our lives. He can destroy us."

"What can we do? Isn't there a way to stop them?"

"I don't know of any way. They have power over us by their lies. All Murtagh has to do is say we are communist spies."

"We don't want to be arrested. We don't want to be deported."

"No, but we can no longer live here."

"Where will we go."

"Canada, Toronto. Many of our people live there."

"What about Milos and his master teacher, Aleksei?"

"We will ask Aleksei to help us find another teacher in Toronto. He has lived there himself and he knows other musicians."

"When do we have to do this?"

"As soon as we can."

"How can this be happening here in America?"

"I don't have the answer, but it is happening to us. We cannot wait."

"What about our house, our furniture, the piano?"

"We will ask Sally and her husband to help us."

"Milos will be so devastated."

"We are all devastated. We have to make a new life for our family."

"Oh, Dimitri, I am so sad for you, after all you have done here."

"What I have done was so we could survive in this country. Now we must find our way in another place."

"Poor Milos and Elias. They will not be friends. When will we tell Milos?"

Dimitri cocked his head and listened to Milos now playing arpeggios in a Chopin etude down the hall in the music room. "When he is done practicing."

"We will have to move the piano and all our furniture."

"We can't wait. We don't have much time before Federal agents come knocking at our door."

"We can't leave everything we own."

"I'll ask Sally and her husband to help us. We can trust them."

Millie sat heavily on a kitchen chair and twisted her hands in a dish cloth. "This is so terrible."

"I know. I'm sorry but there is nothing I can do against Murtagh. At least we are not poor."

"Can they take our money?"

"Tomorrow I will go to the bank and arrange for the transfer of our money to a bank in Toronto."

The final minor chords of the piano etude faded to silence.

"Is he done?"

"I don't know," said Millie. "Sometimes he takes a rest between pieces. Shall I get him?"

"No, no, if he plays again, I want to hear it. His music sounds like pathways through the sky."

"What shall we pack to take with us."

"What we need until we find a place in Toronto."

"Do you think we should call anyone your sister or her friends know there?"

"No, our phones could be bugged, like the secret police did back home. I'll talk with Sally and give her keys to the house. We must leave tonight."

"Drive all night?"

"We'll stay in a hotel in Chicago. See Aleksei in the morning, then drive on."

"Do you think agents are watching Aleksei?"

Dimitri shrugged. "We can only do what we have to do." The opening phrases of a delicate Beethoven sonata drifted to them. "He's playing again."

"Yes."

"Beethoven."

"Yes."

"This is an outrage," shouted Aleksei tugging at his gray goatee. "Even in this country we cannot escape the oppression of demagogues. In 1938, J. Edgar Hoover tried to eliminate my cousin, Yelena Ivanov. She had become a union organizer. Before that, she was a young violist and her sister played the violin until Hoover had their mother and father deported, just for being Russian. His intense dark eyes softened. "I will miss you being my student," he gently rested a hand on Milos's shoulder. "But there is someone in Toronto. A good friend and a master teacher. I will give you a letter to take to him."

He filled five cups of tea from a large polished brass samovar. His long graceful fingers had become gnarled and stiffened with age. He gingerly placed the cups and saucers before his guests, the Woijcek family, seated at a carved oak table in Aleksei Greschenko's large sitting room mainly occupied by an ebony Steinway grand piano.

He sipped his tea. "I hope you will write to me from time to time." He set down his cup. "And now, while you play something to lighten the sadness we feel, a Mozart sonata, I will write the letter for you.

You must let me know when you play your first concert. I will come. I will be there."

Milos touched the keyboard and the tinkling scales and flashing flourishes of Mozart flowed from his fingers.

Elias thought Dimitri, Millie, and Milos and Duska and Radek coming to the house to say goodbye was strange. He still did not fully understand the need for the Woijcek's abrupt departure, except that the man called McCarthy shouting and carrying on with a bloated sense of self-importance every day on the television had somehow forced them to leave. He also heard Dimitri mention Lewis Murtagh's name several times in association with McCarthy.

Elias said he would miss the dog Radek. Sally's husband, Web Dawson, told Elias he would get him a hunting dog.

Chapter 12

The Surrogate

Since the Dawsons had moved in, Elias felt like an outsider in his own home. He had forged a kinship with Sally from the time he and his mother had lived in their small house in Rockford seven years ago. He even called her Aunt Sally and looked forward to her visits when she drove over from Chicago. The visits had become less frequent after her marriage to Web and when Kristina and Elias had moved to their luxury home with Carl Hofstadter near the country club.

Lizzie Dawson's maroon-colored hair topped a silly lopsided face sprinkled with freckles like her dad. Her green-tinged gray eyes reminded Elias of a lake on a cloudy day catching errant rays of sunlight as though from an inner source of humor and joy. Even though he was only nine years older, he felt instantly protective of her. The first time he met her, he said, "You look like a strawberry." She beamed her winning smile at him and he melted inside. "That's a compliment."

"I know."

"How do you know what a compliment is? You're only four years old."

"I know lots of words. I can read."

Elias looked up at Sally's expression of amusement.

"Better be careful what you say around her, buddy," said Sally. "She's really smart."

"Reading at four is pretty smart, but how smart is she."

"She can say the alphabet forwards and backwards and she learns words from the dictionary."

"The dictionary? Who reads the dictionary?"

"Lizzie does. We took her to see a psychologist who studies precocious children. He tested her and said she has a genius IQ and a photographic memory."

"Does that mean she doesn't forget anything?"

"Never, so don't try to pull any tricks on her." Sally laughed. "She might pay you back five years later."

"I don't pull tricks on other kids."

"I know, sweetie. I'm just teasing you."

"Oh."

"We tease a lot in our family," said Sally. "You'll get used to it."

Elias did not want the Dawsons to see him cry. At the funeral, he had watched relatives, friends, and associates of his parents blowing their noses and dabbing at tears. The only man he had noticed crying was Dimitri, although his tears were for Elias's loss of his mother.

Elias did not feel any particular emotion observing the embalmed corpse of his stepfather. The strongest impression he had of Carl was that his stepfather rarely touched him, never threw an arm around him in a comforting or friendly or loving way, and spoke to him only about functional topics such as how he was doing in school, would he like to take swimming lessons or golf lessons at the country club, or take piano lessons like his friend, Milos.

Carl had secretly hoped Elias would at least try golf, especially since both he and Kristina played and the game would provide them a family activity in a relationship that was otherwise devoid of togetherness. Elias compensated by spending more time at the Woijecks and limping home the short distance between their houses if he could not garner permission to stay for supper, even if Millie called to ask Kristina on his behalf. Kristina knew he preferred spending time with the Woijecks, because she and Carl did not offer him their kind of warm, openly affectionate family life. She unconsciously admitted to herself that hers and Carl's marriage was one of economic convenience. They had bolstered each others' careers and financial success. The rest was a performance, a charade of sorts that both accepted.

What Elias silently cried for in his bed at night was the loss of his childhood friend, Milos, and his family.

"You're rid of them," the private investigator confirmed. "They left the country. Moved to Toronto, Canada. The whole family. Not a concern anymore."

"That's good news," said Lewis. "I know about the Blake kid, Elias. He's out of the picture, but that woman who's his guardian isn't. She was a banker in Chicago along with Hofstadter's wife. She's the executor of the Hofstadter estate. That includes fifty percent of the company. Since Dimitri Woijcek has left the country, I'll make arrangements to take his twenty-six percent share. I still have to put up with Sally Dawson coming in here to go over the company finances, not too often, thank God, but enough to be irritating and worrisome."

Through creative accounting and having friends on the board of directors, Lewis had made it appear that he had legally bought out Dimitri's share of the company. Although he knew Sally was suspicious, now that he owned forty-nine percent, he ignored her and barely tolerated her intrusion at board meetings.

He recalled the day he had informed Sally that he had assumed the position of CEO and was managing the company. Sally had reminded him that Elias stood to inherit fifty-one percent of the corporation when he turned twenty-one. Until then, as appointed legal guardian and executor of the Hofstadter will, she would manage his finances. Three months later, Lewis filed with the State of Illinois to change the company name to Murtagh, Inc. and placed an announcement in the Rockford Morning Star.

Sally commented repeatedly to Web that she didn't trust Murtagh. "I think he might try to cheat Elias out of his inheritance if he can get away with it. I can't prove it, but I think he keeps two sets of books. What I see during my company audits to protect Elias only looks legitimate."

Senator Joseph McCarthy Censured

Removal From Senate Ends Reign of Political Terrorism.

Sally was pleased to read the morning headlines of McCarthy's death from alcoholic precipitated hepatitis. That Murtagh had used McCarthy's influence against Dimitri to relocate his family to Canada deeply angered her. But there was nothing she could say or do to bring them back.

She had received a letter with information to proceed with moving the Woicjek's furniture to their new address in Toronto and to place their house on the market for sale. They had transferred their bank accounts. She handled the arrangements with a transport company and hired a real estate broker. Within one month, the Woicjek's home was sold to the franchise owner of a root beer drive-in chain that featured car-hop service by cute gum-chewing teenage girls on roller skates.

"Do you know what I admired most about your mom?" Sally looked at water drops beading on a cold glass pitcher of lemonade. Lizzie noisily sucked the sweet and sour yellow drink from her tall glass.

"You're slurping," said Elias. "I can hear you slurping."

Lizzie removed the tip of the straw from her lips and wiped at the sweat on her forehead. "That's the best way to drink it."

"You get air inside you and it'll give you hiccups," said Elias.

"Your mom was a real go-getter," said Sally. "She wanted to do or be something or just get something done, she went after it. She had the gumption to succeed and that's what she did. It's her gift to you, Elias, something to remember."

"She told me she was a good golfer."

"And a good businesswoman. This house and everything around here happened because of her. Mostly because of her. Have to give your stepfather some credit." She smiled. "He depended on her though. Without her, it would have been difficult."

Her glance shifted to her shirtless husband carrying a weed scythe, swinging it in an occasional swipe near the ground as he walked toward his wife and daughter and Elias sitting on the shaded patio. He had caught the drift of her last few comments on the sultry air.

"I can sure use a glass of that." He sank heavily onto the lounge next to hers creating a stain on the dark green cushion from the skein of sweat that rolled off his sunburned back. "You can't make a businesswoman out of Elias. You know that." An impish grin raised and creased the whiskered jowls and puffy flesh of his reddened cheeks. Elias registered how similar he looked to his daughter, only as a much larger and older strawberry.

"His mother had attributes that can benefit him," said Sally.

"Oh, I know. I know. I'm just pullin' your leg." He listened to the clink of ice cubes against the side of the glass. "Must be close to a hundred out there and humidity you can cut with a knife. Reminds me of back in Texas. Though we got a breeze once in a while come off from the Gulf. Could sure use a breeze here now."

"This is tornado weather, you know."

"Not likely, dear. Not a cloud in the sky." He tipped his glass up and swallowed a gulp of lemonade. "God, that's good. Better with a shot of hooch."

"Better for you. Not for them."

"My old man introduced me to it when I was a young 'un. He was rough on me when I was growin' up. We lived in a backwater town in East Texas, Elias. Taught me how to hunt and fish, and how to fight. Served me well when I graduated high school and joined the marines. I was a natural marksman. Never missed. Killed my share of Nazis during the war and when I was transferred to the South Pacific, any Jap got in my sights was a goner."

He leaned toward Elias and gently punched his shoulder. "Sally told me your dad was there in the South Pacific when you was born. Port Moresby. I know the place. Passed through there on my way to the islands, Tarawa, Kwajalein, Eniwetok, Majuro, Saipan, Guam, Okinawa. She said he died over there and you never knew him. I'm sorry about that. Hard to grow up without a pa, but you find a way. Now me, I can never be your pa, but I can toughen you up, put some muscle on those skin and bones, make a real man out of you, even with a bum foot. I can show you how to hunt and fish. We can go up to them Wisconsin lakes. Have us a good time. In three, four years, you'll have the girls fallen all over theirselves, looker like you. You got them handsome devil looks from your mother. She was a beauty, Elias. I met her at her wedding to Hofstadter. Even though he was in the Navy, a Seabee, not cut from the same cloth as me. I can teach you things that'll do you well for the rest of your life and we'll have a good time doin' it."

The brown squirrel was aware of the man and the boy on the ground thirty yards away. She had heard them approach, their hunting boots crackling the twigs and dry leaves. Her tiny nose wriggled and then she could smell them, and there was another scent, a dog. They were being very still. She sat upright balancing on her tail twitching synchronously with each anxious chittering sound that whistled sharply from her narrow rodent mouth. Hanging tree leaves partially concealed her where she had been foraging for ripening acorns that had not yet dropped to the base of the tall oak that cradled her nest and three babies among the higher branches, clearly visible from the trail below.

Elias squinted over the sight blade along the barrel of his .22 rifle. A sensation of dominance and control over the life of the unsuspecting squirrel rose in his mind. He slowly squeezed the trigger like Web had taught him. An adrenaline rush shocked him at the instantaneous crack. The squirrel disappeared from the branch and her headless body plummeted crashing through layers of twigs and leaves to the ground, landing with an audible thump.

Elias's black Labrador looked up expectantly at his face, waiting for the hand gesture to retrieve the fallen game. The dog sprang forward in a quick dash, sniffed the squirrel, gently lifted it in his jaws, and trotted back to deposit it at the feet of Elias and Web.

Web bent down and picked up the dead squirrel by its tail. "Look at that. Head shot. Good eye. You've got a knack for this. You'll be ready when deer season comes around. Won't take this one home though. Might upset Lizzie." He tossed the carcass into the surrounding brush. The dog trembled, looking for a command. "No, Max. Leave it. Not this time. Good boy." He patted the dog on his head. "You do real good for bein' just a year old. We'll head back to the truck now. You might be able to take out a crow or two along the way. Saw 'em on the fence by that corn field."

Web had included Elias in Max's training, starting with the visit to a kennel to select a pup. "He's your dog. I'll teach you how to raise 'im like my old man taught me. You're responsible for him. Give 'im his food and water. Play with 'im. Make 'im your pal. Take 'im out in the fields. You can train 'im to fetch a tennis ball to start with. Learn the basic commands, sit, stay, come, heel. Marking will come later on. Labs are good duck dogs, but we can train 'im to fetch game birds too, pheasants, quail. Lots of 'em around. We'll go up north to the Wisconsin woods come deer season."

Within one month, Elias had lost his sense of intimidation in the presence of this rough man who showed his affection by becoming his mentor and treating him with respect as an equal. He showed Elias his gun collection, which he kept locked in a case, with the admonition to never take any one of them out without his permission and supervision. "This here's the key and this is where I keep it. So what does that mean to you?"

"I know where the key is, but I can never open the case without your permission."

"Right. Don't ever forget it. I'll start you off with that .22 caliber. Down the road when I think you're ready, I'll tell you and you can take it out on your own. But not 'til then. You savvy?"

Elias nodded.

"Somethin' else you should know. Web is short for my real name, Webster. But don't never call me that. Don't know why my parents called me that, namin' me after a dictionary. Never did much in the word department. Now I have me a daughter who does. Life is strange. Never know what to expect."

A week later, Web had taken him to a sporting goods store to buy hunting clothes, boots, a camouflage cap, jacket, and trousers like the photographs of men posed next to their kills in Web's hunting and fishing and outdoor magazines scattered about on the side tables in the den.

Events continued to unfold. Elias watched with curiosity the day Web brought home weight training equipment, barbells, a bench press, and an adjustable nautilus counter weight system. A textbook on human anatomy also showed up in the mailbox.

Web unwrapped it and handed it to Elias. "Here. Study this. Learn where your muscles are and how they work together. You're gonna build 'em by repetition. I'll be training right along with you. It'll be good for me too. Puttin' on too much weight in the wrong places from

Sally's cooking. Get your gym shorts on and a T-shirt or no shirt. Tennis shoes are good."

Lizzie came in to the den to watch and comment on their efforts until Sally escorted her away. "Leave the men alone to play with their toys."

"But those aren't toys. What kind of toys do you call that. It makes their faces turn red and all they do is grunt all the time. It looks like they're trying to take a poop without sitting on the toilet."

Elias studied the photos and diagrams in the book of his upper body, torso, legs and the bone, ligament, and muscle structure of his crippled foot. He strengthened his body and watched his muscles increase in hardness and size. He dedicated himself to weight training and body building from that time forward through high school and college.

Elias sensed something gently shaking his shoulder breaking into his dream of floating in warm water. He opened his eyes begrimed with sleep and squinted up into Web's unshaven grinning face. A symphony of warbling birdsong competed with the raucous cacophony of a jay from the wall of forest behind them. The aroma of strong coffee and frying bacon wafted from the crackling flames of the cooking fire and aroused his hunger. As Web's face moved away, Elias responded to an immediate need to relieve the pressure in his bladder.

Yawning, he unzipped his sleeping bag and sat up to jam his stocking feet into his hiking boots. The air mattress insulating the bag from the ground and a bed of pine boughs had deflated slightly and the remaining air displaced by his movement squished inside the plastic. He stepped away from the campsite into the surrounding brush to urinate.

A rising mist steamed from the dark glassy surface of the pristine lake and dissolved into the towering spires of spruce and pines crowding the meandering shoreline. Elias walked to the edge near a long aluminum rowboat pulled up onto the narrow gravel beach. His cupped palms scooped up the cold clear water and splashed it boldly onto his face. The sharp chill shocked him into alert wakefulness. He studied the multitude of concentric ripples where bass and crappie rose to feed on winged insects that dotted the surface. A cloud of black gnats swirled in an erratic frenzy in a spear of sunlight.

"Breakfast is ready," Web announced from where he bent over the cooking fire transferring scrambled eggs, fried onions and potatoes, and crisp bacon from a large black iron skillet onto two aluminum plates set on a flat tree stump nearby.

With the back of his hand, Elias wiped a drop of mucous caused by the acrid odor of ash and rising wisps of wood smoke tinged with pine sap. Web poured coffee into aluminum mugs. Elias picked up a fork and a plate of food and sat on the wide circular stump. Web balanced the second plate on his lap. Loud chewing and intermittent slurping of coffee displaced conversation.

"Sleep okay?" Web finally spoke.

Elias grunted. "Yeah."

"Sleeping out in the fresh air – that really does it. Nothing beats it."

Elias nodded.

"Saw hoof prints up a ways in the shore mud. Three deer came to drink judging from how fresh. Two does and a buck. This could be our lucky day."

"The food's good," said Elias. "Tastes even better outdoors than at home."

"Hard to beat Sally's cooking, but have to admit, I have a bigger appetite when I'm out in the woods."

They had driven Web's Ford pickup truck north into the Wisconsin lake country dominated by dense evergreen forests that concealed a few remote log cabins in the vicinity of general stores posting crude hand-painted signs advertising outfitting services, camping, hunting, and fishing gear, taxidermy, guide service, live bait, boat rentals, groceries, beer, and gas available from a single red metal pump in the narrow gravel parking area.

Web had stopped at one such place to rent a boat and single cycle engine and discuss fishing and hunting location options with the proprietor, a tall grizzled balding Swede who filled the cramped store with the maple aroma of his pipe smoke. They pored over a regional map of the local lakes and streams and Web attended closely to the advice being rendered in the Swede's stuttering Scandinavian accent.

Elias pulled at a bottle of orange Nehi and roamed about perusing the fishing tackle and hunting rifles and boxes of ammunition in a glass display case. The heads of an eight point buck and of a black bear overlooked the dim interior from vantage points on the thick log walls shared with shelves of outdoor clothing merchandise. Over the entrance door, a large mounted grayish-green Northern Pike with jaws agape showed saw-like rows of razor sharp teeth.

Before they left the low-lying wooden dock, Web gave Elias instructions on how to operate the motor attached to the stern of the twelve foot aluminum rowboat. Cans of food, packaged bacon, jerked venison, and a bag of flour, baking powder, Crisco, two loaves of bread, a block of butter, and two dozen eggs filled three rucksacks that shared the center of the boat with Elias's and Web's backpacks, sleeping bags, fishing rods and tackle, and rifle carriers. Web cautioned Elias to wear one of the stained orange life vests over his camouflage hunting clothes whenever they were in the boat out on the water.

Elias rode in the bow as they navigated along a chain of lakes into the back country. He missed having his dog, Max, with them, but Web had explained the Lab would just spook the deer. Elias could take him during duck season.

"Lab's are born to retrieve ducks," said Web. "They're great swimmers and they even have webbed toes." He had lifted one of Max's feet to show Elias the black membranes linking the dog's toes.

They cleaned their plates and cookware to ensure no traces of food would draw the attention of bears to the campsite. Web returned their provisions to packs hoisted high overhead by a thick rope looped over the end of a stout branch.

Elias followed Web along the shore to the spot where he had discovered the small cloven hoof prints.

"They could still be in the area," said Web, "but it's also likely they moved on."

Cradling their rifles with safeties on and barrels pointed at the ground, they hiked cautiously along the narrow game trail taken by the deer into the woods until they came to a wide meadow bisected by a stream that irrigated the surrounding tall grass and abundance of wild flowers. Web froze in mid-stride and signaled with his free hand to Elias not to move. He slowly pointed to the open area where three deer grazed beyond the edge of the tall trees. They were unaware of the humans concealed downwind behind a scrim of leafy low-lying brush.

Web motioned Elias forward next to him for a clear shot at the buck who snatched mouthfuls of grass and chewed vigorously with raised head offering a clear display of his six point antlers. His mule ears flicked back and forth to detect any threatening sound. Elias was close enough to see flower stems dangling from the corners of the soft black lips and, being downwind, he could smell the rank odor emanating from the brown hide.

Elias slowly raised his rifle and snugged the reinforced stock against his right shoulder. He sighted over the barrel. His thumb eased off the safety. A shell waited in the chamber. The sensation of control blood-rushed through his head. His finger squeezed the trigger. He barely felt the recoil as he saw the buck leap forward then collapse kicking and scrambling in the tall grass while the does white tails flagged their terrorized flight into the trees at the far side of the meadow.

Elias restored the safety and he and Web walked out into the meadow and gazed down at the inert animal. "Good clean shot," said Web. "Right through the lungs and heart."

He handed Elias his rifle and grabbed the buck's head by its antlers. The weight of the carcass pressed down a swathe of grass as Web pulled it a short distance to an oak tree. He strung it up on a branch that left the deer's hind legs dangling a few inches off the ground.

The long thick blade of Web's hunting knife sliced the underbelly from the neck to the anus with a single stroke that released the stomach and intestines in a steaming bloody heap on the ground, drawing an immediate swarm of large buzzing black flies.

Web loosened and pulled away the hide exposing red striations of muscle and sinew. He quickly butchered sections from the haunches and stuffed them into plastic trash bags which he distributed to the backpacks he and Elias carried. Then he severed the head from the remaining carcass which folded in on the empty abdominal cavity and collapsed in a mound next to the viscera.

"We'll get this meat to the camp and get it smoked before it spoils. Then come back for your first trophy head. I'll have it mounted and you can hang it in your room."

"What about Lizzie?"

"Well, she is a problem. But you can take home just the antlers. No face. No eyes."

"Okay."

"We should've brought a camera. Didn't think about that. You'll have more of these, bigger and better ones. But your first kill is special. That was a great shot."

Elias grinned.

"Need to get moving. Bears 'll find the guts."

They walked to the stream to wash the blood from their hands, then hiked back along the trail to the lake.

162

Chapter 13

Secrets

1985

Elias sniffed the perfumed scent of the pink envelope addressed to him from Lizzie Dawson. He was now a college senior and had recently received his acceptance notification to graduate school.

At sixteen, Lizzie had just sent him a personal note accompanied by a color photo of herself in a saucy pose wearing her cheerleader uniform and with one pom pom blooming from her jutting hip and the other raised high over her head of shining shoulder-length hair. He read her letter sent along with the photo telling him she was in the cast of her annual high school musical and inviting him to come and see her perform. He picked up the phone to call and ask if he could bring a friend.

"A girl friend?"

"Yes, she is a girl."

"You never told me before that you have a girlfriend."

"You never asked."

"I shouldn't have to ask you something like that. Remember, we don't keep secrets from each other."

"You're absolutely right. I stand reprimanded. How's your boyfriend?"

"How did you know I have a boyfriend? I never told you."

"Ah-ha! Gotcha! There, how long have you had a boyfriend?"

"Only about a month. He's really cute and talented. He plays the guitar and has a rock band with his friends. He's also smart. Gets straight 'A's in everything. Almost as smart as me."

"As I."

"As I. I was just testing you to see if you're listening."

"Oh, I'm listening all right. I always listen when you talk. Can't help myself. How old's your boyfriend?"

"Seventeen. He turns eighteen next month."

"What's his name?"

"Andrew – Andy Clark. He doesn't like to be called Andrew."

"Sounds like a nice guy."

"He is. He reminds me of you."

"That makes him super nice."

"You're such an egotist."

"I think that's why we got along so well when I was living at home. It was nice being adored like a big brother."

"You're just so adorable, Elias. What else can I say?"

"What college is Andy going to after he graduates?"

"He's been offered scholarships, but he's really worried about being drafted when he turns eighteen."

"Can't he get a deferment?"

"He said he'll try, but it doesn't always happen. I don't like to talk about it. I don't know what I'd do if I lost him."

"You won't lose him, Lizzie. Don't even think about it."

"You're lucky you didn't have to go because of your foot."

"Never thought of it as a lucky foot, but maybe I have some rabbit in my DNA."

"I know what I want to study when I go to college."

"What's that."

"Biology and chemistry."

"Tough sciences."

"I love those subjects. I want to become a doctor someday."

"You'd be a great one."

"I wouldn't even care about making a lot of money. I want to help people. I was reading how many poor people there are in the world."

"You know more than I do. I want to be there when you graduate from medical school."

"That won't be for a long time – years and years."

"They'll fly by."

"Are you and your girlfriend serious?"

"We are so serious we never laugh – at anything," said Elias. "We just walk around frowning all the time and call each other names."

Lizzie laughed. "You're such a dufus. That sounds like you're serious. But you know, she has to have my approval."

"I do know and that's why I want to bring her with me to see you in the musical, see what kind of competition she has to measure up to."

"Listen, you will never know another girl like me." Lizzie suddenly sang the line as a song lyric.

"Where did you get such a great voice?"

"From my father."

"That's right.   Web did have a good singing voice."

"And my mother taught me how to dance when I was a little girl and then, of course, I've had all kinds of dance lessons, ballet, tap, jazz. Mom says I dance like a pro."

"I don't doubt it."

"What's your girlfriend's name?"

"Dorothy Banacek."

"Her name sounds foreign."

"She was born here. Her parents were immigrants."

"She sounds romantic."

"That's because you're such a romantic. Actually, she is too, in a practical way."

"Call me when you need advice."

"I'll do that. How much do you charge?"

"For you, *pro bono*, because you're like my big brother I never had."

"Are you sure you're not studying to become an attorney? *Pro Bono*?"

"I know what *pro bono* is. I saw it on a television lawyer show."

"I'm surprised you watch television, what with cheerleading practice and games and rehearsals for the musical. You do study, don't you?"

"I study, but I don't have to that much and I still get straight 'A's."

"Oh, that's right. You have a photographic memory. I always had to work hard at getting good grades."

"Well – "

"Well what? That's a deep subject."

"That's trite."

"Best I can do."

"I was born naturally smart and I do have a photographic memory."

"Just popped out of the womb and started quoting Shakespeare, did you?"

"Don't be silly. I had to read a few plays first when I was a month old."

"You started reading when you were a month old?"

"A year old, silly. Children's books."

"When did you start reading adult books?"

"A year after that." Lizzie's infectious laugh filled his ear.

"You're an astounding girl, Lizzie, an astounding girl."

"You better prep your girlfriend so she can pass."

"Pass what?"

"My approval, buddy."

"You sound like your mother. She always called me Buddy. I'll give my girlfriend a heads up. But I think you'll be impressed."

"I'll reserve judgment."

"Reserve judgment – There you go again sounding like a lawyer."

"Well, lawyers and doctors have a lot in common."

"They use big words that are hard to understand."

"They use big words but they're only hard to understand for people who aren't lawyers and doctors."

"I agree. And with those words, I'm signing off, since I have my own exam to study for."

"For which to study, Doobie. Where did you learn to speak English?"

"Lower Slobovia."

"Oh, go study. Love you, Elias," she called out.

"Love you too, sweetie. Go get 'em. Rah – Rah – Rah!"

"Who was that?" asked Alan Erdman, his roommate.

"Lizzie Dawson. She's sort of like a kid sister, though not really."

"Your guardian's kid?"

"Yeah. I've known her since she was four years old. She's one of those kids who's a smart-ass genius. She has a photographic mind."

"I take it you get along."

"Oh, sure, we do. She's special."

"I never had a sister, or a brother. My parents thought one of me was enough. My father started grooming me to become a lawyer when I was five, but I wasn't a genius."

"You're a nice guy, Al. You sure you're going into the right career field? Aren't attorneys parasites and assholes? You're not like that."

"My father was my role model. I can do all that, but in a nice way."

"What do you do? Smile sweetly as you withdraw the knife and it makes everything okay."

"Something like that. Attorneys have a bad rap just because of a few rotten apples. The media likes to feed on those guys. But most of us do good work on behalf of our clients."

"Clients? You already have clients? You haven't even graduated yet. Did you take the bar early and pass with flying colors?"

"No clients yet, except one."

"Who's that?"

"You."

"Come off it. Have another beer."

"You told me you were stiffed by that asshole partner your mother and stepfather had – Murtagh."

"I'm not ready for that. I have one more year."

"You need to start preparing now. Your twenty-first birthday ain't that far off."

The phone rang. Elias picked up.

"Hello, Elias, it's Sally. I have some good news."

"Good news is always welcome."

"Murtagh is in the hospital with stage four liver cancer. It's terminal."

"When?"

"Yesterday. Tests came back. He's in shock. The cancer has metastasized."

"How long does he have?"

"Two months on the outside. As soon as you graduate, you need to take over. I'm keeping an eye on things here for you. No hanky panky from any of the staff."

"You're my fairy godmother."

"I wouldn't go that far. I'll make sure the financials stay in order."

"I love you, Sally. What would I have done without you. You're a gem."

"Silly boy. Party time on campus is over, buddy. You have to get serious about your future. You've got a company waiting for you."

"Thanks to you."

"It's really thanks to your mom. She drove a hard bargain in setting up her contract with your father."

"I still miss her, but you've made up for her."

"No one could match your mom."

"I just got off the phone with Lizzie. Now she's someone special. What a fox."

"Now now. Don't let her hear you say things like that. Just gives her a big head. She's looking forward to seeing you. She and Web and I will be at your graduation ceremony."

"Do you have the information?"

"Of course."

"Need directions?"

"You forget – I'm a Chicago girl. I know all the streets."

"Come early so you get good seats."

"Front row for us."

"Thanks, Sally. Thanks for everything you've done for me."

"You're my son. Maybe not in name, but my son."

Elias hung up the phone. Alan stared at him. "Well, I'm waiting."

"For what?"

"Something big has happened. I can tell from the look on your face."

"Murtagh is dying of cancer."

"I knew it. I just knew it. Couldn't be better timing for you."

"You want to come and work for me?"

"Not right away. After Harvard law. You're gonna do great things and I want to be along for the ride."

"Well, I don't want to lose contact."

"There's the phone."

"You're studying corporate law, right? You're not thinking of becoming a divorce attorney."

Alan laughed. "Aren't you the joker."

"How about another beer."

"Sure, have one on me. Comin' right up, partner."

A week later, a small package arrived in the mail. Elias opened the manila envelope and removed a gray and white furry rabbit's foot on a key chain. A note contained two words: For luck. Love, Lizzie.

Chapter 14

Origins

Elias Blake's son, Burton, wondered how his mother had ever agreed to marry his father in the first place. But she had explained how different he was when they first met in college while she was completing her Masters in teaching and working toward her credential.

They had met at an outdoor anti-Vietnam war concert. A tribal percussion beat and gut-wrenching guitar riffs competed with the indecipherable chanting and howling of the long-haired lead singer wearing a tattered American flag shirt. The steady stream of pile driving hard rock catapulted out over the throng of bobbing heads wreathed in the sweet acrid hay-like scent of marijuana smoke.

The odd moment of the encounter between Elias Blake and Dorothy Banacek was a mutual recognition that they were both standing at the rear edge of the swaying crowd only as onlookers. Even though they both wore flared jeans, heeled boots, and beaded denim shirts, they considered their clothes an outer costume, a fashion of their generation.

"I have a teaching career ahead of me," she told him afterward over coffee. "I'm against the war. I support women's rights and civil rights, all of it, but I can't risk having an arrest on my record because I attended an anti-war protest rally. I can do more good becoming a teacher than sitting in a jail cell, an act that no one will care about or remember."

Her comment fueled his belief that massive protest did little or nothing to influence outcomes and that power was wielded by those who controlled wealth. This perception became the foundation of his business.

Dorothy described him to Burton as being fun-loving, overly attentive, even submissive at times, saying, "He met me every morning to walk me to my classes. We both lived in apartments off campus. My roommate was a dance major and was often at rehearsals, which left Elias and me alone during the evenings much of the time. He brought steaks over to grill two or three times a week and, occasionally, Atlantic lobster flown in from Maine. He said he had a friend of the family who was a fisherman.

Whenever I asked him about his family, he sidestepped the subject except that he explained his father had been killed stationed in the Philippines during the war and his mother had remarried someone in real estate. When he told me they had died in a car accident, he said he didn't want to talk any further about them. But he showed me a high school photograph of his stepsister, Lizzie Dawson, although she wasn't really his stepsister. She was the daughter of his guardian, Sally Dawson. Lizzie was sixteen at the time of the photo. She was a cheerleader, petite, very cute. He said he wanted to take me to meet her when she was performing in a cheerleading competition. I really didn't have time. I was in the middle of writing my dissertation. But he insisted and I went. I did enjoy it and Lizzie's father treated us all to dinner at a posh country club. I began to suspect that Elias was somehow connected to their wealth, but there weren't any details given.

"The life he was leading me into was alien to me. I was raised in dire poverty. My mother and father were Czech immigrants who came to this country in 1936 to escape the Nazi invasion. They had no formal education. My father was a coal miner. He and my mother barely spoke English. My brother and two sisters and I were born and raised in a Pennsylvania mining town. Our living conditions were harsh. My parents, your Gramma and Grampa, came to see us at the mansion only once. They felt so intimidated and out of place at Elias's display of wealth that they never wanted to come back. So I used to take you and, after they were born, Eugenia and Darren to visit them. You were all more comfortable in their small home on Elm Street in Rockford than living in Elias's country mansion.

"Elias did make a small effort to relate to Gramma and Grampa Banacek by telling of his boyhood friendship with Milos Woijcek, the famous pianist who moved to Canada. But Gramma and Grampa didn't care for Elias. He reminded them of the ruling class in Austria – Hungary before the Second World War."

Even though he wasn't a tall man, to Burton as a small boy, his maternal grandfather was imposing, gentle, strong, powerful, and commanding of respect. He called him Grampa, like it was his name, rather than the more formal grandfather. And he called his grandmother Gramma. Burton liked his Grampa's warm strength and how he hugged him rough and hard with a wrestler's grip.

Gramma smelled like cooking and dusty tomato plants on a hot summer day. She let Burton help her pull weeds and pick plants in her vegetable garden. She often wore a *babushka* over her tight brown curls and sometimes Burton would have her tie one on him so he would look like her. She was wiry and tough and reminded him of an energetic sparrow darting around the yard or in the house. She told him he was not supposed to pick and gorge himself on the plums and grapes and raspberries growing in the garden. But he would, regardless, whenever she left him outside in the yard alone and if she weren't watching him from the kitchen window. These fruits were too warm and juicy and sweet to ignore.

What concerned Gramma and Burton's mother the most was finding him clinging to a branch in the tall pear tree swaying in the wind and eating the green pears like a Koala bear. He enjoyed the sensation of a squirrel's eye view. It had been his observation of seeing a squirrel scamper up that very tree that had set the example. Gramma would charge out of the house shaking a finger at him and scolding and commanding him to come down. He never immediately obeyed her. He would polish off a pear or two before making his dare devilish descent. She was worried that he might fall. But what she didn't realize was that the fear of falling out of trees never occurred to her grandson. Despite his experience with pain, Burton did not believe he was vulnerable to personal catastrophe. For the present, he considered himself too skilled a climber and was impervious to such accidents. He could climb anything and hang on, even in a strong wind, the stronger the better. He could climb like that squirrel. And he knew that his Gramma could not climb up there after him.

He admitted that he did waste a great many pears whenever he shook the tree, which he did often. He liked to hear the loosened pears crash through the leaves and thump on the ground. More fell than a person could eat. So Gramma used them for canning and storage in her cellar larder. Burton once told her that she couldn't blame him about the cherries, however, because the robins always got to them before he had a chance. And he wouldn't dare eat cherries full of beak holes, especially when you considered all the worms that had dangled from that beak.

For as long as Burton could remember, Grampa had moved slowly and was generally always calm and contemplative, but with an everpresent smile lingering in his blue eyes. Whenever he looked at Burton, his ruddy face glowed with pleasure. He parted his thinning brown hair on the left side and kept it trimmed short with a bimonthly visit to the local neighborhood barber two blocks away at the corner. His wife's (Gramma's) hearty European meals kept his body solid.

They had migrated from Czechoslovakia to New York City in 1936 and brought their culinary gifts with them. *Halushki* and *pierogi*, handmade stuffed pastas accompanied the rich broth and noodles of beef or chicken soup. Flavors drawn from scrap meat and bones that simmered for two days in large pots commingled with the aroma of garlic and paprika pervaded the house like Bohemian perfume.

Gramma told Burton most of the incidents about how they had come from "the old country" to America. Burton never tired of hearing them. Even several years later, when Burton was no longer an only child, he would urge his grandparents to retell their stories as he and his brother, Darren, and sister, Eugenia, sat enthralled at hearing about their colorful past and adventures. They enjoyed the tales because of the insight they provided as to the man and woman behind Grampa and Gramma who loved them in that house. The stories also provided them an expanded sense of their own heritage and identities. But most of all, listening to them narrate the events was a warm entertaining experience. Burton could recall the Sunday evenings when they visited their grandparents and sat gathered in the living room after a heavy meal, sharing each other's company. He remembered their accented voices, Grampa telling them of the strength and exuberance of his youth. . .

"Yes, I was only sixteen, a young man, young and handsome. I walked in front of all the girls, you know? I was best dancer. I walk up and down at dance hall in Hoboken and twirl umbrella and the girls would all watch me. That was 1936. I see Gramma, Maria, and I say to myself I know I want to marry her. She doesn't even look at me. She goes off and dances with some other fellow, not so good dancer, not so handsome, like me. That make me want her more than ever. We keep seeing each other at dance hall but she will not dance with me, always with other not so good, not so handsome. I no like. Then one day she say yes. We dance and I ask her to marry me before she go back to 'nother one who not so good, not so handsome. She say no, I don't have enough money to take care of her and a family. I'm just dance hall dandy, she call me. She say I'm too young. She is older than me by three years. We both worked in factory then. When we marry, she would stop work. I tell her I want to marry her more than anything else in world."

Gramma would interject. "When I was young girl in old country, Slovakia, I go up into mountains with cows every day and take care of cows. One cow is my friend I raise from when born. When I fall asleep in grass from warm sun, she always stay and watch over me even when other cows go home. One day, I have to take her to market when she no more give milk. When I leave her there with butcher, she cried. Tears come from her eyes and down her face. I did not want to leave her, but I could do nothing. I ran home and cried for long time. I never forget.

"When I become sixteen, my father want me to marry a man I did not like. My father was burgermeister of our village and want to join his land with father of this other man I did not like. So he arrange for me to marry, but he did not ask me if I want to marry with this man. He say he will make me marry this man. So one night, I pack my things and run away from home. I walk alone all the way across Europe north to Denmark. There I wait for many weeks. I work cleaning fish to make money. Then I get on ship, a freighter that bring me all the way across ocean to New York.

"I did not have enough money to go through immigration check at Ellis Island. So another man share his with me. Then after I go through, we arrange to have it all pass back to him so he can come through. After that, I get job working in bandage factory, Johnson and Johnson."

Grampa would smile, remembering. "I show her my father's bank book so she see I have enough money to marry. She say yes and we have a big wedding – eat, drink, dance. It go on for three days, like in old country. Then she find out the truth. I take my father's bank book and show her. We have same name, see." He chuckled. "Your Gramma chase me from house with broom and tell me not to come back until I have job. Going to dance hall is not work and I did not go to factory anymore. She tell me, I want to be married, I got to act like husband.

"I could not get good job and make lot of money, see. I never go to school like you do. When I was boy, my mother take me back and forth on ship to Austria. She know Franz Joseph and many other people there. I saw many dances, waltzes in great ballrooms with many lights and flowers. There was beautiful music. I listen to Strauss waltzes. It was there I learn to dance.

"My father stay in this country, America. He had own business. He and another man come here and have company to make sewing machines. Before that, he was officer in cavalry in old country. That's how he meet my mother, at ball in palace of Emperor Franz Joseph. I spend many days there living at the palace when I was a boy. I am friend with other boys. We have adventures in great forest outside palace.

"When I marry, my father give me some money at wedding. We go buy farm in New Jersey. Raise family. Farm not give us enough money. Then after that, we move to Pennsylvania and I go to work in coal mines. I drive train with empty cars into mine and bring out coal. There is always dust and it hard to breath. I wear handkerchief over nose and mouth."

Whenever they went to their grandparents to visit, Gramma would lay out all kinds of food, more than they could ever possibly eat at a single sitting. Burton thought it was like Thanksgiving there all the time.

Afterwards, as it grew cool in the evening, Burton would sit out in the back yard on a canvas folding chair with his Grampa and water the garden with a hose. Burton always fought a warm itchy sensation of impatience just sitting or standing there holding the hose, so he would relinquish it to Grampa and dash around in the dusk in energetic pursuit of fireflies. Then later, he and his Grampa would go in on the back porch and each would eat a whole large tomato that had warmed and ripened from sitting in the sun on the window ledge all day long. They would eat them with salt and pepper and large hunks of Gramma's freshly baked bread. Then they would listen to the news and the weather report and music on Grampa's radio. Grampa loved listening to music, especially when they played waltzes by Strauss and Liszt. The music reminded him of the days when he was a boy.

One of Burton's uncles, his mother's brother, had played the violin. Grampa had thought his son would become a great musician. He had bought the violin when his son was a young boy, handsome like his father with blond curls. Mick had always had to be careful about his fingers and was never allowed to play baseball or football or any kind of sport. He was also exempt from doing heavy work around the house and he was never supposed to fight back if some other boy attempted to bully him. Burton's mother or all of his sisters always interceded and fought for him. The three sisters were a fearsome trio.

Mick played his violin on a local radio program when they lived in Pennsylvania. When he auditioned for a chair in the Cleveland orchestra and was told by the conductor that his playing was not yet mature and to come back in a few years, in great despair, Mick stopped playing the violin. Nothing his father said or did could make him seriously take up the instrument again. Later in his life, he would occasionally play for family members as they sat about in the living room. Burton liked the emotionally charged gypsy music and Slavonic dances the best. But he also came to love the waltzes that his Grampa treasured.

Burton noticed that his Grampa always wore soft worn slippers when he came home from work during the evening and an old undershirt and baggy gray trousers and he always sat in his stuffed leather easy chair. In the summertime, loud crickets squeaked along the foundation of the house outside in the night and moths came flying out of the darkness like owls and pounded on the windows with their powdered wings trying to reach the light.

Soon, Grampa would open his eyes and carefully put on his old fashion wire rim glasses, then open his Bible. He would read for a while, mark his place with a red pencil, then close the Bible and gently place it on the lamp table next to him. Burton looked in it once and discovered that it contained red pencil marks on nearly every page.

Grampa would remove his flimsy gold wire glasses and return them to their hard leather case wrapped inside a maroon silk cloth.

There were always numerous small magazines and pamphlets lying about on side tables. The drawings of lions and tigers and horned African beasts with a man and a woman and children walking among them intrigued Burton. Steeped in religious mythology, his Gramma told him that someday the earth would be like those pictures. There would be no more wars or disease and food would be plentiful for everybody. People and wild beasts would not be in fear of each other. Children would play with the beasts. Those who were Jehova's Witnesses would have everlasting life and they alone would survive Armageddon.

His Gramma would sometimes take him with her to go from house to house and give the pamphlets and magazines to people so they could read about Armageddon and how they could achieve everlasting life in a Utopian existence. He also watched from the dining room when small groups of people would come to the house and his Gramma would lead meetings where they read from the Bible and talked about everlasting life. She told him she was a missionary for Jehovah.

When he was still a young boy and would occasionally stay overnight with his grandparents, Burton noticed how they watched him from the doorway while he kneeled down beside the bed to say his prayers. He seldom said his prayers, since it was not a practice encouraged at home. His grandparents always said grace at the table and prayers at bedtime. And they always silently prayed after reading the Bible. Burton always complied when he stayed at his grandparents'. It would have hurt their feelings if he did not. At home, if he did say his prayers, he would do so while lying in bed. His mind would wander, however, and generally he never made it to the end because he would fall asleep. With his grandparents, he had to recite his prayers out loud and they would often say them along with him. Burton figured those were the only times he completed the Lord's Prayer.

The bedroom clock ticked so loudly that its sound echoed in the room. Burton wondered how he could sleep with such a loud sounding clock on the night table near his head.

Sometimes the wind blew the thin white curtains like friendly ghosts airily floating in through the second story window. The old house creaked and groaned as though it too were settling itself for sleep. Sometimes the sounds were caused by his grandparents moving about. Occasionally, he could detect their voices downstairs in the distance. He was tucked in and felt safe and secure. He would listen and concentrate to hear as many individual sounds as he could. Then pretty soon he wouldn't hear the ticking anymore.

Grampa would wake him at five o'clock in the morning and fry several eggs in butter for their breakfast. Together, they would sop them up with large hunks of Gramma's warm bread. Then Burton would walk with him down to the bus stop and wait until he had boarded and gone on to work at the factory.

Dorothy had told Burton that when she was a girl while they lived in the small coal mining town of Colver, Pennsylvania, her dad had tried developing occasional small sideline enterprises to supplement his meager income. The chickens he had ordered through a catalog had all died of some disease. She told him of the time she had seen an entire carcass in the smoke house of one of the hogs he was raising. The vision had shocked her and made her ill. She explained that she still saw that dead pig hanging in the smoke house and for the rest of her life she would never eat meat.

Burton's mother had confided that she had always hated living on a farm and raising a few farm animals during the period they lived in the mining town. She just didn't feel comfortable in the country. She feared to go out in the woods and fields to pick blackberries with her sisters because of the snakes. While picking blackberries, one of her friends had been bitten by a copperhead and had nearly died. As a small girl, Dorothy would break out in a severe rash and her legs would swell while walking through tall grass.

She told Burton and his younger brother, Darren, and sister, Eugenia, that when she was a child, their family had been so poor she and her brother, Mick, and three sisters would look through the Sears and Roebuck catalog and dream about what they would like to buy someday.

She told them that she did read many books. Her older sister, their Aunt Ann, would spend hours with her reading in the local library.

"Aunt Ann actually enjoyed living on a farm. She would even go out and help the men cut hay and she would pick berries anywhere and wasn't afraid of snakes."

Dorothy said that Ann had been the tomboy among them, but that she herself was the highest achiever in school. She had earned straight 'A's throughout. What depressed her most of all was that her parents could never afford to send her to college. There was not even a celebration after the high school graduation ceremony. Just waiting out the hot humid summer in the farmhouse adjacent to the mining town. In the fall, she rode the bus back and forth to Wilkes-Barre to attend secretarial school. She was motivated to improve her lot in life.

"Even though we didn't have much money in those days, we did have good times together," she said, "sitting around the stove telling stories and helping Gramma can food in enormous jars for the winter. In the winter, we went sliding down the surrounding hills on flattened cardboard boxes. One time when we'd been sliding a long distance from our house, I had diarrhea and had to go right there in the snow.

I didn't have anything to wipe with, so I borrowed the belt from Ann's coat and used it for that purpose."

When Dorothy told her children about the incident, they laughed uproariously, rolling about on the floor. They enjoyed hearing stories about her childhood and were always astounded that their mother had done such things.

Dorothy and Ann had left home at eighteen and traveled to Chicago to find jobs. Eventually, they moved on to Rockford. Ann worked as a telephone operator and Dorothy as a secretary for the director at the Chamber of Commerce. She earned enough to pay for a college education. After meeting Elias Blake in 1966, they had married.

When his Grampa went off to work on the bus, Burton would return to the house and spend the rest of the day helping his Gramma make dough for bread and rolls, cakes and pies and cookies. Then they would wash clothes together in the old tub and wringer down in the cellar and hang them out on the clothesline to dry in the sun and wind. Following that, there were weeds to pull in the garden and beans and tomatoes to pick. By then, Burton would no longer wear a *babushka* like his Gramma.

* * *

Several years into the marriage, she realized there was something seriously wrong with him. He had married her and needed her and their children as a balance against an impulse to be cruel. He would take every opportunity to go to the shooting range and to go off on hunting safaris for big game, especially to Africa. The trophy heads of animals he killed covered the walls of his office and various rooms in his mansion.

What alarmed her even more than the hunting expeditions, was his gruff manner bordering on meanness with their three children,

Burton, Eugenia, and Darren, and exposing them to potentially dangerous situations. When she objected that what he was doing could be considered child abuse, he scoffed at her. "You're too lenient. You're too soft with them. They need to be challenged. I'm not going to let anything happen. But they need to be challenged."

"Not like what you've been doing."

"What, did they say something? Did they complain to you?"

"The last time you took them sailing, you made them jump off the boat into the lake."

"They were wearing life jackets. It was a drill. That's all. A drill."

"Your boat was not sinking. There was no good reason for you to do that a mile out on Lake Michigan."

"Actually, they got a kick out of it. I'm sorry. I'm truly sorry. What I do with them is character building. It toughens them. The world is harsh. "

"That doesn't mean you have to be, especially with your own children. What you do with them is making them neurotic. It's more than that stupid exercise you tried to pull when they were three and four ordering them to hold back until the last possible moment before going potty. That is not character building."

"I'll make it up to them."

"By doing what? They don't think you even love them. The other day when you stayed home from the office, Eugenia and Darren begged me to take them with me to my school. They're afraid to be alone with you. What does that tell you?"

"It tells me I need to make it up to them."

"What it tells you is that you can't continue what you're doing," said Dorothy.

"Meaning?"

"Start acting like a father who loves and cares about his children."

"I just have a different way of expressing it."

"You don't express it. You've always been indifferent and domineering with them. You don't play with them or read them stories or talk nicely to them when you're at home. You rarely see them enough to even interact with them."

"I have a corporation to run."

"Don't try to use that as an excuse. You don't have any problem going off to Africa or Alaska on junkets for weeks at a time."

"Those are business trips. I take members of my staff and customers with me. You know that."

"There are things I didn't know about you, but I'm discovering. You're a different person than the one I met before we were married. Even though you withheld secrets from me about yourself, your wealth, you actually seemed loving and kind. "

"That hasn't changed. I'm still loving and kind."

"If you believe that, then you're deluding yourself. That is not how you act toward others and it is definitely not how others see you, especially your family. You're incapable of separating your business from your family life."

"By the way, I never withheld secrets from you about myself. I revealed certain information at the appropriate time. I didn't want to scare you off."

"Scare me off? Why did you think that?"

"You're very different than I am, the kind of person I'm not. You've known poverty and from what you told me, you came from a loving family, parents and brother and sister who loved and cared for each other. I envied you. I never had that."

"Is that why you insisted on a small civil ceremony for our wedding? You didn't want to suddenly expose your lavish inherited wealth?"

"That's part of it. I also wanted to hang on to a final moment of what we had together in college before everything would change, as I knew it would."

"It didn't have to change just because of money. I'm still the person I was then and I'm trying to raise our children in the same way, to experience what I experienced as a child."

"There's a difference. They won't experience poverty."

"It's not about the money, Elias. It's not about the money. They're fortunate in having advantages I never had, but there needs to be a balance and it can't come from just me."

Elias remained silent, then took a sip from his glass of scotch. The ice had melted down to a floating sliver. "I'll work on it," he said. "I'll work on it."

Chapter 15

The Bear

Burton had not wanted to go. He appealed to his mother, Dorothy, and they sat together with Elias, who shared his proposal in a calm contrite mood with no hint of his usual dominating manner. He explained that this was a step in reconnecting with his ten year old son, an adventure they could share while Burton was still a boy. Elias paid scant attention to Burton's younger sister, Eugenia, and brother, Darren. But for some reason unknown to his wife, he now suddenly focused on Burton, who had just turned ten.

"In a few more years, you'll be off doing things with your friends and want mom and dad to stay out of the way. Isn't that how it is with teenagers?"

"I guess I won't know 'til I'm a teenager."

"An Alaskan fishing trip is like nothing you've ever experienced. It's a different world, a vast untouched wilderness of mountains and glaciers and rivers teeming with salmon and endless forests filled with wild animals who've never encountered humans. We'll be explorers, the two of us. Of course, we'll fly in to the Kenai and stay at the company lodge, but we'll go out on expeditions every day and fly back in-country to uncharted wilderness, parts unknown. It will be an experience of a lifetime."

"It does sound exciting," said Dorothy, "as long as it's safe."

"Safety is our first priority. We won't do anything risky. Don't want an accident to ruin a good time. And you said yourself, Burt, you do like to camp."

"With the Scouts. But that's different. I'm with my friends and we do projects to earn merit badges."

"I know being with me is not the same as being with your friends, and I understand that. But this will be special, between the two of us."

"Won't anyone else be going? From your company?"

"I'm flying in a chef from Seattle. We are going to eat well. I promise you that. And I'll hire a guide to take us where the fish are biting."

"A guide?"

"Sure, Noah Kaganuk. He's a local native, from the Yupik tribe that's lived in that area for hundreds of years. I use him on all my trips up there."

"Can I think about it?"

"Of course, and if you really don't want to go, I'll understand. I'm not forcing you."

"Okay."

Piloted by a gray bearded veteran who had retired from the Air Force and settled in Anchorage ten years ago, the small yellow and black painted bush plane droned inland high over the dense green forests of the Kenai Peninsula and paralleled the glacier-covered Kenai Mountains and wide stark blue river flowing from the north. Burton shaded his eyes against the sun and peered out his window at small villages and settlements hugging the shoreline passing far below and a cluster of lakes dotting the flat marshes to the west.

Elias had purchased the hunting and fishing lodge eight years ago on his first trip to Alaska and then had it further customized the following year, expanding and modernizing the kitchen to include an eight burner central range, and adding a sauna, spa, and four more bedrooms to the original four. Other than installing a few pieces of leather furniture, he didn't alter the rustic living and dining rooms, which had prompted his interest in the sprawling pine log structure in the first place. A fully racked moose head, the head of a grizzly, and heads of an eight point buck and a mountain sheep he had hunted and killed contributed to the dark wood stained wall décor.

As the plane dropped into a long angular descent, Burton saw the small figure of a man wearing hunting boots and a mackinaw jacket waiting at the end of the dock.   The plane gently settled onto the surface of the water and the roar of the twin engine props diminished as it taxied over to the moss coated wooden pilings. Bobbing in its own shallow wake, it stopped alongside the dock.

The man secured the aircraft with three rapid twists of heavy braided rope around metal brackets embedded in the wood. As the person bent down, Burton noticed shoulder length raven black hair contained under a tan baseball cap that accentuated his weathered brown skin. He steadied the plane's wing against the chop and cold shearing wind sweeping across the river's open expanse, carrying the scent of spruce and pine that clashed with the nauseating odor of a decaying salmon deposited by a shallow side current on the gravel beach. With his free hand, he assisted Elias through the cockpit side door as it was pushed open.

"Noah, it's good to see you. We're looking forward to some great fishing." Elias turned to provide support to Burton stepping from the pontoon onto the dock. "Burt, this is Noah, our guide I've told you about. Noah, my son, Burt."

"It's nice to meet you, Noah."

The flat nose of the imposing man lifted at the corners with a broad smile, a flash of strong white teeth across his aquiline jaw. "It is good to meet you, Burton." He placed a hand on the boy's shoulder to ease his tense expression.   "Your father has told me about you."

Burton wondered what he had told him. The gentle touch of Noah's hand grasping his own surprised Burton and all other thoughts and distractions momentarily fled to that impression and erased his feelings of anxiety and intimidation.

He stood back and watched Noah and Clay Burgess, the bush pilot, remove packs of food and supplies and stack them on the dock.

"Your cook's been here since yesterday," said Noah. "Landed about noon. Brought your special food for a week. Six storage containers. Didn't know quite when you'd arrive, but he has lunch waiting. You can go on up to the lodge. Clay and I'll take care of these."

"Thanks, Noah. I've got this." He picked his encased Winchester rifle from among the provisions. "You both join us for lunch."

Noah nodded.

"Never disappointed when I fly you in," said the bush pilot.

Drying his hands on a white apron, Henri Tambeau came out of the kitchen as Elias and Burton entered the living room at the front door. *"Bonjour, Bonjour, Monsieur* Blake."

"Bonjour, Henri, good to see you. Glad you could make it."

"Although I have an impossible schedule, I was able to make arrangements for the week. And this young man, I assume is your son."

The insistent firm grip of the slightly built little man belied the strength of his slender fingers and thin wrists. A white chef's cap concealed most of his shaved head and contrasted with his brown eyes and clipped Gallic features.

"You assume right. Burton, meet Henri Tambeau, a first class chef who is with us all week to delight our palates."

"Nice to meet you, Mr. Tambeau."

"The pleasure is mine, Burton. In addition to having a fishing adventure, you will have a culinary one."

"Henri owns a five star restaurant in Seattle and one in Vancouver," said Elias.

"I do French cuisine and occasionally a little fusion for my Asian customers. But for lunch today, I have prepared corn beef and cabbage on Russian rye with, of course, Russian dressing and *pomme frites*.   Tonight, we will have venison with a special red wine sauce reduction and move on to salmon I expect you will catch during the following days. And by the way, your guide, Noah, brought me two grouse already plucked and frozen when I arrived. And, of course, there will be soups, blackberry pies and pastries and other such indulgences. And I brought along a variety of cheeses I know you enjoy, Elias."

"Very thoughtful, Henri. Thank you."

"If you would like to wash up, lunch will be waiting for you when you return."

"You can have your pick of the bedrooms," Elias said, as he led the way down the hall, "except for the front one and whatever one Henri has taken."

As the four men and the boy finished eating their lunch and sipped at strong dark coffee to accompany warm chocolate chip cookies, (Burton drank a glass of milk), Noah suggested they would make a short run up the river that afternoon to a spot they would be certain to catch salmon.

The buzz of the departing bush plane faded into an overcast sky on its return to Anchorage. The two Winchester model 1984 rifles loaded with 200 grain class bullets with enough fire power to penetrate a grizzly's heavy muscle and bone and the .357 magnum handguns in shoulder holsters carried by Noah and Elias disconcerted Burton. He looked away out over the river and watched the passing shoreline trees where a huge white-headed bald eagle soared on black wings from its nest of woven branches.

Elias noticed his son's anxious glance. "In case we encounter bears. The reason for the shoulder holster is if one sneaks up behind you, you just draw and shoot him in the face."

"Will we see any bears?"

"There are always bears," said Noah, "especially where there are fish. Salmon is their main food. We won't fish where they are. This is their territory and it is dangerous to go near them. We will stay away from them."

"Noah knows a lot about bears," said Elias. "He's a good hunter, the best."

"Do you live around here?" asked Burton.

"In a small settlement about a mile down the river. Mostly we catch and eat fish. We do hunt moose and deer and we grow and harvest vegetables during the summer months."

"Have you lived here all your life?"

Noah adjusted the throttle on the two cycle engine driving their aluminum longboat slowly upstream against the steady current. Burton felt the motor's vibration and the rhythmic thump of wavelets against the hull.

"Most of my life. My brothers and sisters and I all went to school in Kenai, but I also went to the University in Anchorage to study biology. I worked for the Department of Fish and Game as a naturalist and guide for some years when my children were younger. I have a wife, two sons and two daughters and a pack of sled dogs."

"Huskies?"

"Malamutes. We travel by sled in the winter and by bush plane when the roads are closed and waterways turn into ice."

"Is it hard to live here?"

"Not when you know how. We live in harmony with our environment. The wilderness is more powerful than we are and can easily overcome us. We are guests and caretakers of its forests, mountains, and rivers. My ancestors settled here thousands of years ago. We are still here. Our tribes and societies populate most of the state."

"Do you have a tribe?"

"I am of the Yupik people."

"Are there many tribes?"

"We own land. There are many of us."

"Do you know much about bears?"

"I've studied what they eat, their mating habits, how they raise their young, how far they range."

"Did one ever attack you?"

"No, I have been careful, and lucky."

"Did you ever kill a bear?"

"I have killed bears, but there is no satisfaction in killing them. If I do, it is for meat."

"What do you mean?"

"I do not hunt bears for trophies."

"Noah is a Native American," interjected Elias. "He has a spiritual kinship with wild animals, especially bears. Tell him about the spirit bear."

"The species is known as the Kermode Bear named after the man who researched them. They're white, but not albinos and not polar bears. When you see them in the forest, their white fur gives them the appearance of a ghost or spirit. We do not hunt and kill them. They are an endangered species. We want to preserve them as we do our wilderness and its inhabitants from commercial exploitation and the ruination of our homes and environment. Although there is an abundance of fish and game, we take from our forests and rivers only what we need to eat and survive. We do not fish and kill game for sport. The law provides limits for those who do."

Burton noticed a blush rising up his father's neck, but Elias tactfully withheld comment.

Noah rigged Burton's spinning rod and reel with a Kwikfish lure while Elias attached a Tadpolly to the leader of his fifty pound test line. Noah nosed the boat about to drift downstream and allow the trailing lines and lures to slowly back troll. The boat was passing through a stretch of the river where he had seen dense schools of Chinook King Salmon migrating upstream to spawning beds in feeder creeks and the Anchor, Kasilov, and Ninilchick Rivers.

The first strike took Burton's lure and nearly jerked the rod and smoking reel from his grasp.

"Keep your rod tip up and hold tight," said Noah. "He's well hooked."

The fish suddenly shot up from the depths with a violent explosion of spray. Its red body twisted in a gyrating dance elevated by its thrusting flipping green tail. Burton could see the lure attached at the corner of its hooked beak mouth.

"Sockeye," said Noah. "Not a Chinook. He will give you a fight. Don't force him. Let him play himself out."

Fifteen minutes later, Noah gently netted the exhausted fish as Burton steadily reeled it in to the side of the boat. "You did well," he said. "It's about a twelve pounder."

Burton smiled at his father, who gave him a wide grin and a thumbs up just before his rod bowed and his reel buzzed at a strike.

That night, Burton fell asleep to the distant haunting howl of wolves.

Four days later, Noah took them up a narrow shallow side river and beached the boat so Burton and Elias could step out and fish wading along the shore. Noah showed Burton how to cast a Pixie Spoon lure upstream and bounce it off the bottom rocks as he slowly reeled it in.

Elias took his Winchester and rod and reel from the boat and walked downstream following a game trail.

"No bears spotted in this area," Noah called after him.

"That's okay," Elias shouted back. "Just playin' it safe." He had walked fifty yards upstream and seen the day old paw print of a grizzly in the mud and had come across a pile of dried bear scat. He assumed the bear had probably crossed the river and moved on until he noticed movement in the tall grass on the opposite bank and the characteristic hump of a silvertip boar. Elias thought the bear might be eating fish pulled out of the river and, since he was downwind, hadn't detected him. Elias quietly back-tracked to the boat but said nothing to Noah about seeing the bear he intended to kill.

Once he was out of sight of Noah and Burton, he moved away from the river and circled back through the tall dense tundra brush reddening into its traditional autumn color and established a hidden position where he could observe what the bear might do next.

The bear finished eating the ten pound Coho salmon it had sent sailing out of the river with a powerful swipe of its paw. The fish was no more than a morsel and did little to satisfy his hunger. He raised his head at the cloud of black flies pestering his mucous drooling snout and wriggled his furry pig-shaped ears to test the air for threatening sounds. Hearing none, he pushed back through the grass and slid down the embankment to the edge of the water and stopped. He reared up on his hind legs to his full eight foot height and sniffed and listened to something he detected downstream, obstructed by a slight bend in the river. Because his eyesight was weak, he decided to go and investigate. His thick abundant fur caught the sunlight and rippled over his powerful fifteen hundred pound body as he waded across the stream with quick long strides.

Noah and Burton heard the voluminous angry roar seconds before the bear charged out of the brush no more than thirty yards away. Noah realized instantly he would never get back to the boat for his rifle before the bear would be on them. He drew his .357 magnum and fired three shots that momentarily slowed the animal who paused to swipe at the sting, roared again and continued moving toward them at a lumbering gallop.

Noah heard the crack of a rifle shot and saw the bear's head snap around as the bullet shredded his brain followed by three more rapid fire shots penetrating his heart and lungs. The bear's momentum propelled him forward in a floundering heap, wheezing blood through its nostrils in a final gasp of death and a wave of rank stench that caused the trembling boy to stagger back away from the open jaw at his feet and vomit.

He and Noah looked up as Elias stepped out of the brush and walked over to them with a grim smile.

"Lucky I carried my rifle, eh?"

"You knew he was there," said Noah. "You saw him, but you didn't tell me. You put your son in harm's way. After today, I will not guide for you."

"Burt is safe and you're safe. I've been a crack shot since I was a boy. I knew I could bring him down."

"There is something you should know," Noah spoke to Burton. "Do not blame the bear for trying to kill you. We have intruded onto his territory to take his food. That is how he saw us. If your father had warned me, we would not have stayed. This killing would not have been necessary. We are done here now. We will go back."

"I want this bear for my office," said Elias. "The whole bear."

"I'll send someone for the carcass. The taxidermist at Kenai will do the work and ship you your trophy. After today, you and I will never see or speak to each other again."

"It'll be a while before I come back up here. I'll pay you three times your fee for the trouble. Maybe you'll reconsider."

"I will not take your money. It is time for us to go."

"You going to report the attack to Forest and Game."

"It is the law."

Burton remained unmoving, staring at the bear until his father nudged his shoulder to return him to the boat.

* * *

"So how was the trip?" Dorothy released her son from a barrage of kisses and a crushing embrace.

"I really liked it. I had fun. I liked it a lot. Even the bear, because everything turned out all right."

"Bear? What's this about a bear?"

"I was attacked by a grizzly."

"How's that? What did you say?"

"He didn't get to me, because dad shot him first. Noah told me I should not blame the bear."

"Who is Noah again?"

"He was our guide."

"How is it you were anywhere near a bear?"

"We were fishing from shore. Noah said we intruded on the bear's territory."

"Intruded?"

"The bear thought we were taking his fish."

"Thank God you weren't killed. If the bear was not to blame, who was?"

"Noah said we should not have been there."

"But you were there. Why?"

"Dad wanted to shoot the bear."

"You mean he used you as bait?" Her eyes bore into Elias. "You used your own son as bait?"

"No," Elias shook his head. "Burt was perfectly safe. The bear could not have gotten to him. Noah was right beside him."

Her gaze returned to her son. "How close did he get to you?"

"He died on the ground right in front of me."

Dorothy's balled fists turned to raised claws at her husband. "I can't believe what you've done. You're a monster. Won't you be satisfied until your children are killed?"

"Look at him," said Elias. "He's okay. He's fine. He had an adventure. It's a story he can tell his friends."

"I'm not letting you go any further with this. I'm leaving you and I'm taking the children with me."

"I'm sorry you can't see things my way."

"Unbelievable! Unbelievable!"

Bile rose into Burton's throat as he tried to reconcile being caught between his bickering mother and father. "Except for being afraid of the bear, I still had a good time, Mom. I'm all right."

"The damage is done."

"You should listen to him," said Elias. "Believe what he says. He's all right."

"The damage is done."

"I saved him from the God damn bear!"

"You didn't save him. You used him as bait. This is just another incident like what you did to them on the boat out on the lake."

"That was an adventure."

"No, no it wasn't. One mile out on Lake Michigan. The water was freezing enough out there to cause hypothermia. And Burton said you pulled away from them. He thought you were going to leave them stranded out there and they would have to try to swim to shore. He was shouting at you and you just laughed. Are you crazy? Darren is only six years old and Eugenia seven. They're terrified to go anywhere with you anymore, and for the same reason, Burton tries to avoid you. The damage is done. The damage is done."

Chapter 16

Youth

1970s

Burton and his best friend, Russell, had been young typical American boys, pure and untainted in their exuberant youth. Although Burton stood a head taller than Russell, short and blue-eyed like his glowering father, who had intimidating bushy white eyebrows, Russell was experienced and knowledgeable in subjects and activities in which Burton was not. So Russell became the leader in their relationship.

Russel was small-boned and athletic like his mother. The owner of a construction company, Russell's father's passion was fresh water sports fishing. He had taught his son the skills of handling rods and reels and bait and tackle. Russell passed along the fishing basics to his new friend and taught him how to cast. Burton persuaded his mom and step-dad of his new necessity for a rod and reel, tackle box and artificial lures, along with extra Eagle Claw hooks, various sinkers, corks, and plastic bobbers.

During their first summer together, Russell showed Burton his favorite fishing holes along Spring Creek which originated many miles out in remote farm country and passed through the hills and knolls of their community gradually being transformed into a suburban landscape. The creek was a draw for their adventurous impulses, although it yielded little more than chub, tiny blue gill, frogs, turtles, and crawfish. The wildlife had not yet been displaced by residential development. They saw pheasants, quail, rabbits, chipmunks, skunks, possum, muskrat, and a variety of harmless snakes. They discovered a fox's den containing small broken bones and pieces of gray fur. They crawled on their hands and knees following animal trails through tangled briar patches and stumbled into tall itch weed that caused them to break out in a spreading rash that worsened with scratching.

At the end of each day before going to bed, their parents inspected their hair and bodies for wood ticks. Distinguishing the tiny brown parasites was often difficult because of their resemblance to skin moles and pepper spots. Russell's father used the lighted end of a cigarette to cause the ticks to back out. Burton's step-dad, Tom Linden, used rubbing alcohol. There was always concern that a tick's head would break off and become absorbed into the skin and that the germs they carried would cause Rocky Mountain Spotted Fever. Such cautions expressed by their parents did not keep the boys out of the woods and fields, because the Rocky Mountains were far far away.

Her children would have advantages along with moral values. This was Dorothy Linden's goal as a wife and mother. She had escaped the poverty of her childhood in a Pennsylvania coal mining town, had endured being the wife of Elias Blake for ten years, and now rushed to embrace the promise of the post-Vietnam '70's with her second husband, Tom Linden.

For Dorothy, her house was a symbol of middle class prosperity, a status level of satisfaction that suited her comfort zone out of which Elias Blake had ruthlessly and relentlessly driven her by endangering their children and by having an open affair with another woman. Dorothy could not live up to his expectations of being a socialite and posturing as a trophy wife. The other woman, Alexis Andamiano was born to it.

A house was also a home, an environment to create a family culture in which Elias had had no wish or desire to participate. Her vision of that culture included certain aspects of what she considered gracious, but not opulent, living as she had briefly known with Elias Blake.

Mealtimes with well-prepared food and interesting and educated conversation were important to her. She also lavished a love and caring the like of which she had experienced from her own parents and brother and sisters. She wanted to hold back nothing for her children, but during her marriage to Tom Linden, money became an issue.

In severing her life with Elias Blake, she had not wanted any of his money, not even for child support. Despite the personal ignominy that came with it, she never brought up her previous marriage as fodder for her current discontent. Instead, she took a teaching job to supplement Tom's income. She furnished her house simply and affordably. Blonde wood and pastel accents were the mode with one exception, a George Steck console piano made from mahogany and cherry wood. Her children would learn music.

Their first two houses had been rentals. Their third had a mortgage with their name on it, a major milestone. The selection of the house had been carefully evaluated. The price and the neighborhood were of primary importance. The name of the area had caught their imagination, as the family drove along a two lane road in a semi-rural area where farmland was being converted to residential tracts.

Spring Creek featured semi-custom ranch style homes on quarter-acre lots. Tom and Dorothy selected a corner location directly across from the elementary school. They were among the first residents. Most of the surrounding grassy hills and fields had not yet been touched by earth movers and construction equipment. Plans were being laid for a small shopping center a half-mile away along the narrow main road. The Linden family grew accustomed to the nearly constant distant buzz and whine of power saws and tapping of hammers carried on the warm Midwest spring and summer winds like suburban background music.

The house was a single story model made of stained redwood siding and a shingled roof. Within two years, Tom added an enclosed breezeway for a family room and converted the carport into a two car garage. A red brick chimney rose from a fireplace at the front of the living room next to two picture windows facing onto the narrow street where no sidewalks or curbs existed. People's lawns tapered raggedly into the composite of tar and gravel streets. In the new young all white community, there were no clean edges.

The back yards of seven houses on their block faced on each other and merged to form a few acres of a shared inner complex undivided by fences. This playing field rang with the jubilant shouts and cries of the neighborhood children. Spring Creek was a safe haven for Tom's and Dorothy's children, a fitting place for a middle-class family.

Burton shared a bedroom with his younger brother, Darren. The room housed two twin beds and was paneled with knotty pine. The boys envisioned animal shapes in the grain and whorls of the lightly stained wood. Burton's bed was next to the windows facing out onto the front lawn. Darren's was snugged against the inside wall. Their sister's, Eugenia's, room was on the opposite side of the wall. Burton soon discovered with what ease he and his brother could slip outside late at night through the bottom window, which was nearly at ground level.

Burton was older than his sister by two years and his brother by three. Being the oldest, he felt protective of them and responsible for their safety and well-being. At the ripe old age of eleven, he became a worried parent long before his time. Being responsible was expected of him and was positively reinforced by his parents and every other adult he encountered in his young life. Adults held him in high regard for his grown-up behavior and he liked the way that made him feel.

He didn't goof around and screw up and he was always respectful. He was "a good boy," who lived up to their expectations.

His demeanor also was acknowledged by his peers who held him in high esteem for the kind way he related to them. He always deferred to what his siblings and friends wanted to do, what card games and board games they wanted to play, who would be "good guys and bad guys," and where they would fish "down at the creek." Because he cared about them, he made them feel good.

Along with responsibility came the need to be perfect. Any flaws you might possess must not be revealed in public. The recognition by others of his deficiencies caused Burton intense incapacitating embarrassment. His younger stepbrother and stepsister had a knack, however innocent, for pushing his primary deficiency button which was that he had long toes.

He dreaded when their mother took them to the shoe store. Invariably, Eugenia and Darren would loudly chorus (enough for everyone in the store to hear) that "Burton has long toes! That's why we call him Burton Long Toes!"

The blood would surge up into Burton's face leaving him apoplectic and wanting to depart immediately from the store. But his brother and sister would wait until his shoes had been removed and the salesman was about to fit him with a new pair so he couldn't escape the insolent remark he knew was forthcoming. To make matters worse, they would giggle and tee-hee during the fitting and their mother did nothing to shush them. He thought she was amused by his discomfort, because he saw her try to hide a smile. But he noticed. He always noticed such expressions on the faces of other people.

He loved the fine features, brown wide-eyed enthusiasm, and golden-haired perfection of his brother. He loved the cherubic flatter features of his sister, her curly auburn hair and serious eyes tucked in above wide full cheeks, similar to her Czech grandmother. The corners of her nostrils turned white and quivered whenever she cried and caused a rush of sympathy in Burton. He did not like to see his brother or sister unhappy or in pain.

The day Darren was clobbered on the head with a rock wielded by a neighbor boy, Bobby Klein, Burton wanted to immediately go and exact revenge. He ranted and raved, but his mother would not allow him to leave the house. He could only mentally project his anger from the back stoop across the lawns to the Klein house high on a knoll in the next block.

From the dull expression in Darren's eyes and the open gash on his blood-stained blonde head, he had suffered a mild concussion. In retaliation, Burton spread the word among his friends of Bobby Klein's aggression, and Bobby Klein was black listed, no longer invited to play among them.

Continuing to carry his original father's surname, Burton Blake believed that balance must be restored, that justice must be done, the bad guy must lose in the end. He did not yet realize that life was uncertain and unfair, that he and his friends were not invincible like movie and fiction heroes. They were transparent and vulnerable and subject to pain, and they could lose, as well as win.

Spring Creek was populated with young families. Fathers were employed in median income jobs. A few in the area managed their own companies. With one or two exceptions, wives and mothers did not work outside the home. They cleaned and cooked and maintained the household and ensured the education and well-being of their children. A few were also Cub Scout den mothers or Girl Scout group leaders. The community shared the values of wholesome family life and economic security.

From Burton's youthful perspective, all of the families appeared to be healthy, happy, and stable. When he played in the homes of his friends, he became only peripherally aware of problems. He heard snippets of conversation between adults and had no context or reference to understand.

Mrs. Lane was "frigid." She had never had an orgasm. The wife of a doctor, Mrs. Thurman was an alcoholic who felt inadequate in the shadow of her husband. She had to go to a detox clinic once a year. Mrs. Olson was unhappy because her husband never showed her affection. Mrs. Mason was known to throw wild parties and was thought to be promiscuous by the tight knit dresses she wore and the cleavage she exposed in public. Only the wives seemed to have problems. Burton never heard anything about husbands having problems. All the husbands were okay.

Burton's first and best friend was Russell Johansen. Russell lived three houses away and he and Burton had quick and easy access to each other through their connected back yards.

Burton was impressed with Russell's realistic western six gun and holster rig and persuaded his mother that he needed to have one just like it. He could load blank cartridges containing little round caps into the revolving chamber. Their guns were just like the ones Clint Eastwood used in the movies and on television. The boys galloped about the back yards and fields surrounding the school grounds on their imaginary horses and provided the sound effects of whinnies and snorts to add an element of realism to their make-believe.

Burton parted from his friend as they reached Russell's yard and trudged across the expanse of two more yards to his own which rose in a mild slope to the back door. He stomped his tennis shoes against the door stoop and wiped the loosened dried mud on the black rubber mat before entering the laundry room adjacent to the kitchen where his mother was preparing dinner. The smell of beef and vegetables and biscuits browning in the oven set his gastric juices flowing and caused his stomach to knot up with hunger.

"Are we having French fries?" he called through the door, as he placed his rod and reel and tackle box in the broom closet. "Yes, supper will be ready in about thirty minutes. That gives you just enough time to practice the piano."

"I thought Eugenia would be practicing."

"She finished an hour ago and went to her Brownie meeting."

"I'm too hungry to practice right now. I'll do it after supper. Can I have some milk and cookies?"

"They'll spoil your dinner. Have a carrot instead."

Burton always wondered why his mother thought cookies would spoil his dinner. He never had trouble eating his dinner even when he did sneak cookies when she wasn't looking. He settled for one of three peeled carrots on the kitchen counter and was about to walk back to his bedroom.

"Wash your hands first."

"They're clean."

"You've been handling worms."

"We used lunch meat and cheese. We only caught crawfish."

"Wash anyway."

Burton held the carrot between his teeth so that it protruded from his face like Pinocchio's long nose and washed his hands at the kitchen sink, then used his mother's white dishcloth to dry them. His fingers left dirt smudges on the dishcloth. He bit off a piece of carrot with a loud chocking noise.

"If you're not going to practice, run over to the Thurmans and tell Darren it's time to come home."

Burton crossed the dining room into the breezeway and went out the connecting door through the garage. As he crossed the narrow street, he watched the Olson's tan-skin boxer come over into his yard, raise a hind leg, and pee on one of the low-lying junipers. Burton had helped his step-dad plant the shrubs. He was responsible for mowing the big yard. They didn't own a power mower, so pushing required concentrated labor, during which Burton made frequent stops to drink from the garden hose. He usually ignored the intense heat and humidity of summer as long as he was at play with his friends. When he mowed the lawn, the steaming air aggravated him and made the job unpleasant.

"Hee-yah!" Burton waved his arm at the dog. "Go pee on your own bushes."

The dog ignored him, finished his pee and trotted further into the side yard to investigate new smells. Burton continued across the road into the Thurmans driveway littered with the evidence of five children -- tricycles, a wagon, two hula hoops, and various noise-making push toys. He could hear his brother's loud voice and the softer one of Darren's friend through the screen door. Darren raised his voice on a regular basis to overcome being interrupted by everyone in his own family whenever he tried to say something. His desire to be heard caused him to be vocally dominant when playing with his friends.

Peering through the screen's mesh, Burton saw the shape of Ellen Thurman in somnambulant motion in the kitchen. He always felt embarrassed for her in her alcoholic stupor and avoided engaging her in conversation. He had difficulty understanding her slurred speech and never knew quite what to say to her. He considered going back to his own house and calling on the phone. Past experience told him that the phone rarely got answered. He knocked gently on the aluminum door frame. "Hello."

"Who's there?"

"It's me, Burton."

"You can come in."

"Can you tell my brother it's time to come home for supper?"

"Sure, I'll tell 'im."

"Thanks."   Burton waited a moment to be sure she followed through with what she said. When he heard her speak to the boys in the living room, he quickly left the back door and crossed the road again to his own house where his step-dad's gray Chevrolet sedan was pulling into the driveway.

He was home in time for dinner, an event that eased Burton's anxiety. Whenever his step-dad was late, it upset his mother's expectation of family togetherness and she would angrily scold him as he walked through the door. Burton disliked emotional tension and confrontation of any kind. His dad handled it well. He handled everything well when it came to dealing with people. He understood why his wife was angry and accepted it calmly, just as he accepted all things that came at him and to him. Burton never saw him become angry or outspoken in return to anyone.

Burton knew what emotional stress was. He had experienced it himself in school (particularly when Miss Wersen was teaching math) and sometimes at play as high excitement. He had observed his father laugh gently and smile, but he had never seen him excited or agitated. What Burton didn't know was that his stepfather internalized his stress and his anger instead of letting it out and getting rid of it.

The first time Burton heard the word stress mentioned was late one night. His mother raced into his and Darren's bedroom and shouted at them, "Wake up! Wake up! Go get Doctor Thurman! Your dad's having a heart attack!"

As Burton and Darren leaped from their beds and into the hall, they paused a moment to glance into their parents' bedroom and saw their father clutching his abdomen and writhing and gasping for breath while their mother tried to get him to remain calm. The boys dashed out of the house and across the street to the Thurmans.

Ray Thurman was a general surgeon. Burton and Darren knew him as a tall kindly man with a gregarious assertive demeanor. He had dark hair and eyes that twinkled good-naturedly under bushy eyebrows. Accustomed to being called out of bed to respond to emergencies during the middle of the night, he answered the ringing doorbell and (barefoot, wearing only his pajamas) did not hesitate one moment to follow the two boys jabbering up at him about their dad having a heart attack.

Burton especially liked Doctor Thurman, because of a medical problem Burton had experienced during the sixth grade basketball season. (Their local school covered first grade through eighth.) Burton was convinced that the reddish brown spreading rash throughout his groin area that itched to distraction was cancer. His mother had arranged for Burton to see Doctor Thurman at his office downtown. At the doctor's request, Burton had pushed down his blue jeans and Fruit-of-the-Loom underpants in an embarrassed obligatory manner and exposed his scabrous inner thighs.

"How long has it been since you washed your jock strap," Doctor Thurman asked.

"I don't know. A couple of months, I think."

"Do you keep it in your locker at school?"

Burton nodded.

"How many do you have?"

"Just one."

"You should have at least two and rotate them. Have your mom buy you another one. What you have is called jock itch."

"Jock itch?"

"Yes, I'm going to write you a prescription for an ointment you can apply and it should go away in a few days."

Burton grinned with relief. "I thought I had cancer."

Doctor Thurman swallowed his sudden impulse to laugh. "Nope, just old-fashioned jockstrap itch." He finished scribbling his signature on a prescription form and handed it to Burton, who quickly pulled up his pants. "Have your mom pick this up for you."

"Thanks." Burton took the little piece of paper while fumbling awkwardly with his belt and zipper. He felt incredibly embarrassed. It concerned him that now, every time Doctor Thurman saw him in their neighborhood, he would associate Burton with jock itch. So thereafter, Burton did his best to avoid seeing or talking to Doctor Thurman. At the moment, however, as they raced back across the street to save his father, the thought of jock itch didn't even occur to Burton.

When they arrived, Ray Thurman sat on the bed next to the boys' father. "Hello, Tom, it's Ray. Now I want you to concentrate on my voice and relax your body. Stay focused on my voice." His voice was soothing and calm.   He took one of Tom 's hands and slowly unclenched the tight fist. Keeping the fingers spread, he massaged them while also gently rubbing Tom's abdomen, which was tight and knotted with cramps. His breath came in little gasps, grunts, and wheezes.

A few minutes later, the boys and their sister saw their father's body visibly relax and his shallow breathing expanded into a normal pattern of inhaling and expulsion of air. "What happened?" he asked. "Did I have a heart attack?"

"No," Ray observed with a kindly smile. "You must be under a lot of stress. You had an anxiety attack. The symptoms are similar to a heart attack. But you're fine. You might want to consider taking a couple of days off work and play some golf."

The distressed father nodded. The president of the company had given territory and customers that Tom had established to a newly hired employee, a friend of the president's family who would take over Tom's commissions. Tom had been directed to go out and develop another sales region which meant extensive travel and longer periods of time away from home. Every moment lost away from his family could never be recaptured – each meal, each bedtime snuggle and kiss, each "I love you and I like you goodnight." To be gone saddened him and caused him great emotional suffering.

Burton studied his elongated features in profile. His step-father's previously frightened expression was once again calm. Burton felt a sudden rush of shame at the remembrance of a moment at the dinner table when he had told his step-dad he didn't like the way he chewed his food.

Although probably deeply hurt at the criticism, his step-father had said that Burton's observation was okay and that it was a normal part of growing up for children to be critical of their parents. The memory of what he had said to his step-father was the equivalent of Burton's jock itch association whenever he met Doctor Ray Thurman. The only difference was that Burton did not try to avoid his step-father, who was very attentive of the three children. He never failed to sit nearby and listen to them practice the piano, although Eugenia was musically gifted and the most advanced, and he was patient and helpful when they had difficulty with their homework. Burton fumed with anger at his math, but his step-dad taught him how to logically figure out the story problems.

Burton approached the car from the driver's side, as the door opened and his step-father emerged. He had removed his gray suit coat, but still wore a tie.

"Hi, Dad."

"Hi, Burt. Will you help me with these?" He handed him an expanding file containing sales records. "Sure."

Darren dashed across the street from the Thurmans. "Hi, Dad."

"Hi, Son." He gave his wide smiling golden haired boy a hug. Together they traipsed into the house.

"Tonight's rec night," Burton reminded his mother. I have to get there early to set up the movie projector."

"You'll be ready in plenty of time."

"I have to get there early." Burton emphasized. He had been asked by the science teacher if he would run the movie projector at the Friday Recreation Nights. The combined elementary and middle school provided the facility for the children of local families to come and dance, do crafts, play games, and watch a full length sixteen millimeter black and white movie. Mr. Rowley respected Burton and considered him among the most responsible students in the school.

After dinner, Burton took a quick shower and vigorously brushed his teeth and swallowed a glob of Colgate toothpaste so that his teeth sparkled and his breath was smiling fresh.

"I'm going now, Mom," he shouted as he passed through the laundry room and headed out the back door.

"Have a good time. Be careful crossing the road," she called out from washing the supper dishes at the kitchen sink.

The school loomed across the street from the Linden home as though it were an extension of where they lived. It was an omnipresent influence in the life of the community. The elongated tan brick building contained pockets of experience and information that the children came to gather each day.

The school was a natural cocoon for young people. Burton's teachers and the rows of desks in classrooms with walls and bulletin boards lined with his work and that of his peers formed the chrysalis of their development.

Burton liked the security of being with the other children, gaining his identity from them, from his teachers, from his mother and father and sister and brother, and from his friends. He liked the smell of paste and water colors, of old wooden desks gouged with initials. He and the others shared their idealistic young lives with no realization of what lay ahead.

Burton especially liked the gymnasium bounded on one side by a stage on which were presented school plays, holiday pageants, and assemblies, when the principal would make "announcements" speaking into the stand up microphone.

The gym was also where the local Boy Scout troop met every Tuesday night and where the initial impulse to embrace a strong sense of morality was reinforced and nurtured in Burton.

Chapter 17

On his twelfth birthday, Burton sat in his favorite chair in the living room, opened his newly purchased *Boy Scout Handbook*, and began to read.

Today, you are an American boy. Before long, you will be an American man. It is important to America and to yourself that you become a citizen of fine character, physically strong, mentally awake, and morally straight.

Boy Scouting helps you become that kind of citizen. But also Scouting gives you fellowship and fun.

Yes, it's fun to be a Boy Scout! It's fun to go hiking and camping with your friends...to swim, to dive, to paddle a canoe, to wield an ax...to follow in the footsteps of the pioneers who led the way through the wilderness...to raise your eyes to the heavens...to stare into the glowing embers of a campfire and dream of the wonders of the life that is in store for you.

Burton immersed himself in the handbook, imagining himself according to the description of what he would do in "the great outdoors," learning the skills of Scouting as a member of a troop and a patrol, living life according to the Scout Code, providing service to others, saving someone's life who was drowning (like in the picture), learning about rank and insignia, camping skills, how to navigate using map and compass, tie knots and build shelters and bridges out of logs, and learning about duty to God and country and the world brotherhood of Scouting and living according to Scout ideals. The handbook was a Bible of how a boy should live his life and, as an adult, become a moral American citizen. As he read the final page, Burton realized that he had much to accomplish, each level of rank, each merit badge, an incremental step in achieving his goal of becoming a worthy human being.

* * *

Burton listened to the throbbing beat of the Indian drum. The fire at the center of the outdoor amphitheater threw writhing flames high into the night sky. Surrounded by two hundred other boys, he was halfway up on the rustic tiered seating made of split logs. All eyes were focused on the drummer and another man wearing buckskins, moccasins, and a full double tail eagle feather headdress that flowed down his back to his heels. He raised his arms toward the brown uniformed boys and the drummer stopped. The crackling of burning wood was the only sound in the forest darkness. The man's deep voice carried clearly in the surrounding natural amphitheater.

"The Order of the Arrow is the national brotherhood of Scout campers. Its purpose is to recognize those who best exemplify the Scout Oath and Law in their daily lives and to develop and maintain camping traditions and spirit. The honor of becoming a member of the Order of The Arrow is bestowed on a Scout by his fellow campers when he has proved himself worthy of receiving it by being an outstanding Scout in his patrol and his troop. You have been chosen by your fellow Scouts to receive this honor. Tonight and tomorrow, you will undergo an initiation to test your courage and your commitment to work for the benefit of others. You will be taken out into the woods, each in a different place where you will stay until sunrise. You will be given only a blanket."

Ten older Scouts dressed as Indian braves stepped out of the surrounding shadows into the circle of firelight.

"Starting with the first row, you will follow one of the guides in groups of twenty. As you pass by the table behind the drummer, you will be handed a blanket. Those of you seated in the first row may now rise and proceed."

Burton followed the boys on the lower seats standing and filing in an orderly manner down to the floor of the amphitheater where they linked up with the guides who led them away into the black wall of thick trees. A few minutes later, depending on the movement of the boy in front of him, Burton stumbled along an unseen trail through the woods. The only illumination was the guide's bobbing light from a battery powered lantern thirty yards ahead. The smooth worn path descended gradually to the river where the group turned and walked parallel to the swift dark flowing water toward the sound of distant drums. A half mile further, Burton saw a reddish-pink glow of lights reflected off a range of sandstone cliffs with a labyrinthine network of trails and openings into shallow caves. Dressed as Indians, several older Scouts stood solemnly at the cave entrances like spirits and watched them pass.

The drumming and the strange scene receded far behind them when Burton became aware of the line ahead growing progressively shorter and that he was moving closer and closer to the guide at the front. He noticed the slightly frightened expression of the next boy, as the guide pointed into the brush at the side of the trail and ordered him to "take ten steps. Where you stop is where you will spend the night. Unless you have an emergency, you may not call out or talk to others at either side of you." The boy gingerly pressed his way into the undergrowth.

Fifty yards further, the guide halted and directed Burton to step ten paces into a thorny briar patch. Burton hesitated, then using his blanket as a shield, thrust deeper into the thicket. He stepped on and crushed enough of an area to create room to lie down. He placed his blanket on the ground, lay down, and looked up at the stars through the trees. His pulse raced with apprehension. Remembering he was not out there alone, he grew calm and thought back over the events that had brought him to this time and place.

Mainly, Scouting had all been fun. He enjoyed the association with his friends. He had progressed rapidly through the ranks to become an Eagle Scout, although the final experience had not been pleasant.

*   *   *

Wearing his full uniform, Burton sat waiting in the hallway of the civic building. He clenched and unclenched his right fist and watched the knuckles leap up under the taut skin. His stomach churned with unease and his bowels murmured with a queasy flutter. He did not know what to expect from the four men sitting behind the closed door. Two other boys had gone in before him and had come out smiling. They didn't stick around so he could ask them about the interview.

His mother had driven him to this late appointment, eight o'clock. She waited outside in the car and did homework for one of the college courses she was taking. Burton had been told the interview would last forty-five minutes. What would they talk to him about for forty-five minutes, everything he had done as a Scout? For him, the focus of Scouting had been the outdoor activity, hiking and camping.

His troop leader, Gordon Fueher, a warm-hearted dad with thick dark hair and the ability to jokingly interact with the boys, had ensured that they all had ample experience, since he himself was an outdoorsman. He took them to regional jamborees, summer Boy Scout camp, fishing trips up in the Wisconsin lakes, a canoe trip down the Rock River, a ten day canoe trip into the Canadian wilderness, the twenty mile Lincoln Trail and Black Hawk Trail Hikes, for which he received patches that his mother had sewn on to his awards sash clustered with merit badges. They had been presented to him at troop ceremonies.

"You have reached an important goal," Gordy, as he preferred to be called, had said. "And having reached it, you immediately set yourself another." Achieving goals had become Burton's consuming passion reinforced by not so subtle influences of rightness and goodness and paranoia.

The often repeated theme of patriotism pervaded the *Boy Scout Handbook*, even to the extent of giving your life for your country. The blind obeisance to "God and Country" had little to do with the boyhood reality of Burton and his friends. The Government's fictitiously manufactured fear of nuclear death and the Cold War with Russia did.

He mumbled his allegiance to the flag at school assemblies and at Scout meetings in disjointed unison with the other mumblers. He differentiated between good guys and bad guys, heroes and villains. His Scout handbook told him to "Do your part as a citizen in the big task of upholding the strength of the Government and overcoming its weaknesses. Remember that America is not a gift that is freely given us. Each of us must deserve it. We must work for America, live for it, and, if the call should come, die for it!"

In a section of the Scout Handbook titled "Morally Straight," the page featured a drawing of a Scout and his alter ego giving him advice. The accompanying text appealed to Burton's sense of who he was and who he was becoming.

Deep within each human being is laid a precious thing, possessed by no other living creature --- the thing we call a conscience. No one can tell you where it is located or what it looks like --- but it is there just the same. Occasionally, in some people, it seems fast asleep. But in most people, it is like an inner voice that is very much awake. Sometimes it whispers to you, at other times it seems to yell out loud. It is your conscience that makes it possible for you to distinguish between right and wrong, that helps you follow the right trail through life.

Your conscience speaks to you of yourself – of the moral obligation you have to make your life count. Your conscience speaks to you about your relationship to other people – respecting their rights, treating them justly, giving them a fair chance. Your conscience tells you to obey the laws of our country. Those laws were created to benefit all our people – to keep them safe in their persons and in their property, to protect them in their homes and on the streets and highways. Let your conscience be your guide. Know what is right. Do what is right.

Burton's mother came in to check on him and found him still sitting in the hall waiting for his turn. "How much longer do you think it will be," she asked.

"I don't know. There's still one guy in there ahead of me."

"It's getting much too late."

"They only do this every three months. So they have to get everybody in."

"I hope they hurry."

Burton nodded. "So do I. I'm getting tired of sitting here."

"I'm going back to the car."

Burton raised his hand in acknowledgment. The hall was warm and quiet and caused Burton to feel drowsy. His mind drifted and he thought of the good times he had experienced during his years as a Scout.

III THE CULT OF WEALTH

Chapter 18

The Message

2012

Burton felt like he was being abducted.

The speed and reckless maneuvering through the Johannesburg mid-day traffic gave him the sensation that the two tense men in the front seat wanted to avoid a confrontation. He could still back out and tell them he had changed his mind.

Until one hour ago, he had believed he was free and independent of the inexorable reach of his father. Since he was ten years old, his unforgiving mother had fought a legal battle to prevent Elias from coming near or trying to influence her children.

What Burton didn't know was that after several attempts, out of respect for her, Elias had decided to honor what he called an unreasonable request. But his children remained in his thoughts, particularly Burton.

He felt he had begun to form a bond with his son until the incident with the bear. Burton had told his mother how much he had enjoyed the Alaskan fishing trip and appeared to take some innocent pride in his father's act of killing the bear. In retrospect, Elias knew that what he had done was foolhardy and that saving his son had been a fantasy that he was playing out. Instead of saving him, he had lost him in a different way.

Love had always come about as a distortion for Elias. People he loved were always taken from him. The realization that he could not own love like he owned his company devastated him, a repressed thought he never shared with anyone.

At twenty-four, Burton had traveled halfway around the world on an impulse to seek adventure and to follow a personal calling to help others. For three years, he had experienced a variety of cultures in foreign countries like he had never imagined.

His life was about to change because his whereabouts had been discovered and because of four words he had just heard.

"Your father is dead."

The two well-built men wearing dark suits looked out of place shouldering their way through the crowd of sweating shouting African refugees to where Burton was distributing clothing and cans of food with several other Red Cross volunteers. At first he thought they might be missionaries or perhaps government officials and paid them little attention until one called out his name above the jumbled voices of the exhausted men, women, and crying children pushing and shoving in the heat and dust. "Burton! Burton Blake!" They closed in on him as though anticipating he might bolt and run.

"Who are you? How do you know my name?"

"We're from your father's company."

"What? Can't you see I'm busy? I can't talk to you." The intrusion of the two company men and the mention of his father set Burton back.

He quickly thrust bundles of blankets and clothing into the waiting arms of a man wearing a bloodied bandage across half his bald head and over his left eye. The man's place was immediately taken by a mother, a migrant from Zimbabwe, carrying a malnourished dark wide-eyed infant in a torn cloth sling. The woman's cut and bruised bare feet trembled. Dried mud stained her yellow-faded sarong. Her soiled plum dyed caftan tilted askew as though an external symbol of her life out of balance.

Burton turned away and busied himself taking boxes handed down from a stake-bed truck by another volunteer.

Battered and beaten and driven from their homes, thousands of displaced foreigners were pouring into Johannesburg from surrounding provinces and townships. They brought news that many had been killed and many more injured in their escape from Zimbabwe.

"You're getting in my way," Burton shouted and shoved the men aside thrusting a large box onto a long line of serving tables.

"You want some help?"

"Sure, make yourselves useful."

The two men stepped over to the truck and quickly hefted one box after another, allowing Burton to concentrate on distributing their contents to the indigent and needy victims.

The slightly taller of the two, the one with the lean jaw and shaved head, spoke as they worked.

"Your father's attorney sent us to find you and bring you back."

"Why? I'm not going back, not for anything."

"Your father is dead."

Burton paused. "When did he die?"

"One week ago. He had a massive stroke."

"I haven't had anything to do with him in years."

"We're not here about that. There's other business his attorney needs to discuss with you. Has to do with your father's will. That's all we were told. That's all we know. But we do have orders to escort you safely home."

"Orders? From whom? And if I won't go?"

"Your mother has asked you to return."

"I don't believe that. My mother has had nothing to do with my father for twenty years."

"She said there's something about the will you need to know."

"You talked to her?"

"No but your father's attorney did. She agreed that you should come back."

"That doesn't sound like my mother. And she wouldn't ask you to be her messenger."

The spokesman reached into his inside coat pocket and pulled out a sealed envelope. "Here," he handed him the letter. "This is from her."

Burton recognized her perfect penmanship of his name on the front of the envelope. He carefully opened the seal and removed the single handwritten page. Her brief message requested that now that his father had died, would he please return home and help her take care of some legal business. It was signed love, Mom, and her married name, Dorothy Linden, by her second marriage to the man who had become Burton's stepfather when he was eleven years old.

He folded the letter into the envelope and stuck it in his hip pocket.

"Well?"

"I have work to finish here. When I'm done, we'll talk more about this." He continued to hand out clothes and blankets. The days were hot, but the nights were cold.

"Okay, we'll wait for you. You won't just walk out on us."

"By all rights, I should. But since my mother asked me, I'll cooperate. I'll at least talk to you. But I don't promise anything. If this letter really isn't from her, then no. You'll never find me again. I'll make sure of that."

"We were there when your father's attorney watched her sign it. It's from her. Our SUV is parked just the other side of the last row of tents. It's a black Lincoln Navigator."

"I'll find it."

"My name is George and this is Nikos."

Burton ignored his extended hand and furiously pulled more garments from the boxes. George cocked his head at Nikos and they moved out into the surging crowd of unwashed closely packed bodies that, despite the size and strength of the two men, barely let them pass.

Agonizing memories of his mother's mental suffering emerged from Burton's subconscious. He had been ten years old the day his mother packed their bags and rushed him and his younger brother and sister out of their father's mansion never to return. His father had been traveling on business and didn't realize they were gone until one week later. To deter him from following or attempting to track them down, Dorothy had not left any written message except to say she and her children were no longer part of his life. Her attorney would contact his.

Except occasionally in the news media, Burton had never seen nor heard from his father since. What he remembered most was the fishing trip to Alaska and the bear.

By nightfall, the numbers of refugees arriving and seeking aid had not abated. During emergencies, most volunteers, including Burton, worked fourteen hour days. He forged his way along the serving tables in search of his group leader, Abena Ekwensi, a Gauteng Province woman.

She had been the driver of the Red Cross ton-and-a-half truck that had stopped to give the tall slender young man a ride when he was hitchhiking along the highway to Johannesburg. The passenger and center seats were occupied by an older gray-haired African man and a child between them. A mix of seven volunteers, men and women, rode in the rear seated on wooden crates on the flatbed.

Abena shouted to him in Afrikaans.

Burton shrugged and shook his head that he didn't understand. "English," he said. "I'm an American."

"There's plenty of room in the back," she shouted in English. "Jump in."

Not understanding their language, he listened to their rhythmic voices discussing what he assumed were events of the day. During his travels, he had witnessed poverty and suffering of people in third world conditions in many countries. In Johannesburg, he discovered an opportunity to give something of himself.

Abena dropped him near a hostel. He thanked her and asked how he could get in touch with her. She gave him her business card.

After checking into the hostel and securing his scuffed back pack with the clerk, he went out and roamed the adjacent streets, taking in the sights and sounds and smells of Indian bazaars, fruit sellers, hawking street vendors, and African medicine shops in the troughs of towering skyscrapers and glistening blue glass office buildings reflecting mirrored clouds and fractured sunlight.

The next morning, by asking directions, he found the location of the South African American Red Cross Society and asked to speak with Abena Ekwensi.

She came down from her office to the lobby to meet him and suggested they go to a café for coffee. She wore western style clothing, a cotton shirt, green nylon windbreaker, faded jeans, and Nike tennis shoes. Black curls sprung from her head like tightly wound springs of energy. No makeup adorned her smiling slightly pudgy face, only a trail of freckles. Her brown eyes glistened with good will.

As they negotiated the bustling downtown traffic, business people, and shoppers who vied for space on the sidewalks, she commented, "I'm sure this is not the Africa you've envisioned and heard about. Johannesburg is not much different than Los Angeles, California. I have been there and seen that place for myself. We have the same kind of urban sprawl. Joburg goes on for miles in every direction.

"Big cities have changed the culture of my country. We still have the rural villages and hunting and gathering and agriculture, but as you can see, we are walking through a modern landscape. By the way, I majored in cultural anthropology at the University of South Africa. So what is happening all around us is of great interest to me and has a bearing on what we do at the Red Cross Society."

"That's what I want to talk to you about. I'd like to learn more about what you do."

She suddenly swerved and guided him by the arm into a small side street café. "Doesn't look like much, but Nikiru brews the best coffee and makes the sweetest cakes and pastries."

She exchanged greetings with the proprietress, Nikiru, a thin African woman wearing a traditional orange and black batik dress and with her long brunette hair swept back into a French twist. When Abena and Burton were seated at one of ten occupied tables, she came over to take their order. Amid the rising aroma of toasted coffee beans and fresh bakery, Abena told him of the transition that was occurring in South Africa and her role in providing emergency relief.

"Urbanization has changed our way of life. The rearing and development of a child used to be a shared responsibility of the village. We used to say a child has many mothers and develops his or her values from the extended family. It is not so anymore. People come to the city to find jobs. Children do not receive the care they once had. Their parents cannot afford to live in good houses in nice places. You saw all those mothers with their babies begging on the street. There are thousands of people here and work is often just not available. Family planning is not well received. Therefore, you see so much poverty and hunger. Perhaps you have heard of Soweto." She referred to the extensive slum south of the city. He nodded.

"Many of the poorest in Johannesburg live in Soweto. Conditions have improved, slowly. But many Roads are unpaved, and there was a time residents had to share one water tap between four houses. Soweto was originally created as a dormitory town for Black Africans who worked as domestics and servants in the homes of whites or in the mines and factories. To this day, the food supply cannot meet the demand for the poor. The Red Cross tries, but it is never enough. Children drop out of school at an early age to work and help support their families. Boys join gangs and girls marry young or become prostitutes for higher earnings. They have unwanted teen pregnancies and abortions. The number of abandoned babies and infants and child abuse and neglect is on the rise, and of course, the horror of aids. We do what we can, but it is never enough."

Burton had great respect for this woman whose drive to give to others reminded him of his mother, an elementary school teacher. Abena spoke of her family and her childhood growing up in Capetown. She was the third born of eight children, four girls and four boys of mixed ages. All were adults now and successful in their chosen occupations.

At the refugee site, Burton watched Abena consoling a middle-aged woman distraught over the loss of her home and the killing of her husband who had fought their gang of attackers. He waited until she had finished listening to the woman's story and asked another volunteer to accompany her to a food kitchen line. She turned to him. "Hard work today. So much suffering. So many people."

He nodded in agreement. "I apologize," he said. "I have to leave, but I don't want to. Those two men you saw me talking to came here to tell me there's been a death in my family, my father. I have to return to the States."

"I am so sorry, my friend. It is a sad thing to lose a loved one."

Her hand reached out and gently cradled his tanned smooth young face. "There is always love lost, especially in hate." She brushed back an errant lock of his long blonde hair that insisted on rakishly residing over his left eye. "You came here on a journey. Now that journey continues. I hope you find what you are seeking."

"I already have. It's right here."

"You are welcome back to Joburg any time. I hope to see you again."

"I hope to see you. I'll do my best to come back."

"Farewell. Travel safely. God be with you."

"God be with you."

He quickly turned away to hide the unexpected tears that rimmed his gray-flecked brown eyes. He shouldered through the throng of refugees that congested the midway of the one-hundred communal tents erected to house them and farther along, a row of fifty maximized outdoor toilets that over one thousand native people had to share.

Doctors Without Borders had set up a field hospital and were systematically addressing the medical needs of a long line of sick and injured patients. Municipal healthcare workers and local church volunteers circulated among the stumbling crowd to assist the South African Red Cross Society employees and volunteers by directing people to cooking and food areas, trauma counseling, and other emergency relief services.

Unable to hear the conversation of the two men, Burton maneuvered through the crowd and approached the SUV.

"He looks a lot like his old man," said Nikos.

"Don't let him hear you say that," George muttered. "The attorney told us the son hates his father. We're not supposed to say anything more than he died."

"I'm getting hungry," said Nikos. "We've been waiting a long time."

"We'll eat once we're on the plane. We can have a few drinks then too without any problems."

"I can use a few drinks. It's going to be hard guarding someone who doesn't want to be looked after. At least he seems pretty tough. That helps."

"He's been traveling alone out in the world for three years. He probably is tough. He's also smart. College degree and all that."

"I don't have a college degree and I'm smart."

"You're a trained fighter and you're street smart, Nikos. There's a big difference."

"I feel like we're protecting our little brother."

"He's that and more. He's our meal ticket. Anything happens to him, you know what happens to us." George left the thought unfinished.

Nikos touched the bulge of a handgun snugged into a holster under the left lapel of his suitcoat as a reminder.

"He's here." George stepped out of the SUV and held the passenger door open for Burton as he approached the vehicle.

"So, where are you taking me?"

"Airport. There's a plane waiting."

"Would you swing by the hostel where I'm staying. I want to pick up some personal belongings."

"Of course, Mr. Blake."

Burton hesitated getting into the car and stared at him. "What is this Mister Blake stuff?"

"It's a sign of respect, sir. We work for you."

"I don't mean to put you out of a job, but you don't work for me. I never hired you."

"Someone important high up in the company did."

"Who would that be?"

"Your father's attorney."

"I wouldn't know anything about him."

"When we get to Chicago, he'll be the first person you meet."

Judging by their bull necks and protruding pectoral muscles, Burton could tell his two escorts were body builders. The main physical difference was the heavy jowls of the driver, Nikos, and his partner's testosterone lean jaw shadowed with a day's growth of dark beard. Otherwise, they were cut from the same mold of virility.

After repacking a few loose items at the hostel, Burton informed the male clerk he was leaving. Dispelling second thoughts of escaping through the back door of the hostel when he saw George waiting in the lobby, he reluctantly rejoined his guardians for the race to the airport.

With Burton securely in the vehicle, Nikos outmaneuvered the local traffic to arrive at OR Tambo Airport in one hour. They drove to a secure private hangar. As Burton stepped out of the SUV, he looked with uncertainty at the long white glossy Lear Jet 85 with its descended steps inviting him to enter.

"We're flying in that?"

"We're flying in that. Your father owned six of these babies and a 737."

Burton shook his head and resisted approaching the aircraft.

George and Nikos followed and crowded him close behind. He could not back out. The pilot and co-pilot greeted him as he stepped into the elegantly appointed cabin.

"Mr. Blake," the distinguished middle-aged man with precisely trimmed gray hair extended his hand, "I'm Jay Patton, your pilot, and this is my co-pilot, Marty Lang."

"It's a pleasure to meet you, sir." Marty, the slightly younger man with a clipped dark mustache offered an enthusiastic smile of respect. Both men wore black and gold striped epaulets on their white uniform shirts. Their dark blue trousers were pressed to a sharp crease and barely touched the tops of their black shoes polished to a high shine.

Expected to respond to their courtesy, Burton shook their hands.

"You're welcome to have any seat. The galley is fully stocked and the two gentlemen who accompanied you here will see to your needs," he referred to George and Nikos waiting halfway up the steps behind Burton.

Burton caught a glimpse of the avionics suite with multiple digital displays behind the pilots. He settled into the first of the off-white leather reclining club seats.

"As soon as we take off, I'll announce the flight plan," said Jay, "Please make yourself comfortable."

Burton nodded. "Thank you."

"Have you ever flown in a Lear before?"

"No."

"It's a great experience. I'm sure you'll enjoy it."

Burton gave a noncommittal nod.

The two Pratt & Whitney turbofan engines turned on with a smooth steady rising whine.

"Please fasten your seat belts, the captain's crisp voice sounded clearly over the intercom."

The Lear taxied out of the hangar and moved into the queue waiting take-off instructions from the control tower. Five minutes later, it catapulted into the evening sky, climbed rapidly to thirty-thousand feet and headed north.

Looking out his passenger window at the western shoreline of the massive African continent, Burton promised himself he would return. He stared at the encroaching endless night and clouds laced with heat lightning through which the flying missile passed at great speed and experienced the sensation that he was hurtling through some interplanetary gateway to a distant unknown destination.

Chapter 19

The Obituary

While George and Nikos enjoyed the entertainment center and made frequent trips to the galley for wine and cocktails, Burton drank only water, ate a microwaved gourmet chicken dinner and a chocolate fudge cake dessert, then drifted off to sleep until they landed in London six hours later to refuel.

Refreshed from his long nap, Burton drowned out the snores of George and Nikos by wearing a headset and watched three current movies during the flight over the Atlantic. He hadn't seen a Hollywood movie for the past three years. The surreal violence, repetitious car crashes and gun battles in the first disturbed him. He selected comedies for the next two. He nodded off again between New York and Chicago O'Hare International Airport. George gently touched his shoulder to wake him. Burton's eyes snapped open in bewilderment.

"You're home," said George. "Time to go."

Burton yawned, rubbed his eyes, then returned his seat from a reclining to an upright position. Yellow flashing airport lights festooned the tarmac. He unfastened his seat belt and stood up stretching in the aisle. The pilot opened the door, admitting a rush of warm humid air from the Mid-west night.

"It was a long flight. Hope you were comfortable and slept well," he said.

With rising anxiety at not knowing what was about to happen to him, Burton thanked both pilots and went down the steps.

Standing next to a white limousine, a slightly overweight man of about sixty years waved and came forward to greet him. "Burton,

Burton, it's good to finally meet you." He extended his thick right hand. "I'm Alan Erdman, your father's personal attorney and general counsel for the corporation." He smiled. "You do resemble him, only at a much younger age. I started working with your dad thirty years ago. How was the flight?"

"Comfortable, but I don't want to make another one any time soon."

"Not to worry. You have a full agenda ahead of you here. Lots to do."

"I'm here only because of my mother. She sent a letter."

"I know. She told me you wouldn't come unless she asked."

They were walking to the limousine where a Black chauffeur held the passenger door open, waiting for them.

"We can talk a little on the way to the hotel. After you." Alan stood aside and gestured for Burton to enter the vehicle ahead of him. He raised his hand to George and Nikos walking quickly around to a black Cadillac SUV parked to the side and rear of the limousine.

Alan waited until they were pulling away from the terminal before continuing. "Your father's death came as a shock to many people. He was out pheasant hunting on his estate when he died of a massive cerebral hemorrhage. I know you haven't had any contact with him since you and your mother left when you were ten years old. I don't know what she has told you, but there is a great deal you don't know about him. It's my job to fill in that gap to whatever extent I can."

"I don't need to hear anything more about him than I already know." Burton avoided direct eye contact with the lawyer, who sipped from a half-empty glass of Jack Daniels black label. A deep tan from many hours spent on the golf links accentuated the premature aging of his skin, including liver spots on the balding area of his receding silver-gray hairline. A small sunken scar called attention to his protuberant nose where a spot of skin cancer had been removed five years ago.

"Like one of these? It's thirty-year-old bourbon."

"No thanks."

"Your father's funeral is arranged for next Sunday, seven days from now. He wanted you to read his obituary before it's released to the press." He handed Burton two double-spaced printed pages.

"What do I care about his obituary?"

"Once you read what's there, you'll understand."

As he proceeded to follow the words, Burton became visibly agitated. "You can't publish this. Who wrote this? *These are all lies. That was not the man at all.*"

"He wrote it himself, a year before he died. He had become a changed man from the time you knew him."

"Because of who he was, the media will be all over this. Everyone will know that these are lies."

"He wants you to create a legacy for him. He wants you to carry on his business and to make what you're reading there into truth."

"That's crazy. That's impossible."

"It's done all the time. You can rewrite his history and frame his life accordingly. You can bring out things about him that were never revealed and were previously unknown. You're good with words. Even if you have to make them up."

"I'll have nothing to do with this."

"You are his primary heir, Burton. Your task is a condition of his will. I'll show it to you at the office tomorrow morning so you can read it for yourself."

"He should have named someone else. He has children by a second marriage and there's my brother and sister, and what about my mother? I don't even want his money."

"He knew that. That's why he gave you the majority of his personal assets, nearly everything. He knew you are ethical and honest and would not have some hidden agenda for the disposition of his wealth which is now yours."

"Does that mean his second children aren't ethical and honest?"

"There are issues with them and they don't need the money. They're subsidized by their mother. She's a billionaire."

"Well, let me tell you there are issues with me. I don't need his money and I don't want it. I don't want the responsibility for its stewardship."

"Stewardship is not the issue. You inherited his corporation. He expects you to run it."

"I don't know anything about running a corporation and he doesn't have any expectations. He's dead."

"His expectations are stated in the will."

"That sounds like him. I suppose he's trying to force me to live like him, to become like him. I don't really hate him but I won't do it. I don't need his twenty billion dollars to live the way I do."

"Thirty billion. Legally, you don't have a choice."

"There's always a choice."

"Other than you physically resembling one other, you're not at all like your father. Elias and I were close friends. He knew the kind of person you are. Actually, he was always interested in what you were doing."

"How would he know what I was doing?"

"Not in detail. About being a Rhodes Scholar. He relied on business contacts in countries you visited and the work you were doing to help them. He even made anonymous charitable donations in support of what you were doing."

"He spied on me?"

"No, no, nothing like that. Donations were designated specifically to agricultural and infrastructure projects.

"His name was never mentioned."

"He wanted to remain anonymous."

Burton shook his head. "If what you're telling me is true. . ."

"It's true."

"I'm sorry he didn't contact me."

"That's the way he wanted it."

"I feel really strange about this, about coming back here after he's gone. He died of a stroke?"

Alan nodded.

"I would have at least liked to say goodbye."

"Bringing you back is his way of saying goodbye to you. He considered you as his redemption.

"For what?"

"Not being the father he intended."

Burton remained silent.

"There are others more qualified, but what I'm telling you is why he wanted you at the head of the company. We can talk more tomorrow."

They continued the ride in silence. From time to time, Alan stole a sidewise glance at the young man.

 As they drove into the downtown Chicago financial district, Alan resumed the conversation. "We have a meeting to introduce you to the board tomorrow morning at 9:00."

Burton noticed the Ritz Carlton sign as the limousine pulled up to the entrance. "Why are we stopping here?"

"You have an open reservation to stay here for a while until you make other more permanent living arrangements."

"Are your two goons going to follow me everywhere?"

"They are your bodyguards. They're for your protection. Once the news of your father's passing hits the media, you could become a target."

"A target? Because I inherit a fortune, someone wants to kill me or hold me for ransom?"

"We don't know that. It's just a precaution. Your father made many enemies over the years."

"That's not surprising."

"The concierge is waiting for you. Just walk in and give him your name."

The elegant statuary, crystal chandeliers, and tastefully opulent décor alienated him. Wearing jeans, a long sleeve faded denim shirt, bush jacket, and hiking boots, he stood out from the upscale dressed businessmen and women lounging on stuffed leather chairs and divans among enormous potted green plants and coming and going with important strides across the spacious theatrical lobby.

He considered waiting until the limousine pulled away, then leaving the hotel to find common lodging, but the concierge was already approaching him and calling his name. Burton guessed that Alan Erdman had alerted him by cell phone.

"Mr. Blake, welcome to the Ritz Carleton. It's our pleasure to serve you." The concierge motioned to the bell captain standing near the entrance to take Burton's pack, but Burton shook his head. "Thanks, I can handle it."

The bell captain bowed slightly and backed away.

"We have you in the penthouse suite on the uppermost floor. You have a panoramic view of the city lights and Lake Michigan. Lars will take you there. Is there anything you need or anything we can immediately provide you?"

"No, it's been a long flight. I'd just like to go to the room."

"Very good, sir. Should you need anything, I'm only a phone call away." The concierge nodded at Lars.

"Please come with me," the compact athletic Swede gestured toward the block of elevators.

"If you'll just give me my key card and the room number, I'm sure I can find it."

"Of course," Lars handed him a folder containing the electronic card. "Just take the elevator to the top floor."

"Thank you."

Burton left the two men standing there looking after his departing figure. They quickly returned to their stations as other more traditional and appreciative guests came through the front entrance.

When he was in his suite, he placed a call to his mother to let her know he had arrived. "I'm here only because of your letter," he said. He did not mention his conversation with Alan Erdman. "Tomorrow, I'll find out what the urgency is about. How are you and the girls?"

"We're all fine. When will we get to see you?"

"From the looks of things, probably not 'til after the funeral. I don't imagine you plan to be there."

"Not for the ceremony." She paused. "Perhaps you and I could visit his grave at some other time. Where are you staying?"

"The Ritz Carlton, downtown Chicago. Not my choice."

"Sounds like you've been thrown into the pool."

"Something like that. Cesspool maybe."

"It's so wonderful to hear your voice. We look forward to hearing about your travels. Your room is pretty much as you left it. When you come, will you stay the night or just for dinner?"

"I'll stay the night. Have to get reoriented."

"I'm glad, Burton. We love you. We all love you."

"I love you too."

"Make the best of it. I'm sure you can."

"We'll see. Goodnight, Mom."

"Goodnight, Dear. Goodnight. Welcome back home."

Chapter 20

The Team

At seven the next morning, the Ritz Carlton room service called to take Burton's order for breakfast. He scanned the printed leather bound menu on the desk and decided on a ham and cheese omelet, corn beef hash, wheat toast, juice, and coffee.

At eight o'clock, a tailor knocked on his door and explained he had been requested to take Burton's measurements for his suits, dress shirts, and to get his shoe size. Burton turned him away. "Thank you, but I didn't order any suits or anything else."

"I believe the order was placed by a gentleman from your company, a Mr. Erdman."

"Oh, yes, I see. I'll speak with Mr. Erdman. I'm not in need of a suit."

"Very sorry to inconvenience you, sir. Should you change your mind, my extension is listed in the service book in your room." The short squat dark-haired tailor bowed slightly and returned to the elevator down the hall.

At eight-thirty, followed at a respectful distance by George and Nikos, Burton walked the eight city blocks from the hotel to the Blake Corporation building on Michigan Avenue. He entered the forty-story high rise through the revolving glass doors and crossed the polished black marble threshold to the security desk.

From that moment on, his life would never be the same.

"Welcome to the team."

"It's great to have you on board."

"We look forward to working with you."

"Our condolences on the passing of your father."

"He was a great leader. A great man."

The hollow greetings and accolades rang in Burton's head long after the introductions, over-extended smiles that showed too much teeth, firm handshakes and tight-lipped feral grimaces intended to pass for friendly grins. There were fifteen of them, a mix of board members and senior management representing the eight divisions of Blake Industries, the major subsidiary of the parent company, Blake Corporation.

Burton detected an unspoken wariness and resentment at who he was and, given his young age and inherited status, the practiced repression of a latent shared lethal impulse. These men ranging in age from forty-five to seventy and representing a variety of personalities and lifestyles from thin and insecure to athletic hard bodies to corpulent epicurean indulgence looked him over as though sizing him up for their next meal.

Alan Erdman sat next to Burton and facilitated the introductions from the head of the massive polished teakwood conference table that could easily accommodate up to twenty-five participants at a given meeting with an additional twenty more black leather chairs aligning two recessed panel walls.

Two women were in the room.

The attendees had helped themselves to coffee, juice, fresh fruit, pastries, lox, bagels and three flavors of cream cheese from a serving table at the rear prior to Burton's arrival. Alan inquired if he cared for anything, to which Burton shook his head.

"Gentlemen," said Alan, "there are many names and faces here for our new president and CEO to remember. So if you will briefly introduce yourselves and your positions in the company, I will bring Burton around to your individual offices throughout the day to familiarize him with working details of your divisions. Lunch will be served in the corporate dining room at noon. You will have an opportunity to become further acquainted. Lawrence, as Corporate Vice President, your company overview will be next on the agenda, after which Mr. Blake will meet with the human resources manager."

Burton observed and listened attentively as each senior officer stated his name and job title. The six additional board members came from banks, a law firm, (the two women were attorneys), and an investment firm outside the company. He had never been interested in the business world and the vocabulary they used sounded like jargon about which he had only a limited knowledge from occasional news media comments he had chanced to hear and to which he did not relate nor understand. He silently acknowledged that he was clearly out of his element and considered the potential downside of openly expressing his deficiency and showing weakness.

He wondered how much they actually knew of his private life, especially the recent few years following his graduation from college. Maybe Erdman had exercised discretion and not revealed his past, especially his estrangement from his father. Burton couldn't yet read Alan Erdman, whether he was a sympathetic ally, or might be using him to further some hidden or unknown corporate agenda. Just being in the company of these men elicited an impulse of suspicion and paranoia. He did not know their values, their culture. He was an outsider thrust into their midst. Discovering and learning about his father could be accomplished only through working with them. These circumstances, then, were the unexpected reality of the personal journey Abena Ekwensi had mentioned when he said goodbye to her in Africa.

The room emptied quickly at the adjournment with the exception of Lawrence Harden, who fiddled with the laptop computer hardwired for presentations on a six by four foot flat screen that silently descended against the back wall. With his trim gray crew cut, taut facial muscles, and tall well-conditioned body for a man of sixty-three, Lawrence reminded Burton of an aggressive retired military officer, relaxed and in charge.

"Gentlemen," said Alan, "since I'm quite familiar with the information, I'm going to leave you together and come back in about an hour. You both comfortable with that?"

"Of course," said Lawrence. "We'll take up any questions of a legal nature with you when you return."

Burton nodded.

"Oh, Burton, I'll arrange for a tailor to come in and measure you for some suits this afternoon."

"Don't bother. I don't wear suits. A tailor was at the hotel."

"I know. He called me. You're the company president. You can change the dress code if you want. How about at least one for your dad's funeral?"

Burton nodded.

Alan shrugged and grabbed a remaining pastry as he left the room.

The digitized logo of the Blake Corporation appeared on the opening slide followed by a dynamic four color organization chart and a pictorial review of the divisions and world-wide scope of its operations. Lawrence explained the structure of the company with a sonorous narration.

"The Blake Corporation is the parent company with a number of diversified divisions under Blake Industries. Elias Blake formed the company in 1970 with private investment capital."

Burton studied the photograph taken of his father forty years ago. The physical resemblance to himself was startling. They could be mistaken for brothers.

Lawrence noticed Burton's interest in the photo. "That was ten years before I met Elias and joined the company. He was a pioneer in chemical engineering."

"I never knew much about him as a businessman. He and my mother were divorced when I was ten years old."

"He was my mentor when I came out of college. We were good friends. I'm going to miss him. He did a great job of building this company and making it what it is today."

Lawrence moved on to the next slide, a photographic collage of Blake Industries facilities and installations visually establishing their identity in the petroleum and power and coal and energy industries, including bio-fuel sourced by several hundred thousand acres of corn-growing farms. Labyrinthine branches extended into plastics and paper and forest products manufacturing in addition to metal fasteners, forming, and fabrication for aerospace, defense, and automotive markets. The final division was a medical device company with offshore production operations in Puerto Rico.

"As you can see, you have inherited the responsibility for an extensive business empire. Elias left you a tremendous gift."

"I know the scope of all this seems overwhelming. But once you become familiar with the organization and its people, you'll discover you have all the support you need. We'll help you learn from the ground up. " His smile appeared genuine. "Not everyone has to have a degree in business. Your dad had a knack for it. I'll bet he passed at least some of that along to you."

"Not business but after I learn about the company, I might be able to contribute some new ideas?"

"That's how Blake Industries grew, Burt, out of new ideas. We're an innovative company."

Burton inwardly cringed at the all too soon familiar use of his name.

"The direction we're headed is working quite well. Strategically, technologically and every other way we're a fine tuned organization moving into the next century, your century. Once you start working with us, you'll discover we operate on the basis of consensus."

Burton grinned. "I can't imagine my father consented to anything but what he wanted."

"He was a visionary. We didn't question his leadership. We followed him and he gave us what we needed to meet the policies and financial goals he set for us. Here, look at this slide, our mission statement."

Burton silently read both paragraphs of the overriding policy statement.

Blake Industries is committed to meeting customer requirements through the application of quality management standards in support of corporate and division goals and objectives. Highly trained and fully qualified personnel are actively involved in our continual improvement program. Further, we pledge to maintain a safe and environmentally friendly workplace in recognition of our responsibilities to our employees, our customers and our communities.

This policy has been formulated by the President and executive management of the Blake Corporation. The policy is explained and discussed at the general orientation training given to all existing and new employees and is also posted in conspicuous locations throughout all divisions of the company.

"Sounds inspiring," said Burton.

"It's more than that. We have systems and procedures that make it happen and we hold our employees accountable."

"How many?"

"How many what?"

"Employees.

Lawrence scrolled up another slide. "In our various industries world-wide, we employ about fifty thousand people. Most are in the United States. In the interest of cost control and fair competitive pricing, we also subcontract certain production to offshore operations in China, Puerto Rico, and *mequiladoras* in Mexico. We're an ethnically diverse company, as well, as you'll see when you visit the sites."

The next slide appeared. "And unlike most companies in the current economy, we are profitable. Our earnings to date total thirty billion. Our projections are to reach forty billion in the next five years. We are actively traded in U.S. and foreign stock exchanges. We control our costs and," another slide materialized, "invest in product research and development."

"What's the Blake Foundation?" Burton referred to a line item on the graphic showing eighty million dollars.

"You might not have known your father was a philanthropist. His foundation is a charitable arm of the company donating to worthy causes that provide the company with tax write-offs. From the way your father described you before he died, I imagine you'll be interested in worthy causes."

Burton did not give any outward sign that he acknowledged the comment. He gave only polite attention to the remaining sequence of the presentation expanding on division operations, profit and loss totals for each, and financial goals and projections for the next five years."

"Thirty-billion dollar company – seems like you're doing okay."

"That's it." Lawrence turned off the computer projection and the screen went black "That's the nickel tour. Any other questions or comments?"

"Ah – no. I guess I have a meeting at human resources."

"Yep, let me call Alan." Lawrence raised his I-Phone to his left ear. "Mr. Erdman," he spoke with false gusto. "Our new man is ready." He signed off. "Alan is on his way. Care for a snack? There's plenty left."

"No, thank you." Burton stood and crossed the room to gaze out through the wide expanse of a panoramic window at a dozen small boats bobbing through the wind-driven chop on Lake Michigan.

"You sail or fish?" Lawrence's voice boomed at him from behind.

"I have in Southeast Asia. We used nets."

"Big game fishing was a passion for Elias. The company has a lodge up in Alaska, on the Kenai River. You might like to try the salmon and steelhead sometime. Beautiful country, wild, untouched. You like nature, being out in the woods?"

"I do. I was in Scouts when I was a boy."

"Your father was like that. Preferred outdoor clothes to suits, just like you. He was an outdoorsman, a sportsman. He hunted up there too, moose, bear, elk. You like to hunt?"

Burton shook his head. "No. I don't care for guns and killing animals."

"Well, when you see the trophies in his office, excuse me, in your office, you'll understand what I'm talking about. There are some big game pieces from Africa too. I understand that's where George and Nikos found you, in South Africa."

"They did."

"What were you doing down there?"

"Working as a volunteer for the Red Cross."

"No kidding. You're a good guy, Burt."

"Yeah, I try to be."

"You're one of us.

Burton remained with his back toward Lawrence. "I'm not really one of you. We're a generation apart. I know the purpose of a corporation is to make money. That's not my background."

"What do you have against wealth, Burt? Everyone wants wealth. It's what we all work for, live for."

"Personally, I have nothing against wealth, just the means that my father and, apparently, all the rest of you use to acquire it."

"That's what economics is all about, son. It's called free market enterprise."

Burton turned to face him. "Along with free market enterprise goes social responsibility," he said calmly. "Making money is fine, but I'm also in the social responsibility camp."

"We're in business to make a profit for ourselves and our stockholders. The rest of the world is not our concern. We leave that to the politicians. I know you haven't been exposed to that kind of thinking and how a company like ours operates. But you will be. We'll guide you along. You're a college professor of some kind, aren't you?"

"I have a Master's Degree in English. No, I'm not a professor. I'm a freelance journalist."

"That makes you an academician, not a businessman."

Burton chuckled. "For which I'm truly grateful."

"What good does a degree in English do you?"

"To learn about life. Literature is a mirror of the human condition."

"Sounds academic to me. So what do you know about the human condition?"

"Probably more than you."

"How do you figure that?" Lawrence smirked.

"I've spent the past three years traveling, visiting other countries, seeing how other people, other cultures live."

"And now that your extended vacation is over, we're here to help you."

"Help me to do what? Become like my father? Not interested."

"That's a rash thing to say when you don't know what you're talking about. The fact is you're now among the wealthiest men in the country. You're among the elite, the one percent. You're rich."

"I don't need it and I don't really want it. The house you live in – how much is it worth?"

"Which one – I own five."

"Five houses. How much is the biggest?"

"Thirty million dollars."

"Thirty million. The people I know who I call my friends live in shacks made from cardboard, mud, and tin. The roof leaks when it rains. The water they have to drink is contaminated. They live in conditions of filth and disease."

"So, what difference does that make to you and me? We're not one of them. We're above them."

"I'm one of them. We share the planet. We're responsible for each other."

Lawrence's bemused expression further angered Burton. "How's that? That's an unusual position to take for a CEO."

"No, I'm just not being what you expect me to be."

"How do you presume to understand your father's business and ours?" asked Harden.

"Contrary to what you believe, everyone does not desire extreme wealth. They just want the bare necessities, food, water to drink that won't poison them, shelter, and police and soldiers that don't shoot them and rape their women and torture their children. There are other social values that either you're not aware of or don't care to acknowledge."

"You sound like a bleeding heart liberal. But what you are now is the president and CEO of an American corporation. You need to step up to that."

"What I am most certainly not is your kind of capitalist. And I'm not a socialist or a communist or some other political label. I'm a human being."

"We're all human, Burt. We're just as human as you are."

"There's a whole spectrum of what that means. So I suppose you are, at a different end."

"Ah, come off it, Burt. This is no way for us to get started. I was an idealistic young man once. I believed and said things like you're saying. But I grew up and accepted reality. You will too. You'll soon find we're right and we know we're right. We own the world, Burt, and, like it or not, you are one of us. We need to revisit this discussion at another time."

Burton wanted to escape the suffocating atmosphere of the conference room, the fish bowl view of the lake, the condescending smug expression on the face of the company vice president.

Alan entered the conference room. "You ready? Jim Eckdahl and his assistant are waiting for you."

Burton gave a curt nod to Lawrence, "Thank you for the presentation," and followed Alan out into the hall.

Lawrence's voice trailed after him. "Glad to oblige. I look forward to working with you." Lawrence raised the third finger of his right hand at the closed door.

A moment later, the Vice President of Power and Energy, Earl Fredricksen, entered and pulled the door shut. "So?"

"Actually, he sounds like Elias the year before he – died. I think he'll make us a good poster boy."

A low chuckle shuddered across Earl's unshaven jowls. "Doesn't care much for us, does he?"

"He's just a young upstart. Doesn't know yet the value of what his father's left him."

"We still have to do something about him."

"As long as he plays in the charitable foundation sandbox, he should be okay."

"For the rest of it, he only gets to know what we want him to."

"We can't be ham-fisted about this. We have ways to deal with him that are – civilized."

"Control the information and we control him."

"He's not stupid, Earl. He was a Rhodes Scholar. To qualify, he had to demonstrate he was a protector of the weak. In addition to being extremely intelligent scholastically and in literature, his moral focus had to be unquestionable. That's the material we have to work with."

"I know. He's a very intelligent liberal and, therefore, he can be dangerous to us." Earl swiped a hand front to back across the bald dome of his head. Until a year ago, he had flirted with the vanity of maintaining the thin tapered graying follicular patches above each ear, then decided it conflicted with the image of himself as a former college athlete. The image was further impacted by the steady downward migration during the past thirty years of his bulked up massive chest, shoulders, and biceps to his expanding mid-girth and a weight gain from two-hundred forty-five pounds to two-ninety.

At six foot five, he had been a defensive tackle and offensive lineman at Penn State on a full ride scholarship. A fondness for twenty year old Glenfiddich and Glenmourangie Scotch and expensive French and California wines (one thousand bottles stored in his wine cellar) along with a diet rich in red meat, cheeses, and carbohydrates had contributed to his pre-diabetic condition, which he rigorously attacked by having a treadmill installed in his office so he could walk five miles a day while conducting business and watching NFL games on a giant flat screen on the wall.

Following his physician's diagnosis and recommendations, he had requested his personal Chinese-American chef at home, Stephen Nong, to change his culinary regimen. He no longer ate red meat of any kind and only wild-caught fish, organic chicken, wheat and multi-grain pastas and brown rice and large servings of steamed vegetables. His beloved cakes, pastries, pies, and Hagen Das ice cream were traded in for fresh fruit desserts. As a consequence, he had begun to shed the excess pounds.

In addition, his socialite wife, Berniece, had expressed an interest in his physical remodification and renewed their fading sexual relationship. Having intercourse three times a month gave him a fresh outlook on life.

Earl stepped up to the challenge of modifying his life style while continuing to enjoy his pursuit of another benefit of extreme wealth, the breeding and racing of thoroughbreds. He owned a thousand acre farm in Kentucky where he flew down in his Lear twice a month to visit.

Stemming from his degree in electrical engineering, the twelve patents he had developed for Elias Blake had been recognized and rewarded with advancement from the Director of Engineering to Vice President of Power and Energy, a position he had held for ten years. Along with Lawrence Harden, he had been among the two most influential members of Elias Blake's senior management staff. With the passing of the old man and replacement by his liberal oriented son, they stood to have the most to lose.

Chapter 21

The Funeral

The appearance of a ruby-throated humming bird hovering and sampling nectar from the wreath of flowers draped over the heavy oak casket caught Burton's attention and diverted his thoughts from the attendant throng of businessmen and their wives dressed in black. Upon his arrival with Alan Erdman, they had stared at him as though he were a celebrity.

The rays of the Mid-west summer afternoon sun sliced through the intense green canopy of tall oaks and elms that forested the spacious cemetery gardens. Humidity steamed off the one hundred yard line of cars parked along the narrow road to the gravesite.

Burton steeled himself to endure Lawrence Harden's voice droning on and on with praises for the lifetime accomplishments of Elias Blake as a loving father and benevolent business leader and philanthropist.

Alan Erdman had decided not to pursue the reading of the eulogy by Burton and had delegated the task to Harden.

When he concluded, at a signal from Lawrence, a five piece Dixieland band seated nearby burst into a wailing rendition of *Just A Closer Walk With Thee* followed by the upbeat *When The Saints Go Marching In*. Lawrence reached under the speaker's lectern, brought out a bottle of Jack Daniels bourbon, and raised it high above his head to show the crowd. He opened the cap and proceeded to pour the caramel colored liquid over the length of the casket.

Burton had not bothered to search for and read the obituary in the Chicago Tribune, but others did, many others who had a vested interest in the aftermath of his death as he detected from several parting comments at the conclusion of the outdoor service.

"Sorry for your loss. I'm sure you'll live up to his legacy."

Burton assumed the public relations department had issued a press release to the media about the family survivors and his "taking the helm of Blake Industries."

"Carry the torch he handed you, young man, for him, for yourself and for the rest of us."

"So sorry for your loss. Will you be issuing a statement to the investors?"

"A little early for that," said Burton graciously. "Have to get my feet wet."

"You'll need waders. Your father was a great businessman."

"I'm sure I will. From all the people here, I guess he was. Thank you for coming." Burton inwardly cringed at his own words.

Elias Blake's obituary had prompted a business editorial and email backlash. The fallout had forced Lawrence to field calls from aggressive journalists until he published that a press conference would be announced for the following Wednesday. Accusations assailed him from stockholders immediately following the announcement of Elias Blake's death. Blake Industries stock had dropped by fifteen dollars a share. Lawrence said not to worry. The board had made a selection of Elias Blake's successor. Wall Street was just waiting to see who would replace Elias and regain a comfort level with the new leadership and operational consistency of the company.

The press conference would field questions and concerns of whether Burton would carry on the traditions and management style of his father. Lawrence explained that Elias Blake had built a strong management team that would continue to run the company and provide support and guidance to Burton while he learned the ropes.

Off in the distance, local police and Blake security guards kept television and news journalists away from the funeral site where the service was being conducted. The raised cameras and microphones jockeying for position resembled the shining tentacles of predatory insects seeking a way to the source of food. There had not been a church service, since Elias Blake had been an avowed atheist and afforded few opportunities for media access to the event of his burial.

Alan Erdman approached Burton to introduce Elias's widow, Alexis Blake, and her daughter Savannah, and son Richard.

One month after divorcing his first wife, Burton's mother Dorothy, Elias had married a Texas socialite and heiress to an oil fortune. Elias was fifteen years older than Alexis Andamiano Blake. Now 60, other than her high fashion couture and lustrous coiffed silver hair, there was little about Alexis Blake you could call delicate. A long leggy woman who had to work at concealing vestiges of physical awkwardness, she topped six foot three in her bare feet. Her social signature was a loud raucous laugh more fitting to a smoky red neck sports bar than genteel company. Her departure from a room left a hole of silence.

"Will you be attending the reception?" Alexis leaned in close and, to Burton's surprise, planted a light motherly kiss on his cheek.

"No, I'm sorry I won't be able to. I'm going to visit my family in Rockford. I haven't seen them for three years."

"Don't think badly of your father. He loved and admired you."

"So I've been told."

"When you return, perhaps you'll have dinner with us one evening." She wrinkled her narrow nose, slightly bent from an encounter with a volley ball forty-five years ago in a high school gym class. She could easily afford to have it straightened, but believed it gave her an air of distinction. "We have important matters to discuss." Her luscious brown oval eyes caressed him.

"There's nothing to discuss. If it's related to his will, you can take that up with his attorney."

"You don't know much about your father, do you?"

"I'm afraid not."

"I'm sure you will be interested in what I have to say. We were married for twenty-five years."

Burton shrugged as Alexis's son stepped up to him. Burton noticed the marked resemblance of Richard and his sister, Savannah, to their mother. They lived in the shadow of her elegance and influence. Both were blessed with the pristine beauty of youth, Richard, twenty-one, taller than his mother and favoring her beguiling brown eyes and former dark hair; Savannah, nineteen, tall and slender, a graceful counterpoint to her mother and blindingly blonde with an eternal cosmetic and natural tan. Both projected the fitness and confidence of athleticism from long hours at tennis, running, riding horses, sailing, and basking in the sun on hidden private beaches on Caribbean islands and Mediterranean shores. Both wore expressions of smug complacency typical of the privileged and elite that Burton had often encountered in countries plagued with cultural and economic disparity.

Richard's telegenic features loomed before him. "Congratulations on being handed the company. Even if I were in line for it, I wouldn't want it. As it is, I have the benefits without the responsibility." He laughed.

"Coincidentally, I feel the same way," said Burton, "only I have the responsibility and no interest in the benefits."

Richard moved aside to make room for his sister. "It's nice to meet you, Burton. For some reason, I thought you'd be older."

He gave her extended hand a firm gentle shake. "I'm beginning to feel older."

Alexis and her children aligned themselves next to Burton to accommodate what had grown into a reception line as friends, associates, and well-wishers passed by to express their condolences. Among them was a grinning young man who, despite his peach-colored mustache and goatee, looked more than vaguely familiar to Burton.

"Hi, Burt," he extended his hand. "Remember me? Jerry Olson. We were friends and neighbors back in Rockford."

"Hi, Jerry, of course I remember."

"Didn't know if you'd recognize me since I put on all this weight and grew this." He tugged at his beard.

"Looks good on you, Jerry. How have you been?"

"Great, doin' just great. I'm a stock trader. Do a lot of work with the Blake Corporation. Got to know your dad. A great guy. I'll miss him like the rest of these folks. I asked him about you. He told me you were out traveling around the world, having adventures, something like that. I went right in to investment banking as soon as I graduated. Worked for Morgan Stanley. After three years, I formed my own company, Olson Capital Investment. Listen, since you're back now and have taken over for your dad, maybe we could get together, get reacquainted. I'll send my email address and cell and office phone numbers to Darcy. I'm assuming she'll continue as your secretary, you lucky dog. If she wasn't already married, you know what I mean. Have you met her?"

"Darcy and I have met and, yes, she will continue as my secretary, and, yes, she's a looker, and a really bright person."

"Oh, I know she's smart. Wish I found someone like her."

"Tell you what, Jerry, people are lining up behind you here. I'll get in touch."

"Okay, Burt, great! It's so great to see you again. Too bad it's not under other circumstances. Your dad was a great man."

"So I'm told, repeatedly."

Jerry moved on with a wave and what Burton thought was a silly grin.

Burton began to sweat under his dark suit. He had debated with himself about wearing the suit and having his haircut at the hotel and had bowed to convention. He had decided he would have to use other means than clothing to express the differences between himself and his father. He also understood that his image would be a factor in dealing with the management team and board of directors of the Blake Corporation and Blake Industries.

Two days earlier upon Burton's arrival, Darcy Schumacher did not know what to make of the ruggedly handsome young man who entered her office unescorted and unannounced looking like he had just returned from a camping trip. She noticed he carried a folder containing documents handed out to new employees at orientations by the human resources department. Although he looked vaguely familiar, she knew she had never met him before.

She perched her red-framed glasses on her forehead. "May I help you, sir? Is there someone with you? You appear to be lost."

He looked around the vast space appointed with oil paintings of forest and meadow scenes displayed on the dark wood paneled walls and strategically placed live indoor green plants in large porcelain pots. "

"No, I was told this is where I'd find my office."

"Oh, my goodness," she rose abruptly from behind her desk and computer work station. "That explains the resemblance. You must be Elias's son." She came quickly out onto the thick pile grayish-white carpet to greet him. "I'm Darcy Schumacher, your father's, now your secretary." She extended her hand and bent her right knee with a slight curtsey.

"Burton. Nice to meet you, Darcy. You look pretty young." He guessed she was in her mid-thirties. "How long did you work for my father?"

"Only the last five years. I was the executive assistant to his actual secretary for six years, Juliana Smeets. She retired after thirty-eight years and I was promoted." Burton immediately liked her friendly elfin face and self-conscious grin that colored her cheeks and emerged as a sparkle in her hazel eyes. She seemed refreshingly out-of-place, almost a contradictory personality to other staff members he had met so far that morning. Her styled reddish-brown hair lay feathered on the back of her neck prompting him to want to reach out and stroke it. Her light blue-gray business suit did not conceal the bulge of her breasts and provocative symmetrical curve of her hips emphasized by a tight skirt.

Burton noticed photos on her desk of her clean-shaven bald husband and two beaming young boys, ten and twelve, and stopped letting his thoughts wander to her inviting sexuality. He envied her husband.

"Oh, by the way," she picked a note from her desk top and handed it to him. "There was a phone call from Robert Ostraich, a journalist with the Chicago Tribune. He said he would like to interview you and that he had critical information about Blake Industries and your father you might want to know. I told him you were not even in the company yet and why was he calling."

"Sounds like the PR department leaked something and he got wind of it. I'm not giving interviews. He probably knows more about the company than I do anyway, if he wants to give me information. There's supposed to be a press conference sometime after the funeral. He'll just have to be one of the herd. Have the receptionist forward any media calls to public relations."

She nodded. "I'll get right on it." She picked up the receiver from its flashing red light display panel. "Nobody told me you were coming in today."

"I don't think they knew until I arrived."

"Did HR give you a personal company cell phone?"

"Unfortunately, yes."

"I'll get the number from them. Is there another number where you can be reached – where you're staying."

"At the Ritz Carlton, downtown."

"Nice."

"I won't be there for long."

"Your father often stayed in a penthouse not far from here. That's available to you. In fact, you own it now.

"I'll probably be looking for a place in the suburbs. Living in the city isn't for me.

"Have you contacted an agency?"

"Not yet."

"I can get you listings on-line. My girlfriend's a real estate broker. Pekka Rasmussen. Actually, she's a mom too. We were college roommates, now lifetime friends."

"That will be helpful, after I return from visiting my family. I think I have someone I could call a lifetime friend, in South Africa."

"South Africa? Wow! I'd like to hear about that sometime. Is your family local?"

"No, Rockford."

"That's pretty local. Some countryside and farms in between."

"Where do you live?"

"Lincoln Park. It's a great place to raise kids."

"How's your commute?"

"Not bad. My husband drops our boys off at school and I get them on the way home."

"You have a nice looking family."

"Thank you. I'm proud of my man and boys."

"You should be. Okay if I go in?" Burton moved toward the closed wide oak door of his father's office.

"You don't need permission. It's yours." Darcy thrust open the door.

Burton stood just inside and stared with dismay at the twenty taxidermied heads of wild animals from a water buffalo, deer, elk, moose, big horn sheep, leopard, lion, wart hog, and antelope, to a snarling silvertip Alaskan grizzly standing full height in a far corner.

Darcy noticed his consternation. "If it's not to your liking, you can always redecorate," she laughed.

He smiled and shook his head. "I'll leave them. They're memories of my father, especially the bear. I'll tell you about it sometime."

Following the funeral, Burton returned to the Blake Corporation building garage and transferred to a 750 series glistening black BMW company car waiting for him. As he left the city, he was followed by George and Nikos in their Cadillac SUV on his drive to Rockford. He tried to ignore them in his rearview mirror, maintaining a steady five car lengths behind.

During his orientation with Fred Dolby, a former Federal agent who had worked as the Blake Corporation Director of Security for ten years, Dolby explained the program and the need for Burton to cooperate in every way for his own safety. "You are as important to us as the President of the United States is to the FBI," he said. "We will be looking after you twenty-four/seven."

Burton had to repress his rage at the involuntary loss of privacy. He felt like the company had put him on a leash, which, in fact, it had. Unknown to him, a tiny chip had been installed in his cell phone to track his movement and trace and monitor his calls and conversations by the security department via satellite GPS.

Although he would explain to his mother why the black SUV was parked outside her house, Burton would not invite them in and introduce them. He wondered if they had good bladder control.

The neighborhood of Burton's youth had expanded over the years into miles of multiple residential tracts of single family homes and condominiums interspersed with shopping malls that had displaced farms and the rural landscape of cornfields and dairy cattle browsing over green pastures he remembered as a boy.

He relied on the BMW's GPS navigation system to guide him through labyrinthine freeways and highways and surface streets that had not previously existed.   They served as a reminder of the rapid pace of population growth even in the American heartland compared to the crowded impoverished millions he had seen during his travels in foreign countries.

His mother never appeared to age. Only a slight transition from her sun-streaked brown layered 60's coif to a salt and pepper gray gave evidence to the recent years that had moved her with stubborn resistance and denial into her mid 60s. Her skin remained smooth and unwrinkled over a small straight nose and prominent high cheekbones that narrowed to a compressed mouth and narrow chin. With the exception of a few tiny creases at the outer corners of her warm, unyielding blue eyes, she showed little evidence of aging.

She yelped with delight upon opening the front door to discover her Burton standing there greeting her with, "Hi. Mom."   His smile broadened into a low chuckle, as she threw her sinewy arms around his neck and pressed kisses into his face.

"Burt, Burt, you're here. You're finally here. You didn't have to knock. You could have just walked in."

"I didn't want you to think I was an intruder."

"Oh, my gosh! You, an intruder?" She lead him by the hand as he closed the door behind him. "Come in. Come in. Let me look at you. You're so tall and handsome. My son. My son."

"Dad home?" He referred to his stepfather.

"He's out playing golf. We didn't know you would be arriving today or he'd be here. He should be home by four. He will be so delighted."

"Eugenia and Darren around?"

"Eugenia's at the university."

"How's she doing?"

"Wonderfully, wonderfully, finally. She's nearly through the second year of her Master's in psychology."

"Good for her. That's good news." Burton glanced across the living room at the George Steck console piano on which he had practiced for hours daily from the time he was seven. He had stopped playing when he went to college. Music was something he enjoyed. He had never had any intention of pursuing the field as a career.

"And what about Darren?"

"He'll be home from Afghanistan and out of the National Guard by the end of the year. He plans to finish classes and graduate next June in biochemistry and has started some on-line classes in pharmacy at Wisconsin U."

"I've thought about him often, worried about him."

"He's halfway through his second tour over there. All I care about and pray for is that he comes home alive and whole. He sends me emails. He and the others in his unit are close friends. He says they survive by looking out for each other."

"Darren and Genie are such high achievers. You and dad must be busting at the seams with pride."

"Oh, as soon as Darren comes home, we'll be on cloud nine, and now for you."

"Listen, I'm not a high achiever. I'm just a wanderer."

"Oh, don't say that. Look at what you've accomplished in third world countries. And now you're the president and CEO of a corporation."

"Not by choice, Mom, not by choice. This is like some sort of fantasy. I wouldn't be here if it weren't for your letter. You know that. I'd still be in Africa. I was planning to stay there."

"What's in Africa?"

"I didn't say much in my emails. I'll tell you about it when Tom gets home so I don't have to repeat myself."

"I always thought you wanted to right your father's wrongs."

"That's a strange thing for you to say, Mom. Are you sure you're not talking about yourself? Is that why you wanted me to come back? You left him thirty years ago. I never stopped thinking about him but I stopped caring about him. I didn't think you cared either. From the time I was ten years old and the incident with the bear, you put him behind us. I consider Tom my father, not Elias Blake. Why did you want me to come back? I was happy where I was. I'd found what I wanted."

"Right after Elias died, his widow came to see me. You never met her, Alexis Andamiano. She told me some things about Elias that convinced me you should come home and run the company."

"What things?"

"She said that about a year before he died, he started to change, became almost a different person. I don't have a vendetta with your father. Once I married Tom and we started a new life, I didn't give Elias a second thought."

"I still don't understand why you wanted me to come back."

"I read it in your emails. You were traveling the world searching for something you could do to benefit humanity. You had that goodness in you as a boy. You clearly implied and once even stated that when you wrote me from India. I didn't know what was in your father's will until his attorney brought it to me. I thought his giving you the company was pretty remarkable. I never imagined him doing that. In his own way, he must have cared about you. I thought this would be an opportunity for you. It would give you financial resources."

Burton grinned. "I don't need financial resources. I think you were just looking out for me. You wanted me to be successful like my brother and sister."

"You are successful, but in a different way, your own way. I've always wanted success for all of you. That's my role as your mother."

"There are a number of other roles wrapped up in that, but okay."

"You're not blaming me? You don't hate me for asking you to return?"

"Of course not. I'm here and I'm dealing with it and you're right. I do see some opportunities to do good things for others. My comment about benefiting humanity was overblown, probably a moment of passion, anger, an impulse that passed with rational scrutiny, acknowledging reality. I saw a lot of suffering on a massive scale that prompted a meaningless phrase."

"I don't think it's meaningless. All my children are meant for great things."

"With a reasonable perspective."

"You start with a vision, a goal, and you work to achieve it. I know. That's how I lived my life. You don't let anything stop you. When an opportunity presents itself, you seize it."

Burton laughed. "You sound like a motivational speaker."

"These are not empty words. Considering where I came from, I mean them. I believe in them. Elias and I were once alike in that regard, but he went off the deep end. He didn't have integrity. We're better than that as a family. You're better than that. You have integrity. You have always had it. You are everything of worth that he was not. I've heard it said that now later in his life, he underwent some sort of change. His attorney told me that Elias turning the company over to you was his way of making a statement."

Burton smiled at the small feisty woman whom he remembered traditionally wore a mother's uniform of slacks, a blouse, and flats and a subtle shade of lipstick, if any.

He glanced out the dining room window that overlooked the connecting back yards of the single story ranch style homes where he, his brother and sister, and neighbor children had played as young children after she had married Tom Linden in 1979.

Chapter 22

Intrusion

After an early breakfast with his mother and sister, Eugenia, Burton waved goodbye to them clustered on the front porch steps. Their image stayed with him as he began the drive back to Chicago with a constant reminder of what lay ahead by the black SUV hovering in his rearview mirror. He slowed to thirty miles per hour, hoping George and Nikos might pass him. They remained in a tailgating position. He increased his speed to ninety-five miles per hour on the toll freeway, but they stayed right with him. They flashed the SUV headlights twice as a signal to slow down or risk having the highway patrol spot him and pull him over. He returned to eighty and received another flash of the headlights.

He saw their presence as a spiritual manifestation of Elias Blake pursuing him from beyond the grave. All Burton had wanted to do as a child was to exist in a world of his own making, free from the orders and harsh demands that he perform to Elias's expectations. In his own way, Burton resembled his father and tried to wrest control of their relationship through subtle and not so subtle passive resistance and by ignoring him. Elias was not one to be ignored.

Darcy Schumacher leapt up from her desk and greeted him with a cheery, "Hello, Burt, welcome back," accompanied by a brief hug. "I have several messages waiting for you on your desk and I've screened your emails so only relevant ones pertaining to the business are in the que."

"Thank you for looking after all that."

"How was your visit with your Mom?"

"It was great to see her, catch up on family."

"Will you be wanting to talk with my real estate friend or are you planning to live at the hotel for a while longer?"

"I'll be glad to talk to her, probably sometime next week. I need a few days to get my feet on the ground here."

"There are a number of staff who are waiting to have some of your time."

"I'll work up a schedule."

"Let me know when you're ready."

Burton nodded and walked into his office. Standing full upright in a far corner, the grizzly confronted him. He went to his desk where Darcy had neatly arranged and left a small stack of handwritten messages under a silver paperweight artistically embossed with the letter E.

"He's back," Alan spoke tersely into his speaker phone to Lawrence and Earl in their separate offices. George called in when they arrived and security sent him right up. I checked with Darcy. He's in his office now going over messages. We'll give him fifteen minutes, then casually drop in on him, ask him if he wants to have a staff meeting and reunite with us."

"Shall we bring up any of the deals we've got pending?"

"Not at this time. Too much conflict and publicity going on. Burton is soft in those areas. He's likely to hear about it in the news anyway what with the campaigns."

"We need to get him busy," said Lawrence, "get him so swamped he doesn't know up from down. We have to reinforce for him the importance of keeping the status quo. Put him on a leash so we can pull him back if he goes off on a tangent."

"In good time," said Alan. "Remember, he just started a few days ago."

"It's too bad the old man had to die on us."

"Don't bring up Elias. We'll educate Burton to his father's way of thinking before the – ah - problem. In the meantime, we have him contained."

Burton looked up and rose from his chair at the entrance of Alan, Lawrence, and Earl, who clustered shoulder to shoulder in front of his massive oak desk.

"Welcome back, Burt," said Lawrence. "How was your visit with Mom?"

"Gentlemen." He shook hands from right to left as their arms stretched over the desk top. "The visit was nice. More than nice. We talked over old memories."

"Soon to be adding to your accomplishments," said Earl.

"We were wondering if you wanted to call a brief staff meeting," said Alan, "as a starting point. We can have the management group in the conference room in fifteen minutes."

"Not yet, not today. I have some messages here that require my response and I'd like to visit various other departments, talk with some of the people, basically get informally acquainted."

"Afterwards, I'll take you to lunch," said Alan. "We have a few legal matters to discuss and there's a local deli that makes an outstanding corn beef on rye, lean corn beef."

"Sounds good. Look me up here at eleven thirty. I imagine there's a big lunch crowd."

"That there is." Alan moved toward the door. "Gentlemen." Lawrence and Earl followed him out.

"Mr. Blake, excuse me for interrupting your lunch," Robert Ostraich extended his right hand.

Burton looked up at the tall angular man whose serious creased expression seemed magnified by large black-rim thick bifocals. His faded blue eyes appeared drained of their ability to focus from over-use. Thinning brown hair bespoke his age.

"I'm Robert Ostraich, syndicated journalist and business writer for the Tribune."

"You don't have to talk to him, Burt," said Alan, hastily swallowing a mouthful of his corn beef sandwich. "Mr. Ostraich, please, would you leave us alone. We'd like to enjoy our lunch."

"My apologies, Mr. Erdman, but I won't disturb your lunch."

Noticing the activity at Burt's and Alan's table, George and Nikos, slipped off their stools at the bar where they were eating sandwiches and moved quickly to either side of Ostraich to intervene.

"Your body guards are unnecessary, Erdman. Call them off. They lay a hand on me and you'll be in the evening news with an accompanying lawsuit."

Alan signaled them to back off, but they remained within reaching distance.

"Mr. Blake," he spoke to Burton, "I have been following your father's career for many years. He was an interesting and enigmatic man. I would like an opportunity to just talk with you about yourself, no story, no agenda, just a discussion."

"Don't listen to him, Burt. You don't have to talk to him. He's a news writer. All he wants is a story."

"I want to talk about business, what's happening in the world today."

"On those topics, I speak for Mr. Blake. I'm his attorney."

"This is not an investigation. Mr. Blake is the CEO. I'm sure he's able to speak for himself."

"You know damn well it's an investigation. That's what you do for a living."

"It's okay, Alan," Burton interrupted. "We'll talk. Not here, of course. I'll come and see you at your office."

"Anytime. When is it convenient for you?"

"Wednesday morning at ten o'clock."

"Thank you, Mr. Blake." He again shook hands. "I am grateful. I'll see you Wednesday at ten." Robert turned away and left the restaurant.

"Burt," said Alan, "you're making a mistake. Don't do this. You're going to open yourself up to lies and exploitation. Ostraich is a disreputable news hack. He's been trying to get dirt on the company for the past ten years, even if he has to invent it. He's not to be trusted, Burt. Don't contaminate your father's legacy by doing this."

"Contaminate? What do you mean by that?"

"There are people who want to bring you down. Ostraich is one of them."

"Only a handful of people even know me as the CEO, mostly investors."

"Don't kid yourself. All the Wall Street bankers and traders are watching and waiting to see what you're going to do with your father's company. You're untried and an unknown quantity. If they can profit by it, they'll find a way and you'll come under fire if you attempt to do anything radical so they can bet against you. It's called hedge funding."

"We're a corporation, not a casino."

"Everything our company does is based on risk and is subject to the volatility of the marketplace just like a casino makes its money because people are willing to bet and risk theirs. That's one of the reasons we own three banks that do business with offshore banks. The hedge fund traders are licking their lips in anticipation you'll do something wrong as a financial neophyte so they can make a killing. That's why you need to depend on your advisers. They are among the most skilled and knowledgeable and are dedicated to preserving, protecting, and expanding the corporation's and your financial assets."

"You don't think thirty billion dollars is enough?"

"That figure is just this point in time. It has to be maintained through astute strategic corporate and financial management practices or it can fall drastically. You hear every day in the news what is happening to the big banks."

"I've done some reading about rate manipulation and the unregulated risks they've taken."

"We aren't like that, Burt. The business of the Blake Corporation is conducted in a lawful, legal, and ethical manner. Your father would not have it any other way. Despite what you might see or hear in the news, he was an honest businessman."

"Isn't that why you brought me back here from Africa, to carry out the lies you wrote about him in his obituary? A lot of what he did wasn't honest and still isn't."

Alan's eyes crinkled with a shrewd grin. "Now, now, Burt. There's more than a grain of truth in what was said. But that's a good political position for you to take. In fact, you need to say that for the benefit of investors and the general public, or at least those components of the general public that are casting aspersions and making untrue accusations. That's why I encourage you not to subject yourself to an interview with Robert Ostraich. He's a media spokesperson. He's one of them who would like to find some way to take us down, even if he has to fabricate it."

"Don't journalists have to qualify their sources? They can't just print or say something libelous."

"These days, the media uses spin to twist lies into truth."

"Or truth into lies."

"We don't want to be caught in that trap. You don't want to be caught. That's why we've provided you with advisors in every facet of the business. We don't want anyone outside the company to mislead you and trip you up."

"And inside the company? You noticeably left that out."

"We screen, monitor, and eliminate any individual or group that seems so inclined by thought, word, or deed."

Burton sniffed. "You have a way to read people's thoughts?"

"We profile all Blake employees through extensive background checks, including political leanings and social habits and behaviors. If they don't meet our standards, we get rid of them. We fire them."

"You're saying you spy on them?"

"Background checks are a standard practice for any company. We don't want to hire felons, illegal immigrants, or terrorists. We want qualified people who are United States citizens. That's the purpose of the checks."

"It sounds like you go further, call it an invasion of privacy and violation of personal rights."

"You don't want people, especially the staff, and especially the likes of Ostraich to hear you saying things like that. We do not invade people's privacy or violate personal rights. Most of that kind of information is collateral damage, just a byproduct of any background check."

"But you use it to form opinions and make decisions about people."

"Only as necessary. As I said, anyone who works for Blake has to measure up to Blake's standards. They have to fit our culture."

"Does the culture allow for diversity and new ideas and differences of opinion?"

"Of course, new ideas are what made the company grow. Differences of opinion are encouraged. We're a conservative company. It's a big reason why we've been so successful."

"Do employees have a union?"

"We more than adequately provide for our employees' needs, not only in terms of good wages and substantial benefits, but training, educational, professional and career development for those who want it. In addition, we have an employee investment and bonus program.

Most employees buy shares of stock in the company. The former CEO, Lewis Murtagh, kept it privately held. As soon as he died, we went public within a few months of your father taking over. It helped us diversify and firm our market share position in new industries. You'll learn more about it once you spend time with our strategic planners."

"I noticed they're on my agenda. I have lots of people to talk to."

"And they're looking forward to meeting and working with you. You'll find they're really great loyal employees. Your dad insisted we hire only the best."

Burton nodded.

"Listen, Burt, despite my advice, I know you're going through with your meeting with Ostraich. I just ask that you be very prudent about what you tell him, especially since, at this point, you're just getting started and know very little about the company. I'd like to recommend you take one of our PR professionals along with you."

"The meeting is with me. A PR professional wasn't invited."

"As you wish, but if you don't know the facts about something, just tell Ostraich."

"I think the conversation will not be so much about the company, but about my father."

"Your father was the company and, until you stepped in, the company is your father. His wish is that you continue in his tradition."

"I'm not my father, but I'll do my best." Burton glanced at his watch. "I have an appointment with public relations in fifteen minutes."

"Reid Mumford?"

"Yes."

"About your speech?"

Burton nodded.

"You'll like Reid. He's a good man."

Burton's face twitched with a sardonic grin. "I take it Elias hired only good men."

Alan chuckled. "And women. How do you like your sandwich?"

"I'll become a regular for lunch."

Chapter 23

Dark Money

As soon as they returned to the office, Alan dialed Lawrence's extension.

"What's up?"

"Robert Ostraich waylaid us at lunch. He convinced Burt to meet and talk with him."

"Are you shittin' me?" Lawrence came up out of his chair. "How can you let him do that? Wait a minute. Earl needs to hear this." He dialed in Earl on his speaker phone. "Earl, we're on the line with Alan. You won't believe what he just told me. Burt is going to talk to Robert Ostraich. He's been here only one day and he's pulling this shit."

"I don't want to believe it, but it doesn't sound like I have a choice."

"He's the president and CEO," said Alan. "We know he's a maverick. That's one of the ways we can use him, to adjust the corporate image, but only the image."

"Not Ostraich, anyone but Ostraich. He's been mining us for dirt for the last two decades. Do you have any idea what kind of bullshit lies he's gonna tell our poster boy?"

"That's the whole idea. We want our boy to understand that lies are all Ostraich has to go on. Things he has made up and will be trying to get some form of corroboration from the son of Elias Blake."

"Burton doesn't know anything."

"That's right. So there's nothing he can tell Ostraich. Nothing critical will be said. Nothing is going to happen."

"I sure as hell hope you're right. But what if he tries to get Burton on his side."

"Burt has a lot to learn about what he has inherited, his responsibility. It's not going to be so easy for him to ignore that. We have to educate him."

"He's the President and CEO. If he has a mind of his own, that can be dangerous for the rest of us. Look what happened when Elias pulled away."

"Elias is no longer here. His son is in our hands for a reason. He doesn't understand yet that for business and economic consistency he has to go in the direction we advise him."

"And if he doesn't take our advice, we're doing the same thing to him we did to his father. He doesn't strike me as being compliant in that regard."

"That's the last time I want to hear you say any reference to what happened to Elias," said Alan. "We can't expect Burton to be compliant. Actually, we don't want him to be. We just want him to be himself. That way he doesn't have to pretend or be false about his beliefs and values. He doesn't have to put on a performance for the public and we'll continue to pull the puppet strings and run the company our way. We just have to control him and dilute any controversy that might arise. With Elias, it was the reverse, until last year. We had to restrain him from blundering too far, at least overtly and openly to come under public scrutiny. We're going to show the public and the investors a new side of Elias. Call it the bright side, his son."

Reid Mumford stepped quickly into his secretary's office as he heard her greet Burton by way of announcing his arrival.

"Good morning, Mr. Blake. Mr. Mumford is expecting you."

"Good morning, Mr. Blake," Reid Mumford's tan right hand and precisely manicured and polished finger nails slipped forward from the slender sleeve of his five thousand dollar gray suit coat. A Robins egg blue tie accented his lavender shirt and highlighted his smooth sculpted facial features freshly tanned from a weekend on a country club golf course.

Reid's warm blue eyes and easy smile softened Burton's wariness. He didn't want to come across as blunt or rude with the management staff. He hoped to create the impression that he was friendly and congenial. In the beginning, he would try to keep his opinions to himself.

"Have you had a chance to find a place to settle in the Chicago environs, Mr. Blake?"

"Not as yet. I'll be making some arrangements. And just call me Burt. No need for formality."

"Burt it is. Please come into my office." He spoke aside to his young secretary. "Hold all my calls."

"Yes, Mr. Mumford," her shoulder length blonde hair rippled with her nod.

As Reid closed the door after him, he motioned to a side buffet. "Can I offer you coffee or juice or water and fruit or veggies?"

"No thank you. I just came from lunch with Alan. Nice deli down the street."

"I've eaten there a few times myself. I know what you mean. Please have a seat." He indicated a leather armchair positioned at an angle to a cut glass coffee table in front of a spacious leather couch. He picked up a folder from the tabletop as he took a second chair facing opposite. "Alan informed me of the latest developments in reference to your joining the company and the communications that are scheduled to take place." He smiled, revealing two rows of gleaming white dental work. "It's almost like running a political campaign, something I had experience with in my younger days."

Burton noticed that even though Reid could pass for a man fifteen to twenty years younger, he had not opted for a fashionable spiky crew cut. His dark hair had been trimmed and layered to fit the perfect contours of his head. "Here is the written speech for the investors and board of directors that Alan may have mentioned to you." He handed the folder to Burton.

"He did."

"We hope you're comfortable with it, and of course, it's subject to your feedback and approval. It's structured to be presented over a period of fifteen minutes to be followed with a Q and A session."

Burton opened the red folder and perused the first page. "Who wrote this?"

"We have a team of speech writers. They're pros."

Burton continued reading several more pages. "These are not my words and this is not what I want to say. Some of it comes close, but I'm sorry. I can't present this."

"The topic and approach were recommended by your management team."

"Who specifically?"

"Lawrence Harden and Earl Frederickson. Alan Erdman reviewed it for any legal implications."

"This reads like something they want me to say as though I'm a stand in for them. These are not my words. It's not my language."

"Well, on that basis, we have a few days lead time to go over it with you and make revisions, adapt it to your style."

"I'm not talking about revisions or style. I'm talking about the content. Not to sound ungrateful, but I am able to write my own speeches. I don't need your pros."

"I'm given to understand you're not yet familiar with the company. How can you speak on behalf of it without some guidance and assistance?"

"I've had nothing but guidance and assistance ever since two Blake Corporate body guards nearly abducted me and brought me here from

South Africa. I'm not the kind of person who needs guidance and assistance unless I ask for it."

"That's all well and good, Burt, but we're here to help in whatever way and wherever and whenever. Would you mind my asking what aspects of the speech you object to?"

"I haven't seen my father or had any contact with him since I was ten years old. But my memory of him is sharp enough to realize this speech is an attempt to make me sound like him, or at least give that impression. I'm not Elias Blake risen from the dead, Mr. Mumford, and I don't want the public relations department to attempt to create that image of me. We need to spend some time together so you and your staff get to know me and can put my father out of your minds."

"I think that's an excellent idea, Burt. And please call me Reid. I can be much less formal than I look."

"That's a nice suit. I think you look fine."

"Thank you. I certainly didn't intend for us to get off on the wrong foot together. And I do apologize. I had some reservations about drafting the speech without your input. But now we can move on."

"When is the meeting?"

"Next Monday at noon. It's a sit down luncheon. We will be hosting the management team and one-hundred key investors."

Burton rose from his chair. "Sounds like a manageable number."

Reid mirrored him. "They're looking forward to hearing what you have to say."

"Thanks, Reid, for doing your job."

"I think we'll work well together."

"I'm sure we will."

"When do you want to meet and do you want my writers to be involved?"

"No, they don't have to be involved and I'll have Darcy bring a copy to your office in the morning."

"You don't want to discuss its development?"

"Not necessary."

"You don't need the input?"

"Alan is being helpful with that and I have literature and financials about the company. That gives me a start along with the orientation briefings. I'll know pretty well what I'd like to say."

"As you wish." Reid extended his hand. Burton shook it briefly, but firmly.

Reid escorted him to the door. "Have a good day, Burt."

"Thank you. You too."

Reid watched with a mixture of relief and bewilderment.

"Good meeting?" His secretary asked.

"I'm not really sure. I don't know. He's different. I'll say that for him."

"Good different?"

"I'm not sure. I'll have a better idea after I've worked with him. He hasn't been with us long enough to assimilate."

"At least he's cute."

"Don't get any ideas."

"You know I have a boyfriend."

"Don't get any ideas."

"I'm a blonde, Reid. You know I don't have an idea in my head."

"You wouldn't be sitting here if you weren't intelligent."

"You seem anxious."

"A little. He's not like what I expected as the son of Elias Blake. I expected him to be more like Elias. Maybe he is in a stubborn sort of way. Arrange a conference call with Alan, Larry, and Earl."

"Right now?"

"Right now." He walked back into his office and shut the door. A minute later, the voices of Alan, Lawrence, and Carl came over the speaker phone.

"How did it go?" Lawrence asked.

"It didn't really go anywhere."

"Explain."

"He refused to deliver the speech we gave him. He's writing his own."

"Shit!" Earl's response.

"Did you offer assistance?" Alan's voice.

"Yes, he turned it down. He doesn't want any help except from you and the orientations. He said the words we gave him were not his words. We would be farther along had we involved him."

"Involved him?" said Earl. "He's barely walked through the door. Other than his employee orientation, he doesn't know jack shit about the company. We can't let him talk to the board and investors from a vacuum."

"Are you going to review his speech?" asked Alan.

"He said it won't be necessary. He obviously doesn't want my, our feedback. He doesn't want to be constrained."

"Which isn't a good sign," said Lawrence.

"Jesus, he's a loose cannon," said Earl.

"I suppose not, but I can't force him to do what he doesn't want to. He's our boss now. Whatever he says might turn out to be all right."

"Sounds too risky," said Lawrence. "Maybe we should postpone and cancel his presentation until some undetermined future date when we have a better sense of how our boy is going to play out. We can use the reason that it's too early. He's not ready. He's still getting acquainted with the company. Has expressed the need to learn more before saying anything."

"He pretty clearly wants to learn more but appears to want to do that on his own terms. He comes across as being independent, as well as smart."

"We shouldn't have set up the luncheon. We haven't had time to indoctrinate him and he doesn't respond well to our advice."

"He doesn't respond at all," said Lawrence. "Alan, did you tell Reid that Burton is going to talk to Ostraich?"

"Now he knows," said Alan.

"Ostraich is coming here?"

"No, Burt is going there," said Alan, "to his office. Ostraich ambushed us at lunch and made a pitch. Burt bought into it."

"Christ, there isn't any way I can divert that. You know that."

"We know. We just have to wait and see what the fallout is."

"When?"

"Next Monday."

"Can you have security put a wire on him?" asked Reid.

"They already put a chip in his cell phone we can remotely activate, even if it's turned off. But we have to tread lightly here," said Alan. "If he has any suspicion we're spying on him, he might dump the phone and get his own. So we can't overtly pressure him. We have to let him run and react to whatever intel we can gather."

"We don't know if we have a loose cannon yet, Reid," said Lawrence. "We don't know how far he'll go to fuck things up. If it turns out we do, we'll have to use a different strategy, influence and control whatever he goes after."

"That can be done," said Reid. "Damage control is not a position we want to be in, however."

"We're giving him a little rope," said Lawrence. "Hopefully, he won't hang himself."

"Or us," said Earl.

"Not going to happen," said Lawrence. "Just not going to happen."

"We current?" asked Reid.

"Signing off," said Lawrence followed by three terminating clicks on the amplified speaker.

Walt DeMint swallowed a valium to calm his nerves. It wouldn't do for his new boss to see he had the jitters. Alan Erdman had briefed him on what to expect from the son of Elias Blake and that he might express some discontent with the current operation of the philanthropic division, but to rest assured his job was not on the line. He had provided funds to those charities according to the preferences and direct orders of Elias while he was alive. Alan had explained that regardless of what Elias's son might want to do with charities, plenty of money was available to channel it in those directions and strategically and purposefully capitalize on his choices in support of an adjusted corporate image.

Walt had functioned under the company bylaws of philanthropy that supported lobbyists favorable to company interests and nonprofit organizations. No liberal groups or causes of any kind. Elias had built and expanded his profit-driven company that effectively ignored environmental concerns. Although he loved the wilderness and enjoyed its natural gifts on numerous hunting and fishing expeditions, conservation did not concern him. If he could profit from exploitation of natural resources and the environment, he did so. And Alan had warned Walt that Burton might zero in on that.

"He's a tree hugger," said Alan.

"Too bad. Makes my job harder. Makes it harder for the company on regulatory issues."

"This is a policy Lawrence, Earl, the board and I will allow Burton to change without jeopardizing other covert initiatives that could be misinterpreted. We stay away from things like that," said Alan.

Burton had not met Walter DeMint earlier when his direct reports had come to the conference room to be introduced. In apologizing for his absence, DeMint explained he had been out of the office on business-related travel for two weeks coordinating the funding of a sizeable private charity. From the fresh tan and lawyerly appearance of the man, Burton suspected he had been on a private junket as a guest of the charity's recipient. He reserved comment and confined his remarks to self-introduction and inquiry about the company's philanthropic agenda and gifts to charities. He found DeMint's bulging dark-eyed stare, intended to convey undivided interest, a little unnerving, as if it masked either a personal intrusion or some vestige of insanity.

"I have three assistants on my staff who evaluate and respond to requests, since there are many, as you might imagine, and two others who monitor accountability and performance of charitable gifts and philanthropic endowments. You might have noticed on the organization chart that this department has a reporting function to the finance department. I report directly to Jeff Crowley, the CFO. I imagine you've met him."

"No more than a brief introduction. When I was reading over the annual report, I wanted to talk with you first to gain a better understanding of how you handle charities and corporate philanthropy."

"Although we're vesting large sums of money in qualified programs, our wealth management structure and process are progressive. We partner with an investment company, Olson Capital Investment. We started with a conventional method. When he established this department, your father wanted his company to engage in strategic philanthropy for the public good. As we are both aware, the world and societies are undergoing volatile radical change and needs are widespread and competitive for financial resources. But as we have discovered, just handing out money to organizations without effective planning and implementation and monitoring its use does not give us the results we had hoped for. So we've taken the approach of intervention and change management in certain situations to facilitate sustainable short term and long term goals and, of course, the tax advantages of corporate welfare. We essentially fund a number of operations in foreign countries that manufacture low priced products that are sold for a much higher value in American and other foreign markets. It's called transfer pricing.

"According to Congressional law, the Blake Corporation does not have to pay taxes on those offshore profits generated by Blake subsidiaries in those countries. So we look for every opportunity to move our jobs and operations offshore, especially with our medical and pharmaceutical divisions and, of course, our technology division. I've been involved with philanthropy for nearly thirty years and have a good understanding that to be effective and profitable the process has to facilitate innovative solutions. In addition to my administrative staff here in the office, I have five hundred others, men and women, who I call field agents in various positions. They're essentially business and organizational consultants and accountants versed in international finance law who work directly with beneficiaries of Blake endowments. I like to think of them as our private Peace Corps." Walt blinked twice rapidly with a sheepish smile. "I understand you've had some experience of a similar kind."

"Do you give aid to foreign governments?"

"Not directly. We sometimes affiliate with related Federal programs."

"It sounds like this philanthropy division is a lobby."

"In the purest sense, yes. But any organization or group with an agenda is essentially a lobby trying to influence favorable outcomes on behalf of the business."

"What kind of Federal programs?"

"I'll be happy to share some of the details. Members of my staff have prepared a presentation for you." Walt rose from his chair. "If you'll accompany me into our conference room," he extended his arm for Burton to precede him.

Expecting to meet others, Burton wondered why the room was empty, but withheld comment as he seated himself in the nearest chair and looked at the opening Power Point slide projecting the Blake

Corporation logo amid an artfully arranged collage on the giant digital flat screen. DeMint took a chair to Burton's left at the head of the conference table and pressed a button on the remote controller. He provided a brief narrative that added little to the copy of each slide that Burton read for himself.

Certain special endowments linked to the names of politicians raised Burton's curiosity. They supported programs established by Senators and Governors to benefit a list of obscure charities for urban development projects and poverty assistance in a few southern states and in small third world countries.

Burton attributed a seven million dollar gift to the National Rifle Association as a demonstration of Elias Blake's passion for guns and hunting.   A contribution of ten million for polio research reflected Elias's preoccupation with his own physical defect.

"What about ethnic groups?" Burton asked.

Blacks and Hispanics work in all our divisions. We hire Ph.Ds. from India. We are ethnically diverse."

"I'm letting you know in advance that I am not like my father and I will consider adding a liberal element to Blake charities and philanthropies."

DeMint nodded and continued to the next slide.

One organization that stood out on the list as deviating from what DeMint explained was the Corporation's policy to support socially and politically conservative causes was a sizeable contribution, an endowment for three million dollars, to Elizabeth Dawson, M.D. for Doctors Without Borders. DeMint explained he did not know the rationale behind the gift, although it was a worthy cause, but that Elias had called one morning out of the blue and ordered him to send a check. The impetus for his generosity was known only to the doctor who, DeMint commented, exerted some personal influence.

"I'd like to meet Doctor Dawson sometime."

"I'm sure that can be arranged," said DeMint.

"How much contact do you have with the organizations you support?"

"From the very beginning, face time is important. We verify the validity and extent of financial need and how distribution of funds would be handled. We also require beneficiaries to report the results of their funding. We don't want to be perceived as a free money machine."

"No question there's a lot of it."

"Thanks to Elias Blake. He was a paragon of free market enterprise."

"Interesting description, paragon." Burton flashed a good-natured grin. "Kind of a contradiction of terms,"

DeMint's eyes briefly narrowed. "That's the presentation. Do you have any questions, comments?"

"I'll be getting back together with you in about two weeks to plan some additional strategies. And I'd like to meet your office staff at that time."

"Of course. Of course the field people are out in the field. They act as our eyes and ears so to speak, but we are in regular communications with them thanks to digital technology. Did you want to talk with Jeff Crowley next?"

"Do I need an appointment?"

"No," DeMint smiled. "You're the boss."

"Thank you for your time and information."

"Not at all. I look forward to working with you on your," DeMint hesitated, "strategies."

Burton left DeMint's office and walked fifteen yards down the carpeted hall between oak paneled walls adorned with contemporary art that clashed with the vision and understanding Burton was learning about his father. The glass door to the finance department stood open awaiting his arrival, an indication that DeMint had called to notify Jeff Crowley that "the boss" was on his way.

"An introduction doesn't give much," said Jeff Crowley with a firm grip that matched his firm grin. "I want you to know I'm at your service any time, day or night. The finance department is the heart of the company through which the monetary blood is pumped and flows out through the payable arteries and comes in through the receivable veins, if you don't mind the corny anatomy analogy. Although there's considerable complexity in our financial division, I try to keep things simple and understandable and transparent. Transparency is very important these days as you well know from hearing and reading the news.

"One thing we don't do is take financial risks which are a recipe for catastrophe, witness the Wall Street giants and the UK, Barclays. We're all about risk management here, which is why the company is so successful even with the economy such as it is. Have a seat. Have a seat. I don't mean to keep you standing while I talk, sometimes too much, so I've been told. But," he smiled, "there's always something interesting to talk about. I understand you've had some adventures traveling around the world, hitch hiking, nothing but a pack on your back, working on cargo ships and the like."

"I traveled on a cargo ship, but not as one of the crew. Rode a lot of trains, buses, bikes, an oxcart, a few World War II vintage airplanes."

"Sounds like fun, something a young man should do. Get out there and experience the world, see how other people live. It must have been great. Provides you a perspective now that you're about to settle down with a job beyond the capabilities of most men or women, for that matter. You may have noticed from the organization chart that we do have women in management at the vice president and middle management level at a few of our satellite companies."

Burton decided to let the man rattle on and just listen for insights that might emerge from the flurry of words and ascetic physical gyrations. Crowley paced about the office seeming to dominant the meeting by wanting to impress with his observations, extensive knowledge and experience and leave Burton little space to engage in a participatory manner, let alone take control. His specific sweeping gestures reminded Burton of a tennis player, which he was, judging from the half-dozen photos taken during his college days at Stanford University co-mingled with another signed dozen taken smiling and shaking hands with international stars of the tennis circuit. Although his gray hair was receding, he carried himself with the tanned slender face and body of an athlete. Burton guessed he took good care of himself and, being in his early sixties, was proud of his condition.

He wore a wrinkle-free pressed white shirt and a red tie, dark blue slacks, and stylish comfortable soft leather brown loafers. With the exception of four fifteen-inch flat screens, a computer keyboard extension, and a phone, his immaculately polished desk was free of objects.

"We have real-time live connectivity with all our satellite divisions and, Walt DeMint said you would be interested to know, controlled access to our specialized accounts funded by The Blake Foundation. All financial interactions for the foundation are managed through my office. Walt's staff handles the client interface. We handle the disbursements and monitoring of distributions. I'll be happy to show you the data any time you'd like."

"I appreciate your offer and eventually I'll take you up on it."

"Excellent, I'm sure you'll not only be pleased, but pleasantly surprised how well we do."

"I do have a question."

"Shoot."

"In the annual report, I saw a category called offshore investments, but there were no figures."

"At the time of the annual report, all of the financials were not yet available. But, as an American corporation with offshore business generating revenue, we are not obligated to report what the IRS cannot tax. We also benefit from tax credits for our coal fire plants which produce enhanced alternative fuel. The same applies to our stock option transactions. Discount stocks don't reduce profits. So the company takes a deduction on the difference between what employees pay and what the stock might actually be worth at a given point in time. They're not considered business expenses, but the difference is not taxed as profit. We also benefit from accelerated depreciation. Blake is a capital intensive company, but we are able to write off our capital investments before the deterioration of those assets.

"You may or may not know, but when I joined the company five years ago, I left my position as president of a capital investment company with which the Blake Corporation had been in business for over ten years, twelve and a half to be exact. We had been facilitating and managing the Blake hedge funds and off-shore accounts. The current president over there says he knows you from when you were in elementary school. Jerry Olson. The company is now called Olson Capital Investments, basically engaged in arbitrage. In addition to buying and restoring companies that we downsized through outsourcing to create substantial profit margins, we worked with hedge funds and generated profit from price differences. We were well networked with reliable inside sources of financial intelligence. We also purchased and sold securities, assets, and derivatives. With a few exceptions, including the sub-prime mortgage situation, by which we financially engineered a ten billion profit margin, we took conservative risks.

"With my experience in quantitative finance, it seemed only logical to pull me in to the Blake organization to take over the CFO position and responsibilities when the former CFO resigned. I have since provided a firm and steady hand at the financial management helm that has greatly benefited our company in the volatile winds of trade and commerce. We have great diversity and the ability to create, build, and retain our profits. Our off-shore program is a major contributing factor."

"You're talking about off-shore banks?"

"They are only a small part of the overall picture, tools really, financial repositories."

"Off-shore accounts."

"They are accounts we hold off-shore, as a manner of speaking, including Switzerland."

"Can you give me a rough estimate of how much?"

"The profits are so diversified and distributed that I can't begin to give you an accurate figure, not even a valid approximate figure."

"The annual report says the company's net worth is thirty billion."

"Give or take. It can fluctuate quarterly."

"How about a ball park, Jeff? You're the CFO. You must have a figure in your head."

"I say this with great hesitation, since I don't have the current data, but around fifteen to twenty billion."

"Profit."

"As stated in the annual report estimation. "

"Offshore."

"Offshore."

"And those profits aren't taxed?"

"The strategy of legally maintaining a percentage of profits offshore is that it doesn't have to be taxed." Crowley's face flushed a defensive pink. "It's a smart way of doing business and, before you jump to any unfounded assumption, all transactions are structured in a manner that is legal and legitimate with the IRS and current tax law. You can't believe everything you hear and read in the media. We are not a Wall Street bank. We are a for profit company, supported by our stockholders, and in the business of selling products and making money and ensuring that our stockholders are happy."

"I don't disagree, Jeff. I'm just not familiar with how off-shore accounts work. It was just a question. What does the IRS have to say about it?"

"That's the genius of maintaining off-shore finances. We paid zero Federal taxes on pretax profits of three billion reported to our shareholders every year for the past ten years and received refunds from the IRS totaling six billion, which is clear profit. We also benefit from tax laws allowing for accelerated depreciation on our capital investments, deductions on stock options for employees, tax credits for research. We're ahead of the game in oil drilling, enhanced coal and natural gas. And Walt DeMint may have told you the non-profit tax benefits of outsourcing the manufacture of some of our products to low wage labor through philanthropy. If you want my staff to take you through the books, we can do that. I say books, but everything is digital these days. Digital and instantaneous. Do you work much with computers?"

"I'm a rank amateur. I can create a Word file and go on-line to check Email. That's about it."

"Well, we have the best and the brightest business and finance and computer science majors from leading colleges and universities working for us. We've lost a few here and there to the lure of Wall Street investment firms, but we've always been able to recruit and hire qualified replacements. And my staff is ethnically diverse and gender balanced. Seven of my accountants are women."

"There are a lot of young people out there looking for jobs," said Burton.

"Yes, and we tap in to that talent as part of our succession planning here and throughout all our divisions. We're very progressive about that. Very progressive."

"In the near future, I will take you up on your offer of a digital tour through your financial processes. I have a particular interest in tax shelters."

"You do? I mean I'm pleased that you'd like to know more."

"If I'm going to be the CEO of this company, the more I know about it, the better. And I realize I have a lot of learning to do. It's like visiting a foreign country, learning about a different culture."

Crowley smiled and visibly relaxed for the first time since Burton had entered his office. "We do our job here. We're all professionals, among the best in our fields, and we do a good job."

Burton returned the smile and rose from his chair. "What more could anyone ask." He extended his hand. "Thank you for your time and the overview."

"This is your company, Burton. We are here to follow your lead and do your bidding."

"Well, I like to think we all own the company. The company belongs to all of us right down to the janitor."

Crowley's thin lips momentarily creased in a concerned frown. "I couldn't agree more. It's such a pleasure to meet you and it will be an equal pleasure to work with you."

"Likewise, Jeff. Have to finish my rounds. Good to talk with you."

"Good to talk with you. By the way, do you happen to play tennis? You look like an athlete, good shape. I'm always looking for a challenging partner."

"From those photos on your wall, I can't imagine you would have any trouble finding someone to play. I'm sorry, I don't."

"There are some pretty strong players at the club, but most of the men my age prefer golf. Less strenuous, understandable, easy on the knees, but nevertheless. I'm not ready to hang up my racket. Have a regular workout every day, including a five mile run."

"Well, when I get there, hope I can do the same."

"The company places a lot of emphasis on health and safety. Human Resources promotes a health and wellness agenda for all employees. Helps keep the insurance premiums down. Every division has a workout facility, all the latest equipment, including personal trainers. A lot of employees take advantage of that."

"It's good to know the company values them so much," said Burton

"Absolutely. Without satisfied employees, we don't have satisfied customers, and eventually we don't have a company, at least not as successful as we are."

"I couldn't agree more. People always come first for me. Have a good rest of the day."

"You too, Burton. Have a great day."

As Burt left his office, Crowley picked up his phone and dialed Lawrence Harden's extension. "Larry – Jeff. He just left my office. Some things he said concern me but I think he'll do all right by us. I really think he'll be fine, but we have to tread very carefully, very carefully."

Chapter 24

Transparency

Conspicuously tailed by his bodyguards, George and Nikos, Burton made his way along the bustling wind-blown Chicago streets to the rearing Gothic revival architectural spiral of the Tribune Tower within easy walking distance of the Blake Corporation building. He had called Robert Ostraich to confirm their appointment. Ostraich greeted him in the front lobby with a handshake and a "Welcome. We're going to have a private conversation. So your shadows will have to wait here."

George and Nikos shrugged and crossed the glossy tile floor to claim a waiting spot on soft black plastic cushion chairs. They watched Burton and Ostraich until the two men walking shoulder to shoulder talking in a comradely manner disappeared into one of a long line of glistening brass elevators that suctioned them to the fortieth floor. Burton accepted a bottled water from Ostraich's secretary and within moments was encapsulated in the journalist's glass office providing a view of staff employees at efficient high tech communication work stations in the adjacent open bay newsroom.

On the way up in the elevator, Ostraich had explained his interest in the Blake Corporation as a successful business model on the one hand, and on the other, what he termed its "social flaws."

"To continue what I was saying, I met Elias only once, when his company was growing at a phenomenal rate back in the 80's. Despite the recession, it's happening now again. Elias wouldn't grant me an interview, even though the Tribune published a number of editorial praises for many of his accomplishments. He was media shy. In fact, he made it clear that he disliked journalists whether we wrote for a news publication or read the news from a teleprompter. After one press conference where he had to field some challenging questions, and not well, he was clearly out of his element, he never appeared at the podium again. He delegated that task to his public relations director. It was said off the record that Elias preferred hunting and shooting dangerous wild animals to facing off with the press and he never appeared on television. He was hounded by the paparazzi largely because of his wealth, but also because of his marriage to the socialite Alexis Andaniamo. In her younger days, she was a stunning beauty, still is actually, and undisputedly wild, which might have been one of the factors that attracted Elias to her. He was drawn to the wild, not only in the sense of big game, but to this woman. Have you ever met her?"

"Once, briefly, at my father's funeral."

"Well, her son and daughter have taken up where she left off, especially the daughter. She's trying to be the next Kim Kardashian. She desperately pursues the media, wants them, us, to take her seriously. She has a personal website and runs a string of salacious U-tubes about herself. She hungers after fame but has absolutely nothing to be famous about. She is beautiful, not as beautiful as her mother, but rather vacuous, if you know what I mean, and believes being born into a wealthy family entitles her to be treated as royalty. Savannah Blake has no class. Her brother, Richard, is not much better, just a Yale dropout to become a jet-setting cocaine snorting playboy. But maybe you already know this about that family."

"Only superficially. I've never been interested in following their lives and I don't read People Magazine," Burton grinned.

Ostraich chuckled. "Of course, and that's not what we're here to talk about."

"What do you want to talk about?"

"To the point. You clearly are not a younger version of your father. I'm interested in your views, your position as the CEO by inheritance, what direction you'd like to take the company that has been secretive for decades, avoiding transparency and escaping regulation in its power and energy operations and in its finances. Elias maintained fiscal relations with Washington lobbies favorable to his businesses and personal political opinions. I do know that about him."

"Fiscal relations?"

"Pay-offs, bribery. He got away with it. He had his favorite politicians at the state and Federal levels. Certain things don't escape the notice of the media. We shield our sources, but we depend on them. When we can't get direct information, we have to resort to investigative methods."

"Are you planning to write a story based on this interview?"

"No, I just wanted the opportunity to talk with you, have an open discussion, perhaps help clarify some of the puzzling bits and pieces I've gathered from the periphery of the Blake empire."

"You mentioned you were interested in my views and position as CEO."

"Exactly."

"You're not running a tape recorder or surveillance camera, are you?"

"Burton, to do so without your awareness and permission is illegal. No, I never cross that line. But I appreciate your asking."

"I'm just beginning to learn about the company from the inside. I don't know anything about fiscal relations with politicians and lobbies, but I do know how corrupt Wall Street is and many large corporations where corruption is synonymous with free enterprise. From what you've told me and a few other early impressions, I'm assuming Blake is among them. Dealing with billions of dollars is unfamiliar territory to me. From the time I was ten, when my mother and Elias parted company, I've been raised in a normal middle class family.

"I've lived the past three years down in the mud, so to speak, in third world countries. I'm an odd duck when it comes to fitting into corporate culture. I had issues with American and foreign mega-companies before I was dragged back here from South Africa. I don't buy in with third world dictators either or a system of social aristocracy. Given the position I've been handed, I might be able to have a minor influence, minimal, probably not even a noticeable effect. But I think if Elias spent millions or billions to further his goals, those same resources are now available to me to pursue mine."

"You mentioned you don't fit in with American corporate culture. Do you think you'll encounter resistance to change in your own company?"

"I'm not sure in what manner, but, yes, definitely. I'm a young guy dropped into the middle of a closed group of Elias's good old boys. I'm not a good old boy, not even a young good old boy, and don't intend to be. I know they're watching me carefully, all the time, in fact. Those two goons following me around are only partially for my protection." Burton's grin of sarcasm underscored his comment. "The team at Blake is anxiously watching and waiting to see what I'm going to do next. I'm being coached, facilitated, pushed and prodded, groomed, perhaps is what it's called. They're ready to give me all kinds of advice to keep me on their straight and narrow."

"Blake is run by entrenched corporate politics. It's obvious to me as an outsider," said Ostraich.

"I'm getting a good sense of that."

"You don't strike me as being a political person."

"I've never been in a position where I had to be. But I'm a pretty keen observer of human behavior and I'm on the side of the oppressed. I don't consider myself social royalty or possessing entitlements of any kind. I'll always give away before I'll take away."

Ostraich smiled. "My God that's refreshing to hear. I'd love to quote you on that. Most people in your sphere are takers. You know, this is not what I really wanted to talk about. I just wanted to get to know you, Burton, not get mired in the topic of corporate politics. We both see and hear enough of that every day. If not friends, I'd like us to at least be acquaintances. Have a beer and a burger once in a while and just talk about life and what's going on in the world."

"This was never intended to be about me, Mr. Ostraich."

""Oh, please, drop the mister crap. Allow me the good grace of calling me Bob. There shouldn't be mister anything between else. I am curious, though, as to why you agreed to talk to me."

"I'm not all that comfortable telling you this. We barely know each other and I know you're in the business of writing and publishing sensational stories."

Ostraich smiled. "Only if they are vetted and worth writing."

"This sounds like corporate spying, but I need an outside contact I can rely on."

"Why is that?"

"I have to operate with some constraint. I'm sure there are consequences if I step over the line."

"To you personally?"

"It's a gut feeling, but I'm not imagining it."

"Were you threatened?"

"It's not what's being told to me. It's what's not being said."

"That's the part that interests me. I call them symptoms of the Blake Corporation. I've recently been following a lawsuit brought against Blake. A large number of families have contracted diseases and there have been several deaths from toxic waste emissions and contamination from Blake coal fired plants and fracking operations. One man and a pro bono lawyer are attempting to bring the suit into court. They've turned down attempts by the corporation to pay them off and disappear. I have a suspicion that larger sums of bribery are secretly and illegally exchanging hands elsewhere, because they are being denied a hearing. The Blake Corporation is known for buying legal and political influence."

"Do you know the man and his lawyer?"

"I've interviewed them, but I haven't published anything, until they move to the next step. If they continue to be denied a hearing because the Blake Corporate underbelly is paying off judges and the Governor, that will be published. But we're also subject to a gag order regarding the toxicity and the illnesses."

"Blake donates millions to charity, but I've already learned their real purpose is to profit under conditions of controlled risk. I don't want those two gentlemen to be unduly exposed."

"Are you saying they could come to physical harm?" Ostraich moved his glasses further up on the bridge of his nose. "The effects of chemical toxicity have already caused the man and his family physical harm. It sounds like it might prove difficult to trace the cause of those effects, even with court arguments. The Governor, who has obviously been paid off, has issued a gag order to physicians. They can't go public with results of blood tests identifying the source of toxicity."

"I don't believe in killing people for profit," said Burton. "I've seen far too much death and corruption in other countries I've visited in the past few years."

One of the reasons I was brought into the company is to improve its public image. So I have a certain amount of latitude. Making operational changes to comply with environmental regulations and ensuring affected people have their day in court and are appropriately compensated is not likely to be discouraged by my – I'll call them handlers. They'll give the appearance of not advising me to follow through with an act of corporate attrition, but I don't think they'll stand in my way on some issues. They'll try to give me my lines, but for the moment, I have center stage."

"I can't say I envy you."

Burton grinned, "Just think what you could do with thirty billion dollars, Bob."

Ostraich laughed. "I like your sense of humor."

"I'm going to need one to keep all this in perspective. By the way, since we're just having polite conversation, why don't you tell me about you."

"No one has ever asked me that, not even over cocktails. Everybody thinks the only reason I want to talk to them is to get their story. Not true."

"Okay, I'm at least a decent listener and I promise not to reveal my sources."

Ostraich laughed again. "I've been married forty years, to the same woman. We have three children who are all grown up and have careers and families of their own."

"Your children are probably close to my age then."

"In their thirties."

"Not there yet, getting close, about to turn in a few months. When I was a boy, I remember seeing some of your news columns, especially the ones about the last few Presidential elections and 9/11 and the recession brought on by Wall Street and profiteering in the war with Iraq."

"I'll be making a speech to a roomful of investors tomorrow and I have to be accommodating. I can't just blow off the company."

"I'd like to be a fly on the wall for that one."

Burton smiled. "Sorry I can't invite you. I have to make some concessions to – the team. I'm sure you know what I'm talking about."

"Clearly. Good night and good luck, as a famous news anchor said. Edward R. Murrow, well before your time."

"Things haven't gotten any easier."

"That they have not."

Their continued discussion ranged over Burton's travels and how his experiences in third world countries influenced his political thinking. Topics also touched on contemporary youth culture and the future outlook of the millennial generation of which Burton was a member. Two hours went by before Burton realized he had other appointments waiting back at the office and apologized for having to end the interview.

"It was good talking with you, Burt. I hope we can have another conversation or two down the road."

"I'm sure we will. It's been a pleasure meeting you." Burton rose to leave.

Ostraich walked him to the elevator. They shook hands and parted.

Burton's body guards were waiting for him in the lobby.

There was no applause at the conclusion of Burton's speech, only confused baleful stares as though he were some intruder who had come before them to deprive them of their dividends. He saw a mutual shudder of reproach ripple from one suit to another like a reflexive herd response accompanied by an underlying animalistic grumble.

The Q & A that followed was what Burton had expected. He noticed that the Blake corporate team did an admirable job of concealing their discomfort.

"Why do you want to tamper with what has worked so well? We are experiencing record revenues despite the recession and now it sounds like you might introduce some new thinking that could threaten the profits we enjoy. The board's purpose is to provide advice and direction supported by the investors."

"I'm still learning about the company and I'm not making any changes in staff or business policies. Blake is a complex group of companies and affiliates. There is no intent to ignore the importance of investors and I'm relying on the board to help me in my efforts," said Burton. "Adding new thinking and direction to the company is in keeping with changes in society and changing world conditions. We live in a global community."

Burton noticed a few disapproving expressions.

"The point is we can't ignore the needs of the larger ethnic populations and societies not only in our country, but throughout the world. The demographics have changed, ladies and gentlemen."

"The company addresses those needs through philanthropy."

"Those programs will not be disturbed, but they will be expanded and enhanced."

"In what way? This is a free market economy, Mr. Burton. The Federal Government doesn't have any business interfering with Blake operations by imposing outrageous regulatory constraints. That's what drives up the cost of everything and loses jobs. You want to be responsible for people losing jobs? You don't sound at all like your father."

"Employees are not going to lose jobs by the company complying with regulations. They will lose jobs if Blake doesn't comply and our plants are shut down and the company pays billions in lawsuits and fines and people lose lives. The Blake Corporation has never been socially responsible when it comes to environmental issues like the health of citizens. I'm asking you to help me find a way to change that."

"You sound like a god damn tree hugger!" A loud voice pitched from the back of the crowded room.

"We want to be known as a company that wants to preserve the planet, not destroy it," said Burton.

"As long as you don't tamper with the core profit making ability of the company," shouted another.

"You don't have to worry about that. This isn't about one person. It's about all of us working together to sustain profitability. With the exception of my father, the other management and staff who grew the company to where it is today are still intact. They're not going away. They'll continue. They'll be technically engineering compliance and continued profitability. The two are not incompatible."

"That's the first refreshing comment we've heard from you."

"Comments just touch the surface. The actions that follow are what are important. Ladies and gentlemen, thank you for attending." As he left the podium and exited by a side door, he glanced back and noticed several of the investors who had been sitting in the front row cluster and hover vociferously around the company's senior managers.

Chapter 25

Olivia

George and Nikos followed Burton from the moment he left the hotel and drove through the city to an outlying suburb. Maintaining contact with Fred Dolby seated at his console digital video displays in the basement headquarters of the Blake Corporation office tower, George spoke into his Bluetooth phone, reporting the route being taken by their objective.

Burton pulled up to the curb of a modest 50's style ranch home with tall elm trees shading a neatly trimmed lawn edged with eye-catching flower gardens. George relayed the address to Dolby, whose aide quickly traced the satellite map location on the large wall screen and proliferated a data stream that identified its occupants.

An attractive young woman with nut brown skin answered the door at Burton's knock. "Yes? May I help you?"

"Hello, my name is Burton Blake. Are you Dr. Elizabeth Dawson?"

"No, I'm her daughter."

"I'm very pleased to meet you. I've come to speak with your mother. She's the recipient of an endowment from the Blake Corporation."

"Oh, that. She told me about that. I think I know now. You're the Burton Blake of the Blake billions?"

"That was the company my father founded."

"She told me about him. We read in the newspaper that he died recently. The obituary was quite long, but interesting. Mom told me stories about when they were kids. We visited his grave yesterday."

"That's why I'm here. There's a family connection."

"How do you mean? We're relatives?"

A deep rich female voice came from within the house. "Olivia, who's there? Who's at the door?"

"He says he's Burton Blake, but he didn't show me any ID," her impish grin captivated him.

"Let him come in."

As Olivia opened the door wider, Burton saw the ruggedly elegant woman with tousled red hair step forward from the kitchen. "How do you do, Dr. Dawson. I'm Burton Blake, Elias's son."

"Please, come in. I know very little about you. Elias was several years older than I, when we came to live at his house. My mother was his guardian until he was old enough to inherit his father's company. Please do come in and sit down. Would you like something cool to drink?"

"Yes, thank you."

"I would too. Olivia, would you fix up three ice teas and join us. This is an unexpected surprise, Mr. Blake."

"Burt. Please call me Burt.

Olivia slipped into the kitchen and returned with three ice teas.

"Thank you, dear. Please, everybody sit down. It's wonderful to meet you, Burt. Your father and I only briefly kept in touch over the years. I was often away in foreign countries working with *Medecins Sans Frontieres*, Doctors Without Borders.

"Who are those two men out there parked in the black SUV behind your car?" asked Olivia, who had noticed them when she opened the front door to admit Burton.

"George and Nikos. They're my bodyguards."

"Bodyguards. That's heavy.   I guess when you're who you are, you need them."

"I don't have much of a choice. The company considers me more of an asset than a person."

Olivia smiled. "You remind me of James Bond. Not quite Sean Connery, but handsome, mysterious, a world traveler. I read your profile on the Internet."

Burton laughed. "I don't know what that says, something PR made up. Have to agree with the handsome and mysterious part though."

"Oh, and egotistic. Just kidding."

The security department assigned them to look after me so I don't get abducted. They tell me I could be worth a sizeable ransom. I don't share that inflated opinion of myself, but I have to humor them."

Olivia took a sip of her tea. "Executive ransom. What if I abducted you. How much money do you think I could get for your safe return?" She laughed.

"Bit of a problem there," said Burton with an amused grin. "Those guys are serious."

"Here's the scene. I could charm them into letting me take one of their SUVs with you in it. We could say we're just going on a date. Then later, they'll receive my phone call demanding the ransom. Oh, say a couple of million. Of course, I would disguise my voice."

"You have quite an imagination."

"She gets that from her mother," said Lizzie. "We made up all kinds of plots and scenarios when she was a kid."

"I also read extensively," said Olivia. "Mysteries and thrillers are my fav."

"I used to read a lot in college," said Burton. "Got out of the habit when I was traveling."

"All work and no play, you know what they say," said Olivia.

"Well, I hope you don't find me boring."

"No, maybe after a little more conversation, but no, definitely not boring. I should introduce you to my friends sometime. They would enjoy meeting you. They're kind of nerdy but I think you'd get along. Do you like nerdy people?"

"Ah, sure, I like all kinds of people."

"That's probably for the best because there are so many different kinds of people." She laughed.

"You laugh a lot," said Burton. "I think that's great. When I was traveling, I met a lot of people who laughed. They didn't have much, but they still found things to laugh about. They taught me to laugh with them."

"Sounds cool. When I was growing up and traveled to different countries with my Mom and Dad, I played with children there. We had good times and laughed a lot. Life has funny moments."

"I think that's great."

"Awesome great or just great great?"

"Awesome great. I didn't know about awesome until I heard my sister say it. I visited my Mom and sister when I got back."

"How is your Mom?" asked Lizzie.

"Wonderful, showing a little age, but still the same booster Mom. She had a hand in getting me to come back. I was working with the Red Cross in Johannesburg. That's when those two guys out there showed up. Actually, we've grown to like each other."

"Bravo," said Olivia. "It's important to be fond of your body guards. How can you stand having them follow you around all the time. They would drive me bonkers. It's a total invasion of your privacy. Do they stand guard in your house at night?"

"I don't have a house."

"Where do you live?"

"For the time being in a hotel."

"An expensive hotel?"

"A modest room at the Ritz Carlton."

Lizzie and Olivia burst out laughing.

"Do they carry guns?" asked Olivia.

"Yes, it's pretty obvious when you're standing next to them. There's a bulge.

"I can do a lot of damage with my IPhone." She held it up.

"I'm not at all like you might think I am. I have to tolerate my two chaperones. It's written into the company bylaws. I just returned from South Africa to manage the company. It's not something I asked for. I was told I inherited the job. I've been here only a month. I'm planning to make some changes, but I have to assimilate carefully, which means I have to compromise on most things."

"Since you own the company, why do you have to compromise on anything?" asked Olivia.

"That's not how it works. There are other people with responsibility and authority and, of course, there are the stock holders, who are always concerned about the return on their investment."

" Hedge fund buddies."

"I'm not one of them. Like I said, I have to proceed carefully."

"Your bodyguards should help you, no doubt."

"They're actually not so bad, a little slow on the uptick. It's like having a couple of big dogs following me around. If I tell them to stay, they stay."

"But if you tell them to go away, they don't go away."

"I'm stuck with them, at least for a while."

 Olivia sipped her tea. "There are conspiracies and conspirators out there you know. Have you ever read how the super-rich are running the world? I've made a study of it with my best friend, Zach Lubinsky. He's a super hacker. He calls himself a consultant because he sometimes works for Google and Microsoft and even the FBI, but he's really just a hacker, a super smart one. Graduated with a PhD in computer science from Harvard. He discovers some of those radical conspiracies and the FBI quietly takes them out. You know."

"Olivia," Lizzie found an opening in her daughter's chatter and interrupted. "Give the poor man a break. He didn't come here to talk about politics."

"Well, I happen to be political," said Olivia.

"I've never paid much attention to politics," said Burton. "Had more important things to do. And I've been out of the country for the past three years."

"Traveling around. And here you are running your Dad's company. Talk about irony."

Burton looked at Lizzie.

"One of the reasons I wanted to meet you is to learn more about Elias. I never really got to know him past the time I was ten years old."

"How did you travel?" asked Olivia.

"Mostly hitch-hiked, rode on a few freighters and worked on native fishing boats in Southeast Asia."

"You were a free spirit, a vagabond."

"You could say that and I enjoyed every minute of it."

"As much as you enjoy what you're doing now?"

"I enjoyed doing what I was doing. I didn't know what to expect when I came here today. I didn't know you had a brilliant daughter."

"Hold that thought," said Olivia.

Burton turned back to Lizzie seated at the opposite end of her orange and brown earth tone fabric couch. "How well did you know my father?"

"For a short time, we were like brother and sister. Although he was seven years older than me, I had him twisted around my little finger. After his mother and father died in a car accident, my mother became his guardian. She and Elias's mother were close friends. So I grew up like his kid sister until he went off to college. Elias adored me, but what's not to adore about a precocious freckled smartass little red head. He never got over the fact I have a photographic mind. I helped him study for his exams when he was in high school. He made straight 'A's but he never told anyone I was his secret weapon." Her effusive burst of laughter was catching. Like mother like daughter.

"Will I never hear the end of your photographic mind," Olivia waved her hand as though to sweep away the reference.

"Sounds like quite a gift," said Burton.

"It has made a difference in my life and career."

"I was curious to discover my father made a large charitable contribution to your career."

"You mean Doctors Without Borders. That wasn't my career. That was helping those who were suffering and less fortunate in third world countries. That's where Olivia gets her gene for service. It's also where I met my husband, Joachim Quintana. He was a doctor from the Philippines. That's also where Olivia gets her natural tan. Beautiful young woman, isn't she?"

"Without question. What do you do?" Burton asked Olivia.

"Have you heard of Next Millennium?"

Burton shook his head.

"They're a non-profit. I work for them as a program coordinator for awards and implementation. Our primary goal is to maximize the value of the funds and connectivity with other organizations. We can't single handedly stabilize the world, but we can and do target underprivileged people, societies, and areas who for any reason are oppressed, whether politically or from other circumstances, drought, flood, famine, disease, you name it."

"Who provides your financial resources?"

Olivia grinned. "Generous people like you, if you'd care to get involved. In the past, except for your father's charitable donations to my Mom, The Blake Corporation shunned us like we were a social disease."

"I've learned they use philanthropy for different reasons that are not all philanthropic," said Burton.

"Sure, the people at Next Mill suspect they do. Your company is in it for profit. I'm sure someone benefits, some low wage employees who are exploited in offshore operations. We aren't so inexperienced or uninformed to realize that philanthropy is used to create a favorable image for corporations in certain industries, like oil companies polluting oceans and coastlines and destroying nature and wildlife and then pouring millions into media campaigns that claim they are doing research to protect and preserve the environment. Mining companies are blowing away mountain tops in the Appalachians and contaminating aquifers and ruining people's health by fracking. I imagine you've heard about that, since there's a lawsuit against your company. It's in the news."

"I only recently learned about it."

"Are you going to do something?"

"I'm learning."

"Well, don't wait too long. The plaintiffs could die before they get back into court. And the court did shut down the claim, which I'm sure makes your lawyers and investors happy."

"The issue will be reopened," said Burton.

She held up her I-Phone and captured his surprised image in a digital photograph." My secret weapon. Better than a gun." She briefly glanced at it. "Not bad. Better than a DMV license photo. If you do good things, I can spread the word through my Facebook and Twitter networks and Next Millennium to millions worldwide. What you do can go viral. If you do bad, Uh Oh."

"Sounds like extortion."

"It is, but for a good cause."

Lizzie smiled. "Like mother, like daughter. You didn't realize what you walked into here, did you, Burton?"

"I'm not unhappy about meeting you, both. What you're telling me reinforces what I have to do."

"See, Olivia," said her mother. "It takes a woman."

"You've got that right. Like a refill?"

"Thank you, no. But maybe you'd let me take you to dinner some evening."

"How about that, Mother. You're a witness. He's hitting on me."

"Are you going to accept?"

"We can eat some great food and drink some French wine or hang out with your friends," said Burton. "Whatever you'd like."

"We can do both. Just don't show up wearing a suit and tie. And tell your body guards to stay away. My friends are, very smart, very bright, just can't get jobs because there aren't any. She finger-tapped her iPhone. "I'll text you, so you can text me back. You probably have an iPhone, don't you?"

Burton pulled his from his pocket and held it up. "Just like yours."

"Probably not. You don't have the apps I do, but, if you want, I'll share."

"I have to leave in a few minutes. Have some things to do."

Lizzie laughed. "Places to go, people to see, things to do."

"Mother. Be kind. It's all true." She nudged Burton with her elbow. "That's why I miss my Dad. He never belittled me. But Dr. Lizzie Dawson, MD of the jungle thinks she can because she has a photographic memory."

"I know I can because I'm your mother," said Lizzie.

"Oh, Pshaw." Olivia rose from her chair and extended her hand. "Nice to meet you, Burt. I'll watch for your text." She blushed.

"Glad to meet you." He watched her walk away down the hall.

"She and her friends are a nice young crowd," said Lizzie. "They're smart and good-hearted and dedicated to helping the down trodden. You'll fit right in."

Burton smiled and embraced her with a strong hug. "We'll get together again." He heard the door gently click shut behind him as he went outside to his body guards.

Chapter **26**

Fracking

Burton's secretary, Darcy Schumacher, arranged a tour of homes in upscale Chicago suburbs accompanied by her real estate broker friend, Pekka Rasmussen. Burton left his car parked at the agent's office and together they drove along sun dappled shady streets lined with a mix of traditional stone and brick and occasional geometrically canted modern architectural styles set back from the sidewalk on wide spacious manicured front lawns.

George and Nikos were intrigued by the ravishing wide-eyed brunette at the wheel of the white Cadillac who was escorting Burton. They were unconcerned that he had left his car and were unaware that Burton's cell phone was not traveling with him. It remained hidden in the glove compartment of his BMW.

After stopping at three houses with Rasmussen Realty signs posted at the curb, and going inside, Pekka pulled into the driveway of the fourth home, a two story English Tudor gabled structure with three stone fireplace chimneys thrusting upward from the gray composite shingle roof. A slightly disheveled man greeted Pekka and Burton at the front door. George and Nikos parked at the curb and cranked their seats back to take a snooze.

Burton nodded to Robert Ostraich and the two strangers with whom Darcy had arranged the meeting using Pekka as a go-between. The man with the gray unshaven scruffy appearance had answered the door. The second man, Harold Esser's attorney, Michael Pollock, fiddled with the button of his navy blue suit coat stretched across his slightly protruding belly. His brown eyes peered myopically at Burton from behind thick black rim glasses. After the introductory handshake, he ran his right palm back over his thin, sprung rust-colored curls as though to transmit some of the good fortune Burton possessed to his own personal aura.

Ostraich quickly dispatched their names, Harold Esser, the plaintiff, and Michael Pollock, his attorney, as they sat around an oval hardwood dining room table. A tall skinny third man with an aquiline nose suddenly appeared from down the hall where the receding noise of a flushed toilet could be heard. As the man approached the table, Ostraich gestured toward Burton.

"Burt, this is Brian Bishop. He's an environmental scientist, a physical chemist who served as an expert witness on behalf of Harold. Although the judge allowed his testimony at the hearing, he still would not let the case go to trial. Brian can flesh out some of the legal issues Michael encountered."

"Before I say anything, I think my client needs to share what he and his family have gone through," said Michael, looking from Harold to Burton. "Harold, this appears to be the man who can make restitution for what was done to you."

"I can't make any promises," said Burton. "I'm sorry for what has happened to you and your family. I'm not sure my meeting you is going to help but I want you to know I care about you and I'm subject to the legal decision, as well. I can't personally have a gag order lifted any more than the doctors who diagnosed your medical condition."

Harold rubbed at his unshaven throat and stared for several moments at Burton before he spoke. "They tell me you're new," his voice was coarse and raspy, his breathing labored. "My attorney and Mister Ostraich, they're my only friends and allies I have in this fight. There are thousands of others like me, not only farmers but people living in suburbs, in towns." He coughed and slowly blinked his bloodshot eyes. His weathered ravaged face bespoke internal and mental suffering. Burton could see he was quite ill.

"There are ten farms in my sector. The Blake Oil Company came to us and offered each of us a half million dollars in cash for the right to drill on our land. In these bad times, we were glad to take their money, but the suits lied to us. They said everything would be done in a safe way, that every precaution would be taken to protect our families and our land and our livestock. We were fools to believe 'em. When the drilling started, nothing happened the way they said it would. After the derricks went up, the tanker trucks cut across my land back and forth day and night and parked at the well. There was fifteen of 'em. We couldn't sleep for the noise.   The suits and engineers said they'd put casings down the well shafts to keep gas and chemicals from leaching into the aquifier that has given all the farms and nearby towns pure water for over thirty years. Now we can't even drink it. It comes out of the tap brown and smells so bad, we had to move out of the house. They've got methane stacks shooting off flame into the air day and night that sounds like rockets from a launching pad. My kids came down sick and all their pets and half my lifestock died until I trucked in water for those who didn't. My three acre pond was so polluted the fish died and floated to the surface to add to the stink from fracking. Even the schools had to shut down. The frackers put up holding tanks not far from the house and pipes and conduits all over my fields. Blake Oil said it wasn't possible these things happened because of them. They flat out lied. My crops failed. I couldn't harvest corn, wheat, hay, nothing. Not a damn thing. If it wasn't for the royalty payments, we would've had to go on welfare. Hell, that farm was our life. In less than a year, we couldn't live there anymore.   I took soil samples to a lab and the tests proved it was toxic, contaminated with the chemicals the frackers put down the well. Our doctor said he had a gag order not to tell us what the chemicals were in the fracking mixture. Said Blake Oil claimed they were trade secrets. Trade secrets, bull shit. Your company paid off the judge."

"The company was managed by my father then, not now. That's why I'm here but, as I said, there isn't really more I can do to help. The case has to be tried in court."

"I'm familiar with the tests," said Brian Bishop. "I conducted several additional tests myself and confirmed the presence of benzene and strontium. What Blake Oil is after is oil, but the extraction process makes the fuel more dirty than coal and becomes a major factor in climate change. It isn't so much the vertical drilling that's the issue, it's the horizontal. Explosives are used to fracture the shale and release methane gas. Fracking fluids and sand and ceramics are pumped in under extreme pressure to force the fractures to stay open. The health and environmental problems happen when the chemicals and other contaminants flow back to be recycled. In the meantime, the extracted gas is transported in trucks and pipelines from the wellheads."

"Blake Oil claimed in court that fracking was only the fluid forced under high pressure into the crevices created by the explosions" Michael Pollock interjected. "Their attorney excluded everything else associated with the gas extraction process and the judge bought his argument. We know now he was paid off. But every step of the process collectively causes the contamination, negative health issues and environmental effects."

"I'm sorry that all I can do is offer an apology."

"Then you're no better than the rest of 'em," said Harold. "Comin' here is a waste of time."

Michael pulled a thin volume of paperwork from his briefcase and placed the legal document on the table in front of Burton. "This is a request to reopen the trial. That can only happen if you agree to Blake Oil's fiscal liability for the health problems incurred by residents in the fracking region and that you will stop the environmental contamination. That means you agree to cease drilling until you can provide EPA inspected and accepted methods to stop and to prevent the pollution. In addition, there will be damages brought forward in the suit, not only for Harold, but for many others who have suffered."

"You know as the CEO I can't sign this. I don't have the legal authority. You have to take it through the legal process. I have to have my legal department investigate this and see if they can reargue the case to have the gag order lifted. That would be the first step.

"I would like to provide Mr. Esser everything that is warranted, but I can't do it single-handedly. I'm a person, not a corporation. That's why we're sitting here talking to each other. I'll do everything I can within the limits of the law to help you and others who have been victimized by Blake Oil. I promise but it will obviously take time."

As Burton and Pekka returned to her car parked in the driveway, he took a moment to walk over to George and Nikos in their black SUV. "I know that took a while inside," he said through the open window. "I'm impressed with the house. I like it. I'm going to buy it. You've got a nice parking spot here where you can wait. Nice view, plenty of shade on a hot day."

"Congratulations, Mr. B," said George. "You won't have to stay at that old hotel anymore."

"It will be a relief. But the Ritz Carlton is a great hotel if you have to live in one. You should try it for a week. It's on the company, a reward for your constant vigilance."

"You're serious?"

"I'm always serious."

"Thanks, Mr. B. You're a generous boss."

"That's how it's supposed to be." Burton turned on his heel and walked to the open passenger door of Pekka's Cadillac.

* * *

Alan Erdman stormed past Darcy into Burton's office and slapped a legal document down on his desk.

"What you're asking me to do, we'd be up to our tits in alligators. We contested the Esser vs. Blake case months ago and the verdict was clear. Blake Oil is not responsible. A Federal judge issued a gag order.

"This is among the changes I presented at the stock holders meeting. Blake Oil and every other subsidiary that has anything to do with the health and welfare of people and in support of a clean environment is on the table for compliance with EPA regulations. We have to bring Blake Oil and Blake coal fire plants into compliance according to EPA audits. That's the law. And there's another issue."

"And what's that?"

"We have to clean up all hydraulic fracturing operations anywhere near cities, towns, suburbs, and farms by Blake Oil. All wells are to be dismantled and removed from private and public property and clean up operations are to be undertaken immediately and, to the extent possible, the restoration of whatever land and natural resources that have been contaminated. Anyone who has been affected by a Blake operation is to be duly compensated, including medical treatment. Those actions will also be subject to regulatory compliance and audit."

"My God, Burt, where do you get this?."

"Blake is in violation of EPA laws. If we don't comply, you and your staff will spend the rest of your lives fighting lawsuits that will cost the company billions, more than it will cost to clean up our operations and there's the risk of senior management being indicted. That's the downside of non-compliance, profit loss and job loss, not gain."

"As soon as this hits the media, Blake Corporation stock won't be worth a fucking dime."

"No, we'll be okay. Clean energy upgrades are critical to the future of this company and the health and well-being of people. Other companies are doing it and they're reaping the benefits. The upgrades will make us more competitive on the operational cost front and will continue to draw investors to our compliance with the clean air law for greenhouse gas pollution. I've read the studies on this and consulted with a leading environmental scientist."

"How about consulting our scientists. In case you're not aware, Blake has environmental scientists and engineers too. They do not recommend going down the road you're directing us."

"I wouldn't expect them to. We both know they're well paid company minions loyal to my father and Blake management. Our coal fire plants emit millions of metric tons of carbon dioxide and sulfur dioxide gases into the atmosphere every year. Combined with all the other plants in the country, those tons total in the billions."

"We're talking about your father's legacy."

"I would like it to be positive rather than negative. I also want to bring division managers and their employees more into the decision-making process in defining, supporting, and implementing compliance."

"Hold on there, Burt, son. Hold on. You haven't grabbed the bull by the horns. You grabbed its tail. It's a dangerous position. Let's get Larry and Earl in on this." Alan stepped back through the door into Darcy's office. "Darcy, call Larry and Earl. Tell them there's an emergency meeting in Burt's office happening right now. Whatever they're doing, tell them to drop it."

"Yes, sir, right on it."

* * *

Four of them met that night in the den of Lawrence Harden's opulent mansion. In addition to Harden, Earl, and Alan, another key manager had been ordered to join them, Fred Dolby, the Director of the Blake Security Division.

"He's going rogue on us," said Lawrence gulping at his glass of three hundred dollar Scotch. "Just like Elias flipped on us. The fucking son-of-a-bitch is going rogue. He's doing serious damage to our company, and more importantly to our plans – to us. What did you find out, Fred?"

"George and Nikos never let him out of their sight. Although we know Burton met with Ostraich and that lady doctor, Lizzie Dawson, and her daughter. Her name's Olivia Quintana. Her father died. He was a Filipino married to the lady doctor. The daughter is some kind of social organizer, one of those millennial do-gooder types. We also found out she's a member of the Occupy horde of rats."

"Our native son is obviously impressionable." said Earl.

"He's a fucking tenderfoot," Lawrence crunched an ice cube. "He doesn't know the realities of running a global business. All he has to do is keep his hands out of it and take our advice. Shit! He's gonna put us all in deep shit if we let him go any further with this!"

"I would recommend we go along with him on the environmental compliance," said Alan, "or we'll be in deep legal trouble. Could even be indicted if we don't. Actually, he'll come across in the media as the poster boy we intend for him to be."

"Do you realize how many billions of dollars we're going to lose if we stop fracking? I'm not just talking about domestic markets. I'm talking about export of liquified natural gas. We make more revenue in foreign markets than we do at home. But if we let him cut that off …"

"Not cut off," said Alan, "just clean up. We can at least do that."

"We have ways to look like we're in compliance," said Earl, "and we can make sure whoever comes to inspect our operations is in synch with us. We use our lobbyists to their best advantage."

"But what if all this doesn't work? What if he sticks it to us?"

"He doesn't want to stick it to us," said Alan. "Compliance isn't sticking it to us. It's a little effort that will help us."

"And if it doesn't, what's our plan B?"

"What it's always been," said Fred.

"We bring in Reardon."

Fred nodded. "This is really good Scotch. Where did you get it?"

"A distillery in Scotland."

"Do we own it?"

"Yes, you should visit it sometime."

"Not much of a Scotch drinker, but I could convert, like moving over from one religion to another."

"What religion are you?" asked Earl.

"Atheist, but I could become Scotch."

They shared uproarious laughter.

"Not a time to be humorous," said Lawrence. "We're into some serious shit."

"That we are," said Earl. "But we've always been serious about our shit and we've always come out on top."

"I can't get over the feeling he knows more than he lets on."

"He's just smart. Picks up on things," said Alan. "He could've made a decent lawyer."

"Why don't you send him down that path. Hold his hand."

"He's too pure, too ethical. Trial lawyers would have him for lunch."

"Somebody's having him for lunch. Maybe he's being blackmailed. Maybe he walked into a trap."

"I'm more concerned that he's setting a trap for us."

"What makes you say that?"

"The way he takes in information. It doesn't play back the way we want to hear it. It's almost like he's a spy."

"Who the hell's he spying for?"

"Nobody that I can think of. He's just on the other side. He isn't pro-business. He's anti-business. Elias would never have done what his son is doing to this company."

"But, in fact, Elias tried. You think there's some connection?" asked Lawrence. "Something about the will?"

"I wrote the will with his blessing and approval. Elias signed it. There's nothing hidden there. As a matter of fact, it's one of the cleanest documents he ever turned out. No tricks, no twists. We're just dealing with a different personality. Burt keeps telling us he's not like his father. Well, he isn't. It's up to us to handle him."

"For how long?" asked Earl.

"Only as long as we have to. I'll have another." Alan handed his glass to Lawrence leaning against the bar.

Chapter 27

The Warning

Tailed by George and Nikos in their black SUV, Burton turned in at the gated road lined with spreading oak and towering elm trees to a massive three story mansion patterned after an 18th century English baronial country estate surrounded by two hundred acres of forests and fields bisected by a stream that fed into a small lake stocked with bass and trout. Alexis's ten show hunters roamed a large green pasture adjacent to a stable constructed of the same heavy stone as the house to which it was connected by a wide crushed granite path.

He parked in the circular driveway and walked up the masonry steps to the front door. His hand tapped a heavy brass knocker twice. He waited and the solid oak door opened to reveal a black-uniformed African American maid. "Hello, Sir. Welcome. Please come in. Mrs. Blake is expecting you."

The vision of the stunningly attractive sixty year old socialite returned to Burton. By her expression and demeanor, her high fashion couture and lustrous coiffed silver hair, Burton sensed her strong aggressive personality. He remembered her legginess and that she had to consciously work at concealing vestiges of physical awkwardness. She topped six foot two in her bare feet. Although he hadn't heard it before, he was about to experience her social signature, a loud raucous laugh.

"Hello, Burton, dear, I'm glad you agreed to come and see me. Frankly, I wasn't sure you would. I'm concerned about what might happen to you with that nest of snakes you've been thrown in with. You might be surprised that your mother and I talk, but I haven't told her about this. She's a very nice woman. I don't want to worry her. May I offer you a drink?"

"A cold beer sounds good. I'm not much for the heavy stuff."

"So unlike your father. You don't mind if I indulge? I am much for the heavy stuff." She reached into a refrigerator behind the entertainment bar tucked along the oak paneled wall of a massive living room illuminated by a clear three story dome. "Alaskan beer okay? Elias had a thing for Alaskan beer and Canadian whiskey. Said it reminded him of the wilderness."

"That's one part of him I guess I'm familiar with. My real reason for coming is to learn more about my father."

"Curiosity can be a strong motivator. Do you know, if it had not been for the bear, it's not likely I would have ever met and married your father," said Alexis. "He would have stayed married to your mother."

"Did he tell you about what happened?"

"Yes, and surprisingly, or perhaps not so surprisingly, he never really got over your mother's reaction."

"Did he ever do anything like that with your children?"

"No, I think the grizzly bear incident cured him of the impulse. That sort of thing wouldn't have worked with my children anyway. They're too lazy, spoiled and egocentric. The only way he was able to relate to them was spoil them further instead of challenging them. He lavished everything on them they wanted to the point they became putrid, rotten little putzs, even by my standards, and I tolerate a great deal because I accept what we have as our due."

"I take it, then, you don't think much of them."

"Oh, not at all. I love them. I love them dearly. Spoiled and all, they are beautiful and endowed with unsocial graces. What has been done cannot be undone."

"Sounds like our father kind of went overboard." Burton sipped from the chilled pilsner glass.

"I think your father was always trying to compensate for his crippled foot," said Alexis. "Only he went from one extreme to the other."

"Did his foot ever bother you? As I recall, he pretty much ignored it."

"No, he was an extremely handsome and virile man. How often do you get hung up on someone's feet?"

"Unless you have a foot fetish."

"No, not me. How manicured someone's feet are is unimportant. Depending on where you live, they're meant to get us from point A to point B."

Burton looked at her highly flexed arch and precisely manicured red toe nails prominently displayed in one thousand dollar soft leather Gucci sandals. "Your feet look well taken care of. Quite beautiful."

"Why thank you, Burton, what a nice compliment."

"I've seen a lot of beautiful feet. Dancers in Thailand and Bali. They take very good care of their feet. They're works of art. Their entire bodies are works of art in costume and in motion, the way they move in dance."

"So you have an eye for bodies."

"An appreciation is a better term, for artistic line and form."

"So, those dancers represented only art, not sex."

"Not with me. That's their business."

They both laughed.

"I'm sorry we never became acquainted before this, Burton. Elias told me he was honoring your mother's request not to contact her chidren and asked me to do the same. But I was always curious about you, interested I should say. Elias tried whatever means he had available to find out how you were doing."

"So I was told by his attorney."

"Alan Erdman and I are close friends. Elias told me himself he was anonymously donating money to your third world projects. He certainly preferred you to our son, Richard. Much of that was my fault. We got into some heated arguments about how I was spoiing him and our daughter. Other than that, Elias and I got along well. Maybe because I was a hell raiser like my father. Elias was quiet and private. He valued his privacy. Hated it when I threw a party. Wasn't at all comfortable with society types. Where I got it, my pa was my hero. To me, he was larger than life, loud, brazen, told me wild stories about himself, mostly lies looking back, about climbing mountains and exploring jungles, fighting off lions and tigers. He worked in the oil fields until one night he hit the jackpot. He was an inveterate gambler and heavy drinker. Knocked my mother around until she left us. I got my share of beatings too. Even so, I wanted to stay with my pa and moved back in with him three years later. I loved him in spite of himself, or because of himself. He'd used his winnings to buy oil property in Texas. The first well came in big. He used some of that money to sink more wells and buy more land. In five years, he became a billionaire. But didn't live much longer after that. Booze killed him. What's coincidental is that your quiet, soft-spoken father, the man I married, actually did hunt big game, climb mountains, and explore jungles. He was the real McCoy. That's what attracted me to him. Not his money. I had already inherited a fortune. I was bored with money. All it could do was buy me expensive clothes and homes, a yacht in the Mediterranean, a private jet, skiing junkets in the Swiss Alps, show horses, more houses than I could live in, and on and on. Not that I would ever give all that up, mind you. I enjoyed every minute of it then, and I do now. It's what I have to pass along to my children when my time comes. I expect to live to be a hundred. Your father infused my life with something greater, another dimension that I only imagined my pa had. Elias was a source of energy, a life force. Sounds trite, but true, at least for me.

"When your parents' divorce was made public, I wanted to meet your father. His exploits in the business world, as well as an adventurer and hunter had my attention. I knew I'd never get to meet him in a social setting. He avoided them. So I decided to approach him with a business proposition that partnered our companies. Of course, I wore an expensive stylish business suit. There was cleavage and plenty of exposed leg to whet his imagination. That meeting was repeated with the involvement of our attorneys and CFOs. Andamiano Oil merged with the Blake Corporation. I cemented the deal by inviting Elias to accompany me on a hunting safari in Africa, which Elias found very appealing. My father had taught me how to handle a rifle and I was a crack shot, which," she grinned, "along with other personal attributes, caused Elias to fall in love with me. Our son, Richard, was conceived one night on that safari while hyenas howled and lions roared out beyond the camp in the African night. Pretty amazing story, but we both led and continued to lead amazing lives.

"Our daughter, Savannah, was born three years after Richard. Elias named Richard after Richard The Lion Heart. Savannah was named after the savannah grasslands of the African veldt. His only regret was that you and your brother and sister weren't part of our family. He felt great remorse over what he had done, risking your life to kill a bear. He never put me in that position on any of our hunts, believe me. He didn't have to. I was always a step ahead of him in making a kill."

"I have to say I don't share your enthusiasm," said Burton. "I sympathize with the animals."

"Oh, posh, animals are on this earth for our food and entertainment. Think of the zoo, the circus, horse racing. I own five German Hanoverians for dressage and five English show hunters for riding cross country. I have a Rotweiller and a Wolf hound for household pets and professional trainers for all my animals. We own a buffalo ranch in Montana and shoot our own meat when we feel so inclined. We also own a cattle ranch in Wyoming. Our prime beef is shipped to us here through a Chicago meat packing company Elias bought shortly after we were married."

Burton grinned. "No ducks or chickens?"

"Elias shot ducks during duck season, doves and quail during their seasons, and deer. He was partial to venison. We have chickens on the property here. Fresh eggs every morning if we want."

"In learning about the company, I noticed there's an agricultural division, corn and dairy."

"A small percentage of the business dabbles in bio-fuel, ethanol and methane. But we favor what comes out of the ground, coal and oil. Elias didn't think highly of alternative fuels and sources of power, and he didn't believe there was any truth in what the environmental fear mongers had to say about global warming until about a year ago. Then something changed him."

"What about you?"

"I believe what the scientists tell us," Alexis tossed back the rest of her drink, then rose from her chair to fix another. "The greenhouse effect is real. I'm not about short term profits for oil companies over the destruction of the environment, which may sound strange to you, since I own an oil company."

"Then this shouldn't surprise you. I'm taking the company in the direction of environmental compliance and research and development of renewable and alternative energy sources."

"I know. That's the real reason I wanted you to come and talk to me, to give you a warning. I never got involved in the day to day operations of the company. I was a silent partner until Elias died. When I tried to step in, the board and management blocked me. I only know what happens because of an informer."

"I plan to manage the company as a socially responsible organization," said Burton."

Alexis turned to face him with a clink of fresh ice in her cut glass. "Elias was right. He told me you had ethics, but they weren't learned from him. They were learned from your mother. Elias didn't give a damn about laws and regulations if he could find some way to circumvent them. He had his lawyers and accountants and a capital investment firm working on it full time."

"I know. I've been briefed."

"You're boxed in. You know that. Elias worked a lifetime to build that corporation. He tried to make it impervious to invasion by regulatory agencies. You've got your hands full and you'll be up to your ass in alligators if you don't go with the flow. They'll stop at nothing to get their way."

"I'm aware of what I'm up against."

"That's why Elias put you in his will. He knew you would carry out the changes he intended. Whatever happened to him, he told me he regretted much of what he had done and said he was taking the company in a new direction. A year later, he was dead. Despite the autopsy report, I think he might have been murdered. He collapsed when he was out pheasant hunting a few miles from the house and the investigation implied that his gun went off as he fell and killed him. The groundskeeper found him with his two setters curled up next to him."

"Now I understand why my mother called me back from South Africa. She believes I can rectify what he has done."

"Well, you're one of the young people, Burton. Your mother and I know each other. Not well, but we occasionally talk. The future rests in the hands of young people now. You're a new generation. You have different goals and values. I'm just sorry my two kids didn't turn out like you. But they never had a chance with Elias and me for parents. He told me a strange thing about what happened in Alaska. He always had a fantasy about saving you. That's another reason he funded your projects. That was his way of loving you."

Burton remained silent.

"I wish you the best, Burton. I know it won't be easy. Thank you for coming here. It means a lot to me."

Burton rose from his chair and crossed to her. She leaned toward him slightly, hoping for a kiss on the cheek. Instead, he shook her hand.

"Please be careful," she said. "Watch your back."

"Goodbye, Alexis."

"Goodbye. Don't be a stranger."

Burton turned away and let himself out through the front door just ahead of the maid scurrying to open it for him.

Chapter 28

Regulated

In a large rural region in Central Illinois, a blistering Mid-west summer sun and ninety percent humidity beat down on Burton and his entourage of two EPA inspectors, the plant manager, two Blake senior engineers, Lawrence Harden and Earl Frederickson, who had sworn they would accompany and witness each and every audit of Blake coal fired plants. Wearing bright orange visitor hard hats and safety glasses, they toured the fifty acre facility riding in golf carts and walked the physical factory process on foot to access locations and check calibrations where equipment had been installed.

Devices to control and measure the output of emissions had been retrofitted throughout the acres of labyrinthine pipes, furnaces, turbines, stacks, and holding tanks according to an EPA approved plan. Now, the inspectors were visiting all six of the plants in Illinois and neighboring states to ensure the equipment had been accurately installed and was functionally effective. The follow-up would include the measurement and test data required to be reported on a monthly cycle.

The cost of the carbon dioxide scrubbers and absorbers for each plant had been substantial, three billion dollars per unit. There had been additional construction costs of eight million for flue gas desulfurization, sulfur dioxide removal, and polishing to meet the minimum requirement of ten parts per million per kilowatt. Nitrogen Oxide removal had to meet the standard of 0.07 million pounds per btu or less, a cost of three hundred dollars per ton for NOx scrubbing.

Nine months earlier in the Blake Corporation conference room, studies and recommendations had erupted into caustic arguments over whether to retrofit the plants or convert them to natural gas power sources which could draw from Blake hydraulic fracturing operations. A decision had been made to retrofit three of the plants and convert the remaining three to natural gas, then assess the results in terms of cost, efficiency, and compliance with clean air regulations, which would be more easily achieved since natural gas was a clean-burning fuel and did not produce and emit carbon dioxide into the atmosphere.

Few words passed between them other than questions asked by the inspectors and a discussion with process operators sitting at a deck of seven flat screens populated with four color diagrams showing the status of the plant systems in real-time twenty four hours a day.

As much as he had wanted to avoid public notice, thanks to Robert Ostraich, Burton had been thrust into the forefront of media news focusing on the actions and ethics of the new young CEO.

Darcy screened a plethora of threatening phone calls and Emails.

The television network interviews immediately appeared in U-tube format and went viral on the Internet within one day. A fourth U-Tube segment of which Burton had not been aware showed him entering a restaurant with Olivia Quintana in downtown Chicago. It was particularly noted by the Blake Corporation's security office. Fred Dolby reported it to Alan, Lawrence, and Earl. They met in the conference room and he called it up on the wall screen.

"Who the hell is that?" asked Lawrence.

"Her name's Olivia Quintana. She lives with her mother who's a retired doctor in Lincoln Park. George and Nikos followed him there."

"They look pretty cozy," said Earl.

Lawrence belched. "A little too cozy."

"You know, we're not going to get Burt to change," said Lawrence. "The board and some of the investors want to either curb him or get rid of him."

"We can't curb him," said Alan. "And we obviously can't influence him. The one thing that makes him like his father is he is strong minded. Once Elias set his sight on something, you couldn't get him to budge either. It was like he was looking down a gun barrel at some game he was determined to kill. You never wanted to get in his way. It wasn't healthy."

"Burton isn't dangerous," said Lawrence. "At least not to us personally. He's a danger to the company. The Blake Corporation is bigger than any one of us, bigger than all of us. It has an identity and an existence of its own. It's a living breathing being, a corporation, our corporation. We're here to serve its existence."

"It's purpose is to make a profit, to make money," said Earl. "The rest of it just sounds like hocus-pocus."

"Well, I believe it like religion," said Lawrence. "It is religion, not in the spiritual sense, but in the material sense. We're on this planet to make as much money as we possibly can. That's our purpose. That's what life is all about."

"I'll take what money can buy," said Earl.

"Alan grinned. "We're getting to be a bunch of grumpy old farts with all the side effects. Fifty years ago, we might have been out there marching with those kids. We had different causes then, Vietnam, segregation." He chuckled, "Women's rights."

"Did you march for women's rights?" asked Earl.

"No, but I prosecuted a few cases of discrimination and sexual harassment, even assault and rape."

"We're off topic," said Lawrence. "Our wayward boss is out there in the public eye. We gonna isolate him?"

"He has a lot to learn," said Alan. "He's still wet behind the ears."

"We can use an indirect approach," said Dolby. "We can bring in Reardon and move slowly. It's a persuasion strategy some of my contractors used in the Middle East. You don't go for the center. You nip around the edges so he gets the message that we are in control. You only go for the centerpiece when there aren't any more options. That's plan C."

"When and where do you want to begin?"

"I'll get in touch with Reardon and offer the same terms the last time we used him. Of course, the stakes are much higher. His price is likely to go up."

"Offer him a million," said Lawrence. "If he wants more, offer two. Price is not the issue here."

"What if he wants more than two?"

"Ask him to name his price."

Fred nodded. "You want me to handle the payment the same?"

"Half up front, half when it's done."

"I'll give him what he needs to know."

"Give him a completion date. We're running out of time."

"I'm sure he can handle that."   Fred watched a close-up of the young woman, Olivia Quintana, on the screen.

"I could fuck her," said Earl. "She's got a nice body"

* * *

Reardon parked his jeep on a narrow side road that afforded him a clear view of the Esser farm house and the gas rig a quarter of a mile away in what had been a cow pasture. From his concealed location on a low wooded hill, he could see anyone coming and going from the house, now abandoned by the Esser family because of the contamination caused by the fracking operation. He panned his high powered binoculars slowly away from the house to the gas rig operation, which was completely deserted by a pre-arrangement. No crew members moved about the high reinforced composite fence enclosure and the fifteen high-pressure diesel trucks that had been parked within the compound only a day before were now gone. No vehicles approached along the remote country road to the site. He started the engine and drove the jeep slowly down the dirt track to the farm house.

He parked in the driveway and lifted a small tightly wrapped burlap bundle from the back seat and walked around to a side window on the garage wall. Pulling on a pair of latex gloves, he shattered the glass with a hammer taken from the package. He probed inside and released the window lock, raised the frame, tossed the package inside, and scrambled through. Searching about, he selected a location on a shelf cluttered with hand tools and placed the package among them. Then he exited through the window and returned to the jeep.

Crossing the narrow gravel road that bisected the farm house property from the well site, he stopped at the gate and unlocked it with the key provided him by Fred Dolby during a secret meeting the day before. He drove through the open gate, parked next to the well platform, and removed a second package similar to the first from the back seat floor of the jeep. He climbed the platform steps, opened the package, and laid out its contents of high explosive plastics materials, dynamite fuses and caps and timing devices on the surface. Working at an unhurried pace, he planted the explosives at strategic locations at the base of the rig and lowered a tightly wrapped bundle of dynamite on a rope down into the drilling shaft. He set a timer in the control box for detonation in thirty minutes. He returned to the jeep, drove back outside the compound, locked the gate, and drove quickly away from the area.

He was just turning onto the main two lane highway when he heard the massive explosion erupt like a volcano several miles behind him.

Two days later, police arrested Harold Esser at the home of his sister in Peoria where he and his wife and children were staying. He protested that he knew nothing about the bombing of the gas rig on his farmland. But crime scene investigators had discovered the explosives stored in his garage. There was no question regarding the broken glass pane on the side wall of the garage, since the blast had shattered every window of the house.

Following publication of the incident in The Tribune, Robert Ostraich called Burton to tell him he was convinced the damning evidence had been planted, but there was no way to prove it. Although Harold would be indicted and imprisoned, his wife and children would still benefit from the compensation paid them by the Blake Corporation.

Human social behavior fascinated Reardon. Descriptions, commentary, and live footage were accessible to him through a variety of media from numerous sources. He remained invisible, a voyeur to the amalgam of conflict and hysteria that filled the world. People, their cultures and societies were replete with differences in beliefs, values, opinions, influences, and power for which there was no possibility of consensus, any form of agreement, and resolution. Therein lay the source of his occupation like a writhing seething intangible morphology.

From time to time, he entered that world, provided his service for a substantial sum of money, then disappeared again. Like all other commodities, trading in death and destruction was profitable. He perceived that people were basically amoral and made the world such. The artifice of religion intended to provide rules and regulations prompted violent confrontation and the laws of governments and society were created only to be circumvented or broken.

He existed among the covert periphery of mercenaries and hired killers and assassins who had found a new market for their combat skills learned in the most clandestine military units and as CIA contractors. He recognized the inextricable link of commerce, U.S. Government interests and its associated militarization of politics and war, economic empire building, and the influence of billions of dollars circulated through lobbyists, personal bank accounts and other public and private exchanges. Greed and corruption were the way of American life called free market enterprise and the life of other societies and they provided him a very good living. He perceived that what he did, the services he offered, in a small way and occasionally in a large way, facilitated free enterprise by removing obstacles to someone's or some organization's financial goals.

He had known Fred Dolby when they served together in a secret commando unit. Their friendship had grown out of the camaraderie they shared with the other men and their station in the warrior class, leaders in the forefront of military superiority and supremacy. With the advent of technology, he recognized that the tradition of soldiering was becoming obsolete, but that he could use technology to move his career in a different direction.

He had converted the cellar of his mountain home in Northern Idaho into a virtual command center, a repository of data and information that allowed him to capture and interpret social and political and economic events and trends that identified opportunities for him to offer his services through carefully vetted and well-paid go-betweens. Many of the interventions were arranged through Fred Dolby, who was an insider and overseer for the security of financial and physical operations funded through Blake Corporation philanthropy by Walt DeMint.

The advent of Burton Blake had created a problem that could alter and reveal what had been a profitable and seamless operation for the past three decades, the system to which the journalist, Robert Ostraich, had alluded, but could never prove.

Experienced in psychological warfare, Reardon had introduced the Blake management team to what he termed his nip and tuck method of persuasion. The demise and sometimes intentional accidental death of a related someone who mattered to the target invariably brought him into line. The strategy was Reardon's unique form of extortion by collateral damage.

Reardon spread a thick smear of butter and lingonberry jam on a large spherical slice of San Francisco sourdough bread. The label bearing the cityscape of its namesake kick-started his memory of a weekend he had enjoyed with an escort one month ago in The City by The Bay.

Given his chameleon-like life style, he had presented himself as a wealthy stock broker to the sophisticated sexy brunette who had come to his room at the Top of The Mark. He had divested his image of boots and jeans and western style shirt and replaced them with expensive Armani suits, silk shirts worn open at the collar, and one thousand dollar leather shoes. His hair was fashionably trimmed short with a slight spike and his jaw-line shadowed with a fashionable day's growth of dark beard. A gold Rolex encircled his left wrist. She had cost him twenty thousand dollars for the two days and nights and he had sent her on her way with an additional five-thousand dollar tip for her services. He did not plan to ever hire her again. The next time would be a different woman. He did not want to encourage or engage in any kind of personal relationship, hired or otherwise.

On a Blake Corporate jet, Reardon made a pre-dawn flight from Boise and landed at O'hare International four hours later. Avoiding traceability through any rental car transaction, he rode public transportation into downtown Chicago, checked into a hotel under an assumed name and paid five hundred dollars in cash in advance for the room.

Olivia stepped out of the shower and toweled herself dry, checking on a split toe nail which she quickly filed smooth before dropping the towel and taking up a brush and hair dryer. With her reddish hair whipping and flying about her face, she hummed a tune whose source she couldn't remember, but that stuck in her mind until the next one would come along as they constantly did throughout her busy day while she worked and listened to her IPod set on shuffle providing a range of different musical styles and genres. For her, the auditory stimulation was more effective than coffee, although she always picked up her first cup of Starbucks to go in the lobby of the office building that housed Next Millennium.

After dressing in her usual skinny jeans, layered tank top over a half- blouse, and ballet slipper shoes, she checked her IPhone for messages, returned a text from a friend, then hurried downstairs for a quick breakfast of multigrain toast coated with butter and strawberry jam, fresh orange juice, and a bowl of fruit and granola cereal.

Other than exchanging a morning greeting with her mother, she concentrated on reading Emails and text messages while she munched down her food.

Dolby had provided Reardon with information about Olivia's daily routine, route from home, the parking structure and location of her blue Kia a block from her office, and her habit of buying a grande cappuccino from the local Starbucks in the lobby. Reardon checked the digital image of her on his IPhone as she entered and walked over to the Starbucks counter. He knew she would take an elevator to her office on the tenth floor and that he would next see her when she came down with associates to go to lunch at one of three nearby eateries that catered to local business patrons.

Dressed in running shoes, shorts, T-shirt and carrying a sports bag, he left the lobby and walked to the parking structure to locate the level and space occupied by her car where he would be waiting for her that evening.

He dozed on the flight back to Boise and was in his mountain home by midnight.

Burton learned of Olivia's assault from her mother. Lizzie called him in a hysterical rage, blaming him for the attack on her daughter because of her association with him. "She's in a coma in the hospital. I'm with her now."

Burton did not know how to respond to her except to ask when and where she had been assaulted. He called the police for details and was told he had to come down and see them. Before they would give him any information, they questioned his whereabouts at the time of the assault and determined he was not a suspect. An investigating detective described the scenario he had pieced together.

She had been discovered lying on the concrete floor next to her car. Her right hand was clutching the car keys and her purse had not been disturbed. She was unconscious and did not respond to efforts by the paramedics to revive her and was diagnosed by a doctor as being in a coma when she arrived at ER.

Burton suppressed the inclination to go to Lizzie's house and commiserate with her. He had almost immediately decided against it, as he realized a pattern was beginning to emerge in what had happened to Harold Esser and now to Olivia. He knew he was being watched and tracked, probably through a chip in his cell phone. Any further association with Lizzie would make her vulnerable to what Burton perceived as an attempt to control him and prevent him from pursuing his corporate agenda. He also had to be wary of indicating he suspected a level of conspiracy in the company. He knew that to react, he had to make himself the target and divert attention from others.

Something in the arrangement had changed. Burton noticed the absence of his bodyguards. George and Nikos were no longer following him around when he was on foot and their black SUV had disappeared from his rearview mirror. He didn't miss them, nuisance that they were, but he suspected something else was about to happen. The thought of Blake Security as a kind of in-company Gestapo that would set up Harold Esser and assault Olivia sickened him. They were a function within the company, his company. Ultimately, he held himself responsible, and ultimately, only he could change that. It would have to be done in a special way, but he could not do it alone.

"Next Mill has some awesome computer geeks." Burton remembered Olivia saying when she had invited him to visit her office.

Among the staff to whom he was introduced, he remembered a recalcitrant techy working with spreadsheets of financial data at a bank of computers. He did not remove his headset to acknowledge the introduction and barely glanced up and nodded at Burton's outstretched hand.

Given his earlier lack of reception by Zach Lubinsky, he was uncertain how to approach the lanky young man with the shoulder length wavy brown locks streaked with red and green and a drooping mustache and goatee. His proposition might completely turn off the computer engineer, but then again, he might appeal to Zach's empathy for Olivia. If not lovers, they had obviously been close friends, more than just office buddies.

Burton worried that by going to the offices of Next Millennium, he might be unknowingly establishing the next target for the assassin. He hoped that the fact he and Zach had never been seen talking together would obfuscate the contact being made and deter any action against an individual. But Burton did not put it past the Blake senior management team financially taking down an entire organization if it actively opposed them.

He waited until a few minutes before five o'clock before entering the building from around the corner and taking the elevator up to the tenth floor. He was relieved to find that most of the staff were leaving or had already gone. Zoning on reggae music channeled through his head phones, Zach intently scanned his four computer screens while his fingers raced over the keyboard in a staccato rapid-fire dance as though he were playing an orchestral instrument. He did not look up when Burton seated himself in a vacant chair at a neighboring work station. Zach suddenly stopped clicking the keyboard, slowly removed his headset, and turned his chair to face him, peering at him through thick tortoise shell-rimmed glasses as though he were some kind of organism other than human.

"It never would have happened if you had not contacted her. She could have lived her life doing good for the world. But now she's in a coma because of you."

That Zach seemed to intuit why he had come startled Burton, but he thought there would have been no other reason for him to be there. "She could be brain dead because of me. I admit that. Had I known the kind of people I'm dealing with, I never would have gone to see her. I never would have exposed her to any of it."

"They aren't people, Blake. They're fucking monsters, blood sucking slugs that live under rocks."

"I want to take them down. That's why I've come to see you."

"What do you think I am, dude? Do I look like a hit man?"

"Of sorts. Olivia told me about your capabilities. She called you a techno-wizard. Said you could do anything with computer systems, that you even worked for the FBI helping them solve cyber crimes and that you do contract work for the information and social networks. I hope you'll work with me. I'll pay you any amount you ask."

"This isn't about money, Blake. I don't want your dirty money. Most of it was come by dishonestly anyway. I know very well how corporations like yours operate."

"It's mine in name only. I inherited the company when my father died. I've been trying to change it and now, this."

"I loved Olivia, not like a girlfriend, but as the dynamic, sweet, laughing, intelligent, life-enjoying, giving, wonderful person she was. So, no, if you want me to do something in Olivia's memory, this isn't about money."

"It is and it isn't. You don't have to take any payment. I understand how you feel about her. In the short time I knew her, I felt the same. I admired her. I would have done anything to prevent this. But it's too little too late."

"Then what do you mean it is and it isn't?"

"I want to drain 50% of all Blake offshore bank accounts directly into IRS data banks, then move the rest of the off-shore corporate accounts and all the top manager's private off-shore accounts into an anonymous domestic account that I can use to finance agricultural, alternative energy and environmental causes and anything and anywhere else I want to spend that money. Don't tap into the domestic corporate financial systems with domestic banks. There is more than enough there for the company and all its divisions to continue operations and to be profitable. And leave the Blake managers domestic accounts alone. They'll feel the effects of losing their private offshore holdings and they aren't going to starve. If they feel squeezed, they can sell some of their twenty and thirty million dolar homes. They're still coming out of this as multi-millionaires. I'm just pressing down on the greed factor."

"I'm with you, Blake, but what you're asking me to do is called cyber crime and could put me in prison for the rest of my life."

"I think of it in the reverse. I see it as decriminalization. Can you do it so none of it is traceable?"

"That's the easy part. It's a world class hacker's bread and butter. You're telling me you want to take down your whole company, all those billions like so much digital toilet paper."

"Not take it down. Recreate it. Use the money that's there for the common good instead of for the obscene personal wealth of the people who want to keep running it the way it has always been. If stock holders want to stay with me, they're welcome, but on my terms, not the cabal that minds the store. I'd like to turn various divisions over to employees as ESOPs. There's no reason employees can't own the means by which they make their products. If they want to open their operations up to investors, that will be their call. They will become members of the board of directors instead of a clutch of cronies."

"This is really radical, Blake. I never thought I'd live to see anything like this happen. You're not weird and twisted like the suits and their lobbyists and politicians. They must really hate you. Don't you fear for your own life? People like you get whacked by assholes like them. Don't you know that? The Mafia isn't the only mob."

"I'm sorry," said Burton. "Maybe I shouldn't bring you into this. It's not your life. It's mine. But I don't know who else can help me."

"To give it to you straight. I'd rather you were the one who was in the hospital, not Olivia. On your other comment, it is my life. We're all in it. We're all involved. It's just a matter of whose side you're on. I am going to help you, Blake; but it doesn't mean you're going to come away clean. You're going to have to answer to somebody and you and I never talked. We never met. We don't know each other. After today, we'll never see each other again. I won't exist and you'll never find me. But there's no doubt in my mind that someone will come after you."

After Burton departed, Zach locked the main office doors, then returned to his work station. First, he cleared the screens of all the data and sites on which he had been working. Within minutes, he discovered how the Blake Corporation automated systems had been fire-walled. He encountered the encryption methods and, through experimentation, determined he needed twenty algorithmic decryption keys to decrypt and convert the ciphertext .

Three hours later, he was looking at the architecture of the entire financial system of the Blake Corporation, including all of its offshore accounts. Using the Blake passwords, he emptied the offshore accounts by digitally transferring ten billion dollars from the offshore banks into the IRS database for the corporation. Then he proceeded to follow the links of the personal offshore accounts belonging to each member of the Blake management team and digitally depositing them into a private domestic corporate bank account that was not traceable to Burton but was available to him under another name. All other domestic corporate finances he left untouched.

At the conclusion of all transactions, he re-encrypted the entire system at several levels so no manager or information technology staff member could ever access, restore, or in any way get back into the offshore accounts.

*   *   *

"We've been hacked! Holy shit! We've been hacked? " Crowley screamed as he ran down the hall to Lawrence Harden's office. He pushed open the door with such force that the impact at hitting the end of its hinges cracked the glass. "We've been hacked! I can't access and execute transactions with any of our offshore accounts!"

"What the hell do you mean?"

"I can't see what's going on with any of our offshore corporate accounts. We're blocked out! I can access our local banks and that's all! No one should have been able to do this!"

"Shit! You have got to be shittin' me!" Lawrence swiveled around in his desk chair and quickly tried accessing one of his private offshore accounts. After three warning messages that his user name and password were not recognized, he reached for his phone and called the bank in the Cayman Islands. He impatiently explained his dilemma and held the phone. Then the reply came.

"What is it?" asked Crowley. "What are you getting?"

"Nothing! I'm locked out!"

"Whoever did this laid a new encryption program over ours."

"What the hell does that mean?"

"It means someone has stolen all our offshore financial resources and locked us out."

"How are we gonna get back in?" He tried another bank, this time in the Bahamas. "Hello, this is Lawrence Harden. I'm calling concerning the following account number at your branch." He stated the number and waited. When the response came, he bolted from his chair.

"We have no record of your account with our bank or any of its branches."

"Bull shit! That's bull shit! I have ten accounts totaling fifteen million dollars with you!"

"I'm sorry sir. No such record exists."

Lawrence slammed down the phone. "Oh, Christ! Oh fuck! I can't believe it! I fuckin' can't believe it!"

A sudden flurry of movement in the hall caught their attention as twelve black suited agents converged on the offices. Their spokesperson, a trim attractive woman with no-nonsense eyes, stepped forward and showed her badge.

"Excuse me, gentlemen. We're from the IRS, the Attorney General's office. We need to talk to the Director of Finance and the CEO."

"Where is our fuckin' CEO?" shouted Harden. "Why isn't he here?"

By ten o'clock that night, each member of the management team had been subjected to interrogations and had expressed their individual reactions to millions hacked out of their offshore bank accounts. Crowley also had to explain the disappearance of the company's offshore accounts and how suddenly billions in years of back taxes had flooded the IRS data banks.

Other than to question his disappearance, Burton's name did not come up and Lawrence and Earl and Alan and Jeff Crowley avoided bringing his name into the questioning, since they couldn't respond to any requests for information about him. When the IRS agents had departed, Lawrence voiced what was uppermost in all the minds of the Blake management team.

"Are we still a company?" asked Earl. "Are we still in business. I don't know what the hell is going on."

"We're still in business," said Crowley. "The only thing that's changed is our corporate and personal offshore financial resources have disappeared, the nest egg, the reserves, yours, mine, ours."

"Shit!"

"All of the corporate and our individual domestic bank accounts weren't touched."

"Thank God for that."

"For the offshore to be targeted like that, Burton has some connection with this," said Harden. "I want to find out what."

"He has no reason to destroy the company," said Alan. "Whoever he had help him, he left adequate resources for the company to continue to operate. He just took out our offshore profit holdings. He said he wanted to improve on the company, make it better. It never occurred to us that someone else out there, maybe some group, some individual who hates what Blake stands for hacked into the system. Maybe it's not Burton at all. He doesn't have the technical skills and knowledge to pull off something like this, something on this scale. He had to have help."

"If that's the case, then who is the son-of-a-bitch?"

"I thought you might want to wait until the agents were gone before you hear this," said Dolby. "We lost track of Burton for twenty-four hours but picked up his signal again."

"Where the hell is he?"

"Alaska."

"Alaska?"

Dolby nodded. "Up on the Kenai. Looks like he's at the lodge."

"So what does that tell us?" asked Earl.

"What we want to know," said Lawrence. "It's time to get rid of our fucking poster boy. No wonder Elias wanted to bring him in."

"You have to admit he's done his job," said Alan.

"If he's behind this, then he's a criminal. He needs to be arrested and indicted. "

"We'd have to prove that," said Alan. "Also, his prominence makes it difficult to do anything against him without proof. Elias knew that. That's why he set up the will the way he did."

"We can use the media in our favor. Burton Blake has become a criminal, an outlaw."

"I don't think so," said Crowley. "The company is a target for the media. Always has been. They don't like us."

"Dolby," said Lawrence, "it's your show."

"Bring him back?"

"Is that an option?" asked Earl.

"It has to be," said Lawrence. "We need him inside the company to work through this. We have to get him under control. We can't have him running around loose out doing more damage."

Dolby shrugged and left the conference room.

"Look at us," said Alan. "We've turned into a bunch of old men. Maybe we should just leave this alone. Let it play out. We all have money, millions. We'll die soon enough, just like all our generation, and all this effort to make millions and billions of dollars will be meaningless. My father once told me he who dies with the most money doesn't really win anything. When the poorest man dies, he is equal to the wealthiest man in the world."

"Go fuck yourself, Erdman."

When the story of the Blake Corporation was presented to the media as a voluntary disclosure, surprisingly, only a small number of Investors pulled out. Others decided to take a wait and see attitude. Darcy discovered a personal check signed by Burton Blake in her desk drawer written to her for three million dollars. Employees throughout the company and its divisions had received thousands of bonus dollars in automated payments from an anonymous source.

In Johannesburg, South Africa, Abena Ekwensi received an automatic payment from the Blake Corporation for five million dollars in her organization's non-profit account.

IV REPRISAL

Chapter 29

The Bait

Noah Kaganuk combed out and plaited his long straight gray hair into a braid that hung down to the center of his back. He remembered Burton Blake as a ten year old boy and had not expected to see him again as a young man. Noah heard the distant buzz of the bush plane and watched it appear low over the trees and angle down upriver from the village at the location of the Blake hunting and fishing lodge. He had set out on his boat to inquire about the plane's landing.

The last time the lodge had been used was by Elias and a few of his cronies. Despite being offered a great deal of money, Noah had refused to be their guide. He had not known of the death of Elias Blake until Burton arrived.

The news from Burton that a man would come who wanted to kill him was unsettling to Noah. What was more unsettling was Burton's plan to stop the killer. He wanted to know if the grizzlies were active fishing for salmon in the area upriver where he had been attacked as a boy.

Now, Noah listened each day for the arrival of another plane or the sound of a boat coming past the village from downriver. Thus far, he had heard nothing. He and Burton had kept in daily contact using their cell phones.

At dawn of the fourteenth day, Noah awoke to the sound of the fishing cruiser approaching his village from the south. He rolled out of bed without disturbing his sleeping wife and stepped outside onto the raised porch of his cabin set back several hundred feet from the river.

When Reardon arrived, he docked the cruiser. The chop and cold shearing wind sweeping across the river's open expanse carried the scent of spruce and pine that clashed with the nauseating odor of decaying fish deposited by a shallow side current on the gravel beach. Carrying his high-powered rifle with safety off prepared to fire, he approached the lodge.   He walked up the porch steps and pushed open the unlocked door.   Peering over the gun barrel into the main room, he saw the lodge was deserted. He cautiously searched the interior, checking every room.   Then he spoke through his wireless microphone attached to an ear piece that linked him via satellite to Fred Dolby in Chicago.

"He's not here," said Reardon. "It doesn't look like anyone has been living here for some time."

"He has to be nearby then," Dolby's digitized voice came through the ear phone. "We're getting a steady and consistent signal from his cell phone in that area."

"Well, this is a big area. How precise is your target?"

"I'll give you a coordinate and you check it against your IPhone map."

Reardon waited for several minutes, listened to the information, and coordinated the location on his IPhone satellite tracking map. "He's upriver a ways, maybe a mile or two."

"He's probably fishing. You'll find him. He'll be there."

"I'm heading out."

"Good hunting."

Reardon returned to his boat at the dock, stepped on board, started the engines and navigated the channel to the north.

The signal in Burton's company-issued cell phone lured him near where two boar Grizzlies and three sows were feeding on salmon along the shoreline and at the center of the river rapids.

On shore, Reardon noticed paw prints of a grizzly in the mud and came across a pile of dried bear scat. The satellite location indicator on his IPhone and the encouragement from Dolby that he was getting closer convinced him to continue. If Burton Blake could survive being in the vicinity of killer bears, so could he. He assumed the one bear had probably crossed the river and moved on until he noticed movement in the tall grass on the opposite bank and the characteristic hump of a silvertip boar. Reardon thought the bear might be eating fish pulled out of the river and, since he was downwind, hadn't detected him.

Once he was out of sight of the bears, Reardon moved slightly away from the river and circled back through the tall dense tundra brush reddening into its traditional autumn color. He established a hidden position where he could observe what the bear might do next while he tracked the location signal from Burton's cell phone coming from among a pile of dead logs near the river bank.

As he watched Reardon moving closer and closer to within range of the grizzly, Burton had a vision of himself as a defenseless unaware ten year old boy positioned to be smelled and seen by the bear and to draw the animal to him within easy range of his father's rifle.

The bear finished eating the ten pound Coho salmon it had sent sailing out of the river with a powerful swipe of its paw. The fish was no more than a morsel and did little to satisfy his hunger. He raised his head with a mucous drooling snort at the cloud of black flies pestering his snout and wriggled his furry pig-shaped ears to test the air for threatening sounds. Hearing none, he pushed back through the grass and slid down the embankment to the edge of the water and stopped. He reared up on his hind legs to his full eight foot height and sniffed and listened to something he detected downstream obstructed by a slight bend in the river. Because his eyesight was weak, he decided to go and investigate. His thick abundant fur caught the sunlight and rippled over his powerful fifteen hundred pound body as he waded across the stream with quick long strides.

Reardon heard the voluminous angry roar only seconds before the bear charged out of the brush no more than twenty yards away. As he snapped off a wild shot that grazed and infuriated the animal, heavy claws ripped across his torso followed by a second paw that swiped the rifle away spinning it into the brush.

The bear's slavering jaws consumed Reardon's screaming head and, with a twist, severed it from his body, leaving it twitching spasmodically on the ground.   A pack of wolves would discover and devour it later that night.

Burton and Noah walked quickly away from the area to their hidden boat. Noah pulled the cord to start the engine and they moved downriver.

"This is not over for you," he said. "You will have to go back and confront them. Even though they can't touch you now, they will try to destroy you."

Burton stared at beams of sunlight glancing off the surface of the river.

"I know. It's only the beginning."

Chapter 30

The Disconnect

"The contacts are dead. They're gone. We lost them both."

Surrounded by Lawrence Harden, Earl Frederickson, Alan Erdman, Jeff Crowley and Walt DeMint in the security conference center three floors under the Blake Corporation building, Fred Dolby roamed the satellite scan where the day before, two red blips on the wide screen had identified the locations of Burton Blake and Henry Reardon in a region of the upper Kenai Peninsula in Alaska.

"What's odd is that neither of the contact signals moved until this morning. Now suddenly, they're both gone. Something must have happened. Reardon would have reported back to me immediately once he took out Blake. Something didn't go as planned. I don't have any way of investigating from our remote tracking position. Something happened to eliminate the electronics."

"What can you do about it?" asked Harden.

"The old fashion way. If I don't hear from Reardon in the next twenty-four hours, send someone up there to find out."

"Could something happen to him? He's a professional."

"I don't have an answer."

"Burton couldn't have gone up against him," said Crowley. He's not even an athlete let alone a fighter. He wouldn't know how."

"Nevertheless," said Dolby, "we're looking at a blank screen and we lost contact."

"Maybe he had some help," said Alan.

"What kind of help?" asked Harden. "There's nothing, nobody up there."

"Who are you sending?" asked DeMint. "George and Nikos? If Burton is somehow still alive and saw them, he'd know we set him up."

"But they could catch him off guard," said Harden. "Tell him they were sent to help and protect him since security discovered there was an assassin involved."

"Wouldn't work. They're not right for this. It's wet work. George and Nikos aren't killers. Besides, they admitted they actually got to like the kid. They don't know anything about what has happened and I want to keep them out of it."

"You have someone else then?"

"Yes," said Alan.

"Do we know him?"

"He's an agent from the U.S. Assistant Attorney's office investigating us. At this point, the less you know, the better."

"Why is that?" asked Harden.

"At the moment, we're up to our asses in alligators with the IRS and the Justice Department. If you don't know something, you can't give an answer if what happened turns into litigation."

"How much time we lookin' at?" asked Harden.

"We'll give him a lead. He'll fly up there to hopefully find and talk to Burton. Then we'll have to wait for his answer."

"What do we do in the meantime?"

"We still have a company to run," said Alan. "You and Earl particularly in operations. Nothing has changed in the plants and factories. What's happening comes under internal affairs. It involves only those of us in this room. Just go back to work. Fred, you keep me informed. This agent will come to you for information. I have to be prepared for any legalities."

"How could this happen?" asked Harden. "How could something go wrong?"

"We'll find out soon enough," said Dolby.

Five thousand miles away, Burton sat on the pinewood front veranda of the lodge, sipped from a glass of aged bourbon. The residual hum of the engines faded to silence as Noah navigated the power cruiser downstream where, in two days, he would return the boat to the outfitter rental company at Kenai with the story that he had discovered it adrift foundered on a shallow gravel bar along the shoreline near his home.

He and Burton had gone back to the scene of the grizzly attack to remove the electronic tracking device and cell phone from the ravaged body of the dead man. They retrieved Burton's cell phone which had been used to lure Reardon to his death. After smashing both devices with a sledge hammer, Noah had dropped them into a deep channel at the middle of the river.

Now, Burton sat waiting, not certain of what might happen next, although Noah warned him that after he turned in the cruiser, to expect a visit from the state troopers and the Department of Fish and Game at Kenai. He said that when they came, he would accompany them so that their stories were consistent.

Approaching Kenai, Noah throttled down the dual engines so he could navigate the twenty foot white cruiser through a fleet of commercial fishing trawlers anchored at widely spaced intervals across the harbor. He circumvented a cluster of float planes nosed into the landing and came about to take an opening at a weathered gray wooden dock raised on guano encrusted pilings. He cut the sputtering engines to silence and stepped out of the wheel house among rising diesel fumes onto the rear deck. He secured the boat with tie lines at the bow and stern, then climbed the steel ladder and strode to a large single story wood frame building in need of paint. He passed under the rustic plank sign above the door advertising the business of John Korb, Boat Rentals and Outfitter.

Noah exchanged greetings with the bald bespectacled Korb and explained that he was returning the cruiser that had drifted unoccupied to his village.

"Must have broke loose from its mooring," said Korb, who had rented Reardon the boat. He scratched his dark full beard. "Came in here lookin' like he knew what he was doin'. Bought a bunch of stuff, Winchester odd 6, 357 magnum for up close and personal, if it came to that, ammo, tent, sleeping bag, provisions, fishing gear and lures, pepper spray bear repellant. Said he was going for salmon but knew enough about bears to protect himself. Had plenty of money. Didn't even use a credit card. Paid in cash. Had a fat roll of thousand dollar bills. Figured he was just another one of the wealthy dicks who come up here. Didn't care for him much. Didn't say much. Kind of ignored me like I wasn't good enough to be talking to him. But I was glad to get his money. Charged him an extra five-hundred for his attitude. He didn't know the difference and wouldn't care if he did. You want me to call Fish and Game?"

"I'll go there. Since the boat is yours, you should talk to the state troopers."

"I'll do that. Thanks for bringin' it in. Good thing it didn't break up on the rocks somewhere."

Noah nodded, turned and stepped back outside. He paused a moment to look out at the cruiser and the river widening beyond to merge southward with the Gulf of Alaska. He followed the dock front boardwalk to where it connected to Main Street and waited several minutes for the local city bus.

A brisk cold wind off the river buffeted the low-lying terrain dotted with a mix of large flat-roofed metal warehouses and compact two story wood frame homes with steep-pitched roofs intended to prevent collapse from the weight of heavy snow. The nearly empty bus rolled past shops, restaurants, and bars and a super market along the Main Street Loop to Trading Bay Road. Until he resigned from the fish and game department, as a resident Native, Noah had been a fish and wildlife biologist who coordinated research projects with local villages and tribes in support of subsistence hunting and fishing regulations.

At the Department of Fish and Game office, Steve Rappaport looked up squinting from his study of data on one of several fishery projects along the Kenai River and its key tributaries.

"Noah." He unleashed his awkward six-foot-five frame from his desk chair as though flexing individual hydraulic joints. "Haven't seen you in ages." He came forward to greet Noah with a hearty embrace. "What brings you down the river, Brother?"

"A deserted fishing cruiser washed up at the village. Brought the boat to John Korb. He described the renter as a hunter with a big bankroll and an attitude. Thought you might want to find out what happened to him."

"You think he went overboard?"

"Korb said he seemed to know what he was doing."

"Doubtful since his boat went adrift. Doesn't take much in the way of smarts to anchor it and tie it up. He could've hiked to one of the cabins north of you. And everybody has a cell phone nowadays. Why didn't he just call Korb?"

"Unless something happened to him. Lot of grizzlies up that way. Fishing's good."

"You thinking bear attack?" Steve's thick black eyebrows met at the bridge of his large nose with a concentrated frown.

"Possible."

"Can't be too smart goin' off alone up there without letting someone know where he was," said Rappaport.

"Korb said he was a dick."

"Loners always worry me. I'll see Korb before I head up there. He reporting the incident to the police?"

"Yes."

"That'll be Kyle Dickerson. Him and me better go up there together. No tellin' what we'll find."

"You want me along? I've hunted and fished the area," said Noah.

"By all means, old friend. How's the family?"

"Getting' ready for winter. Nets are in the river."

"Kids back in school?"

"My youngest son graduated last year," said Noah.

"What field?"

"Computer science. He's a geek."

"What else. That's the big one for kids these days."

"What about your daughter?" asked Rappaport.

"Started nursing school."

"Good. Good. You need a ride up to your village?"

"Yes, when will you go?"

"Tomorrow morning after I talk with Kyle."

"I'll meet you at the dock," said Noah.

"Guessin' about nine. Where you stayin'?"

"In town, my cousin Benny."

"Thanks for comin' by, Noah. Hope this doesn't turn out to be what I think it is."

"I'll be at the dock at nine."

"Say hi to Benny for me."

"I'll do that." Noah raised his hand and departed.

The stench of his decaying remains made Reardon's body easy to locate. Dickerson and Rappaport shouted and charged at the bickering crows that blanketed the eviscerated flesh and bones. The birds rose and hopped away with raucous cries and a hideous flapping of sharp angled wings.

"Bear took him," said Steve.

"Where the hell's his head?" The investigating sergeant tramped through the nearby ground cover.

Noah and Rappaport shuffled through the hoary green moss-encrusted roots of spruce, hemlock, cedar, and lodge pole pine snaking and looping among the salmon berry, red alder, and devils club.

"Over here," said Rappaport. "Christ, what a way to die. Have your head torn off."

Kyle Dickerson and Noah walked over to look. Crawling with ants and maggots, the head and face crushed into pulp by the grizzly's jaws were unrecognizable. Searching further, Kyle discovered a few smaller bones dragged away by wolves and scattered among large spreading ferns.

"Don't touch any of this," said Kyle. "Have to take photos. I'll get a body bag." As though to escape the scene of bloody carnage, he walked quickly back to the police cruiser tied at the river bank. Of the infrequent murders he had investigated on the peninsula, nothing approached the savagery of what he had just witnessed. Although investigating crime scenes was always interesting, he disliked observing autopsies conducted by the coroner. The process reminded him of dressing out a deer or a moose, which he himself had done many times on back country hunts. Confronting a human corpse disturbed him. Try as he might, he could not emotionally maintain a professional distance and had to move away from the autopsy table to compose himself. His wife empathized with him and reasoned that he was just a sensitive man and not to be ashamed of his reaction. But seeing the condition of a body like this one made him want to swear off eating red meat.

When he returned with the body bag, Steve pointed out the discovery of a high powered rifle in a nearby thicket. Kyle examined the weapon. "One round was fired," he said. "Had no effect on the bear. You see any other blood?"

Steve shook his head. "Probably just pissed the bear off even more."

"Anybody else who might know this guy was up here?" asked Kyle. Noah shook his head.

"What about at that fancy ass lodge owned by the Blake company?"

"There is someone staying there," said Noah. "Don't know if he's connected."

"We need to stop and see, on the way back," said Rappaport. "Ask a few questions. Someone has to be notified. Next of kin. You know that other person?"

"I do," said Noah, "only his name, Burton Blake. He runs the company. Took over when his father died."

"So you talked to this Burton since he came up here?" A sinking sensation weakened Kyle's mid-section that something awful in this scenario was going to be revealed. He did not want to have to arrest this powerful native who could snap his own slender body in two, if it came to a struggle. He stopped himself from leaping ahead of the unknown facts. The man on the ground had clearly been killed by a bear, not by another man or other men.

Back in Kenai, John Korb had said the man was nothing more than an arrogant hunter. Something still didn't seem quite right to Kyle, just a gut feeling, his investigative intuition which had served him well in past cases. He went through the dead man's pockets and his wallet, whose contents had been strewn about. Maybe it was the absence of a cell phone. There was a driver's license and two credit cards bearing the name of George Sibelius. Everyone carried a cell phone these days. There was no sign of one here and he and Korb had not found one on the fishing cruiser. Kyle's suspicions were always aroused when the stink of money was involved. And he knew that anyone with the name Blake staying at the private lodge was a multi-billionaire.

He finished stuffing the attached and loose parts of the corpse the wolves had left into the body bag with the decapitated head last. He zipped the bag closed and peeled off his blue latex gloves slimy with blood. "One of you give me a hand with this."

Rappaport grasped and hefted the lower end. Kyle felt the head roll around inside the bag as they carried it to the police boat.

Noah carried the rifle.

As the police cruiser approached the dock at the Blake lodge, Kyle was surprised to see a young man wearing hiking boots, jeans, and a ski jacket walk out to greet them.

"He's Burton Blake," said Noah. "The son who inherited his father's company. He came up here on a retreat."

"Alone?" asked Kyle.

"He's alone."

"When?"

"He arrived about two weeks ago. He called from Anchorage to let me know he would be arriving by ski plane."

"You well-acquainted with him?"

"I met him when he was ten years old. I knew his father well. He made many trips here, mostly with business associates."

Burton grabbed one of the ropes tossed by Steve Rappaport to secure the boat to a piling. Followed by Noah, Kyle stepped out onto the dock. Steve remained on the boat deck.

"Burton, this is Kyle Dickerson, the investigating sergeant from Kenai. That's Steve Rappaport from Fish and Game, an old friend."

Burton waved at Steve and grasped Kyle's hand. "How do you do, sir. How can I help you?"

"We have the body of a dead hunter on the boat. He was attacked and killed by a grizzly about three miles upriver. His name is George Sibelius. Noah found his boat adrift and brought it down to John Korb at Kenai. Did a man by that name stop here?"

"No, no one has stopped here since I arrived."

"And when was that?"

"About two weeks ago."

"There isn't much left to identify him."

"Were you expecting anyone to join you?"

"No, sir, I came up here just to get away for a while, a little R&R."

"You hunt?"

"No, like to fish though. But mostly I like the quiet and the wilderness."

"Where's your home?"

"Chicago."

"Noah tells me you inherited a company."

"My father's, the Blake Corporation. He had this lodge built. He was an avid outdoorsman. Liked to hunt and fish."

"How long you planning to stay."

"Just another day or two. Have to get back to work."

"You have a business card in case I have to contact you."

"Not on me. Not here. If you have something I can write on, I'll give you my direct line and Email address at the office."

"Sure," Kyle opened a pocket-size notebook he carried and handed Burton a pen. Burton jotted down the information and handed back the notebook.

"How about a cell phone number?" asked Kyle.

Burton hesitated. "Unfortunately, I lost my cell phone. I was texting a message when I was out fishing and it fell in the river. I'll have to get a new phone and a new number when I get back. My direct line is the best way to reach me or by Email. If you call, my secretary can help you. Her name's Darcy Schumacher."

Kyle printed the name on the open page. "The dead man didn't have a cell phone either."

"Some animal could have carried it off," said Steve. "Pack rat or a crow."

"Interesting coincidence, just the same."

"Is there anything else I can help you with, any other question?"

"Afraid not. Need to have this corpse examined. Thank you for your information, Mr. Blake." Kyle extended his hand.

"It's nice to meet you, sir. Thank you for stopping by."

"Have a good trip home," said Noah, as he shook his hand.

Chapter 31

Evasion

Of all the tax evasion cases that Winston Graham Sims had investigated, this one was the most bizarre. In questioning Jeff Crowley, the Vice President of Finance, Sims doubted that the Blake Corporation and its top management had suddenly decided to come clean with their offshore accounts and turn over billions of dollars to the IRS in compliance with the U.S. Attorney General's voluntary disclosure program. By doing so, they would avoid prosecution for tax fraud and tax evasion schemes that had been going on for the last seven decades. Their answers to questions by the investigative team led by Denise Harbridge struck him as being uncertain as to how the transfers had happened, although Crowley expressed responsibility for making the move based on a directive from the CEO, Burton Blake, who was suspiciously not available and his whereabouts unknown.

Sims accurate impression of the Blake management team was that these were not men who capitulated easily as long as they could get away with what they were doing to enrich themselves and not get caught. Something had happened to leave them hanging and now they had come under the scrutiny of the tax division of the Assistant Attorney General. They were nervous and a little over-eager to appear to cooperate. The sudden raid by Denise and her agents had sent a shock wave through them and they were scrambling to protect themselves.

Denise's team had successfully investigated a long list of individuals and large corporations that had defrauded the

Government using offshore tax evasion schemes that amounted to an annual loss of tax revenue to the IRS of two-hundred billion dollars.

A *magna cum laude* graduate of Harvard Law and ten years as a practicing attorney in criminal and tax law, she had been recruited by the U.S. Attorney General's division to coordinate a combined effort of civil and criminal investigations and prosecutions through the Court of Federal Claims. A small stylish mildly attractive brunette with the articulation of a drill sergeant, renown for her hardline approach in going after tax dodgers and Wall Street and lower echelon criminals in the banking and trading industries.

Denise had assigned Winston to learn everything he could about the CEO and work with Fred Dolby, the Director of Corporate Security, to find him. Locating a missing person who might have skipped the country or was hiding somewhere with a changed identity was a task Winston commonly undertook. He was very good at his work.

There had been a time in his past when he hated his full birth name. It sounded wimpy, Winston Graham, the Graham named after his father, a prominent Boston physician who never forgave him for selecting to attend North Carolina University over Harvard, Doctor Graham Sims' *alma mater*. Winston occasionally heard expressions come from his own mouth that sounded like an uptight New Englander. He wasn't prissy, but he consciously tried to avoid giving that impression. That he had been married twenty-seven years and fathered three children dispelled any doubt. He liked the security of his marriage, the consistency and repeatability of living with his wife and children, who had completed college educations and had jobs and young families of their own.

Not being among the FBI hard bodies with whom he had associated during the past twenty years had been an asset and, as an investigator, allowed him to slip chameleon-like in and out of different covert situations. Who would suspect a tall slender bland nonthreatening Winston. Denise used him as her foil during good cop bad cop interrogations.

While in college, he had been a leading competitor in track and field, specializing in the mile and in the high jump at the University of North Carolina where a sports writer stretching for an effect had spun off his last name with the cheesy label of Winston Slim. The unmistakable feminine association with Winston Slims cigarettes for women had outraged Winston. But until he graduated, the name stuck and made him the butt of salacious jokes by frat boys anxious to establish a shared posturing of their own sexual prowess masking their inadequacies. From that point on, he rarely spoke or signed his full first name, preferring the masculine sounding Win.

In addition to degrees with a double major in psychology and criminology, followed up with an LLD in general practice law, he had excelled in math. Mathematical precision was an integral component of who he was, how he competed in running the mile and sailing over high jumps with a graceful Fosberry flop. His wife called him 'Old Reliable'. There were no surprises, no innovation in their relationship. His children benefited from his consistency in their expectations and how equitably and fairly they were treated.

"Tell me about Mr. Blake," Win spoke in a low quiet calming tone to Burton's mid-thirties secretary, Darcy Schumacher, who sat upright and alert behind her desk. "We're trying to figure out how certain financial changes came about and why he's missing and where he might be."

"Well, to be frank, Mr. Sims, I think highly of young Mr. Blake. I was his father's secretary for the last few years of his life. Burton was named in his will to run the company, but he's not like the others you've been talking to. He's idealistic. In the short time I've known him, he has shown himself to be ethical and honest and is probably threatening to the good old boys way of doing things here. He wants to make changes and he has a mind of his own. He's not your typical high-powered CEO who has to dominant everybody and prove himself every day. He's not on the fast track to succeed, if you know what I mean. I worked for two others like that before being hired here."

"Do you know where he is?"

"I wish I could say yes, but I don't. I'm terribly worried about him."

"Why is that?"

"He's been with the company for only a short time, but he can't get the cooperation of the other senior managers. I'm afraid he's discouraged and would just like to leave it all behind, but he can't. He's a young man who was helping people in third world countries before he was brought here."

"How do you mean, brought here?"

"When his father died, security found him working in South Africa. They brought him home. He confided that he never wanted to leave South Africa."

"Do you think he might have gone back there?"

"I don't think he would turn his back on his responsibilities here."

"He's gone and everybody we've talked to doesn't know where."

"Well, he likes the woods. Maybe he went somewhere just to clear his mind. This company has a hard culture for someone who doesn't want to politically toe the line, so to speak, even if he is the CEO. From what I've observed, the management team would like to convert him to their way of thinking, of doing business like their former boss."

"How do they think?"

"They're traditional, top down, do as I say ideological free market types. Take orders. Everything flows down. Nothing comes up. Despite the corporate mission statement, employees don't have a voice. Burton wants to give them one."

"That's the extent of it?"

"I'm sure there's more, but I don't sit in on their meetings."

"There obviously is more. Our agents were told that Mr. Blake issued a policy directive to comply with the voluntary disclosure act. Are you familiar with the directive?"

"No, sir, none of the details. That would be the finance department, Jeff Crowley. I read about it in the newspaper. That's all."

"All of a sudden, the Blake Corporation is trying to be in full bore compliance. That's why we're here. We want to know what's behind it, how it happened. We aren't confident that it was a voluntary act and there's suspicion that Mr. Blake had something to do with it. His absence raises a number of questions."

"I wish I had answers for you, but I'm sorry I don't."

"Is there someone else in the company or outside of the company who might have an idea where he went?"

"Have you talked with Fred Dolby? Security looks after him or at least they have been."

"You mentioned that Mr. Blake likes the woods."

"Burton is an environmentalist. He was taking steps to comply with the EPA on Blake's coal fire plants and was cleaning up fracking operations that were environmentally unfriendly."

"How did management respond to that?"

"They didn't agree, but they went along with him."

"Where can I find Fred Dolby?"

"He's three levels underground. There's an extensive security complex."

Win rose from his chair. "Thank you, Mrs. Schumacher. You have been most helpful. If Burton Blake should contact you, please let me know. Here's my business card."

"Thank you." She glanced at the card. "I'm sure that whatever he's doing he means well."

Win nodded and departed from her office.

"We have a company lodge in Alaska, on the Kenai River," said Dolby. "He might have gone there. We tried calling him on his cell phone, but there was no contact. Turned it off or maybe just didn't take it with him."

"I understand he has two body guards."

"Told me he didn't want them following him around anymore. Said they were embarrassing to him. So I took them off."

"Will you give me the location of the lodge and the name of anyone who maintains it."

"We don't use a property manager, if that's what you mean. But when Elias Blake was alive and took people up there, he used a local Indian guide, name of Noah Kaganuk. He lives in a village near the lodge. Locals up there know him, can show you where."

"I need a number where I can reach you."

Dolby handed him a business card. "Right here. Direct line and cell."

"Thank you. I'll be in touch." Win headed out the door.

"Hope you find him. Hope he's all right."

Sims landed at Anchorage on an Alaskan Airlines connection from Seattle. He had barely dozed on the flight from Chicago and was experiencing the edginess of not having adequate sleep. A hot breakfast of eggs, pancakes, sausages, and two cups of strong black coffee revived him for the final leg of the trip to the Kenai Peninsula.

The pontoon plane landed and pulled in to the same dock used by John Korb outfitters and boat rentals. Win asked directions to the village where he could find Noah Kaganuk and set out upriver in one of Korb's Boston whalers. The large Evinrude engine pushed the craft steadily against the current as Win angled toward the opposite shore until he reached Noah's village. A small group of children stopped playing tag and came over to greet him. He pulled the boat up onto the gravel beach out of the tug of the current and looked around at their grinning faces.

"Speak English?" he asked with a broad smile.

"Speak good English," said a rosy-cheeked girl of seven.

"Can you show me where Noah Kaganuk lives?"

"Kaganuk?"

"Yes, Noah Kaganuk."

She motioned for him to follow her and her giggling gang up a stone path to the main street intersected by five side streets lined with prefab cottages with steep shingle roofs. The children stopped before one of them. "Here," said the girl.

Win knocked on the front door and waited sharing another smile with the gang. The front door opened. Win showed him his badge.

"Mr. Kaganuk, I'm Win Sims from the U.S. Assistant Attorney's office in Washington, D.C."

Noah did not offer his hand. He waited for further information.

"I'm looking for a young man by the name of Burton Blake. He's the CEO of a company in Chicago that bears his name. I was told you could help me find him."

"Who sent you to me?"

"Someone at the company who knows you or knows of you. My business is not with you, only with Mr. Blake. I need to find him."

"Is he under arrest?"

"No, I need to help him." Win put away his badge. He did not want to intimidate this man who showed no affect or concern that he was being questioned by a Government agent at his front door. "His company lost contact with him. I'm here to find him and make sure he's all right. I was told you do guide work for Blake employees who come up here to hunt and fish."

"Mr. Blake came to stay at the lodge for a while, but he left over a week ago."

"Have you seen anyone else up here from the company?"

"Hunters and fishermen fly in and out of here. I don't know if any stayed at the lodge with Mr. Blake. Most hire guides. Some come up the river on boats. If someone has disappeared, you should check with the forest service. There was news of a hunter killed by a bear attack, a grizzly."

"Around here?"

"His body was found upriver about three miles."

"How did they know he was there?"

"His boat was discovered drifting down the river. He was not on it. Police and fish and game went searching for him."

"What did they do with his body?"

"They took it to the coroner at Kenai."

"I guess that answers that. Thank you. I appreciate your help."

Noah gave a curt nod and firmly closed the door.

Trailed by the children, Sims walked back to his boat and returned down river to Korb's landing. After getting directions to the coroner's office, he rented a Honda Civic from a garage that doubled as an emergency road service and drove along the main street to a small clinic next to the hospital. The sign plate on the door read 'Grant Noble, Coroner'. He parked and entered. No one was at the front desk. A small tent sign propped next to a faded chrome bell instructed, 'Please ring bell for service.' His palm tapped the clapper twice. Considering that the coroner might be busy in the laboratory behind the closed door, he waited for one minute, then rang the bell a third time. The vibration still lingered in the air as the door opened and a balding paunchy middle-aged man wearing blue scrubs looked out at him through bifocals perched at the end of his nose.

"Somethin' I can do fer you?"

"My name's Win Sims." He showed his badge. I'm from the Attorney General's office in Washington. A company CEO came up here a couple of weeks ago on a fishing trip, from the Blake Corporation. We haven't heard from him and his security department lost contact. A native villager told me you found a body, someone killed by a grizzly."

"I've got him here now. You can come in if you want. We did a DNA trace on him," said Grant. "His identity didn't match his driver's license and credit cards. His name is Henry Reardon, not George Sibelius. He's retired from the Government. Lived in Boise, Idaho. He the man you're looking for?"

"No, that is not the same man. I'm looking for Burton Blake, the company CEO. But you say this man was mauled and killed by a bear?"

"Not much to look at, but since you're here on official Government business, I can show you."

"Thank you, no. That won't be necessary. What will you do with the remains?"

"Soon as we find his next of kin, we'll ship him home. You might ask the police about Blake. Kyle Dickerson said he talked to him at the company's private lodge near where he found the body."

Win faked a perplexed expression. "He talked to him? Then he must still be there."

"That was a week ago. Kyle Dickerson brought the body in here then.

"Noah Kaganuk said Blake left about a week ago."

"If he said it, then it's true."

"I believe him."

"You need directions to the police station?"

"Actually, yes, this is my first time up here in Alaska. Beautiful scenery, stunning, gorgeous."

"Not too safe though if you don't know what you're doing, especially if you go out alone," said Grant.

"Guess you see a lot of that."

"Not like the lower forty-eight, but plenty enough to give me a job."

Win extended his hand. "I appreciate your help."

"My pleasure. Good luck finding Mr. Blake."

"He seems to be elusive. I was told he likes his privacy."

"Don't we all."

"Yes. Goodbye." Win went out the door and returned to his rental car before calling Dolby on his cell phone."

"Dolby – Win Sims."

"Got anything?"

"A hunter by the name of Henry Reardon was killed by a grizzly bear. Did you know him."

"Not anyone I ever heard of. What about Burton?"

"He supposedly left here a week ago."

"We have to find out what happened to him," said Dolby.

"I'm in town in Kenai," said Win. Want me to go up there and confirm?"

"No, not with what's happened. Who have you talked to?"

"The Native American you sent me to, Noah Kaganuk, and the local coroner who's holding Reardon's corpse in deep freeze."

"No, not much else you can do. We don't know any Reardon. Not one of our employees."

"I'll be returning to Chicago. I need to have some further meetings with Crowley and your other senior managers."

"We will cooperate and do everything we can to help you resolve any issues."

"This is beautiful country. Maybe I'll do a little fishing before I leave."

"Call me when you arrive in Chicago," said Dolby.

"Bye for now." Win terminated the call, then contacted Denise Harbridge. "Burton Blake has disappeared."

* * *

"What the hell are we gonna do?" asked Harden. "Hire another hit?"

"No, not that. There's no target anyway. We don't know where the hell he is. Can't do anything like that again. Now that we're under investigation, we just have to play this out. How the hell did Reardon tangle with a bear? And how could the kid have anything to do with it? Something about the cell phones, his and Reardon's. They both disappeared."

Chapter 32

War

"We're in a bind here," said Alan. "That Sims agent is coming back from Alaska and no sign of the kid. It's likely he'll move in with us along with a few others from the Attorney General's office. According to that Harbridge woman, we're going to be under regulatory surveillance until this blows over. They have to figure out how to allocate all the unpaid taxes for the past seven years and they want to make sure we don't go offshore again."

"What if poster boy permanently skips town, just never shows up?" asked Lawrence Harden.

"I'll arrange for the board to approve you as temporary CEO. Burton is out there somewhere. We just have to find him and bring him in. Sims won't be satisfied until we do."

"At least this catastrophe hasn't leaked out to the media," said Earl Frederickson.

Reid Mumford, the Public Relations Director, held up his hand. "Actually, holding a press conference and announcing voluntary full disclosure has benefited the image of the Blake Corporation as a responsible company acting in compliance with the IRS. It might even strengthen our relationship with our stockholders instead of them hearing about it through some surreptitious leak."

Earl exploded. "What we do with our money is our business, not the Government."

"They just made it their business."

"Our CEO made it their business. If it wasn't for poster boy, none of this shit would be happening."

"He couldn't have done it himself, said Jeff Crowley, the Chief Financial Officer. "He's not a hacker. He's not even all that computer savvy. He had to have an accomplice, some high level pro who wouldn't leave a trail."

"If the kid comes back, we'll make him tell us," Fred Dolby grunted leaning forward in his leather conference chair.

"How you think you're going to make him, Fred?" Jim Eckdahl, the human resources manager, leered at him with a sardonic grin. "Strap him down and torture his nuts with electrodes? He's the CEO. You're talking like he's a prisoner of war."

"This is a war," said Dolby. "A different kind, but a war."

"You think he's going to wait until you die off?" Eckdahl snickered.

"We have to stop him," Dolby snarled.

"So what are you proposing?"

"There are ways to stop him."

"You should hear yourself, Dolby. This isn't Germany circa 1938."

"We've got the money. We've got the power."

"Do you read anything about world economics?" asked Eckdahl.

"I get everything I need to know."

"If, as you say, we are at war with a young up-and-coming, you better understand his point of view. He certainly understand ours and therein lies the conflict."

"He can't do shit," said Dolby.

"He can do a lot of shit," said Eckdahl.

"How? He doesn't have a god damn private army."

"He doesn't need an army because his secret weapon is electronic communications. Just like all that fancy surveillance equipment you have down in the third floor basement. The kid destroyed his IPhone, the one you installed a chip in. Don't be dense, Dolby," said Lawrence. "Isn't it obvious that he's not as in over his head as we thought?"

"Fucking horse shit. I should have stayed in special services. At least there you knew who you're fuckin' enemy was and you could see 'em and take 'em out. We need to find that hacker."

"Welcome to the reality of the corporate world, Dolby. How long have you been with the company?"

"Ten years."

"You just learned something you didn't know before. It might come in handy," said Lawrence.

"Oh, I'll find that punk kid and whoever's helping him. I'll sure as hell find them."

"He's smart enough that he might find you first," said Lawrence.

"You think he's comin' for me? I sure as hell hope so."

"Maybe not for you. But something is coming for all of us and we need to be sensitive to that," said Alan.

Walt DeMint left staring out the window at Lake Michigan and came to sit at the conference table. "More like a parasite has invaded us. He's part of that whole idealistic generation."

"That's a good way to put it," said Dolby, "parasite."

Chapter 33

Invisible

Burton felt like a fugitive, but not from the law. He knew he had to keep moving. Even though he had destroyed the cell phone with the tracking chip, the corporation would have ways of finding him. He had to avoid giving them an opportunity to trace and track him. He had to keep his activity to a minimum in order not to appear on their radar. He had to become invisible to them.

They had sent someone to kill him. He had to live by their rules or die. They were the organization that had ejected him as though he were an alien invader who had disturbed them and caused them harm.

He figured the only way for him to return to the company would be to capitulate and agree to play by their rules. They couldn't undo what he had done.

Noah had arranged for his brother, Benny, to drive him from Kenai to Anchorage. Burton had purchased a sleeping bag, back-packing outfit, and assorted camping gear and hitch-hiked south in a slow progression to the lower forty-eight. He had let his beard grow and when asked about himself by anyone who gave him a ride, he explained he was a recent college graduate traveling through Alaska and across the U.S. to see and experience its sights and diversity. His story satisfied his inquirers curiosity and placed them at ease.

Crossing the border from Canada to Seattle, Washington momentarily concerned him, but the guard waved the driver of the giant motor coach through with only a cursory glance at the California license plate. The retired aerospace engineer husband and his school teacher wife had sold their house in California and now traveled on a nomadic tour of America. Burton graciously declined their offer to take him further south to a destination in Eugene, Oregon where they would be visiting one of their sons and his family.

Burton found his second ride near the docks in Seattle. As he climbed up into the glossy maroon cab of the massive Freightliner eighteen wheeler, the driver greeted him with a handshake and offered a cup of coffee from a large thermos. He was trailering a ton of hydraulic parts manufactured in China destined for oil company operations in Montana and the Dakotas. Ignatius Lindblad, a kind of amateur geographer assumed the role of tour guide when he learned that Burton had never seen this part of the country.

"This entire region was formed by the movement of glaciers during the last ten thousand years," he spoke proudly as though he had witnessed the event. "Pretty damn amazing, don't you think?"

"It is amazing," Burton responded with tempered enthusiasm and encouraged the Redman tobacco-chewing, gray bearded Montanan who fancied himself a modern version of the frontier muleskinner transporting freight in high-wheeled wagons. He wore polished hand-tooled black leather heeled boots and a gray Stetson with a rattlesnake skin hatband. "Killed the varmint myself," he boasted. "With my bare hands. Grabbed 'im up off the ground afore he could strike and broke its damn neck. Big one too, six footer."

They spotted a moose cow and her calf loping across a slope of uncut alfalfa hay just before harvest time on the Coeur d' Alene reservation. The truck continued south along the western autumn foothills of the Rockies and passed through Missoula, Montana and Bozeman.

They parted company in Billings where Burton's encyclopediac guide ended his route to have his load transferred to a large warehouse.   It was in Billings that Burton became aware of the massive equipment staging program taking place to support thousands of acres of hydraulic fracturing for natural gas contained in the Bakken Shale field extending from Alberta, Canada down into Montana and North Dakota.

His next ride, with a roughneck who thought Burton was looking for work in the booming Dakota oil fields, took him right into the heart of operations that bore the name of his own company. He hadn't known the extent of the Blake production out there on the barren Dakota desert. No one back in Chicago had told him that among the jungle of ten thousand drilling rigs intertwined with miles of pipelines they had one-thousand wells pulling tons of barrels of oil out of fractured crevasses in a subterranean sea and transporting it as fast as possible in oil tanker trucks and rail tankers to Texas ports for shipment to overseas markets. The Blake Corporation was making a million dollars a day on their operation and shared the resource with other prominent oil companies that paid billions to the state mineral resources oil and gas division and to thousands of landowners making overnight personal fortunes for the right to drill.

He wasted no time there in the stench and pall of petroleum chemicals and drilling waste that destroyed what was once fertile ranch and farm land. Bypassing hundreds of acres of trailer camps that housed the men who worked on the rigs, he hitched a ride east into Iowa and asked to be dropped in a small farming community crossroads near Marshalltown. From this location, he decided he would deviate from direct routes and wander aimless back roads in certain regions that interested him and would also hopefully confuse efforts of anyone trying to find him.

One morning, as he trudged along a narrow two lane paved road in central Iowa, he looked ahead for a stand of trees or an old deserted barn where he might find shelter to wait out the impending thunderstorm marching toward him across the darkening lightning streaked sky at his back. In the far distance, he could see the rotating white blades of an army of wind turbines as though preparing to do battle with the bellicose rumbling of the storm.

A middle-aged man driving a white Ford F150 pick-up truck with a green wind tower logo and company name on the doors, Lauter Enterprises, stopped slightly ahead of him and waved at him to come forward as he leaned across the seat to push open the passenger door. "I happened along just in time. Once that storm hits, you could drown standing out in it." A glint of humor tinged his concerned expression. "Rain comes down so hard it's like a tidal wave. Hop in. Name's Ralph Lauter."

"Burt. Thanks for stopping."

"What you doin' way out here on this back road?"

Burt removed his backpack and thrust it in onto the floor as he stepped up inside the cab. "Just hikin' my way around the country. Best way to see it is on foot, otherwise it goes by too fast."

"Got you there. You're not homeless, are you?"

"Nope, not a hobo or a bum either. I'm doing this by choice. It was always my goal that after I graduated from college, I wanted to see the world before I settle down."

"Sounds like a great ambition. Too bad most of us can't afford it. Had to go to work right out of high school. If it wasn't for the wind energy industry, Iowa would be in a deep pile of trouble economically speaking."

"You must work in that industry then."

"Seventy thousand people in Iowa work in this industry. We get tax credits for clean energy. Not only are we experiencing global market growth in wind energy, the jobs stay here, tens of thousands of jobs and they stay here. They don't get sent to China like in so many other industries. We're the second ranking state in wind energy and we manufacture turbines, hubs, and generators. We provide power to over one million homes and it's clean energy."

A thunderous roar opened up the black descending skies with a violent wind-driven wave of rain. As the golf ball size drops splattered the windshield and drummed on the cab roof, the wiper blades could not move fast enough to clear the view of the road.

"Have to pull over" said Ralph, "until the main brunt of the storm passes. That's a display of real power. We have these all summer long. Keeps the corn growing and the wind blowing."

It seemed to Burton that everywhere he went, there was an ongoing conflict on the planet over the exploitation and preservation of its natural resources whether he was seated in his high rise Chicago office building or hiking through cornfields in the heartland. The insatiable needs of populations throughout the world for natural resources outpaced industrial growth.

Like it or not, he was steeped in these industries. He knew he couldn't just walk away. Clean energy and regulated exploration and production were part of the necessary response.

His thoughts immediately centered on Olivia and the people she worked with at Next Millennium. They were another significant part of the equation attempting to develop a sense of balance in societies and populations careening out of control at the hands of multi-million-dollar corporations. He recognized that he had a leadership role to play and needed to get back to it.

"Our plant is right near the city, but I'll drive you into town, if that's where you want to go," said Ralph. "Just returning from an inspection of a new turbine we installed."

"I'll just go as far as you were going. Don't want to inconvenience you."

"Not at all. Actually, there's a truck stop at the other side of town I can drop you off. Good chance of getting a ride further east, if that's where you're headed. Where's your home anyway?"

"Chicago."

"Well, heck, you're bound to find someone to take you all the way."

"Thanks for your hospitality."

"Think nothing of it. People here help each other out. It's who we are."

Burton spent that night at a truckers' motel. A long hot shower washed the sour odor of accumulated sweat from his body and greasy hair. He wore his third and last change of clean socks and underwear when he checked out the next morning. He crossed the parking lot through an armada of diesel trucks and trailers to a café the size of a barn filled with truckers wolfing down hardy breakfasts of pancakes, steak and eggs, bacon and sausage, biscuits and gravy, and pots of coffee consumed to background Country and Western music. He selected an empty table, placed his backpack on a neighboring chair, and gave his order to a blonde overweight waitress wearing too much red lipstick that did little to distract from her nicotine-stained teeth. Her friendly smile and harsh smoker's voice made him feel genuinely welcome.

"Hello, honey. We have some specials on the menu. Need a few more minutes?"

* * *

The front porch light came on in response to Burton's knock. He preferred not to ring the bell at that late hour and disturb anyone. His mother opened the door and stepped back in shock.

"Burton, it's you, with a beard. What are you doing here? How did you get here?" She peered past him out into the darkness. "Where's your car? You look like you've been camping out in the woods."

"I have been out in the woods. I was up in Alaska."

"Alaska! Good Lord, you didn't tell us."

"I needed to get away for a while. A little R&R. May I come in?"

"Oh, of course, what am I thinking keeping you standing out there." She tugged him by the arm. "Come in. Come in. It's always so good to see you. At least Alaska isn't the far side of the world." She hugged him and planted a kiss on his bewhiskered cheek. "I've never seen you with a beard before." She closed and locked the door.

"Just part of kicking back. Never cared much for shaving anyway. But I won't keep it."

"You should. It looks distinguished on you."

"Not concerned about that." He shrugged off his pack. "Mind if I stay the night?"

"You are welcome to stay as long as you want, son. It's our pleasure. Tom is out playing bridge with some of his friends. He joined a club. I think it's good for him."

"Not for you though. Did you consider trying it?"

"You know I hate playing cards or any kind of game, for that matter. I'd rather read or do a crossword puzzle. You know, about a month ago, two men from your company came here asking if we'd seen you or recently talked to you."

"Did they give you their names?"

"They did, but I don't remember. They didn't stay long when I told them we hadn't seen you since you started working at the company. When I asked them what they wanted and why they were looking for you, they just said it was business-related and left rather quickly."

"I'll stay in my old room." He hefted his pack. "Need a shower to get the stink of the road off me."

"You must have laundry that needs doing."

"Just a few items, but I don't want to inconvenience you with that."

"I'd feel very bad if you don't let me do your laundry while you're in my house."

"I'll put a pile on the washing machine. Have you heard from Darren?"

"I've been watching the news about the troops coming home. I sent Darren an Email asking if he knew when, but he hasn't responded yet."

"As soon as you find out anything, let me know."

"With bells on."

"Also, can I use your cell phone to make a call?"

"You can use the regular phone, if you want."

"Want to stay incognito for a while longer."

"Incognito? Are you hiding from someone? Those men who came here looking for you?"

"I'm just keeping a low profile over something that recently happened at the company."

"It sounds like trouble of some kind. You don't have to hide anything from me."

"There's nothing to hide, Mom. Nothing to hide."

"Well, I'm used to you kids drifting in and out of here, but this seems different."

"Not a concern. I'm arranging to return to the office. That's why I need to borrow your cell phone."

"You can use the regular phone, if you want."

"Cell is better for this."

"All right. It's on the kitchen counter."

"Thanks, Mom, for being understanding."

"I don't know what I'm understanding, but you're welcome."

Burton went to the kitchen, picked up the cell phone, and walked outside into the back yard. He checked a business card drawn from his wallet, then dialed. A deep male voice at the other end answered. "Ostraich."

"Bob, this is Burton Blake."

"Burt, where are you? There's a lot happening, some of it good, and some not so good."

"I'm nearby, at least not too far away."

"Your PR man held a press conference. All the top management in your company was there, but you."

"For good reason. I'll explain later. What did he say?"

"That the Blake Corporation made a decision to take advantage of the voluntary disclosure program on its offshore accounts. Did you know about that before you left?"

"We'll have to talk details when we meet."

"We're going to meet? Where? When?"

"I'll give you a location in Rockford."

"You're in Rockford?"

"Hold your questions 'til I'm finished."

"Gotcha, I'm listening."

"Come to the strip mall just off the highway at Spring Creek Road on the east side of town. Arrive at eight o'clock tomorrow night. Cruise through the parking lot. I'll be watching for you."

"And then?"

"Then you're taking me to another location. I'll explain when we see each other. Oh, and by the way, I've grown a beard. I'll be carrying a back pack."

"A beard."

"It relates to what happened."

"You've got my curiosity at pitch point."

"For now, I took a short vacation."

"I'll look for a man with a back pack and a beard."

"What kind of car will you be driving?"

"You have a choice between my gray Hyundai Sonata and my wife's yellow Volvo."

"The Hyundai, less conspicuous."

"The plot thickens, Burt. Can you give me more?"

"Eight o'clock tomorrow night."

"Can I reach you on your cell?"

"This isn't my cell. I don't have one. I had to destroy it."

"Sounds suspiciously like trouble."

"It is, or was, and still is."

"I won't push."

"Thanks, see you then." Burton signed off. He glanced briefly over the shared neighborhood back yards where he had played as a boy, then re-entered the house.

As he turned in at the strip mall parking lot, Ostraich drove at a crawl along a sparse row of cars belonging to late shoppers. His eyes squinted through his thick glasses in search of Burton as he had described himself over the phone. When he didn't see him after two passes along the store fronts, he pulled into an empty space next to the main thoroughfare lane, flashed his bright lights twice, turned off the engine, and waited.   He suddenly noticed a movement in the passenger side view mirror and turned his head as Burton pulled open the door, tossed his pack into the back seat, and quickly slid in next to him.

"Don't wait. Head for Chicago."

Ostraich dropped his outstretched hand, started the engine, backed out of the space, and drove to the street leading to the freeway he had recently exited. "I'm curious about all the secrecy, but I'll wait. You said you'd explain."

"I appreciate your helping me out."

"Are you being followed for something, maybe associated with the offshore disclosure?"

"That is a factor, but not the only one. I need to get back inside the company, but with public recognition that I've returned. And here's why. You can't publish or divulge what I'm about to tell you to anyone. I may need it in a court of law, but I need someone else to know about what happened. You said I can trust you."

"I'll help you any way I can. Where can I take you?"

"I need you to drop me a few blocks from Darcy Schumacher's home and wait for me. If it's not inconvenient, I'd like to stay the night at your house and have you drive me in to the office tomorrow morning."

"Done, of course." Ostraich waited.

"We already know that Harold Esser was set up. The attempt just short of killing Olivia Quintana is because of my association with her and the non-profit where she works, Next Millennium. She was attacked by a contract assassin. He came after me in Alaska. The reason I went up there was to see if I would be followed. It happened. As I suspected, there was an electronic tracking device embedded in my cell phone. An old friend of my father warned me when the boat was coming up river to the lodge. I won't tell you his name, only that he's a Native American guide. I met him once when I was a kid. We used the cell phone tracking signal to lure the assassin into an area where he was attacked and killed by a grizzly. The police identified the killer as a hunter. I have no doubt there are people inside the company trying to get rid of me."

"Why?"

"I arranged for all the company's and certain private off-shore accounts to be transferred to the IRS data bank. I won't tell you how this was done, but the insiders know I had something to do with it."

"What about the insiders?"

"I know who they are. I just don't have proof, yet. But I'll get it. I'll have to deal with them."

"You're still in danger."

"I can't stay hidden."

"If you're not safe at your house, you can stay with my wife and me as long as you need to."

"That's a kind offer. I won't impose but this one time."

"How will you protect yourself?"

"Guess I'll have to be a little like my father."

"How's that?"

"He was a gun nut."

"You think packing will make a difference?"

"Not as much as my associations, legal and otherwise and by being visible in the news and social media. The insiders are less likely to try anything physically violent against me, but they may go after me some other way."

"How will you know? How will you find out?"

"I need someone on the inside, an informer."

"Do you know anyone?"

"They're going to use my secretary to get information on me. I know she'll keep them misinformed, but I don't want to put her at risk. She might be able to identify someone."

"You're looking for an informant."

"A whistle blower. I was told there is one but wasn't given a name."

"Who told you?"

"Alexis Andamiano."

"Elias's widow?"

Burton nodded. "I talked with her a while back. I'd met her only once, at Elias's funeral. I didn't know anything about her."

"Other than she's super rich."

"I knew that when I was a kid. Read about her marriage to Elias in the newspaper that my Mom tried to hide from me. She invited me to come and see her. She wanted to warn me. She suspects that Elias might have been murdered. A year before he died, he was planning to make some radical changes in the company that didn't go down well with the board and his other managers."

"Now you're trying to do the same thing."

"I need to persuade Alexis to connect me with her informer," said Burton.

"You've also got me. Criminals tend to shy away from being in the media."

"You're part of my leverage. There's something else that bothers me about this whole thing, my inheritance, making me the CEO. I'm wondering if it's a cover up."

"How do you mean?"

"The possibility that my father was murdered."

"The autopsy report showed he died of a stroke."

"That report could have been bought for a great deal of money."

Ostraich glanced at him. "You want me to look into it?"

"I figured you'd ask."

An hour later, they left the highway and pulled into the quiet suburb of Lincoln Park.

"You going to see Darcy?" asked Ostraich.

"Can I borrow your cell phone?"

Ostraich handed his Iphone to Burton. He dialed a memorized number and waited for two rings before Darcy's voice came on the line. "Hello."

"Darcy, this is Burt. Don't say anything. On the chance your phones are bugged, we have to meet. Don't say anything. I'll answer your questions later. In a few minutes, I'll give you a signal. Your dogs will probably bark. Then I'll let you know where I am. . . . . . I won't come into the house. There are reasons. In a few minutes." He turned off the phone and handed it back to Ostraich. "I'm on my way. I should be back in about twenty minutes."

Ostraich nodded. Burton stepped out of the car and walked quickly away down the dark street partially illuminated by the glow of porch lights and an occasional driveway globe lantern. Crossing the front lawn at Darcy's house, he hurried around to the side and located a kitchen window toward the rear. His light tapping three times with a small stone set Darcy's two Golden Retrievers inside into an uproar of ferocious barking. Moments later, she came to the window and peered out. Burton pointed to the back of the house. He met her outside the throw of the patio light.

"I've been worried sick about you. What happened? Where did you go?"

"I'll tell you another time. I need to know what's happening at the office."

"There was an investigation. Agents from the U.S. Assistant Attorney General's office invaded us, just came in unannounced. They took over the whole building. Nobody was allowed to leave for two days, at least the managers and their direct staff. Later, it came out that there was a massive voluntary disclosure and bringing in off-shore accounts. That was in the news. There were agents who wanted to talk to you, but you had disappeared. They're probably looking for you."

"I'm coming in to the office tomorrow. You can let the the agents know I'll be there. I want them to know I'll be there. The only thing I can say about why I left, and you have to keep this to yourself, is that someone tried to kill me."

"Oh, my God, Burt. What are you going to do?"

"I have a plan, but I can't share it right now. Don't tell any of the managers I'm coming in, not even Alan Erdman. Only the agents."

"I understand."

"And don't even tell your husband. The less you know and he knows, the better for both of you. I don't want you and your family to get caught up in this like someone else I know did."

Darcy gave him a brief hug and kiss on the cheek. "You go now. I never noticed that anyone has been watching me."

"If they are, you won't know it. I'll see you in the morning."

"Where are you staying?"

"Can't tell you" Burton jogged off into the shadows.

Chapter 34

Leverage

"Blake just came in," Dolby barked into his speaker phone.

"What did you say?" Lawrence lurched forward in his desk chair.

"It's Blake, the kid, poster boy. He came back. I just got a call from the security desk. He's on his way up to his office and Ostraich is with him."

"Shit! Alan, Earl, you on the line?"

"Here, right here."

"What do we do?"

"I'll go see him," said Alan, "alone. Try to find out what he knows. Nothing that has happened is traceable to us."

"Let's keep it that way."

"He's gutsy," said Earl, "comin' in like this."

"He's protected," said Alan. "We can't touch him and we shouldn't try, at least not for now."

"How we gonna work with the bastard?"

"We'll work with him. That's all. I'm going over there now." Alan pressed the speaker phone button to terminate his connection. He left his office and walked down the hall with a pronounced limp from his osteoarthritis. "I'm getting too old for this," he thought. He passed through the open door into the front executive office.

"Good morning, Darcy."

"Good morning, Alan."

"Security just informed me that our wayward lad has returned. May I go in to see him?"

"Of course," Darcy spoke into her headset phone. "Mr. Blake, Alan Erdman is here. . . Please go right in."

"Thank you." Alan pushed open the oak paneled door and entered.

"Hello, Alan."

"Welcome back, Burt. Looks like you've been out in the woods, full beard and all."

"Alaska to be exact. Needed a break. Went up to the lodge."

"A valued retreat. How was the fishing?"

"The fishing was good."

"A few things have happened since you were gone. Mind if I have a seat?"

Darcy's clear voice suddenly came over the intercom. "Mr. Blake, Winston Sims from the U.S. Assistant Attorney General's office is here to see you."

"I need to be part of this," said Alan.

"No, you don't," said Burton. "This is a private meeting."

"Then what's Ostraich doing here? You need legal representation with these people, not a journalist."

"Later, Alan. Mr. Sims is waiting."

Alan departed with a brief nod to Sims on his way out. Darcy shut the inner office door.

"I'm glad to finally meet you, Mr. Blake." He extended his hand. "Win Sims."

"Likewise, Mr. Sims. Sorry to have missed you the first time."

"We need to talk about that and what happened here."

"There were extenuating circumstances. This is Robert Ostraich with the Chicago Tribune. With your permission, I want him to hear what we have to say."

"Mr. Ostraich. You're welcome to stay, but everything that is said between us is confidential and may not be published. Do I make myself clear?"

"Understood."

Sims and Ostraich sat in cushioned black leather chairs facing Burton across his desk.

"Let's start at the beginning," said Sims.

* * *

"I couldn't get anything out of him," said Alan. He, Lawrence, and Earl were clustered in Dolby's security office. "We don't know what he knows or what he saw. He acts like everything's normal, like nothing happened."

"But something did happen," said Dolby. "Otherwise, he wouldn't even be here. And with Ostraich? Son-of-a-bitch. What do you want us to do?"

"We're not finished with him yet," said Lawrence.

Alan held up a hand. "I have a feeling he's not done with us. We have to proceed very carefully. He has high visibility and he has others watching us at the Government level. Very carefully."

"I'll send George and Nikos to Reardon's house in Idaho," said Dolby. "They need to remove and destroy all of Reardon's electronics. Cut all the hardwire. Make it look like vandals broke into the place. His stuff could be the only incriminating evidence."

"How did we come to this?" said Lawrence. "Poster boy my ass."

Unable to locate any next of kin through the U.S. Government, Grant Noble, the Kenai coroner, finally arranged with the Veterans Administration to cremate Henry Reardon and scatter his ashes in the Kenai River.

IV THE INNER CIRCLE

Chapter 35

Regrouping

"I'm curious, Mr. Blake, why you weren't here with your company when this event occurred." Winston Sims spoke to Burton across his desk with a casual friendly manner, not at all what Burton would have expected of an interrogation.

"Coming into the company is a significant new event in my life. To be candid, Mr. Sims, I was feeling, shall we just say, overwhelmed by the magnitude and wanted to get away for awhile."

"Do you know what happened?"

"Only what I read in the news and what my secretary told me when I returned."

"Are you saying you didn't have anything to do with the voluntary discovery compliance?"

"Well, I believe I did. I informed my staff that the Blake Corporation would no longer be maintaining offshore accounts and that all current and past taxes were to be submitted to the IRS. They apparently followed my orders."

"However, it happened with a large degree of confusion and no preliminary contact with the IRS indicating your company's intent. Unraveling the details is going to take months, perhaps years."

"I'm really new at this. I apologize for the inconvenience."

"Didn't your corporate attorney, Mr. Erdman, and your CFO, Mr. Crowley advise you of the process, on what to do?"

"They obviously did what I asked them to do. I don't know what the mechanics were. Those are their departments."

"As the assessment and investigation take place, you and your CFO and others in the company will be questioned from time to time. The Assistant Attorney General's tax division has a great deal of history to cover and you'll be seeing a lot of me."

"We are prepared to fully cooperate. I will be available to you whenever you need me. Quite honestly, I really don't know that much about corporate finance. I'm depending on my CFO, Mr. Crowley, to take the lead in those matters. Mr. Sims, I have a great deal to learn about this company and how it relates to the domestic and global economy."

"Which leads me to ask what Mister Ostraich is doing here. He's not a member of your staff. Why is he here with you now? I know you just returned from Alaska. I went up there looking for you."

Burton reacted with surprise. "You tried to find me, in Alaska?

"Yes, your company is under Federal investigation not only because of the sudden transfer of offshore funds, but the implication that various kinds and levels of fraud and tax evasion have been committed."

"How did you know I was in Alaska?"

"Through your Director of Security, Fred Dolby."

"That's interesting. I never told him or anyone else in the company I was going there."

"He explained that all senior managers have chips installed in their cell phones as a means of tracing their location in the event you experience any - problems or difficulties. He said many of you are engaged in foreign travel in particular and in some countries that you are vulnerable due to political instability."

"Oh, well, that explains why you had to come and try to find me. I accidentally dropped my IPhone overboard while I was texting. You can blame it on a salmon that hit my lure and nearly jerked the rod out of my hands. But I have a question for you then."

"Yes."

"Why didn't you notify the police in Kenai to find me?"

"There are aspects of this case in which I wasn't ready to involve the local police."

"What you're saying is beyond what I know. I guess our corporate attorney was right. He needs to be here. I barely walked through the door into this company. I don't know enough about any of its operations to be able to answer your questions. Pardon the excuse, but whatever has happened that you're investigating is before my time. I spent the last three years traveling around the world working as a volunteer with impoverished people. I didn't know my father had died and I sure didn't know I was going to be brought back here to run his company and that basically he had set me up in his will. I never wanted this job, Mr. Sims, but here I am sitting behind my deceased father's desk and trying to figure out what I've done wrong and what I have to do about it."

"You may not have personally done anything wrong."

"Then you're saying I'm a patsy?"

"No, nothing of the kind."

"I'm beginning to feel like one."

"But the Federal Government does need your cooperation in this investigation."

"I will be most happy to cooperate in any way possible," said Burton. "I've been here only a few months and I feel like I've unwittingly opened a can of worms."

"Let's return to Mr. Ostraich. What is he doing here? Why did you bring him with you?"

"We became acquainted shortly after I returned from Africa, not long after my father's funeral. We're friends. He came with me today to hear about my trip to Alaska."

"When you were in Alaska, did anyone else come to see you?"

"No, this was a solo trip. I just wanted a quiet retreat. That's all. No one came to see me."

"You didn't talk to anybody?"

"Yes, I did, a Native American guide I'd met when my father took me up there when I was a ten-year-old boy. We got reacquainted. He took me fishing for salmon."

"Was his name Noah Kaganuk?"

"Yes, how did you know?"

"I met and talked with him."

"And?"

"He corroborated what you've just told me, with one exception." Burton waited for him to continue.

"A man died up there, supposedly a hunter. Did a hunter stop by your place?"

"No. No one stopped by the lodge. It's not really mine. It's owned by the company."

"The dead man was carrying a false driver's license and was later identified as a retired agent of the CIA. We question what he was doing there and with false identification."

"Sounds like maybe he was just on a hunting trip."

Winston momentarily lowered his gaze. "You say you've been traveling around the world for the past three years."

"Yes."

"What countries did you visit?"

"Not to sound uncooperative, but I'm guessing you already know that. So why are you asking?"

"This is not an interrogation, Mr. Blake. My job is to gather information. Did you have any association with the Blake Corporation during your travels to foreign countries?"

"No, I never gave the Blake Corporation a thought until I was brought here from South Africa. What are you trying to get at?"

"There are some questionable associations that your company has had in certain foreign countries".

"You're holding me responsible for something the company did? And I don't even know what it is?"

"The FBI has traced several anonymous charitable donations to projects you were working on."

"I never knew that until our corporate attorney, Alan Erdman told me when I was brought back from South Africa. I didn't know that money even existed."

"Actually, those donations were for worthy causes," said Sims. "Others that the company has made are questionable bribery and money laundering schemes."

"Are you saying the Blake Foundation was being used as a front?"

"We're going to explore this further another time, Mr. Blake, together. There will be others from the Government involved."

"Can you tell me what we're going to explore?"

"Not at this time. What I have to say is not for Mr. Ostraich to hear and to know."

"I'll gladly leave so you can continue your conversation in private," said Ostraich.

"Should I call in my attorney now?" Burton asked.

"It would benefit you and your attorney if he were here."

Burton pressed a button on the speaker phone. "Darcy, would you please call Alan and ask him to return to my office. Thank you."

Ostraich rose from his chair. "I'll show myself out. It was nice to meet you, Mr. Sims. Burt, let me know when you'd like to get together again."

"And remember, Mr. Ostraich," said Sims. "Be aware that you're under a gag order."

"I fully understand."

Winston waited until Ostraich departed. He said nothing further until a few minutes later when Alan entered the office. "Please have a seat, Mr. Erdman. We're getting into areas where it's beneficial for you to be involved."

"I appreciate the acknowledgement," said Alan seating himself in the recently vacated chair.

"Alan has been facilitating my entry into the company and acting as my mentor," said Burton.

"Yet you chose not to tell him you were going to Alaska. Why?"

"Force of habit. In my travels, I never told anybody where I was going. I'm kind of a free spirit in that sense, Mr. Sims. I like to just up and go when the impulse strikes me."

"It never occurred to you to at least tell your secretary?"

"In this case, it didn't occur to me. But I've learned my lesson. She'll always know where I am from now on. Reminds me of tell my mom when I was a kid."

Winston turned to Alan. "So, Mr. Erdman, what do you make of all that has happened?"

"I don't have much to add since our discussion when you were here before. Burt's explanation doesn't shed any light on the situation other than he's still a green recruit with a lot to learn."

"I apologize, Alan. It won't happen again."

"I'm grateful to hear that. You have a mind of your own, just like your father."

"I think the company's intent, Mr. Sims, is for me to carry on like my father," said Burton, "but with the freedom to pursue opportunities as I might see them. Isn't that what leadership is about?"

Winston stared at him with a bemused expression. "I'll bet you're a handful for the veteran managers. But as I said, we have issues to explore. I'll need the cooperation of you and Mr. Erdman and all the other managers and any employees we wish to interview."

After Sims was gone, Alan smiled and warmed up to Burton to reconnect. "Bet you haven't had a good corn beef on rye in some time. How about lunch today?"

"Sure, Alan. Again, I'm sorry for all that's happened, I mean my disappearing on you. I had no idea what was going on financially with what is it called - the voluntary disclosure act? I guess I told Mr. Sims a bit of a white lie to perhaps cover up for you. But among my plans which I haven't shared with you and the others, is that I intended that Blake put an end to hiding offshore profits in offshore banks. I guess all of you anticipated me."

"It's strange that all this happened when it did. From your response to our initial orientation, we anticipated this is a direction you wanted to take the company. It's just that once started, it all happened rather quickly and without any oversight. It was the intent of the management team to have you centrally involved. We're learning from each other."

He paused. "You really didn't know anything about this until you got back?"

"How could I?" Burton's eyes hardened. "Let's just say it's beyond my purview."

Alan stared at him. "Good enough. I guess. Welcome back. You have some catching up to do. I've taken the liberty of calling a staff meeting for ten o'clock. You need to reconnect with the team. That okay?"

"Reconnect. Of course. I'm rested. Time to get back to work."

Alan rose. "Good. See you in the conference room at ten." He left the office.

"There's something strange going on with him," Alan spoke privately with the two vice presidents, Lawrence Harden and Earl Fredrickson, and the CFO, Jeff Crowley. "He's holding out on us. He pretends not to know anything about voluntary disclosure, but he has to. He has to. This is no coincidence."

"And now we've got that suit sniffing around," said Earl.

Lawrence paced his office like a caged animal "As you said before, we're not done with him, but he's not done with us. He's playing us. Otherwise, why didn't he just come right out and say someone tried to kill him?"

"For the record," said Alan, "I'm glad he made it back. It shows he's a survivor. I don't really care for Dolby's strong arm tactics anyway."

The other three men stared at him with suspicion.

"And why's that?" asked Lawrence.

"There are subtle legal ways to exert influence," said Alan. "You don't have to kill or maim someone."

"We don't have the luxury of subtle legalities," Lawrence retorted.

"Maybe the kid is telling the truth," said Earl. "Maybe someone didn't try to kill him. How would he know? According to Dolby, Reardon is dead. Just like he said, the kid might not have ever seen him. At this point, we have to go with that."

"I don't buy any of this," said Lawrence. "There's something going on here. He had to have something to do with the transfer of funds. Otherwise why would he run off and try to hide? There are things going on here." He looked at Alan. "He comes back from Africa because of the will and now this shit happens. He has to be working with somebody. We have to find out."

"You think he suspects?"

"He might, hiding behind his goodie two shoes for humanity bull shit. Maybe Elias was worried something might happen to him and that's why he set up the will the way he did. What do you think, Erdman? You're being awfully quiet."

"There was never any suspicion of a conspiracy. If there were, Elias never mentioned it or even hinted at it. There's nothing about the will that would even imply it. He genuinely wanted to bring his son into the corporation and have him carry out his legacy."

Earl rolled his eyes. "You're talking about when Elias had an epiphany and lost it?"

"To that extent, he did," said Alan. "He knew Burt would pick up the baton."

"We need to bury the fucking baton," said Lawrence.

"It will be much more difficult now," said Alan, "pretty nearly impossible."

"Not in my book," Lawrence growled. "We're still in charge. But we need to know what he's got going for him besides the IRS and that god damn journalist. We need to know his strategy."

"The only way to find that out is work with him," said Crowley. "I'm the one in the hot seat. I've got three IRS agents practically living with me and breathing down my neck."

"We'll work with him all right," said Earl, "up close and personal." He drew a finger across his throat.

"We need to get Dolby back in on this," said Lawrence. "He can't figure out what happened. He's still lickin' his fuckin' wounds. His mercenary pride's hurt."

"Tell him to get over it," said Earl. "Tell him to act like a professional."

"You tell him," said Lawrence.

Alan rose from his chair. "I'll talk to Dolby. We all talked about it, but he sent Reardon to take out Burton on his own, certainly not with my endorsement. What Is happening is more complicated than putting out a hit. Dolby doesn't understand that. He thinks he can still operate like he did in the CIA. He can't be that basic, especially with Sims and the IRS investigating us. The game has changed, gentlemen. It's being played at a much higher level."

"What do you think, Crowley?" Harden turned to the CFO.

"I'm a little shaky, but I'm holding steady. I know the risk and I have no doubt that Burton is the lynch pin. I don't know how he pulled it off, but we won't go down in flames. I won't let that happen."

"Forget the fucking flames," said Earl. "I'm more concerned about doin' time."

"That's my department," said Alan. "None of us are going to do time as long as we cooperate with the IRS."

"We'd better go see Dolby," said Lawrence. "He's dancing on his hemorrhoids. Doesn't know what to expect just like the rest of us."

Burton scanned the eight sullen faces waiting for him around the conference table.

"I've been informed that there have been some changes since I've been gone, hopefully for the better. Although I didn't expect to come back and find the IRS has invaded us." He grinned.

His comment didn't raise a smile.

"Before I left, I was just beginning to get a sense about the company, the departments and their functions, how all of you manage the different aspects of the operation. From this point forward, I'd like to drill down a little deeper, an expression I picked up in my reading, and get to know the organizational dynamics, how all of you and your staff, the employees in the various divisions mesh. From Lawrence's presentation overview when I first started, I understand the corporate organization and its divisions are integrated. I'd like to become acquainted with how that works. Toward that end, I'll be visiting and spending time with division managers and their people in all the product areas. I won't just be sitting at my desk calling meetings and sending out Emails. I want to get to know our employees out there and I want them to get to know me, that I'm available to them, not just through the chain of command, but directly."

"We've never operated that way," said Lawrence. "People will be uncomfortable, especially the mid-level managers. You'll meet with resistance, but you're certainly willing to try."

"It may be a paradigm shift," Burton grinned, "another one of those phrases. At the moment, the only resistance I detect is coming from you."

Lawrence controlled an impulse to leap out of his chair and strangle Burton.

"Change always meets with resistance, in the beginning," said Burton. "But since all of you are experienced veterans in effective management," he grinned, "you'll help facilitate the process with your people."

"Theory is one thing. It's nice to read about," said Earl, "but it doesn't work in the real world of business."

"We'll give it a try and deal with the issues as they come along, as a team. Isn't that why you call yourselves a management team?"

The surliness dripped from their eyes.

"Where do you plan to start?" asked Jim Eckdahl, the Human Resources Manager.

"Actually with you, Jim. Change is about people and communications. What we're going to undertake is a human resources activity that will involve operations, how we make products and run the company."

"You want to bring our strategic marketing folks into it?"

"Yes, we'll be dealing with both internal processes and resources and external influences, global and domestic, social, political, and economic."

"It's a waste of time," said Earl, "considering how well we're doing."

"It's not just about the money, Earl. It's about the people, all of us."

"The people are just fine and they'll continue to be fine as long as we don't mess with 'em," Lawrence growled.

"We're not going to mess with 'em. We're going to ask them if they would like to do some things in a different way, improve how we operate as a company. We need to get their ideas, their opinions."

"And then what?"

"Then we, as management, will make changes at our level. We'll improve."

Earl slowly shook his head.

Burton looked around the table. "Any other comments, questions? If not, Jim, I'd like to meet with you tomorrow morning at nine to get started."

Jim Eckdahl nodded. "My office or yours?"

"Yours, and there will likely be members of your staff we need to pull in."

"Anyone you want. They'll be available."

"Thank you. If there's nothing further, gentlemen, this meeting is adjourned."

Chapter 36

Conversations

Bushy brows drooped above light brown eyes in an expression of perpetual worry and concern over the magnitude of his job and life itself. At fifty-seven, his once taut features were beginning to fold with tension and middle-age.   Despite arranging numerous stress management seminars he had brought into the company, he had never taken one himself, as though he believed he was exempt from and untouched by the vicissitudes of human behavior. Although the title Ph.D. punctuated his name on his business cards, none of his peers or his staff referred to him as Doctor Eckdahl, since he made it clear he was to be addressed as Jim. "I'm just one of the group," he was heard to say, "no better, no worse."

Seated in Jim Eckdahl's office, Burton confirmed his intuition that he was not like the other senior managers. He projected a sense of humility through a quiet tolerance and focused attention when people talked to him. He actually listened, rather than fogging or tuning out what was being said.

A bump of brown hair tinged with natural reddish streaks swept back in a tight wave beginning at the top of his wide forehead and folded in to a carefully trimmed thick growth in which he clearly took pride. His unbuttoned tan corduroy sport coat and pressed gray slacks and brown loafers gave him the appearance of a 1950s college professor, even without the pipe.

Burton had liked him the first time they had met.

A small collection of bobble heads clustered on a cabinet shelf behind Jim. The novelty toys made Burton smile. He did not feel that he had to be wary and guarded with Eckdahl like he did with the other managers.

"So how are things going for you, Burt? Topsy-turvy I imagine."

"Topsy-turvy nails it. But the future has potential. Does the investigation touch you and your department in any way?"

"Indirectly perhaps, as far as hiring practices, background checks and the like. Thankfully, we don't handle any money."

"Most of what I want to do, where I want to take the company, has more to do with its people. Although the purpose of the company is to provide resources so it can make money, that's the part I'm least interested in."

"Then we're simpatico. That's why I chose human resources as a career. I've never been a number cruncher. I'd rather talk to people. However, without intending to explain your responsibilities, which are in the bylaws and your job description," Eckdahl smiled, "you are also responsible for all the rest. You're new at this, so I'm providing a little counseling, which is part of my job, I hope without you feeling defensive."

"Not at all, Jim. I'm being given advice from everyone I've met here." Burton grinned. "I'm sure they think it's their duty since I'm a newcomer, fresh off the boat. That's not to denigrate anybody or what they're telling me. I'm receiving the information and processing it in my own mind. But I'm also using it to make decisions which I know are disappointing to a few others."

"You've landed among some strong personalities who've had things their way for many years. Their opposing positions and opinions are to be expected. It's just part of corporate behavior, corporate politics. Even being CEO, you have to maneuver cleverly and carefully."

"How well did you know my father?"

"We had a smooth working relationship, as long as I did what he told me." Eckdahl laughed. "But that's how Elias was with everybody.

He wasn't close friends with anyone in the company, even his direct reports, perhaps with the exception of Alan Erdman. They were college buddies. You know Alan, of course."

Burton nodded.

"Alan was instrumental in helping Elias recover this company as his birthright, something you may not know. The former owner was not ethical. Alan shared with me the story of what happened to Elias when he was a child, and how the company was inexplicably taken away from him when his parents died in a car crash."

"I didn't know anything about a car crash. Actually, no one ever told me how the company came into being. My mother never talked about it. And I understand what you're saying about Elias. He was a kind of tyrant, and my brother and sister and I experienced what my mother considered abuse from him until I was about ten. Then my mother took us and left him."

Eckdahl leaned back in his over-size black leather chair and placed his hands behind his head in the same motion, elbows horizontally splayed out like wings and his moderate belly pushing at his shirt buttons. "Did you ever meet his second wife, Alexis Andaniamo?"

"Yes, at the funeral and again about three months ago. I went to her house."

Eckdahl laughed. "If you can call it a house. It's a monster mansion."

Burton grinned. "A good way to describe it. I'm not big on mansions."

"After attending some of her dinners and horse shows and soirees, we gradually became friends over the years. She likes to talk and I like to listen. Despite her wealth, she's quite a nice person. She has a keen intelligence and more than a shred of humanity."

Burton seized on the thought that Eckdahl was her informant.

"Speaking of wealth," said Eckdahl, "how are you handling yours?"

"As little as possible." Burton's eyes conveyed a sheepish sense of humor. "I'm not the right person for this. Elias made a mistake putting me in his will."

"Why do you say that?"

"I want to deconstruct a lot of what he did."

"It's not a mistake. Several months before he died, he and Alexis confided in me that this is what they wanted. At the ripe old age of sixty-five, Elias had a change of heart. He wanted to take the company in a new direction, with the humanitarian perspective that you have." Eckdahl leaned forward with arms firmly on the desk top and intertwined his fingers. "This is the legacy he wanted you to carry forward. You're undertaking what he was just beginning to get a taste of."

"That's what Alan told me, not that Elias had changed, but that he wanted me to do what he couldn't do." Burton chuckled. "Alan said it wasn't in my father's nature. He wasn't a people person, an understatement."

"What we're talking about here is confidential and needs to stay between us," said Eckdahl.

"I understand."

"Alan was not privy to the conversations I had with Elias and Alexis. He only witnessed the change in Elias's behavior. He didn't know and doesn't know to this day the reason and motivation behind it."

Burton waited to hear more.

"You're expecting that I'm going to tell you."

"I'm hoping you will but Alan does know. He told me when I arrived from South Africa. Elias was always looking out for me and I never knew it."

"It's said that what you don't know can't hurt you, but what you do know can hurt you even more. Elias and Alexis also wanted to protect you from certain elements in the corporation that can destroy you, given the chance. Now that Elias is gone, I'm placed in the dilemma of having to decide what's beneficial for you to know or not know."

"I acknowledge I have enemies. I'd rather be informed so I can be prepared."

"The problem is, other than myself, I can't tell you who your friends are and your enemies are. I'm not an accepted member of the inner circle."

"The inner circle?"

"I just call it that. It's not unusual for a corporation to have a clique or even many cliques, closed social groups. Your company has a few. The one I'm referring to includes people from outside the company, investors, board members, and the like, even some beyond those groups."

"Sounds clandestine."

"It could be, but I don't have any evidence or proof."

"So the dangers are mine to discover."

"Dangers may be too strong a word, but in a word, yes. Alexis asked me to help you in any way I can, but I have very limited influence."

"But you're able to acquire information."

"Only on occasion. I'm not a snoop. I don't spy on the people who work here, but I'm aware of office politics, even those that aren't all that transparent. Because you're the CEO and I'm the HR Manager, we can have meetings and discussions without fear of repercussions. But we have to be careful what we say or how we say it."

"So you're the whistle blower Alexis told me about."

"Not in the legal sense." Jim grinned. "More like her inside man. The rest of upper management won't talk to her. She gets annual reports. That's all."

"You suspect we're under surveillance."

"It's possible. Fred Dolby's security system can monitor any information technology in the company. The invasion of privacy is always something I've objected to, but my opinion was not, shall we say, well received. Dolby acts more like a State Department enforcer than a security director. He comes from that background."

"Do you ever feel threatened by those guys?"

"Threatened? No, just ostracized, but it's a welcome and accepted ostracism."

"They really don't like you."

"The feeling's mutual. But we get along well enough. I do my job. They do theirs. We don't have to go home together and have supper at night. Differences in a company are acceptable as long as you accept them." Eckdahl broadcast an infectious grinned. "So far, no one's threatened to break my knees."

"That must be comforting."

"Other than what management sees as a catastrophic fiscal event that must have given them the heebie-jeebies, what do you know about organizational change management?" asked Jim.

"A certain amount of common sense, but otherwise, admittedly, nothing," said Burton.

"That's a good place to start, no preconceptions. It's all about commonsense business practices anyway. I've gone through training on it, but the brass in our company has never been remotely interested. As a matter of fact, they're threatened by it."

Burton leaned forward in his chair. "What kind of training?"

"It's called Kaizen. It's a Japanese concept meaning improvement of anything."

"Sounds like something I need to go through."

"If you're intent on pursuing this," Jim pulled a brochure from a desk drawer, "I'll bring in a consultant to provide the training and facilitate the process. You shouldn't try to do it here at corporate. You need to start at one of the lower level product divisions to establish a model and prove that it works. Then bring it up the chain, nurture it and allow it to spread until it becomes the cultural norm. It's not something you can do overnight, especially in a company our size. It involves the participation of people, all of the people, management and employees alike. Since it's a continuous process, it's ongoing and doesn't take just weeks or months. It takes years of incremental improvement just as it took years for the company to get where it is today. There's a certain amount of unraveling that takes place. In this company, that will require a great deal. Blake is too polarized, too political. It has too much complexity."

"Could I see the employment contracts for Lawrence Harden and Earl Frederickson."

"Only because you're the CEO, of course." Jim pressed a button on his speaker phone. "Gretchen, would you bring me the employment files for Lawrence Harden and Earl Frederickson, the ones containing their contracts. Thank you." He pressed off the button and turned to Burton. "I know what you're looking for, but you won't find it in their contracts. They have a protection clause. You can't get rid of them, not any of the inner circle. You can't touch them, force them to resign, retire with a golden parachute, anything. Their contracts are signed and sealed by your father. Until this past year before Elias died, they were thick as thieves. But you're welcome to look over their employment contracts. It's probably a good idea that you do. It will give you more of an idea of what you're up against. The inner circle set up the corporation to have a life of its own."

"And there's no way that can be changed."

"Not without their consent. And that means total consensus of the founding fathers, minus Elias now, of course. They're going to block you at every turn."

"The founding fathers?"

"The original investors and highest ranking members of the Board of Directors. They're actually the Board that tells the Board what decisions to make, how to vote, and what they can and can't do. Their names are not known to the general public and not even to us. They're like a secret society. The published members of the Board have no power. They're just a front for those few who give the orders."

"Who are they? Why can't we know their names?"

"I'd tell you if I knew, but I don't. I only know that they exist as a kind of elite shadow group. I would never know who they are even if they came here. The management here at Blake has to answer to them, even you. That's why you have impenetrable obstacles raised against you, the same that Elias encountered when he tried to take the company in a new and different direction. And despite all appearances, he died of a stroke that involved gunshot wounds, there are some who suspect he was murdered and the diagnosis of the stroke was a cover-up. That's how powerful those few people are."

"But I inherited Elias's authority, his vote, his percentage of stock ownership."

"Not entirely. Elias's widow controls forty percent through stock ownership. She's a silent partner that the boys upstairs and the invisible Board want to be sure remains silent. By majority vote, the Board of Directors doesn't allow her to participate in the management of the company."

"She mentioned something along those lines when I saw her. You said you're friends, or at least well acquainted. I guess that includes sharing with her what goes on inside the company."

Eckdahl grinned. "You mean she didn't give you my name? What a gal."

"That makes at least four of us who are on my side."

"Four?"

"Darcy."

Eckdahl nodded. "Of course."

"Alexis thinks Elias was murdered."

"We've discussed that possibility, but there's no proof, no evidence," said Eckdahl.

"So someone was paid off."

"More than one. I'm sure of it."

"What raised your suspicion that there's a possibility?"

"Elias himself. At first Alexis thought he might be getting a little paranoid and wanted him to get some counseling," said Eckdahl. "He wouldn't have any of it."

"What was he reacting to?"

"A meeting with the boys. They told him that his management team, the board, and investors didn't approve of what he was doing. They were incensed. He basically told them all to go fuck themselves, that Blake was his company and that they were privileged to be along for the ride. If they didn't like it, they could resign. Words to that effect."

"Calling him out in a meeting isn't unusually threatening."

"There's more. He started receiving anonymous emails, which he treated as spam, especially those suggesting he was exhibiting signs of dementia. The board sent him a letter of disapproval. He shredded it and mailed the confetti to a major banking CEO who is on the board. That didn't go down well."

"Sounds like a feud."

"It was, not like the Hatfields and the McCoys, but it grew. Got right nasty walking the halls on the fortieth floor. Elias's top guys went out of their way to avoid him. They started holding their own secret meetings and let Elias know they were doing it. They were essentially informing him that they would run the company as intended, but without him. They were obviously under orders from the clandestine Board."

"How did Elias take that?"

"He created the will that made you CEO and has you sitting here today."

"So I'm the continuation of what he set out to do."

"Yes."

"And I can believe they murdered him in some way, because they tried to do the same to me."

Eckdahl stared at him. "What did you just say?"

"That's why I went to Alaska, as a test. And I was right. They sent someone to take me out. But obviously that didn't happen. The hit man was taken out instead, by a grizzly."

"An accident?"

"No, a setup, using their own technology against them. A chip in my Iphone was being tracked by satellite. What I'm telling you has to remain only between us. I planted the phone where it would do me the most good. The assassin tracked me to where he thought I was and he was attacked by a grizzly. The bear killed him."

Eckdahl continued to stare at him.

"And you're sure you don't know who 'they' are."

"I'm being honest with you. I'm way down the food chain in all this," said Eckdahl.

"Just as with Elias, I can't prove anything either," said Burton. "I'm still a fish in a barrel, but the wild card I pulled stopped them."

"You mean the attorney general."

Burton nodded. "But only temporarily. I'm sure they'll try again, but they have to do it in a way that has no transparency."

"Like Elias."

Burton nodded. "If I can prove they murdered Elias, I have a way to get rid of them, all of them."

"How do you think you can identify them outside the company?"

"I think the answer lies in certain Blake philanthropic venues. I'm certain of it," said Burton.

"You're referring to Walt DeMint."

"He runs the philanthropic division."

"He would only be taking orders from the shadow group, just like Harden and Fredrickson and Crowley."

"So he would get his orders in the same way."

"Yes, through the Board of Directors that has no power. They're just a figurehead to channel messages and directives to the senior managers in the company. If you're going to try to find out who the puppet masters above them are and go after them, I wouldn't want to be in your shoes," said Jim.

"I don't have a choice."

"Proceed with great care, my friend. This company is a mine field."

"Yeah, not a happy thought. When can I meet this Kaizen consultant you mentioned."

"I'll call him this afternoon and set up a meeting."

"Not here."

"Good idea."

"I'm proceeding carefully." Burton reached across the desk and shook Eckdahl's hand. "Thank you, Jim, for everything you're doing."

"I wish I could do more, but – "

"I know. You're not in the inner circle." Burton left the office.

Chapter 37

The Visit

Burton thought he had seen the last of George and Nikos until the afternoon he left his office and stepped into the elevator for the descent to the parking level.

"I thought you guys deserted me." He pressed the button.

"No," said George. "The boss gave us some time off."

"I thought I was the boss. I don't remember giving you time off."

"The other boss, our boss, Dolby."

"We took your advice and took a vacation," said Nikos.

"That's nice. Where did you go?"

"The Ritz Carlton, like you told us. Everything was free, even the girls. Didn't have to pay for anything."

"What a deal. But you boys deserve it."

"Yeah, we thought so."

"So where you off to?" asked George.

"To the hospital, to see a friend."

"Do we know her?" asked Nikos.

"No, but she knows you."

"Ah, a woman. That's good. We noticed you didn't have no female companionship, if you know what I mean, and we were thinking we should do something about it, as part of our responsibility for lookin' after you," said George.

"No, you guys can follow me around, but you really need to stay out of my personal life."

"Just want you to be happy, Mr. B. Just want you to be happy."

Burton refrained from saying anything further.

Olivia Quintana appeared small and withdrawn in the rehab hospital bed, reminding Burton of a child in her crib. An oxygen machine remained at rest against the wall behind her next to electronic equipment that monitored her heartbeat. Her eyes were open and alert and recognized him instantly with a flicker of amusement that surprised him for one who was suffering.

The realization that her attacker had been careful not to kill her occurred to him. He conjectured that her beauty and spirit and energy might have influenced him. The blow to her head was caused by the fall to the concrete floor of the parking garage. The attack was a message, a warning.

He thought it ironic that the killer had lost his own head to the gaping jaws of a male grizzly.

"It's you," she said. A smile blipped beneath the bridge of her nose. "I got whacked and you didn't. That's hardly fair."

"I would rather it had been me. I am sorry."

"You're to blame for this." Another disconcerting brief flash of teeth.

"I take full responsibility."

"That's good, because you're going to make it up to me."

"I intend to," Burton laughed. "I will."

"The doctor said I can be released in another week, all things considered."

"I'm glad to hear that."

She closed her eyes. "I'm not falling asleep on you. I'm thinking."

Burton glanced across the bed at Olivia's mother, Doctor Lizzie Dawson, seated in a second visitor's chair. They shared a grin. She gently stroked her daughter's hand resting on the covers. Olivia opened her eyes.

"So, are you two plotting something?"

Burton abruptly returned his attention to Olivia. "No, no plotting. We both wonder what you're thinking about."

"Since I woke up, I check on myself from time to time to see if I've lost any high level cognitive functioning. Mother was in here with a neurologist the other day doing tests and poking and probing and asking questions."

"Doctor Abbot and I are satisfied you didn't suffer any brain damage. But he's keeping you under observation for a few days to be sure there isn't any delayed reaction to your injury. The blow was quite severe." Said Lizzie.

"I think it rattled loose a few cells that have made me more intelligent than I was before. I can hear and see things more clearly and I now have the power to see into the future."

"So now you're clairvoyant?"

"Not about everything, just some things."

"Are you sure it's not just your imagination?"

"Since it's a newly found ability, I'll have to try it out and see if it works."

"A scientific experiment."

"No, there's nothing scientific about it. It's spiritual."

"Oh, oh, you were spiritual before this happened. Actually, I thought you were delusional."

"New Age spiritualism is not delusional, Mother. It's just not Christian or Muslim or Hindu or Mormon or some other religion."

"I know. I've never had an issue with what you want to believe. They're all of equal value, even the remote jungle tribes I've visited."

"Actually, what I believe is closer to your jungle tribes than to other religions. While I was in a coma, I traveled the spirit world and the universe."

"You were dreaming. Doctor Abbot explained how your brain functions to create dreams."

"This was real. It was definitely real."

"Dream reality is dream reality."

"What do you dream about, Burton?" Olivia asked.

Her question caught him unawares. "I've never really thought about my dreams. When I wake up, I forget what they were."

"You don't remember anything, ever?"

"I guess there is one that reoccurs once in a while."

"What is it?"

"A bear comes and talks to me."

"A bear? What does he say?"

"I don't remember. I never remember."

"Are you afraid?"

"No, he's my friend. This is going to sound weird, but it's just a dream. I feel like he loves me and he's there to protect me."

"That's awesome, Burton. The spirit of the bear."

"Maybe, it's a nice way to think about it."

"So, Mother said you went away for a while, and now you're back at work. I can't wait until I can go back to work. Lying in a hospital bed is really boring. I've been doing some reading, but television is a total wasteland."

Olivia flashed a self-conscious smile and hunched her shoulders.

Chapter 38

Interrogation

"Mr. Sims, we're prepared to walk you through the initial segment of our analysis." The young analyst moved a cursor across the digital display on an oversized high definition wall screen in the Assistant District Attorney's conference room.

Denise Harbridge, the U.S. Assistant Attorney General, had met with Win Sims in a private conference one hour prior to the meeting to receive his briefing on the status of the investigation and regulatory monitoring of the Blake Corporation financial system. He had flown in from Chicago to Dulles International the day before, arriving after the dinner hour.

She sipped a glass of chardonnay while checking a recent spate of Emails received since she had left her downtown office at six o'clock. Her husband had carpooled with a fellow professor from Georgetown University to avoid the gridlock of beltway traffic and was enjoying his second Blue Goose vodka martini by the time she arrived at seven, was greeted by a kiss on the cheek and the chardonnay thrust at her enroute to her office study.

"I'm doing steaks on the grill. Fifteen minutes," he warned her.

"Medium," she called back over her shoulder.

"Of course, you don't have to tell me."

"But I always do."

"And I always get it right."

"Baked potato?"

"In the oven, as we speak."

"Start the asparagus five minutes before the steaks are ready."

"Aye aye, ma'am."

She disappeared into her home office and opened her flat screen desk computer.

The sudden onslaught of the Blake Corporation's financial world underscored the quagmire she and her staff encountered daily in unraveling the endless tax evasion schemes. Digesting the worst economic recession since The Great Depression still weighed heavily on her mind as did the endemic penchant for greed and corruption in politics and business. Her department was mired in an economic stall.

The meeting tomorrow involving the Blake Corporation would offer the first glimpse of how to bring under control what she was calling the attack of the blob.

She peeled off her business suit and undergarments and slipped on a loose flowing lavender lounging dress that swept the tops of her perfectly contoured bare feet tucked into a pair of soft leather backless sandals. Three quick brush strokes electrified her bobbed dark hair. She tossed back the last swallow of her chardonnay and left the master bedroom.

"You hungry?" her husband stepped back from the sudden flame flaring up around two prime beef filets. "Crap," he cursed a few spots of grease that leaped from the stove top grill to speckle his tan apron. Although he acknowledged the purpose of an apron was to protect his clothes from cooking stains, the appearance of splotches reminded him of being attacked, caught unaware, not being sufficiently focused and attentive. He viewed cooking as a kind of primitive battle between the chef and the raw makings of a meal that resisted his culinary efforts despite the assiduous care with which he read and followed written recipes in cookbooks and food magazines.

"So what do you think?" Denise poured a second glass of wine to accompany a dollop of creamy brie on a multi-grain cracker.

"I think what's happening at your company is indicative of what's happening everywhere. A shift is taking place in the world order. It's the topic of the day with my staff and students. "

"With this company, I believe the good old boys didn't willingly come to the table. Something or somebody has forced their hand. Their PR press conference was nothing more than a performance that dripped with false sincerity. They don't know what hit them. I think they're trying to figure it out, but they're fearful about being too visible. They got caught with their pants down and are struggling to pull them up."

"Everyone's afraid of the IRS, dear. You know that. They can't pull up their pants when you've got a strangle hold on their balls."

"Is that your way of saying I'm one of the forces of history?"

"Of course. Criminal capitalism gives you job security."

"And stress."

"You shouldn't be stressed. You wield the big club and you're married to me."

Denise grinned. "You think that isn't stressful?"

"Oh come now, dear. There's no one easier to get along with than your hubby."

"You have to be. I'm the one who's difficult."

"You have all the bad guys to go after. I get off easy and I have an inside seat to the entertainment."

"You think what I do is entertaining?"

"Your fight against greed and corruption is the foundation for every book of political intrigue and police story written or made into a movie. It unravels before you every day."

"If only it were that simple, the unraveling part."

"That's what makes your job interesting, solving crimes. It's challenging and you're very good at it."

"That's why I married you, flattery."

"You married me because not only am I a bottomless reservoir of academic intelligence and intellect, I'm also a great lover for my age."

Denise snorted wine through her nose and choked. "Mainly I married you because I don't like to cook and you do. If you left the meals up to me, we'd be micro-waving Stouffers frozen dinners and eating out more often."

"Do you know a young co-ed complimented me on my hair today."

"How would I know except that it gives you an excuse to tell me. And isn't your use of the word young redundant? Aren't all co-eds young?"

"Just pointing out that age and wavy white hair aren't entirely a disadvantage."

Two days later, she and Win Sims were on a U.S. Air jet to Chicago. They said little other than to comment on a few shared Emails that involved them, then bided their time listening to personal music choices and watching televised news.

Back in Washington, they had discussed potential strategies of how to crack the defensive wall of resistance and legal obfuscation that blocked the ongoing investigation. Having the money was one thing. Figuring out where it came from and what to do with it for tax considerations was a daunting task that now tied up fifty analysts deciphering the chaos of the Blake Corporation's 'financial tsunami', as her second reference to 'the blob'.

The data transfers had come in scattered indiscriminately between the Atlanta, Georgia and Ogden, Utah centers. Denise had decided they must begin by going inside the corporate systems, not only digitally, but behaviorally. With the return of Burton Blake, Win thought they might have an opening.

The Chief Financial Officer, Jeff Crowley, squeezed the yellow Wilson tennis ball rapidly three more times before returning it to a prominently displayed small red clay dish on his desk top. Surrounded by vanity photos of himself with tennis pros covering the walls did nothing to impress Denise when she and Burton and Win walked into his office. His crisp gray haircut and athletic tan added to her original perception of him as a self-indulgent elitist when she had met him during her first visit.

His thousand dollar gray suit, blue shirt and subdued cream-colored tie surprised her. She expected to see him wearing tennis clothes because she suspected he always played the role and lived within the fantasy he had created for himself. That was how she had met him the first time, about to go off to his club. He had been clearly miffed at having to cancel his reservation but changed his demeanor when he realized who she was and her purpose in coming.

Following a few ritual comments of greeting accompanied by brief handshakes, He led them through the back door of his office into an expansive conclave of light blue carpeted cubicles manned by accountants seated at spacious work stations fronted by four flat screens of financial data. Ten of Denise's regulators sat next to ten of the thirty accountants and witnessed the ebb and flow of data related to the domestic and international divisions and vast subsidiaries of the Blake Corporation. The regulators had submitted daily reports to Denise during the past three months of monitoring the financial system with no conclusive trending or quantifiable results. Whatever had been done, as Denise characterized it, was chaos.

Jeff herded Denise, Win, and Burton into an adjacent glass-walled conference room and encouraged them to sit while he directed their attention to a digitized process flow chart representing the architectural systems interface of the financial software at a macro level.

Denise opened her notebook computer on the conference table and tapped a few keys. "The main issue we have in the analysis is determining the sources of corporate income," she said. "The sum of consumption and total accumulated net worth are the factors we have to work with. Matters get very sticky when it comes to international income and foreign tax credits. The daunting task we face with the flooding of the IRS coffers with Blake Corporation billions is tracking and finding the sources and appropriately matching funds to the corresponding regulations. We're dealing with immense wealth here that doesn't have identifiable source locations. We are questioning how and why you made these transfers to the IRS without first notifying us and, secondly, without our collaboration. Our third concern is that, with a few exceptions as to sources of corporate and individual income, you are either unwilling or unable to provide us traceability."

Jeff responded with the alacrity of a return on a blistering tennis serve. "It's because of the enormity and complexity of the financial systems. I have to admit they have separately and collective taken on a life of their own over which we have lost control. Blake finances have become its own creature, if we can call it that. In prompting the tax transfers, there is something somewhere in the labyrinth of programming codes that reached out and pulled in everything Blake has ever touched and beyond, including what we haven't touched or don't have any awareness that we've touched. To put it bluntly, we've been out of control financially speaking for years and we haven't known it. What we do know and can provide is the sum of corporate distributions to shareholders and Blake's increase in net worth. You have to admit there is inconsistency in the Government tax regulations between distributed and undistributed earnings from our wholly owned foreign subsidiaries and we have exercised both. We require that certain ones send us, the parent, the dividends and others keep the earned revenue and make us loans."

"We have been unable to discover any transparency on how you manage foreign tax income," said Denise.

"There has been nothing out of the ordinary. We handle foreign tax income according to tax regulations. It's deferred when we pay domestic shareholders."

"There is no question you have transferred domestic income to offshore accounts and created foreign income through foreign corporate subsidiaries. To be blunt, there appears to be a convoluted, let me say covert investment system to erase the original source and trail of income to escape paying domestic corporate tax."

"That is definitely not true."

"Let me remind you, Mr. Crowley, this is not a hearing. It's a mutual exploration to help us understand how to position your company's voluntary disclosure and payment of funds to the IRS. As of now, we have no way to document it."

"We use only permitted methods, again, I stress according to IRS regulations. The Blake parent company credits foreign tax paid as gross up and does not pay the domestic corporate tax portion. We have also exercised the option of rather than establishing U.S. branches of the parent company, Blake has created numerous controlled foreign corporation foreign sourced business entities."

"We are aware of your foreign entities. But we have discovered that in several instances, these foreign business entities paid dividends to more than 50 percent of the U.S. shareholders in cases where more than 10 percent of the dividends were sourced from the U.S. We consider this an illegal diversion of funds. But, as I said, for now, we are overlooking these anomalies as a kind of asylum from prosecution."

All of our records are open to you. We operate with the currency of those countries."

"What we are seeking" Denise continued, "is how that foreign currency is to be translated into U.S. dollars for tax liability. Our legal issue, that we are putting aside for now, is how Blake avoided this step on a large percentage of its profits and is suspected of maintaining a separate set of financial records to conceal the fact."

"I have no knowledge of that. It hasn't happened. And if it did happen, unknown to me, I had no part in it."

"Our purpose here is to help each other, Mr. Crowley. We seek only clarification. But as you do know, since you are conversant with the tax laws, that the reduced effective tax rate on foreign income is lower than U.S. rates and gives shareholders of Blake dividends an excess credit position. What that means is distributions of previously taxed income become tax free. Your foreign business entities retain income earned offshore and reinvest to earn income which is not taxed. Based on what we have so far analyzed is that Blake arranged for disguised investor dividend distributions as equity investments, interest on loans, and millions of dollars in management fees.

Crowley stiffened. "Under the law, we have exercised our right to do business in countries where we pay relatively high foreign taxes and pursue the margin to move investments into low tax foreign countries rather than into a domestic U.S. company. The high tax investments shelter the low tax investments. If I'm not mistaken, that is allowable in a free market enterprise economy."

"And so it is, Mr. Crowley. So far, I believe we're making progress, but we have much more to discuss and the need for more extensive analysis by my staff."

"Let me reiterate that the software programming codes have a life of their own over which we have lost control. Things have happened that we didn't know were happening, because they were subliminal, hidden in the system. Not much different than a bug or a virus."

"And if there were a bug or a virus, aren't your IT people capable of discovering that?"

"I can't answer for them."

"Or were they told to ignore whatever they might find."

"I have no way to answer that and won't without our attorney present."

"At some point, it will be necessary for us to have that meeting, since the software has come under suspicion," said Denise.

"I'm not unwilling to cooperate. I just don't want to be forced to answer something I don't know about and can't provide you with an answer. Just tell me when you want the meeting and I'll arrange it."

"Thank you, Mr. Crowley. There is no force intended here."

"You can understand my position."

"Of course."

Later, in private, Denise commented to Win, "Something doesn't add up. Crowley can't be that uninformed that he's blaming his software. He claims he authorized the downloads."

"He's afraid," said Win. "He's just trying to stay out of the spotlight."

"I'm doing my best to cut him some slack. It's not easy for me to deal with people like him."

"You're doing a good job."

"Strokes I don't need," said Denise.

"I know, but it's still nice to have one once in a while."

"I feel dirty dealing with companies like this," said Denise.

"We're just getting our feet wet, or muddy might be a better term. You can go for the jugular down the road."

"Work with that poor young CEO. He's way out of his element," said Denise.

"I think we can develop an understanding."

Denise nodded. "That's more than I give myself credit for."

"Stroke for me?"

"No, a flaw in my personality."

Win laughed.

Chapter 39

The Intervention

Burton noticed that although the workers were curious about him, because of his youth they avoided looking at him by keeping busy until he, Jim Eckdahl, Adriana Forbes, the local division human resources manager, and Ivan Trimble, their consultant walked past. Nobody wanted to catch his attention, since other than being told in advance that the big boss was coming to visit the plant, they dreaded that he might actually stop and speak to them.

In the past, they had rarely glimpsed the former CEO, the old man who had died. Only Earl Frederickson, the Vice President of Manufacturing corporate-wide, had come to tour the plant from time to time and he never talked to any of the fifty machinists who operated the computer numerically controlled CNCs spread across the seventy-thousand square foot factory floor.

The sour odor of machine lubricant cascading over the spinning stainless steel drill bits and other tooling for lathes and mills pervaded the air. Burton noticed how piles of steel chips were regularly deposited in waste barrels near the machines. The operators wore blue protective smocks and safety glasses as they moved about their work cells completing set-ups and checking parts to verify machine accuracy and consistency.

Upon returning to the conference room from their plant tour, Jim Eckdahl asked Adriana to provide her perspective about the proposed intervention. She had been the human resources manager of the Rockford plant for twelve years. Reporting to Jim, she was a buffer between the authoritarian mandates that came down from corporate management and the plant employees who understood she looked out for their interests but had no power or authority to influence her superiors. Jim did the best he could for her, as for HR managers in other divisions of the company, but he, too, was a powerless pawn among the rank and file of the Blake work force.

The covert Kaizen organizational improvement intervention that Jim and the young CEO, Burton, were proposing was a risky endeavor that she knew would meet with resistance by the employees out of fear of losing their jobs for participating.

"Present company excepted, the top brass has institutionalized a culture of distrust. People here are afraid of the Vice Presidents, particularly Earl Frederickson and Lawrence Harden. There isn't any encouragement for employees to make suggestions or voice their opinions. They clock in, work their day, and clock out. They come to see me regarding their healthcare and retirement benefits, which they fear losing. When I first started, I tried to have employee recognition and company social events. The turnout for a family picnic was paltry. I was told employees weren't interested. They didn't want to be singled out and have their mug shots posted in the newsletter for doing an exceptional job. They wanted to keep a low profile, stay under the radar, I was told. They didn't want the bosses to see them. We got along just fine." Her rounded features nesting in a sprung brown hair style pouched into a smile. "They're always glad to see me come around to distribute their paychecks."

She shifted her middle-aged sag, widening downward into her lower extremities. She had given up her health club membership two years ago following a knee injury from a fall caused by winter ice on her front steps, for which she blamed her husband for not spreading rock salt after a storm.

"The starting point you describe is really not that uncommon," said the consultant who had been listening and observing leaned forward with his elbows firmly on the table. "Even with senior management, resistance is the beginning of any change and establishes the objectives for how to manage it. No one wants to live and work in a negative situation if they have a better option."

"If you come in here wearing a suit and tie," said Adriana, "no one will give you the time of day. These are working class highly skilled labor and technicians. They don't trust suits. They'll think you're a lawyer and no one trusts lawyers."

"The only occasions I've worn a suit for the past twenty years is to weddings and funerals. I'm very comfortable and get along well with employees who operate machines and use tools to make things and drive trucks and forklifts. My father was a steel worker when I was a kid growing up in Indiana. I'm blue collar, not white. I believe that manufacturing is the core strength of the middle class and the core strength of this country, not financial markets that just move money around to make more money."

"You might get a few of the guys to listen to you."

"That's what I would ask. I don't own the ideas I'd be sharing. The concepts and methods belong to the employees. They have ownership. I just facilitate. And by the way, I started off as a tool and dye maker and I know how to run those machines out there."

"He's been thoroughly vetted," Jim laughed. "Did you have a chance to look at his resume I emailed to you?"

Adriana nodded. "Yes, it is impressive. Throw a hoodie sweatshirt on you and give you two days without shaving, you could pass for one of them. But if you're a guru, they listen to someone who's either clean cut like yourself or has a real beard, not bald on top and a goatee hangin' off your chin. I think they respect someone who still has his hair, either that or they envy him. Mr. Blake, I don't know how you fit in to this. For some, you're young enough to be their son. For others, you're the same age as the up and comers."

"This is my idea, Adriana. It's something I feel strongly about. I don't wear suits either. I'm going to be working with Ivan according to what he tells me to do. I won't be sitting up in the Blake corporate tower in Chicago waving a baton."

"That's refreshing. At this point, I'd like to bring in my plant manager. Dorian started here twenty years ago at eighteen sweeping the floor and doing shipping and receiving. We paid for him to learn machining in trade school and he's taken advance high tech courses and supervisor training since. He's a natural communicator and well respected by his peers."

"Then he's the man you want to lead this."

Adriana pressed a button on the centrally placed conference speaker phone. "Dory, can you join us in the conference room? We need to pick your brain."

"Give me two," his deep voluminous voice erupted from the speaker.

Moments later, rubbing grease from his thick scarred hands with a faded red cloth rag, he entered the room. Burton immediately liked his unshaven face and White Sox baseball cap tugged low over a strong wide nose and stern dark eyes glowering with humor as though he were enjoying some endless personal comedy.

"Come in, Dorian. Have a seat. Gentlemen, Dorian Spencer, our plant manager."

Dorian raised his right palm and beamed it at the others around the table. Dorian, the young guy to my left is Burton Blake, your CEO, next to Jim Eckdahl, who you know and Ivan Trimble. Ivan's a consultant, an expert in lean manufacturing and Kaizen. You know a thing or two about that."

Dorian nodded.

"Dorian talked to me about introducing Kaizen into the plant about three years ago, but we arrived at the same conclusion I've been discussing with you. Dorian, these gentlemen would like to give it a try, but I wanted them to talk to you before making a decision."

"You'll need to talk with more of the guys than me. With all due respect, Mr. Blake, we know who you are. You don't have any power. All you have is a title. The inner circle at the top will do whatever they want to me, to you, to the company, to all of us. They've got so much money they can get rid of us anytime and our salaries and benefits will turn in to short term profit for the shareholders. Even if the market doesn't collapse, they don't need us unless they want to stay in this business. Then they need us to make the products so the profits trickle up. But if the market goes down, we go down with it. We become unemployed and they still get their money. Otherwise you wouldn't be here bothering to listen to me and to try what you're proposing. I've read about Kaizen. Took a seminar. It's a great idea, a great method, a great philosophy. But it'll never work here because it requires all of senior management to support it and be involved. You won't even get off the ground."

"Let's just see how far we can go," said Burton.

"I understand you're trying to connect with us, but I'm afraid you'll be disappointed. Instead of making friends, you're going to make enemies. It's best if you leave things the way they are. At least we have jobs and can support our families."

"Your jobs are not at risk, not with me."

"We appreciate who you are, but like I said, we know where the real power is up in that tower in Chicago. Most of my guys have worked here for a long time. Some of 'em started before you were even born. They adjusted and got used to the way things are. Six or seven are working toward retirement. We have a pretty good take at your boys at the top. We know the kind of money they make and how they live. We don't want to upset the status quo, if you know what I mean."

"I know what you mean. But look at what's happening in the world. Since I inherited this company, and I do own most of it as a majority stock holder, I'm more than a CEO in name only. I can and will do things differently. One thing I won't let happen is that people lose their jobs. I can promise you that."

"That's a big promise and hard to keep these days."

"We can start slow," said Ivan. "Let's just get to know each other."

"I know how Kaizen is supposed to work. And to be fair, I've never seen it in action," said Dorian. "Theory is one thing. Reality is another."

"We live and work in the real world and that's how we approach and implement this. There's nothing academic or mystical about it. We use common sense tools."

"Seems funny, don't it. You'd think companies would naturally run on common sense rather than fuck up. Excuse my French. But we have our work arounds."

"I know," said Ivan. "They're called informal systems. You need them to survive in dysfunctional working situations. We want to turn the fuck ups into an effective common sense process."

"I'm willing to at least start out with you and I'll talk to my crew before you meet with them. But keep this in a low profile, okay?" Dorian stood up from the table. "Gentlemen, I have a machine waiting for me."

"Thanks, Dorian," said Adriana. "See you later."

"Hope it turns out to be a pleasure."

"I'm sure it will."

Adriana led her entourage out of the conference room past the centralized machine programming department manned by five programmers seated at wide screen work stations next to the shop floor and into the glass enclosed environmental quality control lab where three inspectors leaned over their benches to verify dimensions of aluminum and stainless steel parts. The group watched the middle-age Black Quality Manager operating a computerized measurement machine to check a part destined to become a central unit for a fuel pump subassembly.

An uptick in the markets for automotive and aerospace fasteners and parts had prompted Earl Frederickson to expand the machining capacity at the Rockford plant in response to requests for proposals. He had forged ahead with the backing and support of senior management, their board, and investor enthusiasm encouraged by a private equity partner, Olson Capital Investment, established by the corporation's Chief Financial Officer, Jeff Crowley.

Chapter 40

Vicarious

A phone call from Lawrence Harden to Earl Frederickson, vacationing at his thoroughbred farm in Kentucky, notified him of Burton's visit to the Rockford plant and his planned purpose. Initially outraged by the news, Earl succumbed to Lawrence's logic of how Burton was unknowingly playing into their hands.

"We have a way to get rid of him now," said Lawrence, "and without any suspicion of foul play, even while the IRS is camped out in our offices."

"How's that."

"Not over the phone. We'll talk when you get back. Jerry Olson gave me the idea."

"Olson – he got us into this mess."

"It wasn't Olson. It was a combination of things, but mostly bad luck."

"Without giving me the details, what does he have in mind?"

"He has a plan that will implicate the kid."

"Wonderful, hot fucking damn. I can hardly wait. Is this going to blow up in our faces like another Henry Reardon?"

"This doesn't involve anything physical, only money."

"Money's physical."

"It's only good for what it can buy."

"What's it gonna buy us?"

"I'll tell you when you get back. When's that gonna be?"

"In three days. My trainer is starting a colt in training. Shows a lot of promise. Actually, I want to stay away from the regulators in my office as long as possible. They been askin' for me?"

"No, they're spending most of their time with Crowley and his staff. He's the money man."

"Poor bastard. How's he takin' it?"

"Not well. Pretty stressed out. What really pisses him off is the investigation is keeping him away from his tennis club."

"Bet his wife is ready to scream. Crowley gets cranky when he can't play tennis."

"See you in a few days. Life is still good."

"It was better."

"Yeah, it was. We'll get through this. Get back to the way things were."

"Somehow I don't feel certain about that."

"Think positive. We haven't broken any laws. The Feds got our money. They're just trying to figure out what happened. Otherwise, they're happy as fucking clams."

"Gotta go. Trainer's takin' my colt out to the track."

"See you in three."

"Bye." Earl turned off his cell phone and watched the hatless red-headed trainer give a leg up to the young Puerto Rican rider, Ramon Davila, wearing a maroon high neck sweater against the morning chill. The nip in the air invigorated the leggy chestnut colt, Apollo's Son, who executed a skittish side step as the jockey tucked the short crop under his arm and adjusted his helmet strap and goggles.

Apollo's Son created the first trace of prints on the dark loamy track raked with the precision of a Zen garden. The merging sunrise touched his burnished coat giving him the aura of a moving flame with each thrusting stride of his powerful hindquarters.

Three days later, Earl's pilot was waiting for him with the Gulf Stream on the landing strip. Earl drank heavily on the flight to Chicago and wondered what manner of revenge Lawrence Harden and Jerry Olson had cooked up that would destroy their nemesis, the poster boy, Burton Blake.

Chapter 41

Cold Case

Robert Ostraich decided to begin his inquiry with Emory Fliegle, the groundskeeper who had discovered Elias Blake's body on the estate. A tall mild-mannered émigré of German extraction, as a young man, Emory Fliegle had worked as an assistant groundskeeper at a Chicago cemetery before he was hired by Elias Blake to oversee and manage the extensive lawns, terrace, and flower and vegetable gardens, horse pastures, stables, and woodlands of the five hundred acre estate. Emory brought in crews to do the heavy work and to cultivate and harvest hay and corn fields on a seasonal basis. His wife, Alta, worked as a housekeeper and cook for Alexis Andaniamo. They lived on the property in a well-appointed full-size house. Given the attention required by their employers, they had no children by choice.

A smaller second cottage nearby housed a stableman responsible for the care and feeding of the horses that Alexis rode.

Emory wore work boots and khaki trousers and long sleeve shirts with rolled up sleeves during the spring and summer and wool plaid shirts and down jacket and a cap with ear flaps on chill winter days. With his slight accent, Emory reminded Ostraich of a German village burgher whose crisp blue eyes crinkled at the corners of his weathered face when he smiled, exposing slightly crooked teeth.

"This is where you found him?"

"Lyin' right there. His dogs were takin' a nap right alongside him. Woke right up when they saw me comin'."

"So how did you find him? What did he look like?"

"It was startin' to get dark. His wife told me to take one of the ATVs and go look for him."

"Do you remember what time it was?"

"Well, gettin' dark. About this time a year ago. Pheasant season. He had his two bird dogs with 'im. Gettin' dark. Dark and cold. Temperature droppin'. Had to be around five."

"Were there a lot of fallen leaves like this?"

"Best as I can remember. This time of year. Leaves had turned. Lot of 'em comin' down. Half the branches were bare, like this."

"Do you remember anything odd or unusual about the situation?"

"Hard to say," he paused, "except for one thing. He'd shot two pheasants, one male ringneck and a female. Trussed up lyin' on the ground nearby."

"How close nearby?"

"Few yards away, like he'd dropped 'em when he fell, maybe stumbled. The other thing, one of two shells was spent. T'other was still in the chamber, so he had reloaded after shooting the birds. The first shot of the reload was the one that killed 'im when he fell, according to the detective on the scene. Wasn't like Mr. Blake to carry a loaded gun after he was done huntin'. He was a nut about gun safety. Said he'd been taught by his step-dad when he was a boy. But who knows."

"The coroner's report said he died of a stroke first, then the gunshot wound," said Ostraich.

"Don't know about the stroke. Just saw the wound that killed 'im. Least that's what I thought killed 'im. Gunshot opened up his chest."

"Where was the gun when you found him?"

"On the ground, close by, six or seven feet."

"What direction was the barrel pointed?"

"Right at him, like he'd fell back from the blast."

"Did you watch the crime scene investigation?"

"Couldn't get close. Police had the area taped off."

"Did the detective question you?"

"Yes, told 'im just what I'm tellin' you. He recorded what I said."

Ostraich scanned the surrounding woods dense with tall elms, birch and oak and a tangle of brambles and underbrush interspersed with spreading leafy green ferns growing in pockets of shade and damp soil. Calling songbirds flitted in and out among the branches overhead. He shuffled slowly through the accumulation of dappled autumn leaves, their variegated reds and golds accented by spears of sunlight filtered to the aroma of verdant decay on the forest floor.

"Where would he have gone to shoot the pheasants?" asked Ostraich.

"Fields out at the edge of the woods."

"How far?"

"Hundred yards or so on the path."

"Let's walk there."

An hour later, he sank into a soft over-size cushion on a couch opposite Alexis intently leaning forward seated in a chair across from him. "The year before he died," she said, "Elias had two mini-strokes that could have influenced the change in his behavior and might have also impaired his visual perception. He was a fanatic about gun safety. It might be he had forgotten or he was unaware there was a shell in the chamber and when he stumbled and fell the gun went off and killed him. But the autopsy showed he had had a third stroke that cut off the blood flow to his brain. It's hard for me to accept that Elias accidentally shot himself. I know there wasn't any evidence found that he was murdered. I'm just not comfortable or convinced with the results of the investigation."

"Did you pursue that with the police?"

"They did cooperate with me. I have to give them that. I looked at what they looked at. I don't have anything to go on, just my gut feeling. And maybe at this point, it doesn't matter. Elias is gone. My concern is for his son. There's something toxic about the men who are running his company. I should say running away with his company. There doesn't seem to be any way to stop them."

"What recently happened put a crimp in what they've been doing."

"A crimp is nothing. A crimp can be removed."

"They're under the surveillance of the Assistant Attorney General. They're squirming and they don't have much wiggle room."

"The corporation is very complex," said Alexis. "Over the years, it took on a life of its own. The system and way of operating and schemes to generate profit dominated and influenced lives of the people in the company. Influenced is not an adequate term. There is a group outside of the board of directors that runs things. It subjugates them. It rules them. It even ruled Elias. In a way, what he had created overtook him to the point he no longer controlled the company. The others ran it for him. He just spent more and more time on hunting trips and junkets. The last two years before he died, I didn't see much of him. He was gone most of the time. And when he was here, we didn't do anything together. We didn't get along. I have my own life, so his absences and lack of interest in our marriage didn't bother me that much. And besides, we were getting along in years and there wasn't any purpose in a divorce."

"Obviously you still miss him."

"I didn't think I was that transparent."

"Well, you're not. I'm here because Burton asked me to follow-up on something you mentioned to him, that you suspected Elias had been murdered."

"I guess you could call that being transparent in an indirect way, to him. I'm concerned about him as though he were my own son, and not by a family relationship. In some ways, we're related because of the company, the corporation, the scope of what it does and the effects it has on so many levels. There isn't any sense of humanity about it, and Burton is a humanitarian. He's an extension of what Elias was becoming, even if Elias changed because of his mini-strokes. Although I would have to say they were not the primary cause. I think his age factor was changing him, as well, and even more so, the realization that the corporation was controlling him. He was trying to escape it."

"Why didn't he just resign and retire?"

"I don't think he wanted to openly admit to himself what had happened, the shift of who was in charge. I also think he had grown tired of it all, not the nuts and bolts of running the company, but the corporate and outside political forces. He tried to hide from me some of the unethical and amoral things he had supported, or at least looked the other way. It was as though if he didn't know the details, he wasn't personally involved or liable. Someone else was calling the shots, the group I mentioned. He could just let it slip away and let others run with what they were doing, and he would no longer be responsible. His behavior was a signal to his management team that they could do whatever they wanted. They were in charge."

"How do you know this?"

"From someone who's a friend. Someone inside the company."

"Can you tell me who?"

Alexis smiled. "You're a journalist, Bob. I'm sure this is a provocative story for you, but no, I can't tell you. Along with Burton, he's among the people I want to protect."

"There are others?"

"Yes, and they will remain anonymous."

"So you think there's a conspiracy?"

"I don't think it was deliberately planned. I think it happened because of the company culture that nurtured it. When Elias took over the company from his step-father's partner who had cheated him, he hired and surrounded himself with competent, well-meaning people.

Over time, conditions changed and so did they. The outside group infiltrated the company in financial ways."

"And the current management didn't recognize that was happening."

"Perhaps not, but they came around to it and accepted it. They had no option and they were well rewarded. Now it's entrenched as a kind of religious fanaticism, the cult of wealth."

"Yet you don't regret your wealth."

"I'm not critical of it, just of some of the things the company does to acquire it."

"The unethical, immoral things."

"Yes."

"You know, Burton told me the same thing. By the way, he doesn't hold it against you that you're rich."

"I know." Alexis smiled. "I guess we don't have control over our fate."

"I don't have a clue about fate, except from my perspective as a journalist, it's overrated."

"So what are you going to tell Burton?"

Ostraich thought a moment. "That there isn't any answer."

A message from Burton was waiting for him when he returned to his office. He placed the call.

"Burt, Bob here. I saw your message."

"How did your meeting go with Alexis?"

"It didn't turn up anything. Talking with the police and the coroner the same."

"Here's another trail to follow," said Burton. I talked with Jim Eckdahl, the Manager of Human Resources."

"Yes?"

"He's certain there's a hidden secret group, a few major players in the political and banking world that run the Blake Corporation through the Board of Directors that takes orders from them and has ties to the philanthropic division. Even top management at Blake is controlled by them. And without my knowing, including me and, until he died, Elias."

"Alexis told me the same thing. Does Eckdahl know who they are?"

"He says he doesn't and I have to believe him."

"What are you proposing?"

"Find out who they are," said Burton.

"How do the orders come down?"

"Eckdahl doesn't know. There isn't a trail back to wherever they're being issued, but Walt DeMint could be a connection. A few billion dollars of so-called philanthropic endowments are channeled to foreign private banks we've never heard of and become a source of private income to whoever is behind this."

"As intriguing as it all sounds, I'm not sure I can help you on this, Burt. It's beyond the scope of what I can investigate. Maybe you should tell Sims about this. He's your resource that can do something. I'll publish the story if all this comes out."

"I'll talk to him. I do appreciate your trying to learn more about how Elias died."

"If it is a conspiracy, it's well-hidden," said Ostraich.

"Okay, we'll keep in touch."

"Don't forget. I'm under a gag order."

"I know."

Chapter 42

Stocks

From the time he was in elementary school, Jerry Olson had always excelled in math. He loved doing puzzles of all kinds and solving arithmetic problems. As an adult, he breezed through the entire series of Sudoku books and looked for other challenges. He graduated summa cum laude on a full ride scholarship from the Harvard University School of Business with a double major in economics and computer science.

Trading in stocks and investing in the acquisition and development of low performing companies to raise their stock value, then selling stock short at the highest point and gradually degrading the companies by withholding resources until they failed was among his most successful strategies for generating profits on capital investments.

He ignored the human factor, pretended to not even be aware of how the lives of employees were being impacted. A multi-millionaire at thirty, he believed he was conducting business as it was intended to be.

The only child of a Congregationalist minister, he had long ago separated from his father's doctrine of preaching religious faith. Jerry told him that faith was specious, relying on a platform of myths and stories, just like all religions. Faith was not founded on fact. It was a theoretical wish that was not solvable and, therefore, gave him the opportunity to pursue his social and financial goals and objectives according to his own tenets with no regard for humanitarian values.

Rules and regulations, laws, were just obstacles to be circumvented and overcome, another form of puzzles to be solved.

When he married two years after graduation, he denied his father the request to preside at his wedding. He and his graduate student wife, Priscilla, conducted their own ceremony by reciting their vows to each other in the presence of friends standing in a grassy field. The marriage certificate was signed by one of them, a rock musician who doubled as a mail order minister.

"Why don't you invite Burton to have dinner with us?" asked Priscilla. "You said he was a boyhood friend."

"We weren't really friends. More like acquaintances," said Jerry.

"Acquaintances? Children don't think of each other as acquaintances. Look at your own. Either someone's a friend or they're not. They don't even know what an acquaintance is."

"All right, all right," Jerry swiped the air with his hand as though to erase her. "We just went to the same elementary school. We didn't hang out together. We weren't friends. We knew each other's names. That's all."

"But you knew his father. You actually did business with him."

"That was all done through Jeff Crowley when we were partners."

"But we went to some of their dinner parties given by his wife, Alexis, the one with the hideous laugh."

"So what about her laugh. One of the reasons, the main one, we've made so much money is that they made so much money. They had money and made more and Crowley and I helped them along with that."

"Well, regardless, I thought it would just be a nice gesture on your part to invite him for dinner," Priscilla pressed him.

"I don't think there's anything to be gained from it. Why are you so insistent?"

"I thought you might like to have him as an," she paused, "an acquaintance. He's young, like you. All the others you have to deal with in that company are old farts."

"I don't have to deal with them," Jerry retorted. "I want to deal with them. And by the way, in case you haven't noticed, I do have young friends. We get together. We have parties. We drink beer. We golf. You chit chat with their wives and our kids know their kids."

"But Burton is a bachelor."

"So fuckin' what. Burton?"

"That's his name. I saw it in the paper," said Priscilla. "I saw him on a news channel. What do you call him?"

"I don't call him anything. I don't talk to him. I don't even see him."

"You said you spoke to him at his father's funeral."

"That was different," Jerry snorted. "I just expressed my condolences."

"But what did you call him, certainly not Mr. Blake. You're the same age."

"Burt. I called him Burt."

"There, you see?"

"See what? You're making some kind of mountain out of a mole hill."

Priscilla detected he was growing irritated and realized she had to quickly make her point. "Not a mountain, no mole hill. He's not married. I'm thinking he and Natalie might hit it off."

"What? Let's not go there," Jerry stormed aggressively. "Don't you get into this. Have you been talking to Natalie?"

"Why else would I bring her up?"

"About Blake?"

"Now you're calling him Blake."

"That's his last name."

"But the way," Priscilla sipped her orange juice, "you said it was sort of callous. How would you like it if someone you do business with referred to you as Olson?"

"I would be ecstatic. If someone calls me Olson, it's better than them calling me Mr. Olson. Mr. Olson is formal. Olson is familiar, chummy."

"You mean like watching football chummy?"

Jerry gave her a derisive smirk. "Watching football chummy."

"Like locker room chummy?"

"What does a locker room have to do with it. It's just casual, friendly."

"It just sounds rude, calling someone by his or her last name."

"When I was in high school sports," said Jerry, "the coach always called us by our last names. He never used our first names. So my friends and I did the same. We've called each other by our last names ever since."

"It sounds like some sort of guy thing."

"Guy thing, girl thing, what difference does it make? I've heard girls, women even, call each other by their last names."

"There's a difference," said Priscilla. "We do that using a friendly tone, not a rude or a tough tone."

"See. You do it too."

"It's meant in fun and with good humor," Priscilla fluttered her eye lashes.

"Just because my voice is an octave lower than yours doesn't mean it's not fun and not in good humor," said Jerry.

"Well, it occurred to me that," she hesitated, "Blake may not have any friends. Young friends. They say it's lonely at the top."

"Who says? Who's they?"

"The men who work there, at the top. It's a common saying. It's been around for a long time."

"Longer than you," said Jerry.

"Of course, that's why it's part of the jargon."

"Jargon?"

"Corporate jargon."

"What do you know about corporate jargon?" he asked. "You've never worked in a corporation."

"I have so. Just not a behemoth."

"Working for your uncle doesn't count."

"His company has Inc. after its name. It was a corporation. I should know. I was his CPA," said Priscilla. "Is that where you got what you call your buff body, playing high school sports?"

"You know, I work my ass off to support my family in the manner to which you have become accustomed. There's no reason to be derogatory about my physique."

"You could actually have a physique if you exercised and lowered your carb intake and drank only one glass of wine a night instead of five or six."

"I don't just drink wine. I'm a connoisseur. I study it."

"You mean you read the labels," she grinned.

"I don't have time to exercise."

"If you have time to eat, you have time to exercise."

"You do enough for both of us."

"When was the last time you had a physical?" she asked.

"I'm only thirty-five years old. I don't need a physical."

"In another five years, you could drop dead from a heart attack."

"I come from a family with strong hearts," he stated adamantly.

"You've made enough money you don't have to work at it so hard anymore."

"But it's what I like to do," said Jerry. "It gives me a reason to get up in the morning."

Chapter 43

The Set-Up

"This is how we can get him out of the way," said Harden.

"I don't like the sound of it," said Alan.

"What do you mean?"

"We already have one Federal agency in our shorts. You don't want the FDA to come in here too. If they discover something unacceptable, they'll shut the whole company down and management, all of you, will take the hit. You're hurting enough. What you're proposing is too risky. Too much high visibility. Do you have another option? Something that isn't tied to Federal regulations."

The group fell silent.

"Well, I see we don't have any volunteers," said Jerry Olson. "Understandable, none of you wants to sacrifice one of your divisions. So how about we create a new one. One that doesn't really matter to you."

"What about doing a spin-off," said Crowley. "We're diversified in a number of industries. Do we have one that isn't performing, that we can sacrifice?"

"You mean inflate the stock value."

"Exactly," said Crowley.

"But we make it appear the decision came from Burton."

"He won't know until he's discovered by the SEC. We can lock him in so they won't believe anything he tries to tell them," said Jerry.

"Then his buddies from the Attorney General's office won't be his buddies anymore," said Earl.

"That's the general idea."

"What division we going to tap for this?" asked Lawrence.

"Crowley, you know the figures better than anybody here. What do you say."

"Not off the top of my head. I'll have to do some research."

"The opportunity may have already presented itself," said Earl. "Poster Boy is fooling around with his Kaizen project at the plant in Rockford."

"That's aerospace," said Crowley. "You sure you want to touch that?"

"The commercial market with Boeing and Airbus is up right now, but it won't stay that way. It never does. It's the defense side I'm talking about, the fighter jets. With the cutbacks on the defense budget and the greater use of drones, that could be a natural, less obvious."

"I can work with that," said Jerry. "We can float that out there."

"I have a better idea," said Lawrence. "It'll be easier to shitcan the solar and wind energy division. Alternative power is still new and it's suspect, not fully endorsed and accepted by everybody.   We can use that against our infamous eco-fanatic CEO and no one at the Federal level will be the wiser, especially the kid, until it's too late. Then the SEC can have him for lunch."

"Brilliant," said Crowley. "Good thinking."

Lawrence scowled. "That's why I get paid the big bucks."

They all laughed.

Jerry tugged at his reddish brown goatee, freshly trimmed that morning. He had debated shaving it off entirely, since Priscilla's passing comment that "It really doesn't do anything to improve your looks. Did you grow it just because your friends have them? Or the sports jocks have them? It makes you look like a goat."

"That's why it's called a goatee. I grew it because I like it," Jerry had snapped back. He wondered why, lately, she constantly harassed him with critical remarks about his increasing weight, drinking, lack of sensitivity and consideration in their love-making, if you could call it that anymore. She complained that his belly got in the way. So what did he have to do, develop a six pack to please her? Just because she and her friends were into healthy diets and regular workouts at the club didn't mean he had to join them. If anything, without saying, he didn't care for the amount of weight she had lost. She was starting to look skinny and her breasts had reduced from once enticing parts of fleshy interest to a couple of small pears the palm of his groping hand easily consumed.

And now she had brought up her friend Natalie, a lean svelt body building brunette who, in Jerry's opinion, had too much influence over his wife who was filtering her opinions down to him. He suspected Priscilla was confiding in Natalie, sharing all her intimacies that were none of Natalie's fucking business. Introduce Natalie to Burton Blake, not a fucking chance.

Burton's father, Elias, had been great to know and to work with. They had shared the same economic and political beliefs and values. But Burton was not at all like his father.

Jerry continued studying the financial data that filled his three computer flat screens on the Blake Corporation wind and solar divisions. Of particular interest was the fundamental and quantitative analysis with risk management to reconstruct the portfolio.

Because they were new enterprises, less than three years old, developed in response to the emerging alternative power and energy markets, they had been introduced on the stock market with a low valuation which provided for opportunities to stimulate capital appreciation by calling an emergency meeting of the board of directors and shareholders to vote issuing a sudden large number of shares. When the stock reached an appropriately high enough value, with the collaboration of Earl Frederickson and Lawrence Harden, they could fail the companies and bring the stock value tumbling down, but not until Burton Blake's stock had been sold short so that he would realize billions in personal profit. As other investors saw the falling value, they would sell or pull out as quickly as possible. When the IRS came after Burton for insider trading, he wouldn't know what hit him.

Jerry perused the indicators of stock price appreciation, the anticipated earnings growth, the company restructuring that would take place to give the appearance of state-of-the-art management, an effective business model attuned to the environmental demands of the new social economy, and product innovation.

Given the multiple billion dollar capital and operating budgets, the start-up competitive position in a demand industry, and potential for growth and stock price appreciation, the crash of these companies would have an astronomical effect.

The estimated market value of the two companies totaled one hundred million based on Jerry's calculation of the present worth of the future income expected from the operational output of the assets.

Several years before Elias Blake died, Jerry partnered with Jeff Crowley, who was the Vice President of Finance for the Blake Corporation. They made the decision to list with a leading investment bank to manage the paperwork with the Securities and Exchange Commission and to issue shares that created high visibility on the New York Stock Exchange. The investment bank would sell the stock without any guarantee on how much was sold. The arrangement was ideal for Olson Capital Investments to sweeten the insider holding pot with Burton Blake's name on it. Based on a recent meeting with the investment banker managing the account, Jerry knew he was in favor of substantially increasing the number of shares to raise the price of the stock, especially with the support of the new young environmentalist CEO, Burton Blake. Jerry had jokingly referred to

Burton as the poster boy for the stock. The banker agreed that Burton would appeal to progressive investors in the booming environmental markets.

Jerry estimated his scheme would take about six months to set in motion.

Chapter 44

The Device

None of the members of the inner circle thought or suspected that Elias Blake might have been murdered. And even if they did know, neither the fact nor the possibility were important to them, only that he was gone and unable to interfere with their lives.

To them, Henry Reardon was not an actual person, only a symbolic identification of a method to maintain the company's status quo. Fred Dolby had introduced the name as a reference for discussion, "Let's bring in Henry Reardon," whatever that meant in Fred Dolby's mind.

The rest of them knew nothing about the man who had sabotaged the fracking operation on Harold Esser's farm, resulting in Harold Esser going to prison. They knew nothing about the man who had put Olivia Quintana in the hospital in a coma. And they knew nothing about the attempt to assassinate Burton Blake in Alaska that ended with his savage death. The only person who did know was Fred Dolby.

Dolby used the Henry Reardon reference as a device for plotting a scheme of any kind that required extraordinary means to the extent that the members of the inner circle called such an application 'a Henry Reardon'. The name was used by the shadow financial group who influenced the company from somewhere outside. For all he knew they existed in cyberspace. There were never any names associated with where they came from or who they were. The only identification that came to him in an anonymous email was 'Henry Reardon' linked to a coded message that ordered a killing that had no investigative traceability and could never be solved. Having worked in black ops for most of his career, he had ostensibly been recruited by the invisible cabal through the Board of Directors to become the Director of Security for the Blake Corporation. His compensation had made him a millionaire. He never knew for whom he was working. He didn't ask questions.   He did what he was ordered to do.

He had converted his underground cellar into a shooting range where he invited select friends who were gun enthusiasts, ex-military, and free-lanced as security agents on Federal Government installations in the Middle-East and as mercenaries in Africa.

Although he had hired George Papadoupolos and Niko Karzinski from among his circle of acquaintances, he observed and suspected they had grown to like and respect the young CEO he had assigned them to spy on and protect. Now, he had to remove them from their assignment, get them out of the way. He had received a coded 'Henry Reardon' email from Anonymous ordering him to terminate Burton Blake. A repeat of Dolby's failure to do so when Burton fled to Alaska would not be acceptable and the consequence to Dolby would be unquestionable.

He emptied the magazine of his AR-15, his favorite assault rifle, shredding the target posted thirty yards away. He set the weapon on a storage rack, removed his protective ear phone head set and safety glasses, then bent to sweep the still hot shell casings with a hand broom onto a dust pan.

......*

Alan had not been informed about the meeting being held by Lawrence Harden, Earl Frederickson, and Jeff Crowley, along with Jerry Olson.   Burton's secretary, Darcy Schumacher, had overheard part of the exchange on an open shared line linked to her office phone, until the line had suddenly gone dead, when they realized it was open.

"We're going to try this Alan's way," said Lawrence, "With a subtle legality."

The day before, Alan had reminded them, "Burton's father and I were very close friends. He was your friend too, all of you. We wouldn't have achieved the success we have, if it weren't for him. He gave you your first employment and it's lasted most of your adult lives. We owe it to his memory to cooperate with his son."

What had been said the day before was discounted as Alan was becoming a risk and a liability to them. *"We don't owe Elias Blake shit, Erdman. He's dead and gone and just in time for trying to screw up the company with his do-gooder crap. His son is cut from the same cloth, only worse. He has a lot of years ahead of him to do damage, if we let him."*

"It will go easier on all of us with the Feds if you cooperate."

"Spoken like an attorney. You're going soft on us, Erdman. That's not a good sign. The majority rules here and you're just a single vote."

Now, Darcy was hearing. . .

"I have this locked up tight," said Jerry Olson. "There's no traceability. Burton Blake's electronic signature on that stock is better than a wet one."

"The investors expect a high return."

"That's not our concern," said Olson. "Investing is a risky business."

"What you're proposing to do is a risky business," said Earl. "You can be indicted."

At that point, Crowley noticed the red light on the conference room phone and pushed the button to turn it off. Darcy heard the line go dead.

"No one is going to find out, Earl, because no one here is going to tell anybody. If we go down, and we won't, I guarantee it, there's going to be too much mud sticking to Burton. You've got thirty years of history with this company, with us. You've done many things that are under the radar, and that's where they'll stay, as long as we don't cave."

"We have to be careful that Erdman doesn't hear about this. He's an old smoke and fire guy. We give him enough smoke, he'll never see the fire, even after we start it."

"What are you thinking?"

"I'm thinking he's an old man, older than us. I'm thinking he's not in the best of health."

......*

Alan fumbled with his cell phone, the display barely illuminated in the dim overhead light of his car. He listened impatiently for Darcy's voice through seven rings at the other end of the wireless connection.

"Darcy, It's me Alan. I apologize for bothering you so late at night, but I got your message about Jerry Olson and I'm calling to give a warning." He paused. "For Burton. He doesn't carry a cell phone anymore since whatever it was happened in Alaska. He's onto the fact, or at least has a valid suspicion that it contained a chip to track him. You're the only other person I can trust. If something should happen to me, you've got to let Burton know there's a conspiracy in the works to take him down. . . . . No, not kill him, to get rid of him with what I suspect is an insider trading scheme. They're only at the talking stage and they might not try to go through with it. They're risking legal consequences and that they would have no hope of escaping if found out. If and when you speak to Burton about this possibility, tell him not to confront these guys. They'll deny it, accuse him of not trusting them, which he should not, and become adversarial, nasty, worse than they already are. Equally important, I don't want them to know we talked and know about Olson. I don't want to put you in harm's way. In a political sense, but I also mean in any other sense. The top management at Blake is not made up of nice people, self-serving and potentially dangerous is a more apt description."

......*

Six months later, Curtis Meininger, the plant manager for Blake Solar Systems, considered the rise in the stock price a positive sign, but he was concerned that it didn't correlate to recent sales figures and the reticence of the market to embrace solar energy on a scale that would warrant such a dramatic increase.

He noticed that a similar abrupt event had occurred with the Wind Energy division as though overnight the value of both stocks had leapt upward. Since both divisions were barely two years old and still in a start-up position, he questioned what was happening. He picked up the phone and called his boss, Earl Frederickson, the Vice President of Power and Energy at the Blake Corporation Chicago headquarters.

"Earl, Curtis here. Could you explain to me what's happening with Blake Wind and Solar stock? If you haven't seen the New York Stock Exchange report this morning, check them out on-line. Something doesn't jive on the cost per share. It jumped thirty dollars and for no obvious reason. You know something I don't know? Production has been steady, but it's been on the low side for the past year."

"Our strategy boys are reporting that the demographics for power and energy consumption has accelerated," said Earl. "It's bumped up projections. I was about to call you and discuss plans for expanding production to meet what we see as a robust growing market for both wind and solar. For the moment, we don't have what I would call significant competition, but that could change overnight. We don't want to get caught with our pants down and get left behind."

"We're going to have a big issue with lead times on this," said Curtis. "Even if we step up electronic board production in China, it takes six months for containerized product to reach the port in San Pedro, California. Then it has to be transported by rail which takes another month. The demand for metal to fabricate our frames has pushed out lead times, as well. U.S. mills are responding first to demand from China, since the red dragon is willing to pay five times what we are for raw metal. We can't compete."

"We're already being gouged by their labor cost on board production," Earl growled into the phone. "We started out all right with them, but they're raising their rates on us. Now they're grabbing up all the raw material in the world. They're too competitive. They're gonna put us out of business and we should be the world leader on this."

"You trying to generate revenue by raising the stock prices?" asked Curtis.

"It's part of our new plan for the division. Your call is timely. We want to ramp up production to show the investors we can beat the Chinese at their own game."

"Hard to do without the resources, Earl. Impossible to do."

"I know you have at least a half dozen U.S. metal suppliers and there are dozens of qualified domestic electronic board houses you can tap."

"Easier said than done, especially given the economy."

"We can't keep blaming the economy for everything. The corporation will provide an infusion of capital to increase production."

"That doesn't solve the lead time issues."

"Negotiate options with other suppliers. If you can't get what you need, find new ones."

"How much time do we have?"

"We want to ramp up in two to three months."

"It takes that long and longer for the ship to get here from Shenzhen." He was referring to the free trade zone city on the southeastern coast of mainland China. The International Department of the Blake Corporation contracted with one of the high tech companies in the Science and Technology park to manufacture electronic boards for solar panels that were assembled in the United States at the Illinois plant.

"Tell purchasing to work on it. If you have to, fly over there to Shenzhen and light a fire under them."

"The Chinese won't answer to us. You know that. We have to scrap fifty percent of what they send us and rework most of the other fifty. I have more people here repairing and rebuilding boards than I have making the final product. It's a losing proposition."

"You're my plant manager. Find a way to work with them."

I'll have to hire more assemblers and add a third shift."

"Then do it. The budget will be adjusted for whatever you need."

"Like I said, it isn't the budget I'm concerned with. It's the material and subassemblies from China."

"I'm confident you can work things out. Make it happen, Curtis. Just make it happen."

Curtis slammed down the phone, leaped up from behind his desk, slipped on his safety glasses, and walked out into the adjacent production area visible through the glass wall of his office. At fifty-five years old, Curtis prided himself in maintaining his personal health and physical conditioning. He jogged at a fast clip three miles a day and, with the exception of occasional tendonitis and knee joint discomfort, had not experienced any injuries.

His slender pixie blonde wife had been his running partner after her third pregnancy until she turned fifty, then had reduced her activity to light workouts on home Nautilus equipment in their exercise room.

Along with a low fat largely vegetarian diet, his running and weight training workouts kept his long body lean with a corresponding acceptable body mass index that allowed him to easily wear designer jeans and polo shirts to work. His shaved head and constant five o'clock shadow on a chiseled jaw gave him the appearance of a man ten to fifteen years younger.

Returning to his office, he called his plant manager counterpart at the wind machine manufacturing operation.

"Rudy, you hear from Earl?"

"Haven't talked to him in at least a month."

"I suspect you will. It can't just be my operation."

"What's up?"

"He called me this morning. Really turned my day brown."

"What did he say?"

"Ordered me to ramp up production beyond our current capacity, given our problems with China and the long lead times with our metal suppliers"

"We do more work with resin than with metal, so we're not as impacted, and our international customers are picking up, especially Europe and South America."

" Well, maybe he's happy with you. You kind of balance out the solar side of the business. It's a difficult market for us."

"Did he order you or threaten you?"

"To be honest, my gut feeling is we're being set up to fail. At least I am."

"Why would Earl want to do that to us, to you, me, to any of us? Wind and Solar are his baby."

"Who knows what those guys at Corporate are up to? I heard a rumor that the new CEO, the old man's son, Burton Blake, is an environmentalist. If he is, I'm surprised he hasn't come to see our plant."

"The last time I drove up to Chicago, I talked with Jim Eckdahl about some human resources needs and corporate purchasing. It's no secret that the brass favor coal and oil production. That's where they make their billions."

"That's where the market is, no question about it. But it's not our market. It's not our purpose and mission. I'm beginning to think we're just window dressing to make Blake look like the company is environmentally friendly while they create pollution and toxic waste."

"That's for damn sure. Now all of a sudden, we're getting pressed. Maybe we need to bypass Earl and talk to the new CEO, maybe invite him down here to visit us."

"That's what I was thinking. Only we don't want Earl to hear about it. We'll know soon enough who supports Earl's decision or even knows about it."

"How do we handle this in the meantime? We have to do what Earl tells us. Our hands are tied."

"We're both all too familiar with the supplier situation. That's not something we can single-handedly turn around. Even the President can't do that."

"You going over to China?"

"I've been to Shenzhen three times in the past two years. The operations manager there says they will change and improve, but it never happens."

* * *

"Excuse my French, Alan, but you've got to be shittin' me." Alexis was appalled at what her long time friend and Blake corporate attorney had just told her.

Alan shook his head. "I wasn't there. I wasn't invited. Darcy heard only a part of it on an open line that was cut off. She told me."

"Have you said anything to them?"

"I don't want them to know I'm on to them," said Alan.

"Are you afraid of what they might do?"

"To me personally?"

"Yes, to you personally. They're ruthless, Alan. You know that working with them for how long has it been, thirty years?"

"Close enough."

"When is this supposed to take place?"

"I don't have a date and time on it. Olson Capital Investments is handling the stock transaction."

"Jerry Olson. That pig gives pigs a bad name. I never liked him. He was always trying to curry favor with Elias. He did help him to become a billionaire. I guess when that kind of money is involved, he could tolerate having that asshole around. What I'm worried about is how we're going to protect Burton. We can't let Olson get so far down the road with this that Burton can be arrested and indicted."

"No, not Burton, for sure. But Olson, yes, and sweep up Harden and Frederickson and Crowley as accessories, but on a conspiracy charge," said Alan.

"But you don't have any evidence, just your word against theirs."

"I'll work on that."

"Have you told Burton?"

"Not yet."

"Why not?"

"I have to handle this as a legal matter. Burton is my client. I have to protect him. I'll involve him when it becomes necessary."

"So, what's your next step? What's your plan? You must have one or you wouldn't be sitting here in my living room telling me this."

"I have to proceed carefully. I'm sure Earl and Harden told Dolby to put me under surveillance."

"Then they must know you're here."

"Very likely, but they know you and I are old friends that go way back when you and Elias got together. They don't know what we're talking about. This could be just a social visit."

"You know as well as I do that's not what they're thinking. I'm going to start packing a Glock. How are you going to protect yourself?"

"I met with Sims last night and we talked on the phone with his boss, Denise Harbridge, the Assistant Attorney General. So far, Olson hasn't broken any laws. All he did with the approval of Earl and Harden and Crowley was plan to influence the stock price by issuing a large number of new shares. He hasn't introduced the fraudulent involvement of Burton as an insider. That would not be set to happen until Blake Wind and Solar starts sliding and the division fails and Burton collects a few billion from the insurance that Olson purchased in Burt's name. We're looking at six to eight months for that to happen."

"That slimy son-of-a-bitch. So you have some time, a short window, but still some time."

"I've talked to Rudy Benson and Curtis Meininger, the plant managers at Wind and Solar. Burton hasn't been there yet. They're going to invite him to come and visit their manufacturing operations down in Springfield. They'll make him aware of the unrealistic production demands Earl has placed on them, especially Curtis and Solar. For logistics reasons, he can't possibly accomplish the level of production he's been ordered to do. He doesn't have the supply chain and he doesn't have the capacity."

"So he's being set up to fail. The division will fail."

"I want Burton to tell Curtis, and Rudy, they are to ignore anything Earl orders them to do and proceed with operations just as they are."

"Will Burton know what's going on before he goes down there?"

"He'll know. And that's the second part of my plan, a special surprise for Olson and the gang."

"Can you tell me?"

"At the appropriate time. I don't want to put you at risk."

"I have a Glock."

"I know you have a Glock. But it's better that you don't know what happens next."

"I'm not going to go whack Jerry Olson, if that's what you're worried about, although I'd like to. It would give me great satisfaction."

"And a life sentence. I need to have Olson cross the line so the Feds can nail him. They want a live body, not a corpse."

"Not to worry, Alan, dear. It's just my dark side expressing itself."

Alan grinned. "I know. I miss Elias. We had such great times together."

Alexis nodded. "It's Burton's turn. We have to protect him."

"That's what we're doing."

"Just keep me in the loop, okay?"

"Okay, Ali, you've got my word."

* * *

Earl Fredrickson held the phone receiver away from his ear, stared at it in disbelief, then returned it to his ear. "What the hell you mean you're not shutting down. I gave you a direct order."

"I was given an order by your boss, the CEO, not to shut down." It was Curtis at the other end of the line.

"You don't report to him. You report to me. If you don't follow through with what I've told you to do, your ass is fired."

"Mr. Blake assured me that is not going to happen."

"Don't hold your breath, Meininger. There's a pink slip headed your way." Earl slammed down the phone receiver, "Fucking shit!" then immediately picked it up again and called Lawrence Harden.

"Larry, something's wrong. I just got off the phone with Curtis Meininger at Solar and he had the gall to tell me he's taking orders only from Burton Blake. We have to find out what's going on."

"Either someone found out and has talked to the kid or someone is guessing because of Wind and Solar action on the stock market. Otherwise, he wouldn't even be in the picture. He had no way of knowing the order you gave to Meininger. He barely knows that division exists. Can't Crowley stop the money? Wind and Solar can't produce if we cut off their operating capital."

"I think we're getting into some quicksand here, Larry. I don't feel good about this and I don't trust Olson to handle it. You know that if he goes down, we go with him."

"No, we don't. We're legally outside of everything he's doing. As a matter of fact, we don't even know what he's doing and we don't want to know. This is his gig not ours."

"You think he'll tell that to a jury?"

"Earl, calm down. None of this has gone that far. We control production. We can stop the ramp up."

"That's what Meininger wants us to do, keep hands off. We don't control Olson and Blake stock and securities."

"Tell Crowley to deal with Olson. They're buddies. He can make Olson understand. I'm looking at stock exchange reports right now. Blake stock for Wind and Solar has gone way up. There's nothing unusual about that."

"What will be unusual if it suddenly goes down, and I mean rapidly goes down."

"Stay out of it. We have to keep a low profile. Let Meininger and the kid have their way."

"I want to retire to my farm in Kentucky, Larry. I'm thinking tomorrow might be the right time."

"Don't get crazy, Earl. We haven't done anything. We're okay."

"Shit." Earl hung up.

Chapter 45

Black Ops

Burton Blake's death had to appear to be an accident. Just as Fred Dolby had murdered Burton's father, he planned a careful sequence of how to end the life of Elias Blake's son so no traceability back to him would exist.

Timing and invisibility were critical to conceal the method and instrument of death. Dolby had years of experience from the Middle East wars as an operative in the CIA and as a mercenary in South America.

Staging a civilian accident was not as easy as laying a mine field or even placing a plastic explosive under Burton's car or killing him with a sniper bullet.

The murder of Elias Blake had been a covert and complex affair. Through digital surveillance providing advanced knowledge of his location on the pheasant hunt, Dolby's effective concealment and the gunshot wound to Elias Blake's chest was staged to coincide with an injected methadone caused stroke.

Dolby wasn't certain if Burton had told anyone, particularly the Tribune journalist, Robert Ostraich, about whatever happened in Alaska. Not knowing placed Dolby at a disadvantage in covering his own trail in taking out his current target.

Most of what he knew about Burton he had gleaned from impressions and from the senior management staff, who largely disrespected and distrusted him for his youth and oppositional social and economic philosophy. George and Nikos had also been able to feed him details about Burton's personal tastes and preferences in food and entertainment and general life style, and relationships. So Dolby sorted through these impressions in search of the weak point where he might interject a telling accidental end to the young man's physical life. His spirit be damned. It was inconsequential.

Letting George and Nikos go was easy enough. He told them that under the circumstances of the Federal investigation happening in the company, their services were no longer needed. He offered to provide them references for which they expressed their appreciation. He asked for their company cell phones and credit cards. Their guns were their own. They shook hands. He bid them well and they quietly left his office.

With the two of them gone, he had removed the constraint to the execution of his plan.

Following his usual routine, Burton arrived home at nine and prepared an easy microwaveable dinner, which he quickly consumed while watching the evening news on television.

He had spent the day with Sims and Jeff Crowley attempting to navigate and sort through the disposition of billions of dollars that had been transferred to the IRS. Except for the basics, he found the Federal tax laws governing the corporation staggering, complex, and difficult to understand, even with Sims' clarification.

After an hour of news channels that repeated themselves, he switched off the television and lay his head back against the soft rolled top of the rust-colored leather cushion. He would often doze off in that position and wake two hours later and make his way to bed on the second floor of the large five bedroom home he had purchased. This time, he did not wake up. A sharp pain from a hard blunt object striking the right side of his head thrust him into a deep dark unconsciousness.

Dressed in black and wearing a black ski mask with slitted eye holes, Dolby pulled Burton off the couch with latex gloved hands and dragged his body to the foot of the wooden stairs leading to the upper floor. He positioned Burton's body to make it appear he had fallen and struck his head while trying to escape from the fire.

After considerable thought, Dolby had decided to opt for a simple and unquestionable accidental death that eliminated the risk of discovery and left no investigative trail.

He carried Burton's empty food tray to the kitchen table where he placed it next to a lighted candle. He then returned to the television family room and turned on the gas fireplace without lighting the flame. The room began to immediately fill with the distinct odor of carbon dioxide fumes. He looked about the room to make sure nothing appeared amiss, then quickly exited by the back door, dashed around the side of the house to the street and ran to his black suburban three blocks away. He stopped abruptly when he saw another black unoccupied suburban parked directly behind his. At that moment, Burton's house exploded into flames on the first floor.

As he opened the driver's side door and started to step into his car, Dolby heard a deep recognizable voice call his name. "Dolby!"

He pulled his handgun and fired in the direction of the voice and was answered by two .45 caliber slugs penetrating his right lung and heart and leaving an exit wound where his back was pinned to the open door. With a hard grunt, he slid in a wash of blood to the street.

George and Nikos sprinted the three blocks to the house and saw the cyclone of flame creeping up the walls to the second floor. They didn't know where Burton might be inside and they couldn't get through the front door. The heat was too intense.

"Try the back!" shouted George.

As they charged along the side yard, they could see that the majority of the fire was centered toward the front of the house. They kicked open the kitchen door. A gas cloud of flame assaulted them as they stumbled half blind through the intense heat and smoke.

Coughing and choking, they searched wildly through blurred eyes for Burton. Nikos spotted him first. "Over there! By the stairs!"

Flames licked at their clothes as they staggered across a lake of fire that had been the carpet. George hefted Burton's prostrate form up and over his shoulders in a rescue carry and followed Nikos to where he had opened French doors from the dining room onto the terrace. Then they were out into the night rolling on the ground to extinguish stubborn swatches of flame intent on consuming their clothes.

They heard the wail of approaching sirens in the distance.

Chapter 46

Turnabout

"How did he find out? How did he know?" Harden was apoplectic with rage.

"Gentlemen," said Alan, "he has people in this company who support him. They have his back."

"Yeah, we know. And you're one of 'em," said Earl.

"I told you I was."

"We're not going to change the way we do business. We'll get the kid out yet. The Board will vote him out."

"No, you won't and no, they won't. The three million in stock that you and Olson Capital Investments attempted to defraud Burton with as insider trading, is being distributed to investors and to the employees of Blake Wind and Solar."

"The Board doesn't have any love for you, Erdman. Why are you doing this?"

"Doesn't matter. Your days here are over."

"What the fuck are you talkin' about?" Harden's face contorted in a menacing mask.

"Gentlemen, we're now going to leave this room and be escorted by security guards to the main conference room where you will be given a debriefing. Do not attempt to return to your offices. If you do, you will be immediately arrested."

"Jesus fuckin' Christ," Harden hissed. "You're supposed to be one of us."

"It's time to go. People are waiting."

In the main conference room, flanked by the Human Resources Director, Jim Eckdahl, Alan Erdman, and Winston Sims, Burton addressed Lawrence Harden, Earl Frederickson, and Jeff Crowley.

"Gentlemen, this meeting is to inform you that, as of this moment, you are no longer employed by the Blake Corporation."

Harden leaped out of his chair. "What the hell!"

"Stay seated, Mr. Harden," Sims ordered.

"What the hell is going on?"

"Your computers and files are now being confiscated by newly hired security guards," said Sims. "Dolby's security staff has been fired and is now being debriefed in another room. In case you haven't heard, he died in an attempt to murder Burton Blake. At this time, place your keys, company credit cards, and company cell phones on the conference table. In five minutes, security guards will accompany you back to your offices where you will have twenty minutes to pack your personal effects. You will be escorted by security guards out of the building. If you resist in any way, you will be immediately arrested. You may still face prosecution in the future. You will be under surveillance and stopped and arrested at any airport or at any border. Your private jets have been impounded and are now under control of the Federal Government. Also to let you know, Jerry Olson of Olson Capital Investments has been arrested and is being held in detention without bail."

Earl glared at Crowley. "Your friend."

"Not mine. I barely know him."

"You were his partner."

"Twelve years ago. I have nothing to do with him."

"Best to hold your comments," said Sims. "There is an ongoing investigation."

"Shit," Earl slurred out of the corner of his mouth.

"Gentlemen," said Sims, "it's time to go."

"Do you mind if I ask what became of Walt DeMint?" Jeff Crowley hesitated at the door. "He hasn't been here for the past month."

"He has fled the country," said Sims.

"Are you telling me he wasn't involved with any of this?"

"Mr. DeMint has other issues. We're working on finding him."

Crowley shook his head and, flanked by a new security guard, shuffled back to his office.

EPILOGUE

Ice Cream

"She won't leave the house," said Lizzie. "Her assault precipitated agoraphobia. It's a fear factor centered in the amygdala of her brain. It generates a secretion of hormones that prompt her fear response."

"Mom, Burton does not need to hear your clinical explanation. Suffice to say, I'm just not ready to go out into the world yet. Next Millennium has a remote system. So I'm able to work from home and Skype during meetings."

"I just stopped by to see how you're doing," said Burton. "I'm sorry to hear you won't leave your house."

"You have some responsibility for what happened, you know," said Olivia. "I never would have been attacked if it wasn't for you."

"I guarantee you never will be again. The bad guys are gone."

"How did you manage that?"

"It's a long story. I'll tell it to you over an ice cream."

"An ice cream?"

"Yes, and I'm making you a job offer. My HR manager is recruiting and restructuring my senior management team. I was hoping you'd come and work with me.

"Doing what?"

"An agricultural development project."

"You don't know anything about agriculture. You've never been a farmer."

"I worked with farmers in Southeast Asia."

"Agriculture. Next Millennium funds projects like that."

"I'm aware. I need a good project manager."

"I really have to think twice about that."

"There's no hurry."

"I'm not sure I'm ready to go out into the world again."

"I know you don't plan to live here the rest of your life with your mom?"

Lizzie's hand shot up into the air. "Not if I have anything to say about it. You better take Burton up on his offer, dear. It sounds like a great adventure and it's right in line with your work."

"I'll give it some thought." She smiled. "About that ice cream. I like Cold Stone."

"Cold Stone it is."

The Saga of Burton Blake
Book Club Discussion Topics

1. The American journey of three generations locks the neophyte company president, Burton Blake, in a vicious struggle with corporate intrigue, economic greed, and social and financial corruption.

2. Following World War II, Elias Blake's youth is influenced by the adult world's drive for personal material gain. Over the next decades, he expands his parents' original real estate empire into the diversified multi-divisional, multi-national corporation that he leaves to his son, Burton.

3. What events following World War II influence Elias Blake as a child and eventually as a young man and mold him to become the father whom his son despises? How was society different in the 1950s than it is today? What were the prevailing attitudes toward the role of women? How does Kristina Holtzman overcome those prejudices and social standards of behavior?

4. How would you compare Burton Blake's life with that of his paternal great grandmother, Julie Josephson/Holtzman in the novel *The Revolutionist*? What social, political, economic, and technological conditions are different? What has changed since the early 1900s?

5. What is Burton Blake's reaction when he reads his father's obituary? Why does he say what is being asked of him by Alan Erdman, the corporate attorney, is impossible?

6. Why does Burton Blake resist and try to deny his father's legacy, then try to learn more about him? How is he different than his father, Elias Blake, and why? Do they have any character and personality similarities? If so, how would you describe them?

7. As Burton undertakes the challenges of leading the company in a new direction that corresponds to the values of his own millennial generation, who in the company tries to prevent and stop him? What means and methods do they apply? Are they successful? What is Burton's reaction? What does he do to fight against them?

8. How would you describe the corporate culture or the prescribed and shared values of the Blake Corporation? Who and what are the sources of the corporate culture? Social, psychological, political? Describe the personalities of management that dominate the company.

9. What is meant in the novel by The Cult of Wealth?

10. What is the role of the corporation in engaging in various forms of corruption and exploitation of human and natural resources to gain profit at any cost? Who are the victims?

11. Who does Burton discover he can count on as friends, mentors, and collaborators to support him and cover his back?

12. Various social and political forces block Burton's efforts to change the company. Although he is the CEO, he is excluded from the "inner circle." How does his exclusion handicap him?

13. What is the physical and the symbolic significance of the grizzly bear in the story? Why does the hunting and fishing cabin in Alaska

become a sanctuary for Burton? How does he use the location to protect himself?

14. How does Dr. Elizabeth (Lizzie) Dawson provide Burton with a link to his father's childhood years and a new realization about Elias Blake?

15. What confidential information does Elias Blake's second wife, Alexis Andamiano Blake, provide that is further insight into the nature and behavior of Burton's father? In learning more about his father, what does Burton learn about himself?

16. What role does the news media play in the story?

17. What role do regulatory agencies play in the story?

18. Who is the unexpected source that comes to Burton's rescue?

Rob is a graduate of the University of California, Santa Barbara and received his graduate degree in communications from the University of California, Los Angeles. He worked as a business and management consultant to advertising, corporate communications, and media production companies as well as many others. Now retired, he resides with his wife in Southern California where he devotes much of his time to writing. He is a recipient of the Samuel Goldwyn and Donald Davis Literary Awards.

An affinity for family and the astute observation of generational interaction pervade his novels. His works are literary and genre upmarket fiction that address the nature and importance of personal integrity.

Tell-Tale Publishing would like to thank you for your purchase. If you would to read more by this or other fine TT authors, please visit our website:

www.tell-talepublishing.com